Praise for *Cemetery Dance*

World Fantasy Award Winner
International Horror Critics Guild Award Winner
British Fantasy Award Nominee
American Horror Award Nominee

"A very fine piece of work."
—Dean Koontz

"*Cemetery Dance* is beautifully choreographed."
—Robert Bloch

"A fine home for innovative horror fiction. A home that invites in both the talented beginner and the old pro—as long as they bring the best of blood and shadows in their luggage."
—Joe R. Lansdale

"The best magazine in the horror field."
—*The Time Tunnel*

"Unfailingly entertaining. A great magazine."
—Joe Bob Briggs

"Hands down the best horror magazine available."
—*Mystery Scene*

THE BEST OF CEMETERY DANCE

edited by
Richard Chizmar

VOLUME ONE

A ROC BOOK

ROC
Published by New American Library, a division of Penguin Putnam Inc., 375 Hudson Street,
New York, New York 10014, U.S.A.
Penguin Books Ltd, 27 Wrights Lane, London W8 5TZ, England
Penguin Books Australia Ltd, Ringwood, Victoria, Australia
Penguin Books Canada Ltd, 10 Alcorn Avenue,
Toronto, Ontario, Canada M4V 3B2
Penguin Books (N.Z.) Ltd, 182–190 Wairau Road, Auckland 10, New Zealand
Penguin Books Ltd, Registered Offices: Harmondsworth, Middlesex, England

Published by Roc, an imprint of New American Library, a division of Penguin Putnam Inc.
Previously published as part of a hardcover edition by *Cemetery Dance*.

First Roc Printing, November 2000
10 9 8 7 6 5 4 3 2 1

ACKNOWLEDGMENTS

Nine years have gone into the creation of this book. It's been a long journey, and I did not make it alone. So I offer my deepest thanks to the following people who walked by my side: Kara and Max, William and Olga Chizmar, my entire family, the Wilsons, Kara's family (and thanks to Tip and Kelly, the *CD* shipping department!), Mindy Jarusek, Brian and Tracy Anderson, Steve and Dani Sines, Bill and Daniella Caughron, Bob Crawford, Jim Cavanaugh, Pondo, Roy Boy, Bob Eiring, Richard Gallagher, Tom Nugent, Ed and Carol Gorman, Marty Greenberg, Barry Hoffman, Bob Morrish, William Schafer, Tim Holt, Dave Silva, Stephen King, Shirley Sonderreger, Dean Koontz, Peter Crowther, Muffin Spielman, Adam Fusco, and each and every person who ever contributed their creative talents to *Cemetery Dance*, and – last, but certainly not least – all the good folks who supported us over the years.

This book is very special to me,
and I'd like to dedicate it to three very special people:

Mary Wilson
Nancy Chizmar
And the memory of Rita Chizmar

My sisters and my guardian angels.
Thanks for letting me be your little brother.
I love you.

For more information about Cemetery Dance:

Visit the official website: *www.cemeterydance.com*

Or write: Cemetery Dance Publications
P.O. Box 943
Abingdon, MD 21009

THE BEST OF CEMETERY DANCE

INTRODUCTION

Richard Chizmar

Introductions, Afterwords, Editorials — I've always hated them. Actually I love *reading* them. It's the *writing* that I hate. It's not because I'm lazy, and trust me, it's not because of my naturally humble nature. I guess I've just always been one of those editors who would rather have the actual contents of the book or magazine do the talking. I've always been more comfortable outside the spotlight . . . in the shadows.

And that philosophy certainly applies here with *The Best of Cemetery Dance.*

Still — after hearing from hundreds of loyal readers — I knew I couldn't get out of this one. Folks wanted to know the inside story; they wanted to know the history of *Cemetery Dance.* So, instead of sitting down at the keyboard and writing about *myself* for a few painful hours, I did the next best thing — I asked *CD* columnist, Bob Morrish, to interview me. To take us all the way back to issue number one and work up to the present. And, as usual, he did a wonderful job. He even managed to make me sound a little interesting!

Here's how it all started . . .

Bob Morrish: As I believe you've stated elsewhere, your primary inspiration for launching *Cemetery Dance* was David Silva and his *Horror Show* magazine, correct?

Richard Chizmar: Yes, I definitely started out more focused as a writer, and discovered the whole underground of small press magazines. I found out about a lot of them through Janet Fox's *Scavenger's Newsletter*, sent away for some sample copies, and wasn't terribly impressed by much of what I saw. But then one day in a chain bookstore, I came across a copy of the "rising stars" issue of *The Horror Show* and I couldn't believe it. I couldn't believe that [Silva] did the whole thing by himself. And I really liked the mixture of contents that he had — fiction, non-fiction, interviews, novel excerpts — a real broad range of stuff.

So, seeing that issue was the first thing that got me thinking "well, maybe we could do something like this." And I was dumb enough to want to try it.

BM: Did you plan, or hope, right from the beginning to publish a book line, or did that come much later?

RC: No, we just . . . we announced the magazine in the summer of '88, worked on it for a few months, and put out a thousand copies of #1 in December. Our initial plans were just to do the magazine twice a year, and that was really it. A part-time hobby. At the time, I was in college, and really had no idea that it could go anywhere. We took about $600 from [his future wife] Kara's student loan and used that to place a half-page ad in the final issue of *The Twilight Zone* magazine, and that got us a couple hundred subscriptions. It was a good start.

And then I think it was shortly after we put out issue #2, David Silva called and mentioned that he was shutting down *The Horror Show*. So, at that point, we realized that there was going to be a sizeable hole to be filled. And we had just recently decided to go quarterly anyway, so . . . there was no great master plan, things just sort of fell into place and we said, "well, let's try this on a higher level."

BM: In your editorial for issue #1, you thanked a number of people who I don't believe have ever re-surfaced in the magazine in any way — Bill and Deb Rasmussen, Melinda Jaeb, Janet Fox, Donald Miller, and Jeannette Hopper. Were they all publishing their own magazines at that time?

RC: Yeah, that was really the core of the small press back in those days. The Rasmussens were doing *Portents*, Janet Fox was doing *Scavenger's*, and so on. Those folks were very willing to answer questions and give advice. They made me feel like part of the community right from the very start.

BM: You also thanked Chris Lacher, former editor/publisher of *New Blood* magazine, very extensively. He also had a column for a few issues that seemed to suddenly disappear without a trace. What happened with that?

RC: I don't exactly remember. I know that for a while Chris was pretty prominent in the small press, and I can't recall if he just got too busy with his own magazine, *New Blood*, or maybe even if his column ended at the same time that *New Blood* was shutting down . . . I'm not sure.

BM: That first issue of *CD* also credited an Art Director named Willie Ray Caughron. Who was that?

RC: [laughs] That was my college roommate. A high school buddy, and a guy I still play poker and softball with. That first issue of the magazine was produced on an old dinosaur of a Macintosh. We took the disk to the computer lab at the college and printed it on the laser printer there, even though we weren't supposed to be printing that many pages. That's why the second issue was printed on my dot matrix printer, because we couldn't print it on the lab's laser printer. But that first issue . . . most of the illustrations in there were drawn by Willie by hand on the actual print-outs from the laser printer, adding them after the text had been printed. It was truly a home-made operation.

I pretty much designed the first . . . I don't know, thirteen issues or so, myself on a Mac, even though I was, and still am, pretty computer illiterate. I was just happy that we were publishing on a regular schedule, regardless of how simplistic the layout was.

BM: I also noticed that there was some poetry in first two issues of *CD*. Was that just to fill space? It's not something that you've continued to publish . . .

RC: I just stopped buying it. A very large percentage of what I was reading was horrible . . . although I also have to admit that I probably wasn't the best judge of what was good poetry.

BM: Did you get word out to *Scavenger's Newsletter* and other market guides to get a slushpile going in those early days, or did you mostly solicit stories then?

RC: A little of both. I did spread the word very aggressively. A lot of new editors will ask me if there was anything I did in the beginning that made us stand apart from other magazines, and I think the big thing is that I was really relentless about getting the word out about the magazine. When that first issue came out, a lot of people had already heard of us, from either market reports or advertising or free listings or flyers at conventions or whatever. I think our advertising went a long way to showing folks that we were serious and that we planned to stick around for a while.

BM: Initially the magazine was very heavily fiction-oriented, but it sounds like you were planning on having a strong non-fiction presence right from the get-go.

RC: Yeah . . . in the beginning, it would have been difficult to convince some of the professional folks to write columns for us who later wound up doing so. We just needed a bit of a track record first, but we knew right from the beginning that we wanted to have columns and interviews and so forth.

BM: In issue #2, you already had ads from major publishers like Onyx and St. Martins. Did you approach them and drag ads out of them, or what . . . ?

RC: I think in some cases we were able to convince publishers to pay small fees to advertise. In other cases, we went directly to the authors and convinced them to advertise. I don't recall what the ad rates were then — probably something like $50 a page — but I think at that price, they really couldn't go wrong.

BM: Issue #3 seemed like a big step in a number of ways — you went to two-color covers, increased to 72 pages, got an ISSN, picked up some distributors — obviously you were looking to make the step up to semi-pro status.

RC: Yeah, that was our last semi-annual issue; we knew we were going quarterly after that. R.C. Matheson sent us some good material for that issue, and we started a couple of regular columns. It's funny . . . the reviews of that issue were pretty much universally positive, but several of them led off with "*Cemetery Dance* has now become a *Horror Show* clone." And in some ways that was true . . . but the funny thing is I took it as a great compliment, because *The Horror Show* really set the standard for what I wanted to do. But that was definitely a jumping-off point for us; the point where I realized "hey, this could be more than just a hobby that costs me a couple grand a year."

BM: Speaking of the financial aspects of what you do, what does your wife Kara think of your chosen career?

RC: She's always been very supportive. In fact, in the beginning, I was really on the fence about how far I should carry all this, and it was Kara who nudged me over the line, saying "you want to do this, you should just do it." And then she volunteered her help and support and enthusiasm, not to mention the money for that initial *Twilight Zone* ad.

And my family was extremely supportive, too. I was really lucky that way. Here I was, about to get a degree from one of the nation's top journalism programs, and I'm not even thinking about putting together a resumé and hitting the pavement looking for a job. I knew my mother and father were a little concerned, but they just told me that they believed in me and knew I would work hard to make the business a success. Same thing with my sisters and brother and all my friends. No one ever doubted us, and that was a very big key to our success.

BM: In the editorial for #4, you mentioned that there was going to be a *Cemetery Dance* TV commercial, locally sponsoring an episode of *Freddy's Nightmares*. What ever happened with that?

RC: That actually never happened. I just re-read that editorial the other day for the first time in years, and thought "well, there's the first time

that Rich jumped the gun on something." They ran a big article about
me in the Features section of the *Baltimore Sun*, and one of the results
of that article was this woman calling me from the cable company and
proposing this commercial to us. It sounded like a great idea, and we
talked it out, and put some numbers down on paper, and agreed to when
we would film it, and when it would start airing. The woman really
sounded like she understood how small we were, and she offered us a
great deal. But when it finally came time to sign the official papers, the
costs were suddenly much higher. I think I had been prepared to sink a
total of about $3,000 into it over time, but it suddenly jumped to more
than $6,000, so we had to back away.

BM: Then issue #5, your special Rick Hautala issue, featured *CD*'s first
four-color cover . . .

RC: That was a Chuck Lang cover . . . that made a big difference because
it helped us get picked up by Ingram [a major magazine distributor].
And that gave us instant credibility.

BM: . . . and in the editorial you mention that you had decided to feature
"dark mystery" in the magazine. Do you think the tone of the fiction in
the magazine changed significantly after you made that proclamation?

RC: Probably not significantly. I think the biggest thing is that . . . in
the beginning, the magazine was strictly focused on horror. Now I've
always been a big fan of horror — that's why I got into all this in the
first place. I grew up loving this kind of stuff: horror comic books, *The
Twilight Zone* on television, Ray Bradbury, Robert Bloch, the list goes
on. But after the first few issues, I suddenly realized that I was an even
bigger fan of dark suspense, and that was where I wanted to steer the
magazine. I wanted a mixture of the genres, and I wanted to come out
and put the cards on the table for the readers and for the writers, and let
them know that, even though, we'd still have straight horror content,
there would be a strong emphasis on suspense and mystery.

BM: Issue #6 featured your first Gary Braunbeck story, with many to
follow, and it was a special J.N. Williamson issue. Why did you decide
to do a special issue for him?

RC: Primarily because he was such a mainstay in the small press. I think he was probably *the* most visible professional writer who also published regularly in the small press. And he had been a big help to me. He was very supportive of *CD*. And, incidentally, that was actually our first issue that sold out.

BM: How many copies were you printing at that point?

RC: I would say . . . between three and four thousand.

BM: I noticed that #6 also featured the third story you'd published by David Duggins, who I don't believe has since appeared in the magazine. Has he continued to submit to you?

RC: Not for a long time. He's in the military and he was overseas the entire time he was selling to me. He took a long break to write a few novels, and then I just recently heard from him in the last year or so.

BM: Let's see . . . in #7, your Joe Lansdale special issue, you started Matt Costello's column, and you ran a fourth story by Bentley Little and a fifth by Ronald Kelly. Then issue #8 was the last one to feature Joe Citro's column. Why did that come to such a quick end?

RC: He wrote me and said that he was just getting too busy. He did a great job for us, but we weren't paying all that much then, and I think he just had too many other things competing for his time.

This is probably a good time for me to add . . . it never failed to amaze me, how — right from the beginning — we had writers of such quality stories and novels willing to write for us, and to trust us with their work. Citro was one of them in the early days, and R.C. Matheson and Bill Relling and Steve Tem and Ed Gorman, and a whole long list of others.

BM: Jumping ahead to #10 . . . you were up to twelve columns in that issue, along with seven stories — were you at all concerned that you were getting too top-heavy with non-fiction?

RC: We were probably getting a little top-heavy in the non-fiction department then. I did get a few letters from people saying "Hey, I want more fiction." It's interesting . . . in general, the typical readers — the fans — want more fiction, while the writers, the editors, the agents — the professionals in the field who read the magazine — want more non-fiction.

BM: In #11, you had your second story within three issues by Michael Thomas Dillon, another writer who I don't believe has appeared since then. Has he continued to submit?

RC: Yes, on and off. I know he's still out there writing; I've seen him published elsewhere recently. And we've had a few close misses in the past couple years. He was just a new writer, at that time, who submitted to me very regularly and responded well to my critiques of the stories that I rejected, and kept submitting until he found something that I liked. I expect to see him in the magazine again some time.

BM: In the editorial for #11, you invited readers to send letters (an invitation you repeated several times in later editorials), and yet you've never had a regular letters column. Why is that?

RC: I think mainly because of the lack of letters of real substance, letters that warranted being printed, taking up pages at the expense of something else. I'd say that 90% of the letters that we receive are really just complimentary — which is great, but to take up space to print them doesn't make much sense. If I remember correctly, I was actually offering to forward letters of feedback to the various columnists.

BM: You also noted in that editorial that you were receiving four to five hundred submissions a month. Is that still your average for a typical month?

RC: I'd have to talk to William Schafer, one of my new associate editors, but I think we're probably down closer to around three hundred or so.

BM: Number 11 was also the issue in which Lori Perkins' column was discontinued. Why did that column come to an end?

RC: I don't remember 100%, but if I had to guess . . . Lori Perkins was my agent for a time, and I think at about that time she ceased to be my agent. It was not a negative parting of the ways, but I think we just decided to discontinue the column at the same time . . . and also I think I decided to replace her column with someone who would do more reviews; more than just one book per issue like she was usually covering.

BM: Issue #12, which came out in the Spring of '92, was the first to list Adam Fusco as an editorial assistant. How did you know him, and what kind of stuff did he do for the magazine?

RC: He did everything from proof-reading to some typesetting to making some phone calls and so forth. He was a local writer, and worked as a casting assistant on a lot of local film productions, and I met him through one of those channels. We got together after another newspaper article appeared, I think.

BM: In the editorial for #13, you mention that T. Liam McDonald, who was doing a column for you at the time, had a *Cemetery Dance* forum on the CompuServe on-line service. Has that since gone away, or is that still around . . . ?

RC: I'm pretty sure it's gone now. At that time, Tom was way ahead of me in terms of computer knowledge — and he still probably is, for that matter — and he was on-line, and people who knew he was a contributor to the magazine started contacting him, so he put up an unofficial forum where he could kind of act as my mouthpiece on-line, distributing news and so forth.

BM: Speaking of having an on-line presence, I noticed that *CD* has had a web page on the HorrorNet site for a while now. Is that something that Matt Schwartz set up for you?

RC: Yes, Matt contacted us, just like he has dozens of other people in the field, and we were tickled to death to have him put together something for us. I think that by the time this interview comes out, we'll have the covers of all our books available for viewing on that site. And people have responded — we get a few orders a week through there.

BM: In issue #14, you published the Stephen King story, "Chattery Teeth." How did that come your way?

RC: Actually, it sat in my slush pile for almost a month without my even knowing about it. Steve had sent the story down via Chuck Verrill, who I guess was acting as his agent at the time. So it had Mr. Verrill's name and return address on it and it just went in the pile with all the other submissions. Then one day we got a postcard from Chuck saying that he had sent it, and was wondering if we'd had a chance to look at it yet, since Steve really loved the magazine and would really like to see it appear. So, after I almost fainted to the floor, I went through the slush pile and found it about half-way down.

BM: That was obviously a big day for you . . .

RC: You're not kidding! Man, it was like something out of that movie, *Field of Dreams*. I mean, it was King's work that got me into this genre — in a serious way — in the first place. Back in high school, a wonderful English teacher, Richard Gallagher, brought in a copy of the novella "The Monkey," and we read it aloud in class. And that started it all . . . without that day, there would be no *Cemetery Dance*. I'm sure of it.

So, to receive an original story from Stephen King, all those years later. I can't emphasize it enough (and I don't care how corny it sounds): it was a dream come true.

I'll never forget that day, or how I felt.

BM: In issue #14, there was an ad for *Shivers*, an anthology that you were editing for Spine-Tingling Press, but which never came out. What was the story behind that?

RC: They were doing mainly audio books, and then I sold them on the concept of doing a joint hardcover/audio release of an original anthology. I solicited the stories and put together what I thought was a very good book, but then six months later, they decided that the sales numbers on their initial tape releases were so poor that they were just going to cease publishing.

BM: Did most of the stories wind up getting published elsewhere?

RC: I'd say about half of them ended up in *Cemetery Dance*. I think a couple made their way into other anthologies, and a few are still out there.

BM: Issue #15 featured your first Alan Clark cover after ten consecutive Charles Lang covers. Any particular reason for the switch?

RC: I thought it was just time for something different. Ninety-eight percent of the feedback on Lang's covers was very positive, and I'd like to have him do more stuff for us in the future. It was just that . . . change is good sometimes — if you stay with one look, or one focus, for too long it can get kind of stagnant. And Alan certainly gave us a different look.

BM: About that same time you discontinued A.R. Morlan's quiz column. Did she run out of quizzes, or . . . ?

RC: No, in fact I think she kept on with it, publishing them elsewhere. It was just the same thing as with the Lang covers — her column had run for quite a while, and we just decided to try something different.

BM: Your combined issue #17/18 in the Fall of '93 came after you had missed publishing an issue for the first time. What happened there?

RC: The specifics of it were . . . we could've gotten the Summer issue out a few weeks late, but our biggest distributor let us know that it would decrease the amount of time the magazine would sit on the shelves, and increase the number of returns. So that convinced us to just wait and publish a double issue. This was better for the advertisers, too.

I know it caused a little bit of a murmur in the small press community, sort of an "oh-oh, is *CD* in trouble?" reaction. Which just made me realize that we could be publishing for twenty years, and then be a little late with an issue, and *some* people out there were going to get nervous. It's just the small press track record working against us.

BM: Issue #19 was your Fifth Anniversary issue, and you mentioned in the editorial how much your print run had increased since your first issue. So . . . what's the highest number of copies that you've printed of an issue?

RC: We printed about 11,000 of #14, which had the Stephen King story. Nowadays, we probably average in the 8 to 9,000 range. Depends on the orders from the comic and regional distributors.

BM: In your editorial for #22, you summarized your bout with cancer. I thought that was a pretty good synopsis of your ordeal, so rather than ask you to reiterate all that, why don't we just reprint that part of the editorial here, for people who aren't aware of that aspect of your history?

RC: Sure. That'd be fine with me. The big thing to me was . . . as I said in that editorial, I was truly inspired by all the letters and calls and gifts I received from readers. *Cemetery Dance* contributors and readers really went out of their way to make me hear their collective voice — they became like an extended family for me then.

Reprinted from that editorial: Most long-time readers of *Cemetery Dance* know that this issue — issue #22 — is the first to be published in over a year . . . So what caused the hiatus?

In case you *don't* know the story, here it is: In September, of last year, I was diagnosed with cancer. The doctors caught it early and, after two operations (small one in September, major one in October), I was considered in remission with a one percent chance of recurrence. When you're dealing with the "Big C" you just don't get better odds.

So we put out the good word and planned for the return of *Cemetery Dance* in the Winter.

Good thing I don't gamble.

Wouldn't you know it — that one percent came back and bit me right in the you-know-what. And it was hungry. The cancer returned in mid-March with a vengeance. In my lungs, liver, stomach, lymph nodes. The odds had dropped drastically — to 50%.

A flip of a coin.

We immediately began a very intense program of chemotherapy (a twelve weeker), and after six weeks, my blood markers had returned to normal and I was on my way back. We thought of returning to the magazine late in the Summer, but knowing the toll that chemo takes on body and soul, we decided to wait until the Winter Issue before coming back.

As of the day I am writing this — mid-November — I am one week short of reaching the six month mark (of having normal blood markers).

I'm back.

And, I'm delighted and proud to report, *Cemetery Dance* is back, too!

BM: I believe issue #22 was the first to list Mindy Jarusek as an editorial assistant, although I believe she'd been doing things for the magazine for a while before that . . .

RC: Yes, Mindy grew up with Kara and is her closest friend. In the beginning, she mainly helped us with packing and order fulfillment, but over the next couple years, she did a lot of proof-reading for us, some typesetting, handling phone calls, you name it. Her help has been invaluable.

BM: Let's see . . . in #23, you announced that Kathy Ptacek's column was ceasing . . .

RC: Yeah, there just weren't enough anthologies being published anymore to warrant a column dedicated to nothing but anthologies.

BM: . . . and you also announced that there was only going to be one more installment of the "Trash Theater" column from Joe Lansdale and David Webb. I believe time constraints were cited there . . . ?

RC: That's what it came down to. Joe had always been very, very busy, and the fact that it was co-written actually made it a little more work than if it was just one person sitting down and writing it on their own. I know they loved doing it, but I think they just couldn't find the time any more.

And I think it had just about run its course.

BM: In issue #24, you ran your third Peter Crowther story, and you're going to soon be publishing a Crowther collection. Why a Crowther collection as opposed to a collection by some of the other writers who've had multiple stories appear in the magazine?

RC: Probably just because . . . Peter's work has really, really impressed me. And maybe it's because he's this guy from England who writes this great contemporary fiction that's set over here in the US. He's represented twice in *The Best of Cemetery Dance* because I just couldn't decide which of the stories I liked better, so I had to publish both of them.

BM: And then, in the last issue or two, Matt Costello's column was discontinued. Was that another case of time constraints?

RC: Yeah, it's not something he came out and told me, but I could tell that he was getting busier and busier, and it was getting harder for him to get a column to us. So . . . I kind of let him off the hook.

BM: Speaking of time constraints . . . do you have a hard time juggling your *Cemetery Dance* responsibilities with your own writing?

RC: I find it very difficult. For the longest time, my writing took a back seat in a major way because every time I'd have a little free time, I'd think "well, should I help the magazine by doing this task, or help improve the book line by doing that task, or should I sit down and try to write a story that I can maybe sell for $150?" So for a long time I had to look at it from a practical standpoint, and I had to do the things for the magazine and book line that helped pay the bills.

BM: Can you tell us a little about your new editorial team?

RC: Sure. We recently added William Schafer and Tim Holt to help us with everything from reading and responding to manuscripts to designing the interior pages of the magazine. From day one, these two gentlemen have made us a better publication . . . and they're only going to get better with time.

BM: How long ago did you decide that you wanted to do a *Best of Cemetery Dance* volume, and why did you decide to do it?

RC: Not very long ago. I wasn't really thinking about it much, but after *The Best of The Horror Show, The Best of Whispers* . . . I think there was a *Best of Pulphouse* . . . and a few others, people started asking me about it. I guess the first time that I really started considering it seriously was when I came back from being sick. At that point I felt like: one, we had enough material to do it, and two, it just felt like the time was right, judging from all the letters I'd received.

So . . . I started by listing all the stories that we'd ever published (over 200 stories!). I cut the list down, on the first pass, to about 120 stories, then down to about 100 stories, then 80. And the hardest part was cutting from those 80 stories down to the final list of stories that made it into the book. There were some gut-wrenching decisions . . .

And it's only going to get tougher, because I've been told that if we sell the paperback rights, we'll probably have to pare it down even further. Having a mass market [paperback] edition was one of the primary goals with this book because, ultimately, what I really want to do is showcase the authors and showcase the magazine, and do this for as broad an audience as possible. My hope is to find new readers and subscribers this way.

BM: Did you use any rules, like "no one can have more than one story in the book," or anything like that?

RC: No, I consciously didn't want to make too many rules, I just wanted to pick the best stories. And, like I said, it was really tough to choose — there are some writers who had four or five stories in the magazine but didn't make it into the book, and on the other hand, there are people who had only one story in the magazine and that one story got selected for the book. I just tried to be fair and pick the stories I liked the best. That's what it came down to — what *I* liked the most.

BM: Given the number of authors included in *The Best of Cemetery Dance*, and just the sheer scope of the project, has it been a more difficult book to put together than most?

RC: Yes, by far it's been the most complicated and troublesome book that we've ever put together. I have to keep reminding myself that when we're done, and when it's finally in my hands, it'll also be the most satisfying book we've ever done.

The worst thing is . . . we started with four sets of authors' signature sheets, and that's since turned into five sets of sheets, because when we were about two weeks away from going to press, one set of sheets was lost — after it had been signed by 75% of the people whose names were on the sheet. There had been twenty names on that page, so in order to save time in getting the sheets signed again, we printed up two new pages with ten names printed on each. And sent them out again with fingers crossed.

All this, after two other sets were lost much earlier in the process!

For me to ever do a book with more than sixty signatures again, there's going to have to be a damned good reason!

BM: Any final comments?

RC: I guess I just want to make it perfectly clear how appreciative I am for all the support we've received over the years — from writers, artists, readers, retailers — everyone.

And I want folks to know that all this really has been a dream-come-true for me. Trust me, I know exactly how fortunate I am. Back in the old days, when I was 22 or 23, and working those fifteen hour days (every day), and we had four or five credit cards maxed-out (I still tell people that *CD* was built on blood, sweat, tears AND 21% interest!), and we didn't have a clue whether this thing would fly or not — no matter what, we never stopped believing in this dream. We were working awfully hard, that's for sure, but we were having fun, and we truly believed (in our hearts) that it would all pay off one day.

And it did.

And it still is.

Cemetery Dance will be around for a long time to come — I promise.

Thanks for helping us along the way!

Okay, it's time to go now.

Turn down the lights, flip the page, take my hand, and start the dance . . .

THE BEST OF CEMETERY DANCE

CHATTERY TEETH

Stephen King

Looking into the display case was like looking through a dirty pane of glass into the middle third of his boyhood, those years from seven to fourteen when he had been fascinated by stuff like this. Hogan leaned closer, forgetting the rising whine of the wind outside and the gritty *spick-spack* sound of sand hitting the windows. The case was full of fabulous junk, all of it undoubtedly made in Taiwan and Korea, but there was no doubt at all about the pick of the litter. They were the biggest Chattery Teeth he'd ever seen. They were also the only ones he'd ever seen with feet — big orange cartoon shoes with white spats. A real scream.

Hogan looked up at the fat woman behind the counter. She was wearing a tee-shirt that said NEVADA IS GOD'S COUNTRY on top (the words swelling and receding across her enormous breasts) and about an acre of jeans on the bottom. She was selling a pack of cigarettes to a skinny young man with a lot of blonde hair tied back in a pony tail. The young man, who had the face of an intelligent rat, was paying in small change, counting it laboriously out of a grimy hand.

"Pardon me, ma'am?" Hogan asked.

She looked at him briefly, and then the back door banged open. A skinny man wearing a bandanna over his mouth and nose came in. The wind swirled gritty desert dust around him in a cyclone and rattled the pin-up cutie on the Valvoline calendar thumbtacked to the wall. The newcomer was pulling a handcart. Three wire-mesh cages were stacked on it. There was a tarantula in the one on top. In the cages below it

were a pair of rattlesnakes. They were coiling rapidly back and forth
and shaking their rattles in agitation.

"Shut the damn door, Scooter, was you born in a barn?" the woman
behind the counter bawled.

He glanced at her briefly, eyes red and irritated from the blowing
sand. "Gimme a chance, woman! Can't you see I got my hands full
here? Ain't you got *eyes?* Christ!" He reached over the dolly and
slammed the door. The dancing sand fell dead to the floor and he pulled
the dolly toward the storeroom at the back, still muttering.

"That the last of em?" the woman asked.

"All but Wolf." He pronounced it *Woof.* "I'm gonna stick him in
the lean-to back of the gas pumps."

"You ain't not!" the big woman retorted. "Wolf's our star
attraction, in case you forgot. You get him in here. Radio says this is
gonna get worse before it gets better. A lot worse."

"Just who do you think you're foolin?" The skinny man (her
husband, Hogan supposed) stood looking at her with a kind of weary
truculence, his hands on his hips. "Damn thing ain't nothin but a
Minnesota coydog, as anyone who took more'n half a look could plainly
see."

The wind gusted, moaning along the eaves of Scooter's Grocery &
Roadside Zoo, throwing sheaves of dry sand against the windows. It
was getting worse, Hogan realized. He hoped he could drive out of it.
He had promised Lita and Jack that he would be home by seven, eight
at the latest, and he was a man who liked to keep his promises.

"Just take care of him," the big woman said, and turned irritably
back to the rat-faced boy.

"Ma'am?" Hogan said again.

"Just a minute, hold your water," Mrs. Scooter said. She spoke
with the air of one who is all but drowning in impatient customers,
although Hogan and the rat-faced boy were in fact the only ones present.

"You're a dime short, Sunny Jim," she told the blonde kid after a
quick glance at the coins on the counter-top.

The boy regarded her with wide, innocent eyes. "I don't suppose
you'd trust me for it?"

"I doubt if the Pope of Rome smokes Merit 100's, but if he did, I
wouldn't trust *him* for it."

The look of wide-eyed innocence disappeared. The rat-faced boy
looked at her with an expression of sullen dislike for a moment (this

expression looked much more at home on the kid's face, Hogan thought), and then slowly began to investigate his pockets again.

Just forget it and get out of here, Hogan thought. *You'll never make it to L.A. by eight if you don't get moving, and this is one of those places that has only two speeds — slow and stop. You got your gas and paid for it, so just get back on the road before the storm gets any worse.*

He almost followed his left brain's good advice . . . and then he looked at the Chattery Teeth in the display case again, the Chattery Teeth standing there on those big orange cartoon shoes. And white spats! That was the killer. Jack, his right brain told him, would love them. And tell the truth, Bill, old buddy: if it turns out *Jack* doesn't want them, *you* do. You may see another set of Jumbo Chattery Teeth at some point in your life, anything's possible, but ones that also walk on big orange feet? Huh-uh. I really don't think so.

It was the right brain he listened to that time . . . and everything else followed.

The kid with the ponytail was still going through his pockets; the sullen expression on his face deepened each time he came up dry. Hogan was no fan of smoking — his father, a two-pack-a-day man, had died of lung cancer — but he had visions of still waiting to be waited on an hour from now. "Hey! Kid!"

The kid looked around and Hogan flipped him a quarter.

"Thanks, dude!"

"Think nothing of it."

The kid concluded his transaction with the beefy Mrs. Scooter. He put the cigarettes in one pocket and the remaining fifteen cents in another. He made no offer of the change to Hogan, who was not very surprised. Boys and girls like this were legion these days — they cluttered the highways from coast to coast, blowing along like tumbleweeds. Perhaps they had always been there, but to Hogan the current breed seemed both unpleasant and a little scary, like the rattlers Scooter was now storing in the back room.

The snakes in pissant little roadside menageries like this one couldn't kill you; their venom was bled twice a week and sold to clinics that made drugs with them. You could count on that just as you could count on the winos to show up at the local Red Cross every Tuesday and Thursday to sell their blood. But the snakes could still give you one hell of a painful bite if you made them mad and then got too close. That, Hogan thought, was what the current breed of road-kids had in common with them.

Mrs. Scooter came drifting down the counter, the words on her tee-shirt drifting up and down and side to side as she did. "Whatcha need?" she asked. Her tone was still truculent. The west had a reputation for friendliness, and during the twenty years he had spent selling there Hogan had come to feel the reputation was deserved, but this woman had all the charm of a Brooklyn shopkeeper who has been stuck up three times in the last two weeks. Her kind was also on the rise, Hogan reflected.

"How much are these?" Hogan asked, pointing through the dirty glass. The case was filled with novelty items — Chinese finger-pullers, Pepper Gum, Dr. Wacky's Sneezing Powder, cigarette loads (A Laff Riot! according to the package — Hogan guessed they were more likely a great way to get your teeth knocked out), X-ray glasses, plastic vomit (So Realistic!), joy-buzzers.

"I dunno," Mrs. Scooter said. "Where's the box, I wonder?"

The object of Hogan's interest was the only item in the case that wasn't packaged. A crudely lettered card beside them read JUMBO CHATTERY TEETH! THEY *WALK!* They certainly *were* jumbo, Hogan thought — *super*-jumbo, in fact. They were five times the size of the sets of wind-up teeth which had so amused him as a kid growing up in Maine. Take away the joke feet and they would look like the teeth of some fallen Biblical giant — the cuspids were big white blocks and the canine teeth looked like tentpegs sunk in the improbably red plastic gums. A key jutted from one gum. The teeth were held together in a clench by a thick rubber band.

Mrs. Scooter blew the dust from the Chattery Teeth, then turned them over, looking on the soles of the orange shoes for a price sticker. She didn't find one. "*I* don't know," she said crossly, eyeing Hogan as if he might have taken the sticker off himself. "Only Scooter'd buy a piece of trash like that. Been around a thousand years. I'll have to ask him."

Hogan was suddenly tired of the woman and of Scooter's Grocery & Roadside Zoo. They were great Chattery Teeth, and Jack would undoubtedly love them, but he had promised — eight at the latest.

"Never mind," he said. "I was just an— "

"Them teeth was supposed to go for $5.95," Scooter said from behind them. "They ain't just plastic — those're metal teeth painted white. They could give you a helluva bite if they worked . . . but *she* dropped em on the floor two-three years ago when she was dustin' the inside of the case and they're busted."

"Oh," Hogan said, disappointed. "That's too bad. I never saw a pair with, you know, feet."

"There are lots of em like that now," Scooter said. "They sell em at the novelty stores in Vegas and Dry Springs. But I never saw a set as big as those. It was funnier'n hell to watch em walk across the floor, snappin' like a crocodile. Shame the old lady dropped em."

Scooter glanced at her, but his wife was looking out at the blowing sand. There was an expression on her face which Hogan couldn't quite decipher — was it sadness, or disgust, or both?

Scooter looked back at Hogan. "I could let em go for fifty cents, if you wanted em. We're gettin rid of the novelties, anyway. Gonna put rental video-tapes in that counter." He pulled the storeroom door closed. The bandanna was now pulled down, lying on the dusty front of his shirt. His face was haggard and too thin. Hogan saw what might have been the shadow of serious illness lurking just beneath his desert tan.

"You could do no such a thing, Scooter!" the big woman snapped, and turned toward him . . . almost turned *on* him.

"Shutcha head, Myra," Scooter told her. "You make my fillins ache."

"I told you to get Wolf— "

"If you want him back there in the storeroom, go get him yourself," he said. He began to advance on her, and Hogan was surprised — almost wonder-struck, in fact — when she gave ground. "Ain't nothin' but a Minnesota coydog anyway. Fifty cents for the teeth, friend, and for a buck you can take Myra's Woof, too. If you got five, I'll deed the whole place to you. Ain't worth a dogfart since the turnpike went through, anyway."

The long-haired kid was standing by the door, tearing the top from the pack of cigarettes Hogan had helped buy, and watching this small comic opera with an expression of mean amusement. His small blue eyes gleamed, flicking back and forth between Scooter and his wife.

"Hell with you," Myra said gruffly, and Hogan realized she was close to tears. "If you won't get my sweet baby, I will." She stalked past him, almost striking him with one boulder-sized breast. Hogan thought it would have knocked the little man flat if it had connected.

"Look," Hogan said, "I think I'll just shove along."

"Aw, hell," Scooter said. "Don't mind Myra. I got cancer and she's got the change, and it ain't my problem she's havin the most trouble livin with. Take the teeth. Bet you got a boy might like em. Besides, it's probably just a cog knocked a little off-track. I bet a man who was handy could get em walkin' and chompin' again."

He looked around, his expression helpless and musing. Outside, the wind rose to a brief, thin shriek as the kid opened the door and slipped out. He had decided the show was over, apparently. A cloud of fine grit swirled down the middle aisle, between the canned goods and the dog food.

"I was pretty handy myself, at one time," Scooter confided.

Hogan did not reply for a long moment. He could not think of anything — quite literally not one single thing — to say. He looked down at the Jumbo Chattery Teeth standing on the scratched and cloudy display case, nearly desperate to break the silence (now that Scooter was standing right in front of him, he could see that the man was more than pale — his eyes were huge and dark, glittering with pain and some heavy dope . . . Darvon, or perhaps morphine), and he spoke the first words that popped into his head: "Gee, they don't *look* broken."

He picked the teeth up. They were metal, all right — too heavy to be anything else — and when he looked through the slightly parted jaws, he was surprised at the size of the mainspring that ran the thing. He supposed it would take one that size to make the teeth not only chatter but walk, as well. What had Scooter said? *They could give you a helluva bite if they worked.* Hogan gave the thick rubber band an experimental tweak, then stripped it off. He was still looking at the teeth so he wouldn't have to look into Scooter's dark, pain-haunted eyes. He grasped the key and at last he risked a look up. He was relieved to see that now the thin man was smiling a little.

"Do you mind?" Hogan asked.

"Not me, pilgrim — let er rip."

Hogan turned the key. At first it was all right; there was a series of small, ratcheting clicks, and he could see the mainspring winding up. Then, on the third turn, there was a *spronk!* noise from inside, and the key simply slid bonelessly around in its hole.

"See?"

"Yes," Hogan said. He set the teeth down on the counter. They simply stood there on their unlikely orange feet and did nothing.

Scooter poked the clenched molars on the lefthand side with the tip of one horny finger. The jaws of the teeth opened. One orange foot rose and took a dreamy half-step forward. Then the teeth stopped moving and the whole rig fell sideways. The Chattery Teeth came to rest on the wind-up key, a slanted, disembodied grin out here in the middle of no-man's land. After a moment or two, the big teeth came together again with a slow (and rather ominous) click. That was all.

Hogan, who had never had a precognitive thought in his life, was suddenly filled with a clear certainty that was both eerie and sickening. *A year from now, this man will have been eight months in his grave, and if someone exhumed his coffin and pried off the lid, they'd see teeth just like these poking out of his dried-out dead face like some sort of animal trap — a set of footless Chattery Teeth that don't work anymore. And why? Because something called cancer came along and knocked all of Scooter's cogs just a little off-track.*

He glanced up into Scooter's eyes, glittering like dark gems in tarnished settings, and suddenly it was no longer a question of *wanting* to get out of here; he *had* to get out of here.

"Well," he said (hoping frantically that Scooter would not stick out his hand to be shaken). "I have to go. Best of luck to you, sir."

Scooter *did* put his hand out, but not to be shaken. Instead, he snapped the rubber band back around the Chattery Teeth (Hogan had no idea why, since they didn't work), set them on their funny cartoon feet, and pushed them across the scratched surface of the counter. "Go on," he said. "Take em. No charge. Give em to your boy. He'll get a kick out of em standin' on the shelf in his room even if they don't work. I know a little about boys. Raised three of em."

"How did you know I had a son?" Hogan asked.

Scooter winked. The gesture was terrifying and pathetic at the same time. "Seen it in your face," he said. "Go on, take em."

The wind gusted again, this time hard enough to make the boards of the building moan. The sand hitting the windows sounded like fine snow. Hogan picked up the teeth by the plastic feet, surprised all over again by how heavy they were.

"Here," Scooter said. He produced a paper bag, almost as wrinkled and crumpled about the edges as his own face, from beneath the counter.

"Stick em in here. That's a real nice sport-coat you got there. If you carry them choppers in the pocket, it'll get pulled out of shape."

He put the bag on the counter as if he understood how little Hogan wanted to touch him.

"Thanks," Hogan said. He put the Chattery Teeth in the bag and rolled down the top. "My boy, Jack, thanks you, too."

Scooter smiled, revealing a set of teeth just as false (but nowhere near as large) as the ones in the paper bag. "My pleasure, mister. You drive careful until you get out of the blow. You'll be fine once you get in the foothills."

"I know." Hogan cleared his throat. "Thanks again. I hope you . . . uh . . . recover soon."

"That'd be nice," Scooter said evenly, "but I don't think it's in the cards, do you?"

"Uh. Well. Okay." Hogan realized with dismay that he didn't have the slightest idea how to conclude this encounter. "Take care of yourself."

Scooter nodded. "You too."

Hogan retreated toward the door, opened it, and had to hold on tight as the wind tried to rip it out of his hand and bang the wall. Fine sand scoured his face and he slitted his eyes against it.

He stepped out, closed the door behind him, and pulled the lapel of his real nice sport-coat over his mouth and nose as he crossed the porch, descended the steps, and headed toward the Dodge Fiesta camper-van parked just beyond the gas-pumps. The wind pulled his hair and the sand stung his cheeks. He was going around to the driver's side door when someone tugged his arm.

"Mister! Hey, mister!"

He turned. It was the blonde-haired boy. He hunched against the wind and blowing sand, wearing nothing but a tee-shirt and a pair of faded 501 jeans. Behind him, Mrs. Scooter was dragging a mangy beast on a choke-chain toward the back door of the store. Wolf the Minnesota Coydog looked like a half-starved German Shepherd pup — and the runt of the litter, at that.

"What?" Hogan shouted, knowing very well what.

"Can I have a ride?" the kid shouted back over the wind.

Hogan did not ordinarily pick up hitchhikers — not since one afternoon five years ago. He had stopped for a young girl on the outskirts of Tonapah. Standing by the side of the road, the girl had resembled one of those sad-eyed waifs in the velvet paintings you could buy in the discount stores, a kid who looked like her mother and her last friend had both died in the same housefire about a month ago. Once she was in the car, however, Hogan had seen the bad skin and mad eyes of the long-time junkie. By then it had been too late. She had stuck a pistol in his face and demanded his wallet. The pistol was old and rusty. Its grip was wrapped in tattered electrician's tape. Hogan had doubted if it was loaded, or if it would fire if it was . . . but he had a wife and a kid back in L.A., and even if he had been single, was a hundred and forty bucks worth risking your life over? He hadn't thought so even then, when he had just been getting his feet under him in his new line of work. He gave the girl his wallet. By then her boyfriend had been parked beside the van (in those days it had been a Ford Econoline, nowhere near as nice as the Fiesta XRT) in a dirty blue sedan. Hogan asked the girl if she would leave him his driver's license, and the pictures of Lita and Jack. "Fuck you, sugar," she said, and slapped him across the face, hard, with his own wallet before getting out and running to the blue car.

Hitchhikers were trouble.

But the storm was getting worse, and the kid didn't even have a jacket. What was he supposed to tell him? Fuck you, sugar, crawl under a rock until the wind drops?

"Get in," he said.

"Thanks, dude! Thanks a lot!"

The kid ran toward the passenger door, tried it, found it locked, and just stood there, waiting to be let in, hunching his shoulders up around his ears. The wind billowed out the back of his shirt like a sail, revealing glimpses of his thin, pimple-studded back.

Hogan glanced back at Scooter's Grocery & Roadside Zoo as he went around to the driver's door. Scooter was standing at the window, looking out at him. He raised his hand, solemnly, palm out. Hogan raised his own in return, then slipped his key into the lock and turned it. He opened the door, pushed the unlock button next to the power window switch, and motioned for the kid to get in.

He did, then had to use both hands to pull the door shut again. The wind howled around the Fiesta, actually making it rock a little from side to side.

"*Wow!*" the kid gasped, and rubbed his fingers briskly through his hair (it had come loose from the rubber band and now it lay on his shoulders in lank clots). "Some storm, huh?"

"Yeah," Hogan said. There was a console between the two front seats — the kind of seats the brochures liked to call "captain's chairs" — and Hogan placed the paper bag in one of the cup-holders. Then he turned the ignition key. The engine started at once with a good-tempered rumble.

The kid twisted around in his seat and looked appreciatively into the back of the van. There was a bed (now folded back into a couch), a small LP gas stove, several storage compartments where Hogan kept his various sample cases, and a toilet cubicle at the rear.

"Not bad, dude!" the kid said. "All the comforts." He glanced back at Hogan. "Where you headed?"

"Los Angeles."

The kid grinned. "Hey, great! So am I!" He took out his just-purchased pack of Merits and tapped one loose.

Hogan had put on his headlights and dropped the transmission into drive. Now he shoved the gearshift back into park and turned to the kid. "Let's get a couple of things straight," he said.

The kid gave Hogan his wide-eyed innocent look. "Sure, dude — you bet."

"First, I don't pick up hitchhikers as a rule. I had a bad experience with one a few years back. It vaccinated me. I'll take you through the Santa Clara foothills. There's a truckstop on the other side — Sammy's. It's close to the turnpike. That's where we part company. Okay?"

"Okay. Sure, dude. You bet." Still with the wide-eyed look.

"Second, if you really have to smoke, we part company right now. *That* okay?"

For just a moment Hogan saw the kid's other look (and even on short acquaintance, Hogan was almost willing to bet the kid only had the two) — the mean, watchful look, and then he was all wide-eyed, sure-you-bet-right-on-dude innocence again. He tucked the cigarette behind his ear and showed Hogan his empty hands.

"No prob," he said. "Okay?"

"Okay. Bill Hogan." He held out his hand.

"Bryan Adams," the kid said, and shook Hogan's hand briefly.

Hogan dropped the transmission into drive again and began to roll slowly toward Route 46. As he did, his eyes dropped briefly to a cassette box lying on the dashboard. It was *Reckless*, by Bryan Adams.

Sure, he thought. *You're Bryan Adams and I'm really Don Henley. We just stopped by Scooter's Grocery & Roadside Zoo to get a little material for our next albums, right dude?*

As he pulled out onto the highway, already straining to see through the blowing dust, he found himself thinking of the girl again, the one outside of Tonapah who had slapped him across the face with his own wallet before fleeing. He was starting to get a very bad feeling about this.

Then a hard gust of wind tried to push him into the eastbound lane, and he concentrated on his driving.

They rode in silence for awhile. When Hogan glanced once to his right he saw the kid was lying back with his eyes closed — maybe asleep, maybe dozing, maybe just pretending because he didn't want to talk. That was okay; Hogan didn't want to talk, either. For one thing, he didn't know what he might have to say to Mr. Bryan Adams from Nowhere, U.S.A. It was a cinch young Mr. Adams wasn't in the market for labels or universal price-code readers, which was what Hogan sold. For another, he needed all his concentration for driving.

As Mrs. Scooter had warned, the storm was intensifying. The road was a dim phantom crossed at irregular intervals by tan ribs of sand. These drifts were like speed-bumps, and they forced Hogan to creep along at no more than twenty-five. He could live with that. At some points, however, the sand had spread more evenly across the road's surface, camouflaging it, and then Hogan had to drop down to fifteen miles an hour, navigating by the dim bounceback of his headlights from the reflector-posts which marched along the side of the road.

Every now and then an approaching car or truck would loom out of the blowing sand like a prehistoric phantom with round blazing eyes. One of these, an old Lincoln Mark IV as big as a cabin cruiser, was driving straight down the center of 46. Hogan hit the horn and squeezed right, feeling the suck of the sand against his tires, feeling his lips peel away from his teeth in a helpless snarl. Just as he became sure the oncomer was going to force him into the ditch, the Lincoln swerved back onto its own side just enough for Hogan to make it by. He thought he heard the metallic click of his bumper kissing off the Mark IV's rear bumper, but given the steady shriek of the wind, that was almost certainly his own imagination. He *did* catch just a glimpse of the driver

— an old bald-headed man sitting bolt-upright behind the wheel, peering into the blowing sand with a concentrated glare that was almost maniacal. Hogan shook his fist at him, but the old codger did not so much as glance at him. *Probably didn't even realize I was there,* Hogan thought, *let alone how close he came to hitting me.*

For a few seconds he was very close to going off the road anyway. He could feel the sand sucking harder at the rightside wheels, felt the Fiesta trying to tip. His instinct was to twist the wheel hard to the left. Instead, he fed the van gas and only urged it in that direction, feeling sweat dampen his last good shirt at the armpits. At last the suck on the tires diminished and he began to feel in control of the van again. Hogan blew his breath out in a long sigh.

"Good piece of driving, dude."

His attention had been so focused he had forgotten his passenger, and in his surprise he almost twisted the wheel all the way to the left, which would have put them in trouble again. He looked around and saw the blonde kid watching him. His gray-green eyes were unsettlingly bright; there was no sign of sleepiness in them.

"It was just luck," Hogan said. "If there was a place to pull over, I would . . . but I know this piece of road. It's Sammy's or bust. Once we're in the foothills, it'll get better."

The thing was, he did not add, it might take them three hours to cover the seventy miles between here and there.

"You're a salesman, right?"

"Right."

"Right."

He wished the kid wouldn't talk. He wanted to concentrate on his driving. Up ahead, fog-lights loomed out of the murk like yellow ghosts. They were followed by an Iroc Z with California plates. The Fiesta and the Z crept past each other like old ladies in a nursing home corridor. In the corner of his eye, Hogan saw the kid take the cigarette from behind his ear and begin to play with it. Bryan Adams indeed. Why had the kid given him a false name? It was like something out of an old Republic movie, the kind of thing you could still see on the late-late show, a black-and-white crime movie where the travelling salesman (probably played by Ray Milland) picks up the tough young con (played by Nick Adams, maybe) who has just broken out of jail in Gabbs or Deeth or some place like that—

"What do you sell, dude?"

"Labels."

"Labels?"

"That's right. The ones with the universal price code on them. It's a little block with a pre-set number of black bars in it."

The kid surprised Hogan by nodding. "Sure — they whip em over an electric-eye gadget in the supermarket and the price shows up on the cash register like magic, right?"

"Yes. Except it's not magic, and it's not an electric eye. It's a laser reader. I sell those, too. Both the big ones and the portables."

"Far out, dude." The tinge of sarcasm in the kid's voice was faint . . . but it was there.

"Bryan?"

"Yeah?"

"The name's Bill, not dude."

He found himself wishing more and more strongly that he could roll back in time to Scooter's, and just say no when the kid asked him for a ride. The Scooters weren't bad sorts; they would have let the kid stay until the storm blew itself out this evening. Maybe Mrs. Scooter would even have given him five bucks to babysit the tarantula, the rattlers, and Woof, the Amazing Minnesota Coydog. Hogan found himself liking those gray-green eyes less and less. He could feel their weight on his face, like small stones.

"Yeah — Bill. Bill the Label Dude."

Bill didn't reply. The kid laced his fingers together and bent his hands backward, cracking the knuckles.

"Well, it's like my old mamma used to say — it may not be much, but it's a living. Right, Label Dude?"

Hogan grunted something noncommittal and concentrated on his driving. The feeling that he had made a mistake had grown to a certainty. When he'd picked up the girl that time, God had let him get away with it. *Please,* he prayed. *One more time, okay, God? Better yet, let me be wrong about this kid — let it just be paranoia brought on by low barometer, high winds, and the coincidence of a name that can't, after all, be that uncommon.*

Here came a huge Mack truck from the other direction, the silver bulldog atop the grille seeming to peer into the flying grit. Hogan squeezed right until he felt the sand piled up along the edge of the road grabbing greedily at his tires again. The long silver box the Mack was pulling blotted out everything on Hogan's left side. It was six inches away — maybe even less — and it seemed to pass forever.

When it was finally gone, the blonde kid asked: "You look like you're doin' pretty well, Bill — rig like this must have set you back at least thirty big ones. So why— "

"It was a lot less than that." Hogan didn't know if 'Bryan Adams' could hear the edgy note in his voice, but *he* sure could. "I did a lot of the work myself."

"All the same, you sure ain't staggerin' around hungry. So why aren't you up above all this shit, flying the friendly skies?"

It was a question Hogan had often asked himself in the long empty miles between Tempe and Tucson or Las Vegas and Los Angeles, the kind of question you *had* to ask yourself when you couldn't find anything on the radio but crappy syntho-pop or threadbare oldies and you'd listened to the last cassette of the current best-seller from Books on Tape, when there was nothing to look at but miles of gullywashes and scrubland, all of it owned by Uncle Sam.

He could say that he got a better feel for his customers and their needs by travelling through the country where his customers lived and sold their goods, and it was true, but it wasn't the reason. He could say that checking his sample cases, which were much too bulky to fit under an airline seat, was a pain in the ass and waiting for them to show up on the conveyor belt at the other end was always an adventure (he'd once had a packing case filled with five thousand soft-drink labels show up in Hilo, Hawaii, instead of Hilsdale, New Mexico). That was *also* true, but it also wasn't the reason.

The reason was that in 1982 he had been on board a Western Pride commuter flight which had crashed in the high country seventeen miles north of Reno. Fifteen of the nineteen passengers on board and both crew-members had been killed. Hogan had suffered a broken back. He had spent four months in bed and another ten in a heavy brace his wife Lita called the Iron Maiden. They (whoever *they* were) said that if you got thrown from a horse, you should get right back on. William I. Hogan said that was bullshit, and with the exception of a white-knuckle, two-Valium flight to attend his brother's wedding in Oakland, he had never been on a plane since.

He came out of these thoughts all at once, realizing two things: he had had the road to himself since the passage of the Mack, and the kid was still looking at him with those unsettling eyes, waiting for him to answer the question.

"I had a bad experience on a commuter flight once," he said. "Since then, I've pretty much stuck to transport where you can coast into the breakdown lane if your engine quits."

"You sure have had a lot of bad experiences, Bill-dude," the kid said. A tone of bogus regret crept into his voice. "And now you're gonna have another one." There was a sharp metallic click. Hogan looked over and was not very surprised to see the kid was holding a switchknife with a glittering eight-inch blade.

Oh shit, Hogan thought. Now that it was here, now that it was right in front of him, he didn't feel very scared. Only tired. *Oh shit, and only four hundred miles from home. Goddam.*

"Pull over, Bill-dude. Nice and slow."

"What do you want?"

"If you really don't know the answer to that one, you're even dumber than you look." A little smile played around the corners of the kid's mouth. "I want your dough, and I want your van. But don't worry — there's this little truck-stop not too far from here. Sammy's. Close to the turnpike. Someone'll give you a ride. The people who don't stop will look at you like you're dogshit they found on their shoe, of course, and you might have to beg a little, but I'm sure you'll get a ride in the end. Now *pull over*."

Hogan was surprised to find that he felt more than tired — he felt angry, as well. Had he been angry at the girl who had stolen his wallet that other time? He couldn't honestly remember.

"Look," he said, turning to the kid. "I gave you a ride when you needed one, and I didn't make you beg for it. If it wasn't for me, you'd be back at Scooter's, eating sand with your thumb out. So why don't you just put that thing away? We'll— "

The kid suddenly lashed forward with the knife, and Hogan felt a thread of burning pain across his right hand. The van swerved, then shuddered as it passed over another of those sandy speed-bumps.

"Pull *over*, I said. You're either walking, salesman, or you're lying in the nearest gully with your throat cut and one of your own price-reading gadgets jammed up your ass. I get what's in your wallet either way. The van, too. I'm going to chain-smoke all the way to Los Angeles, and you know what? Each time I finish a cigarette I'm going to butt it out on your dashboard."

Hogan glanced down at his hand and saw a diagonal line of blood which stretched from the last knuckle of his pinky to the base of his thumb. And here was the anger again . . . only now it was something close to rage, and if the tiredness was still there, it was buried somewhere in the middle of that irrational red eye. He tried to summon a mental picture of Lita and Jack to damp that feeling down before it got the better of him and made him do something crazy, but the images were fuzzy and out of focus. There *was* a clear image in his mind, but it was the wrong one — it was the face of the girl outside of Tonapah, the girl with the snarling mouth below the big dime-store waif eyes, the girl who had said *Fuck you, sugar* before slapping him across the face with his own wallet.

He stepped down on the gas-pedal and the Fiesta began to move faster. The red needle moved past thirty.

The kid looked surprised, then puzzled, then angry. "What are you doing? I told you to pull over! Do you want your guts in your lap, or what?"

"I don't know," Hogan said. He kept his foot on the gas. Now the needle was trembling just above forty. The van ran across a series of dunelets and shivered like a dog with a fever. "What do *you* want, kid? How about a broken neck? All it takes is one twist of the wheel. I fastened *my* seatbelt. I notice you forgot yours."

The kid's gray-green eyes were huge now, glittering with a mixture of fear and fury. You're supposed to pull over, those eyes said. That's the way it's supposed to work when I'm holding a knife on you — don't you *know* that?

"You won't wreck us," the kid said, but Hogan thought he was trying to convince himself.

"Why not?" Hogan turned toward the kid again. "After all, I'm pretty sure I'll walk away, and the van's insured. You call the play, asshole. What about that?"

"You— " the kid began, and then his eyes widened and he lost all interest in Hogan. "*Look out!*" he screamed.

Hogan snapped his eyes forward and saw four huge white headlamps bearing down on him through the flying wrack outside. It was a tanker truck, probably carrying gasoline, propane, or maybe fertilizer. An air-horn beat the air like the cry of a gigantic, enraged goose: *WHONK! WHONK! WHONNNK!*

The Fiesta had drifted while Hogan was trying to deal with the kid; now *he* was the one halfway across the road. He yanked the wheel hard to the right, knowing it would do no good, knowing it was already too late. But the approaching truck was also moving, squeezing over just as Hogan had done to try and accommodate the Mark IV. The two vehicles danced past each other through the flying sand with less than a gasp between them. Hogan felt his rightside wheels bite into the sand again and knew that this time he didn't have a chance in hell of holding the van on the road — not at forty-two miles an hour. As the dim shape of the big steel tank (CARTER'S DAIRY MILK FROM CONTENTED COWS was painted along the side) slid from view, he felt the steering wheel go mushy in his hands, dragging further to the right. And from the corner of his eye, he saw the kid lunge forward with his knife.

What's the matter with you, are you crazy? he wanted to scream, but there was no time left for screaming, and besides, he already knew the answer — of *course* the kid was crazy. That was the message in those gray-green eyes, and it had been there long before the kid pulled the knife. Pure craziness.

He tried his level best to plant the blade in Hogan's neck, but the van had begun to tilt by then, running deeper and deeper into the sand-choked gully. Hogan pulled back from the blade, letting go of the wheel, and thought he had gotten clear until he felt the wet warmth of blood drench the side of his neck. The knife had unzipped his right cheek from jaw to temple. He flailed with his right hand, trying to get the kid's wrist, and then the Fiesta's left front wheel struck a rock the size of a pay telephone and the van flipped high and hard, like a stunt vehicle in one of those movies this rootless kid undoubtedly loved. It rolled in midair, all four wheels turning, still doing thirty miles an hour according to the speedometer, and Hogan felt his seatbelt lock painfully across his chest and belly. It was like reliving the plane-crash — now, as then, he could not get it through his head that this was really happening.

The kid was thrown upward and forward, still holding onto the knife. His head bounced off the roof as the van's top and bottom swapped places. Hogan saw his left hand waving wildly, and realized with amazement that the kid was *still* trying to stab him. The kid was a rattler, all right, he'd been right about that, but no one had milked his poison sacs.

Then the van struck the desert hardpan, peeling off the luggage racks, and the kid's head connected with the roof again, much harder this time. The knife was jolted from his hand. The cabinets at the rear of the van sprang open, spraying sample-books and laser label-readers everywhere. Hogan was dimly aware of an inhuman screaming sound — the long, drawn-out squall of the Fiesta's roof sliding across the gravelly desert surface on the far side of the gully — and thought: *So this is what it would be like to be inside a tin can when someone was using the opener.*

The windshield shattered, blowing inward in a sagging shield clouded by a million zig-zagging cracks. Hogan shut his eyes and threw his hands up to shield his face as the van continued to roll, thumping down on Hogan's side long enough to shatter the driver's side window and admit a rattle of rocks and dusty earth before staggering upright again. It rocked as if meaning to go over on the kid's side . . . and then came to rest.

Hogan sat where he was without moving for perhaps five seconds, eyes wide, hands gripping the armrests of his chair. He was aware there was a lot of dirt and crumbled glass in his lap, and something else as well, but not what the something else was. He was also aware of the wind, blowing more dirt through the Fiesta's broken windows.

Then his vision was blocked by a moving object. The object was a mottle of white skin, brown dirt, raw knuckles, and red blood. It was a fist, and it struck Hogan squarely in the nose. The agony was immediate and intense, as if someone had fired a flare-gun directly up into his brain. For a moment his vision was gone, swallowed in a vast white flash. It had just begun to come back when the kid's hands suddenly clamped around his neck and he could no longer breathe.

The kid, Mr. Bryan Adams from Nowhere, U.S.A., was leaning over the console between the front seats. Blood from perhaps half a dozen different scalp-wounds had flowed over his cheeks and forehead and nose like warpaint. His gray-green eyes stared at Hogan with fixed, lunatic fury.

"*Look what you did, you numb fuck!*" the kid shouted. "*Look what you did to me!*"

Hogan tried to pull back, and got half a breath when the kid's hold slipped momentarily, but with his seatbelt still buckled — and still locked down, from the feel — there was really nowhere he could go.

The kid's hands were back almost at once, and this time his thumbs were pressing into his windpipe, pinching it shut.

Hogan tried to bring his own hands up, but the kid's arms, as rigid as prison bars, blocked him. He tried to knock the kid's arms away, but they wouldn't budge. Now he could hear another wind — a high, roaring wind inside his own head.

"*Look what you did, you stupid shit! I'm bleedin'!*"

The kid's voice, but further away than it had been.

He's killing me, Hogan thought, and a voice replied: *Right — fuck you, sugar.*

That brought the anger back. He groped in his lap for whatever was there. It was a paper bag. Some bulky object inside it. Hogan closed his hand around it and pistoned his fist upward toward the shelf of the kid's jaw. It connected with a heavy thud. The kid screamed in surprised pain, and his grip on Hogan's throat was suddenly gone as he fell over backward.

Hogan pulled in a deep, convulsive breath and heard a sound like a teakettle howling to be taken off the burner. *Is that me, making that sound? My God, is that me?*

He dragged in another breath. It was full of flying dust, it hurt his throat and made him cough, but it was heaven all the same. He looked down at his fist and saw the shape of the Chattery Teeth clearly outlined against the brown bag.

And suddenly felt them *move.*

There was something so shockingly human in this movement that Hogan shrieked and dropped the bag at once; it was as if he had picked up a human jawbone which had tried to speak to his hand.

The bag hit the kid's back and then tumbled to the van's carpeted floor as 'Bryan Adams' pushed himself groggily to his knees. Hogan heard the rubber band snap . . . and then the unmistakable click and chutter of the teeth themselves, opening and closing.

It's probably just a cog knocked a little off-track, Scooter had said. *I bet a man who was handy could get em walkin' and chompin' again.*

Or maybe just a good knock would do it, Hogan thought. *If I live through this and ever get back that way, I'll have to tell Scooter that all you have to do to fix a pair of malfunctioning Chattery Teeth is roll your van over and then use them to hit a psychotic hitchhiker who's trying to strangle you.*

The Chattery Teeth clattered away inside the torn brown bag; the sides fluttered, making it look like an amputated lung which refused to die. The kid crawled away from the bag without even looking at it — crawled toward the back of the van, shaking his head from side to side, trying to clear it. Blood flew from the clots of his hair in a fine spray.

Hogan found the clasp of his seatbelt and pushed the pop-release. Nothing happened. The square in the center of the buckle did not give even a little and the belt itself was still locked as tight as a cramp, cutting into the middle-aged roll of fat above the waistband of his trousers and pushing a hard diagonal across his chest. He tried rocking back and forth in the seat, hoping that would unlock the belt. The flow of blood from his face increased, and he could feel his cheek flapping back and forth like a strip of dried wallpaper, but that was all. He felt panic struggling to break through amazed shock, and twisted his head over his right shoulder to see what the kid was up to.

The kid was up to no good. He had spotted his knife at the far end of the van, lying atop a litter of instructional manuals and brochures. He grabbed it, flicked his hair away from his face, and peered back over his own shoulder at Hogan. He was grinning, and there was something in that grin that made Hogan's balls simultaneously tighten and shrivel until it felt as if someone had tucked a couple of peach-pits into his Jockey shorts.

Ah, here it is! the kid's grin said. *For a minute or two there I was worried — quite seriously worried — but everything is going to come out all right after all. Things got a little improvisational there for awhile, but now we're back to the script.*

"You stuck, Label Dude?" the kid asked over the steady shriek of the wind. "You are, ain't you? Good thing you buckled your belt, right? Good thing for me."

The kid tried to get up, almost made it, and then his knees buckled. An expression of surprise so magnified it would have been comic under other circumstances crossed his face. Then he flicked his blood-greasy hair out of his face again and began to crawl toward Hogan, his left hand wrapped around the imitation bone handle of the knife.

Hogan grasped the seatbelt buckle with both hands and drove his thumbs against the pop-release as enthusiastically as the kid had driven his into Hogan's windpipe. There was absolutely no response. The belt was frozen. He craned his neck to look at the kid again.

The kid had made it as far as the fold-up bed and then stopped. That expression of large, comic surprise had resurfaced on his face. He was staring straight ahead, which meant he was looking at something on the floor, and Hogan suddenly remembered the teeth. They were still chattering away.

He looked down in time to see the Jumbo Chattery Teeth march from the open end of the torn paper bag on their funny orange shoes. The molars and the canines and the incisors chopped rapidly up and down, producing a sound like ice in a cocktail glass. The shoes, dressed up in their tiny white spats, almost seemed to *bounce* along the gray carpet. Hogan found himself thinking of Fred Astaire tap-dancing his way across stage and back again, Fred Astaire with a cane tucked under his arm and a straw boater cocked saucily back on his head.

"Oh shit!" the kid said, half-laughing. "Is *that* what you were dickerin' for? Oh, man! I kill *you*, Label Dude, I'm gonna be doin' the world a favor."

The key, Hogan thought. *The key isn't turning.*

And he suddenly had another of those precognitive flashes; he understood exactly what was going to happen.

The kid is going to reach for them.

The teeth abruptly stopped walking and chattering. They simply stood there on the slightly tilted floor of the van, jaws slightly agape. Eyeless, they still seemed to peer up quizzically at the kid.

"Chattery Teeth," Mr. Bryan Adams, from Nowhere, U.S.A., marvelled. He reached out and curled his right hand around them, just as Hogan had known he would.

"Bite him!" Hogan shrieked. "Bite his fucking fingers *right off!*"

The kid's head snapped up, the gray-green eyes wide with startlement. He gaped at Hogan for a moment — that big expression of totally dumb surprise — and then he began to laugh. His laughter was high and shrieky, a perfect complement to the wind howling through the Fiesta and billowing the curtains like long ghost-hands.

"Bite me! *Bite* me! *Biiiite me!*" the kid chanted, as if it was the punchline to the funniest joke he'd ever heard. "Hey, Label Dude! I thought *I* was the one who bumped my head!"

The kid clamped the handle of the switchblade in his own teeth and stuck the forefinger of his left hand between the Jumbo Chattery Teeth. "Ite ee!" he said around the knife. He giggled and wiggled his finger between the oversized jaws. "Ite ee! O on, ite ee!"

The teeth didn't move. Neither did the orange feet. Hogan's premonition collapsed around him the way dreams do upon waking.

The kid wiggled his finger between the Chattery Teeth one more time, then began to pull his finger free. Suddenly he screamed in pain, and for a moment Hogan's heart leaped in his chest.

"*Oh shit! MotherFUCKER!*" the kid screamed, but he was laughing at the same time, and the teeth, of course, had never moved.

The kid lifted the teeth up for a closer look as he grabbed his knife again. He shook the long blade at the Chattery Teeth like a teacher shaking his pointer at a naughty student. "You shouldn't bite," he said. "That's very bad behav— "

One of the orange feet took a sudden step forward on the grimy palm of the kid's hand. The jaws opened at the same time, and before Hogan was fully aware of what was happening, the Chattery Teeth had closed on the kid's nose.

This time Bryan Adams's scream was real — a thing of agony and ultimate surprise. He flailed at the teeth with his right hand, trying to bat them away, but they were locked on his nose as tightly as Hogan's seatbelt was locked around his middle. Blood and filaments of torn gristle burst out between the canines in red strings. The kid jackknifed backward and for a moment Hogan could see only his flailing body, lashing elbows, and kicking feet. Then he saw the glitter of the knife.

The kid screamed again and bolted into a sitting position. His long hair had fallen over his face in a curtain; the clamped teeth stuck out like the rudder of some strange boat. The kid had somehow managed to insert the blade of his knife between the teeth and what remained of his nose.

"Kill him!" Hogan shouted hoarsely. He had lost his mind; on some level he understood that he *must* have lost his mind, but for the time being, that didn't matter. "*Go on, kill him!*"

The kid shrieked — a long, piercing firewhistle sound — and twisted the knife. The blade snapped, but not before it had managed to pry the disembodied jaws at least partway open. The teeth fell off his face and into his lap. Most of the kid's nose was still impaled on that wide, naked grin.

The kid shook his hair back. His gray-green eyes were crossed, trying to look down at the mangled stump which had once been his nose. His mouth was drawn down in a rictus of pain; the tendons in his neck stood out like pulley-wires.

The kid reached for the teeth. The teeth stepped nimbly backward on their orange cartoon feet. They were nodding up and down, marching in place, grinning at the kid, who was now sitting with his ass on his calves. Blood drenched the front of his tee-shirt.

The kid said something then that confirmed Hogan's belief that he, Hogan, had lost his mind; only in a fantasy born of delirium would such words be spoken.

"Give bme bag by *dose,* you sud-of-a-bidtch!"

The kid reached for the teeth again and this time they ran *forward,* under his snatching hand, between his spread legs, and there was a meaty *chump!* sound as they closed on the bulge of faded blue denim just below the place where the zipper of the kid's jeans ended.

Bryan Adams's eyes flew wide open. So did his mouth. His hands rose to the level of his shoulders, springing wide open, as if he meant to conduct the opening movement of some amazing symphony. The switchknife flew over his shoulder to the back of the van.

"*Jesus! Jesus! Jeeeeeee —* "

The orange feet were pumping rapidly, as if doing a Highland Fling. The pink jaws of the Jumbo Chattery Teeth nodded rapidly up and down, as if saying *yes! yes! yes!* and then shook back and forth, just as rapidly as if saying *no! no! no!*

"*— eeeeeeEEEEEEEE —* "

As the cloth of the kid's jeans began to rip — and that was not all that was ripping, by the sound — Bill Hogan passed out.

He came to twice. The first time must have been only a short while later, because the storm was still howling through and around the van, and the light was about the same. He started to turn around, but a monstrous bolt of pain shot up his neck. Whiplash, of course, and probably not as bad as it could have been . . . or would be tomorrow, for that matter.

Always supposing he lived until tomorrow.

The kid. I have to look and make sure he's dead.

No, you don't. Of course he's dead. If he wasn't, you would be.

Now he began to hear a new sound from behind him — the steady chutter-click-chutter of the teeth.

They're coming for me. They've finished with the kid, but they're still hungry, so they're coming for me.

He placed his hands on the seatbelt buckle again, but the pop-release was still hopelessly jammed, and his hands seemed to have no strength, anyway.

The teeth grew steadily closer — they were right in back of his seat, now, from the sound — and Hogan's confused mind read a rhyme into their ceaseless chomping: *Clickety-clickety-clickety-clack! We are the teeth, and we're coming back! Watch us walk, watch us chew, we ate him, now we'll eat you!*

Hogan closed his eyes.

The clittering sound stopped.

Now there was only the ceaseless whine of the wind and the *spick-spack* of sand striking the dented side of the Fiesta.

Hogan waited. After a long, long time, he heard a single click, followed by the minute sound of tearing fibers. There was a pause, then the click and the tearing sound was repeated.

What's it doing?

The third time the click and the small tearing sound came, he felt the back of his seat moving a little and understood. The teeth were pulling themselves up to where he was. Somehow they were pulling themselves up to him.

Hogan thought of the teeth closing on the bulge of the kid's balls and willed himself to pass out again. Sand flew in through the broken windshield, tickled his cheeks and forehead.

Click . . . rip. Click . . . rip. Click . . . rip.

The last one was very close. Hogan didn't want to look down, but he was unable to help himself. And beyond his right hip, where the seat cushion met the seat's back, he saw a wide white grin. It moved upward with agonizing slowness, pushing with the as-yet-unseen orange feet as it nipped a small fold of gray seat-cover between its incisors . . . then the jaws let go and it lurched convulsively upward.

This time what the teeth fastened on was the pocket of Hogan's slacks, and he passed out again.

When he came to the second time, the wind had dropped and it was almost dark; the air had taken on a queer purple shade Hogan could not remember ever having seen in the desert before. The swirls of sand running across the desert floor beyond the sagging ruin of the windshield looked like fleeing ghost-children.

For a moment he could remember nothing at all of what had happened to land him here; the last clear memory he could touch was of looking at his gas-gauge, seeing it was down to an eighth, then looking up and seeing a sign at the side of the road which said SCOOTER'S GROCERY & ROADSIDE ZOO GAS SNAX COLD BEER *SEE LIVE RATLLESNAKE'S!*

He understood that he could hold onto this amnesia for awhile, if he wanted to; given a little time, his subconscious might even be able to wall off subsequent memories permanently. But it could be *dangerous* not to remember. It could be *very* dangerous. Because—

The wind gusted. Sand rattled against the badly dented driver's side of the van. It sounded almost like

(teeth! the teeth! the Chattery Teeth!)

The fragile surface of his amnesia shattered, letting everything pour through, and all the heat fell from the surface of Hogan's skin. He uttered a rusty squawk as he remembered the sound

(chump!)

the teeth had made as they closed on the kid's balls, and he closed his hands over his own crotch, eyes rolling fearfully in their sockets as he looked for the runaway teeth.

He didn't see them, but the ease with which his shoulders followed the movement of his hands was new. He looked down at his lap and slowly removed his hands from his crotch. His seatbelt was no longer holding him prisoner. It lay on the gray carpet in two pieces. The metal tongue of the pull-up section was still buried inside the buckle, but beyond it there was only ragged red fabric. The belt had not been cut; it had been gnawed through.

He looked up into the rear-view mirror and saw something else: the back doors of the Fiesta were standing open, and there was only a vague, man-shaped red outline on the gray carpet where the kid had been. Mr. Bryan Adams, from Nowhere, U.S.A., was gone.

And so were the Chattery Teeth.

Hogan got out of the van slowly, like an old man afflicted with a terrible case of arthritis. He found that if he held his head perfectly level, it wasn't too bad . . . but if he forgot and moved it in any direction, a series of exploding bolts went off in his neck, shoulders, and upper back. Even the thought of allowing his head to roll backward was unbearable.

He walked slowly to the rear of the van, running his hand lightly over the dented, paint-peeled surface, hearing and feeling the glass as it crunched under his feet. He stood at the far end of the driver's side for a long time. He was afraid to turn the corner. He was afraid that, when he did, he would see the kid squatting on his hunkers, holding the knife in his left hand and grinning that empty grin. But he couldn't just stand here, holding his head on top of his strained neck like a big bottle of nitroglycerine, while it got dark around him, so at last Hogan went around.

Nobody. The kid was really gone. Or so it seemed at first.

The wind gusted, blowing Hogan's hair around his bruised face, then dropped away completely. When it did, he heard a harsh scraping noise coming from about twenty yards beyond the van. He looked in that direction and saw the soles of the kid's sneakers just disappearing over the top of a dry-wash. The sneakers were spread in a limp V. They stopped moving for a moment, as if whatever was hauling the kid's body needed a few moments' rest to recoup its strength, and then they began to move again in little jerks.

A picture of terrible, unindurable clarity suddenly rose in Hogan's mind. He saw the jumbo Chattery Teeth standing on their funny orange feet just over the edge of that wash, standing there in spats so cool they made the coolest of the California Raisins look like hicks from Fargo, North Dakota, standing there in the electric purple light which had overspread these empty lands west of Las Vegas. They were clamped shut on a thick wad of the kid's long blonde hair.

The Chattery Teeth were backing up.

The Chattery Teeth were dragging Mr. Bryan Adams away to Nowhere, U.S.A.

Hogan turned in the other direction and walked slowly toward the road, holding his nitro head straight and steady on top of his neck. It took him five minutes to negotiate the ditch and another fifteen to flag a ride, but he eventually managed both things. And during that time, he never looked back once.

Nine months later, on a clear hot summer day in June, Bill Hogan happened by Scooter's Grocery & Roadside Zoo again . . . except the place had been renamed. NAN'S PLACE, it now said. GAS COLD BEER VIDEO'S. Below the words was a picture of a wolf—or maybe just a Woof — snarling at the moon. Wolf himself, The Amazing Minnesota Coydog, was lying in a cage in the shade of the porch overhang. His back legs were sprawled extravagantly, and his muzzle was on his paws. He did not get up when Hogan got out of his car to fill the tank. Of the rattlesnakes and the tarantula there was no sign.

"Hi, Woof," he said as he went up the steps, and the cage's inmate rolled over on his back, as if hoping to be scratched.

The store looked bigger and cleaner inside. Hogan guessed this was partly because the sky was clear and the air wasn't full of flying dust, but that wasn't all; the windows had been washed, for one thing. The board walls had been replaced with pine-paneling that still smelled fresh and sappy. A snackbar with five stools had been added at the back. The novelty case was still there, but the cigarette loads, the joy-buzzers, and Dr. Wacky's Itching Powder were gone. The case was filled with videotape boxes. A hand-lettered sign read X-RATED IN BACK ROOM "B 18 OR B GONE."

The woman at the cash register was standing in profile to Hogan, looking down at a calculator and running numbers on it. For a moment Hogan was sure this was Mr. and Mrs. Scooter's daughter — the female complement of those three boys Scooter had talked about raising. Then she raised her head and Hogan saw it was Mrs. Scooter herself. It was hard to believe this could be the woman whose mammoth bosom had almost burst the seams of her NEVADA IS GOD'S COUNTRY tee-shirt, but it was. Mrs. Scooter had lost at least fifty pounds (most of it in the breastworks, from the look) and dyed her hair a dark walnut brown. Only the sun-wrinkles around the eyes and mouth were the same.

"Getcha gas?" she asked.

"Yep. Fifteen dollars' worth." He handed her a twenty and she rang it up. "Place looks a lot different from the last time I was in."

"Been a lot of changes since Scooter died, all right," she agreed, and pulled a five out of the register. She started to hand it over, really looked at him for the first time, and hesitated. "Say . . . ain't you the guy who almost got killed the day we had that storm last year?"

He nodded and stuck out his hand. "Bill Hogan."

She didn't hesitate; simply reached over the counter and gave his hand a single strong pump. The death of her husband seemed to have improved her disposition . . . or maybe it was just that the waiting for it to happen was over.

"I'm sorry about your husband. He seemed like a nice enough sort."

"Scoot? Yeah, he was a good 'nough fella before he took ill," she agreed. "And what about you? You all recovered?"

Hogan nodded. "I wore a neck-brace for about six weeks — not for the first time, either — but I'm okay."

She was looking at the scar which twisted down his right cheek. "He do that? That kid?"

"Yeah."

"Stuck you pretty bad."

"Yeah."

"I heard he got hurt in the crash, crawled out into the desert, and died." She was looking at him shrewdly. "That about right?"

Hogan smiled a little. "Near enough, I guess."

"J.T. — he's the State Bear around these parts — said the animals worked him over pretty good. Desert rats are awful impolite that way."

"I don't know much about that part."

"J.T. said the kid's own mother wouldn't have reckanized him." She put a hand on her reduced bosom and looked at him earnestly. "If I'm lyin', I'm dyin'."

Hogan laughed out loud. In the weeks and months since the day of the storm, this was something he found himself doing more often. He had come, it sometimes seemed to him, to a slightly different arrangement with life since that day.

"Lucky he didn't kill you," Mrs. Scooter said.

"That's right," Hogan agreed. He looked down at the video case. "I see you took out the novelties."

"Them old things? You bet! That was the first thing I did after—" Her eyes suddenly widened. "Oh, say! Jeepers! I got somethin' belongs to you! If I was to forget, I reckon Scooter'd come back and haunt me!"

Hogan frowned, puzzled, but the woman was already going back to the grille area. She went behind the counter, stood on tiptoe, and brought something down from a high shelf above the rack of breakfast cereals. She came back and put the Jumbo Chattery Teeth down beside the cash register.

Hogan stared at them with a deep sense of *deja vu* . . . but no real surprise. The oversized teeth stood there on their funny orange shoes, cool as a mountain breeze, grinning up at him as if to say, *Hello, there! Did you forget me? I didn't forget YOU, my friend. Not at all.*

"I found em on the porch the next day, after the storm blew itself out," Mrs. Scooter said. She laughed. "Just like old Scoot to give you somethin' for free, then stick it in a bag with a hole in the bottom. I was gonna throw em out, but he said he give em to you, and I should stick em on a shelf someplace. He said a travelling man who came in once'd most likely come in again . . . and here you are."

"Yes," Hogan agreed. "Here I am."

He picked up the teeth and slipped his finger between the slightly gaping jaws. He ran the pad of the finger along the molars at the back, and in his mind he heard the kid, Mr. Bryan Adams from Nowhere, U.S.A., chanting *Bite me! Bite me! Biiiiite me!*

Were the back teeth still streaked with some dull rusty color? Hogan thought they were, but perhaps it was only a shadow.

"I saved it because Scooter said you had a boy."

Hogan nodded. "I do." *And,* he thought, *the boy still has a father. I'm holding the reason why. The question is, did they walk all the way back here on their little orange feet because this was home . . . or because they somehow knew what Scooter knew? That sooner or later, a travelling man always comes back, like a murderer is supposed to come back to the scene of his crime?*

"Well, if you still want em, they're still yours," she said. For a moment she looked solemn . . . and then she laughed. "Shit, I probably would have throwed em out anyway, except I forgot about em. Course, they're still broken."

Hogan turned the key jutting out of the gum. It went around twice, making little wind-up clicks, then simply turned uselessly in its socket. Broken. Of course they were. And would be until they decided they didn't *want* to be broken for awhile. And the question wasn't how they had gotten back here, and the question wasn't even *why* — that was simple. They had been waiting for him, for Mr. William I. Hogan. They had been waiting for the Label Dude.

The question was this: What did they want?

He poked his finger into the white steel grin again and whispered, "Bite me — do you want to?"

The teeth only stood there on their supercool orange feet and grinned.

"They ain't talking, seems like," Mrs. Scooter said.

"No," Hogan said, and suddenly he found himself thinking of the kid. Mr. Bryan Adams, from Nowhere, U.S.A. A lot of kids like him now. A lot of grownups, too, blowing along the highways like tumbleweed, always ready to take your wallet, say *fuck you, sugar,* and run. You could stop picking up hitchhikers (he had), and you could put a burglar alarm system in your home (he'd done that, too), but it was a hard world where planes sometimes fell out of the sky and the crazies were apt to turn up anyplace and there was always room for a little more insurance. He had a wife, after all.

And a son.

He summoned up the memory of the blonde kid's crazy, empty grin, and tried to match it to the one tilted up to him from beside Mrs. Scooter's new NCR register. He didn't think they were the same. Not at all.

He lived in L.A., and he was gone a lot. Someday the blonde kid's spiritual brother might decide to break in, burglar alarm or no burglar alarm — rape the woman, kill the kid, steal whatever wasn't nailed down.

It might be nice if Jack had a set of Jumbo Chattery Teeth sitting on his desk. Just in case something like that happened.

Just in case.

"Thank you for saving them," he said, picking the Chattery Teeth up carefully by the feet. "I think my kid will get a kick out of them even if they are broken."

"Thank Scooter, not me. You want a bag?" She grinned. "I got a plastic one — no holes, guaranteed."

Hogan shook his head and slipped the Chattery Teeth into his sportcoat pocket. "I'll carry them this way," he said, and grinned back at her. "Keep them close to me."

"Suit yourself." As he started for the door, she called after him: "Stop back again! I make a mean cheeseburger!"

"I'll bet you do, and I will," Hogan said. He went out, down the steps, and stood for a moment in the hot desert sunshine, smiling. He felt good — he felt good a lot these days. He had come to think that was just the way to be.

To his left, Woof the Amazing Minnesota Coydog got to his feet, poked his snout through the crisscross of wire on the side of his cage, and barked. In Hogan's pocket, the Chattery Teeth clicked together once. The sound was soft, but Hogan heard it . . . and felt them move. He patted his pocket. "Down, boy," he said softly.

He walked briskly across the yard, climbed behind the wheel of his new Chevrolet Sprint van, and drove away toward Los Angeles. He had promised Lita and Jack he would be home by seven, eight at the latest, and he was a man who liked to keep his promises.

THE BOX

Jack Ketchum

"What's in the box?" my son said.

"Danny," I said, "Leave the man alone."

It was two Sundays before Christmas and the Stamford local was packed—shoppers lined the aisles and we were lucky to have found seats. The man sat facing my daughters Clarissa and Jenny and me, the three of us squeezed together across from him and Danny in the seat beside him.

I could understand my son's curiosity. The man was holding the red square gift box in his lap as though afraid that the Harrison stop, coming up next, might jolt it from his grasp. He'd been clutching it that way for three stops now—since he got on.

He was tall, perhaps six feet or more and maybe twenty pounds overweight and he was perspiring heavily despite the cold dry air rushing over us each time the train's double doors opened behind our backs. He had a black walrus mustache and sparse thinning hair and wore a tan Burbury raincoat that had not been new for many years now over a rumpled grey business suit. I judged the pant-legs to be an inch too short for him. The socks were grey nylon, a much lighter shade than the suit, and the elastic in the left one was shot so that it bunched up over his ankle like the skin of one of those ugly pug-nosed pedigree dogs that are so trendy nowadays. The man smiled at Danny and looked down at the box, shiny red paper over cardboard about two feet square.

"Present," he said. Looking not at Danny but at me.

His voice had the wet phlegmy sound of a heavy smoker. Or maybe he had a cold.

"Can I see?" Danny said.

I knew exactly where all of this was coming from. It's not easy spending a day in New York with two nine-year-old girls and a seven-year-old boy around Christmas time when they know there is such a thing as F.A.O. Schwartz only a few blocks away. Even if you have taken them to the matinee at Radio City and then skating at Rockefeller Center. Even if all their presents had been bought weeks ago and were sitting under our bed waiting to be put beneath the tree. There was always something they hadn't thought of yet that Schwartz *had* thought of and they knew that perfectly well. I'd had to fight with them—with Danny in particular—to get them aboard the 3:55 back to Rye in time for dinner.

But presents were still on his mind.

"Danny . . . "

"It's okay," said the man. "No problem." He glanced out the window. We were just pulling into the Harrison station.

He opened the lid of the box on Danny's side, not all the way open but only about three inches—enough for him to see but not the rest of us, excluding us three—and I watched my son's face brighten at that, smiling, as he looked first at Clarissa and Jenny as if to say *nyah nyah* and then looked down into the box.

The smile was slow to vanish. But it did vanish, fading into a kind of puzzlement. I had the feeling that there was something in there that my son did not understand—not at all. The man let him look a while but his bewildered expression did not change and then he closed the box.

"Gotta go," the man said. "My stop."

He walked past us and his seat was taken immediately by a middle-aged woman carrying a pair of heavy shopping bags which she placed on the floor between her feet—and then I felt the cold December wind at my back as the double-doors slid open and closed again. Presumably the man was gone. Danny looked at the woman's bags and said shyly, "Presents?"

The woman looked at him and nodded, smiling.

He elected to question her no further.

The train rumbled on.

Our own stop was next. We walked out into the wind on the Rye platform and headed clanging down the metal steps.

"What did he have?" asked Clarissa.

"Who?" said Danny.

"The man, dummy," said Jenny. "The man with the box! What was in the *box?*"

"Oh. Nothing."

"Nothing? What? It was *empty?*"

And then they were running along ahead of me toward our car off to the left in the second row of the parking lot.

I couldn't hear his answer. If he answered her at all.

And by the time I unlocked the car I'd forgotten all about the guy.

That night Danny wouldn't eat.

It happened sometimes. It happened with each of the kids. Other things to do or too much snacking during the day. Both my wife Susan and I had been raised in homes where a depression-era mentality still prevailed. If you didn't like or didn't want to finish your dinner that was just too bad. You sat there at the table, your food getting colder and colder, until you pretty much cleaned the plate. We'd agreed that we weren't going to lay that on *our* kids. And most of the experts these days seemed to agree with us that skipping the occasional meal didn't matter. And certainly wasn't worth fighting over.

So we excused him from the table.

The next night—Monday night—same thing.

"What'd you do," my wife asked him, "have six desserts for lunch?" She was probably half serious. Desserts and pizza were pretty much all our kids could stomach on the menu at the school cafeteria.

"Nope. Just not hungry, that's all."

We let it go at that.

I kept an eye on him during the night though—figuring he'd be up in the middle of a commercial break in one of our Monday-night sitcoms, headed for the kitchen and a bag of pretzels or a jar of honey-roasted peanuts or some dry fruit loops out of the box. But it never happened. He went to bed without so much as a glass of water. Not that he looked sick or anything. His color was good and he laughed at the jokes right along with the rest of us.

I figured he was coming down with something. So did Susan. He almost had to be. Our son normally had the appetite of a Sumo wrestler.

I fully expected him to beg off school in the morning, pleading headache or upset stomach.

He didn't.

And he didn't want his breakfast, either.

And the next night, same thing.

Now this was particularly strange because Susan had cooked spaghetti and meat sauce that night and there was nothing in her considerable repertoire that the kids liked better. Even though—or maybe because of the fact—that it was one of the simplest dishes she ever threw together. But Danny just sat there and said he wasn't hungry, contented to watch while everybody else heaped it on. I'd come home late after a particularly grueling day—I work for a brokerage firm in the City—and personally I was famished. And not a little unnerved by my son's repeated refusals to eat.

"Listen," I said. "You've got to have something. We're talking *three days* now."

"Did you eat lunch?" Susan asked.

Danny doesn't lie. "I didn't feel like it," he said.

Even Clarissa and Jenny were looking at him like he had two heads by now.

"But you *love* spaghetti," Susan said.

"Try some garlic bread," said Clarissa.

"No thanks."

"Do you *feel* okay, guy?" I asked him.

"I feel fine. I'm just not hungry's all."

So he sat there.

Wednesday night Susan went all out, making him his personal favorite—roast leg of lemon-spiced lamb with mint sauce, baked potato and red wine gravy, and green snap-peas on the side.

He sat there. Though he seemed to enjoy watching us eat.

Thursday night we tried take-out—chinese food from his favorite Szechuan restaurant. Ginger beef, shrimp fried rice, fried won ton and sweet-and-sour ribs.

He said it smelled good. And sat there.

By Friday night whatever remnants of depression-era mentality lingered in my own personal psyche kicked in with a vengeance and I found myself standing there yelling at him, telling him he wasn't getting up from his chair, *young man,* until he finished at least *one slice* of his favorite pepperoni, meatball and sausage pizza from his favorite Italian restaurant.

The fact is I was worried. I'd have handed him a twenty, gladly, just to see some of that stringy mozzarella hanging off his chin. But I didn't tell him that. Instead I stood there pointing a finger at him and yelling until he started to cry—and then, second-generation depression-brat that I am, I ordered him to bed. Which is exactly what my parents would have done.

Scratch a son, you always get his dad.

But by Sunday you could see his ribs through his teeshirt. We kept him out of school Monday and I stayed home from work so we could both be there for our appointment with Doctor Weller. Weller was one of the last of those wonderful old-fashioned GP's, the kind you just about never see anymore. Over seventy years old, he would still stop by your house after office hours if the need arose. In Rye that was as unheard-of as an honest mechanic. Weller believed in homecare, not hospitals. He'd fallen asleep on my sofa one night after checking in on Jenny's bronchitis and slept for two hours straight over an untouched cup of coffee while we tiptoed around him and listened to him snore.

We sat in his office Monday morning answering questions while he checked Danny's eyes, ears, nose and throat, tapped his knees, his back and chest, checked his breathing, took a vial of blood and sent him into the bathroom for a urine sample.

"He looks perfectly fine to me. He's lost five pounds since the last time he was in for a checkup but beyond that I can't see anything wrong with him. Of course we'll have to wait for the blood work. You say he's eaten *nothing*?"

"Absolutely nothing," Susan said.

He sighed. "Wait outside," he said. "Let me talk with him."

In the waiting room Susan picked up a magazine, looked at the cover and returned it to the pile. "*Why?*" she whispered.

An old man with a walker glanced over at us and then looked away. A mother across from us watched her daughter coloring in a Garfield book.

"I don't know," I said. "I wish I did."

I was aware sitting there of an odd detachment, as though this were happening to the rest of them—to them, not me—not *us*.

I have always felt a fundamental core of loneliness in me. Perhaps it comes from being an only child. Perhaps it's my grandfather's sullen thick German blood. I have been alone with my wife and alone with my children, untouchable, unreachable, and I suspect that most of the time they haven't known. It runs deep, this aloneness. I have accommodated it. It informs all my relationships and all my expectations. It makes me almost impossible to surprise by life's grimmer turns of fate.

I was very aware of it now.

Dr. Weller was smiling when he led Danny through the waiting room and asked him to have a seat for a moment while he motioned us inside. But the smile was for Danny. There was nothing real inside it.

We sat down.

"The most extraordinary thing." The doctor shook his head. "I told him he had to eat. He asked me why. I said, Danny, people die every day of starvation. All over the world. If you don't eat, you'll die—it's that simple. Your son looked me straight in the eye and said, '*so*?'"

"Jesus," Susan said.

"He wasn't being flip, believe me—he was asking me a serious question. I said, well, you want to live, don't you? He said, '*should I?*' Believe me, you could have knocked me right off this chair. '*Should I!*' I said of course you should! *Everybody* wants to live."

"'*Why?*'" he said.

"My God. I told him that life was beautiful, that life was sacred, that life was *fun*! Wasn't Christmas just around the corner? What about holidays and birthdays and summer vacations? I told him that it was everybody's duty to try to live life to the absolute fullest, to do everything you could in order to be as strong and healthy and happy as humanly possible. And he listened to me. He listened to me and I knew he understood me. He didn't seem the slightest bit worried about any of what I was saying or the slightest bit concerned or unhappy. And when I was done, all he said was, yes—yes, but *I'm not hungry.*"

The doctor looked amazed, confounded.

"I really don't know what to tell you." He picked up a pad. "I'm writing down the name and phone number of a psychotherapist. Not a psychiatrist, mind—this fellow isn't going to push any pills at Danny. A therapist. The only thing I can come up with pending some—to my way of thinking, practically unimaginable—problem with his blood work is that Danny has some very serious emotional problems that need exploring and need exploring immediately. This man Field is the best I know. And he's very good with children. Tell him I said to fit you in right away, today if at all possible. We go back a long time, he and I—he'll do as I ask. And I think he'll be able to help Danny."

"Help him do what, doctor?" Susan said. I could sense her losing it. "Help him do what?" she said. *"Find a reason for living?"*

Her voice broke on the last word and suddenly she was sobbing into her hands and I reached over and tried to contact that part of me which might be able to contact her and found it not entirely mute inside me, and held her.

In the night I heard them talking. Danny and the two girls.

It was late and we were getting ready for bed and Susan was in the bathroom brushing her teeth. I stepped out into the hall to go downstairs for one last cigarette from my pack in the kitchen and that was when I heard them whispering. The twins had their room and Danny had his. The whispering was coming from their room.

It was against the rules but the rules were rapidly going to hell these days anyway. Homework was being ignored. Breakfast was coffee and packaged donuts. For Danny, of course, not even that much. Bedtime arrived when we felt exhausted.

Dr. Field had told us that that was all right for a while. That we should avoid all areas of tension or confrontation within the family for at least the next week or so.

I was *not* to yell at Danny for not eating.

Field had spoken first to him for half an hour in his office and then, for another twenty minutes, to Susan and I. I found him personable and soft-spoken. As yet he had no idea what Danny's problem could be. The jist of what he was able to tell us was that he would need to see Danny every day until he started eating again and probably once or twice a week thereafter.

If he did start eating.

Anyhow, I'd decided to ignore the whispering. I figured if I'd stuck to my guns about quitting the goddamn cigarettes I'd never have heard it in the first place. But then something Jenny said sailed through the half-open door loud and clear and stopped me.

"I still don't get it," she said. "What's it got to do with that *box*?"

I didn't catch his answer. I walked to the door. A floorboard squeaked. The whispering stopped.

I opened it. They were huddled together on the bed.

"What's what got to do with *what* box?" I said.

They looked at me. My children, I thought, had grown up amazingly free of guilty conscience. Rules or no rules. In that they were not like me. There were times I wondered if they were actually my children at all.

"Nothing," Danny said.

"Nothing," said Clarissa and Jenny.

"Come on," I said. "Give. What were you guys just talking about?"

"Just stuff," said Danny.

"*Secret* stuff?" I was kidding, making it sound like it was no big deal.

He shrugged. "Just, you know, stuff."

"Stuff that maybe has to do with why you're not eating? That kind of stuff?"

"*Daaaad.*"

I knew my son. He was easily as stubborn as I was. It didn't take a genius to know when you were not going to get anything further out of him and this was one of those times. "Okay," I said, "back to bed."

He walked past me. I glanced into the bedroom and saw the two girls sitting motionless, staring at me.

"What," I said.

"Nothing," said Clarissa.

"G'night, daddy," said Jenny.

I said goodnight and went downstairs for my cigarettes. I smoked three of them. I wondered what this whole box business was.

The following morning my girls were not eating.

Things occurred rapidly then. By evening it became apparent that they were taking the same route Danny had taken. They were happy. They were content. And they could not be budged. To me, *we're not hungry* had suddenly become the scariest three words in the English language.

A variation became just as scary when, two nights later, sitting over a steaming baked lasagna she'd worked on all day long, Susan asked me how in the world I expected her to eat while all her children were starving.

And then ate nothing further.

I started getting takeout for one.

McDonald's. Slices of pizza. Buffalo wings from the deli.

By Christmas Day, Danny could not get out of bed unassisted.

The twins were looking gaunt—so was my wife.

There was no Christmas dinner. There wasn't any point to it.

I ate cold fried rice and threw a couple of ribs into the microwave and that was that.

Meantime Field was frankly baffled by the entire thing and told me he was thinking of writing a paper—did I mind? I didn't mind. I didn't care one way or another. Dr. Weller, who normally considered hospitals strictly a last resort, wanted to get Danny on an IV as soon as possible. He was ordering more blood tests. We asked if it could wait till after Christmas. He said it could but not a moment longer. We agreed.

Despite the cold fried rice and the insane circumstances Christmas was actually by far the very best day we'd had in a very long time. Seeing us all together, sitting by the fire, opening packages under the tree—it brought back memories. The cozy warmth of earlier days. It was almost, though certainly not quite, normal. For this day alone I could almost begin to forget my worries about them, forget that Danny would be going into the hospital the next morning—with the twins, no doubt, following pretty close behind. For her part Susan seemed to *have* no worries. It was as though in joining them in their fast she had also somehow partaken of their lack of concern for it. As though the fast were itself a drug.

I remember laughter from that day, plenty of laughter. Nobody's new clothes fit but my own but we tried them on anyway—there were jokes about the Amazing Colossal Woman and the Incredible Shrinking Man. And the toys and games all fit, and the brand-new hand-carved American-primitive angel I'd bought for the tree.

Believe it or not, we were happy.

But that night I lay in bed and thought about Danny in the hospital the next day and then for some reason about the whispered conversation I'd overheard that seemed so long ago and then about the man with the box and the day it had all begun. I felt like a fool, like somebody who was awakened from a long confused and confusing dream.

I suddenly had to know what *Danny* knew.

I got up and went to his room and shook him gently from his sleep.

I asked him if he remembered that day on the train and the man with the box and then looking into the box and he said that yes he did and then I asked him what was in it.

"Nothing," he said.

"Really *nothing*? You mean it was actually empty?"

He nodded.

"But didn't he . . . I remember him telling us it was a *present*."

He nodded again. I still didn't get it. It made no sense to me.

"So you mean it was some kind of joke or something? He was playing some kind of joke on somebody?"

"I don't know. It was just . . . the box was empty."

He looked at me as though it was impossible for him to understand why *I* didn't understand. Empty was empty. That was that.

I let him sleep. For his last night, in his own room.

I told you that things happened rapidly after that and they did, although it hardly seemed so at the time. Three weeks later my son smiled at me sweetly and slipped into a coma and died in just under thirty-two hours. It was unusual, I was told, for the IV not to have sustained a boy his age but sometimes it happened. By then the twins had beds two doors down the hall. Clarissa went on February 3rd and Jenny on February 5th.

My wife, Susan, lingered until the 27th.

And through all of this, through all these weeks now, going back and forth to the hospital each day, working when I was and *am* able and graciously being granted time off whenever I can't, riding into the City from Rye and from the City back to Rye again alone on the train, I look for him. I look through every car. I walk back and forth in case he should get on one stop sooner or one stop later. I don't want to miss him. I'm losing weight.

Oh, I'm eating. Not as well as I should be I suppose but I'm eating.

But I need to find him. To know what my son knew and then passed on to the others. I'm sure that the girls knew, that he passed it on to them that night in the bedroom—some terrible knowledge, some awful peace. And I think somehow, perhaps by being so very much closer to all of my children than I was ever capable of being, that Susan knew too. I'm convinced it's so.

I'm convinced that it was my essential loneliness that set me apart and saved me, and now of course which haunts me, makes me wander through dark corridors of commuter trains waiting for a glimpse of him—him and his damnable present, his gift, his box.

I want to know. It's the only way I can get close to them.

I want to see. I *have* to see.

I'm *hungry*.

For Neal McPheeters

HACELDAMA

Gary A. Braunbeck

"Thus let me live, unseen, unknown,
Thus unlamented let me die;
Steal from the world, and not a stone
Tell where I lie."

—Alexander Pope
Ode on Solitude (1717)

tell me, my torturer, did you ever think i would last this long?
of course not.
i wonder how they would react if they knew the truth.
oh well. the traditor papilio waits.
time to begin. yet again.

1

The customers in the truck stop restaurant paid no attention to the man until he started shooting.

Everyone moved at once, running for doors, throwing themselves under tables, grabbing the loved ones with them or calling the names of those they'd never see again: all were silenced by the cold, contemptuous crack of rattlegun racket.

A dog sat immersed in the unreason of the rainy midnight outside watching blood bloom on the windows.

Five minutes later the man came out.

The dog looked up.

A bloodied hand rested on its head.

"Patience, my friend," said a deep, sepulchral voice.

The grieving howl of an approaching siren echoed from the distance. The dog whirled around, baring its teeth.

"Easy, boy. Here."

The dog accepted what was placed between its teeth.

"Remember, don't eat this. See you soon."

It looked toward the direction of the siren. When it turned back, the man had disappeared into unreason and the rain.

2

Five hours later, as the sun perched above the hills like a vulture examining a field of fresh carrion, Detective Ben Littlejohn stood shivering in a corner of the blood-smeared restaurant and sipped lukewarm coffee from a thermos. The bodies had been examined, counted, and hauled away, the rifle lay on the counter in an evidence bag, and three wallets plus one purse *(which equals four missing bodies,* he thought) were neatly arranged on a nearly table.

He glanced up and saw Captain Al Goldstein in the doorway. "I keep thinking about the guy who walked into that McDonald's in California."

"The 'I'm-going-to-hunt-humans' guy?"

"Yeah. I remember seeing this picture of a cop kneeling over the body of a little boy who was splayed against a bicycle. The kid's hand was reaching out and you could see the hand of another person outside camera range reaching toward him. I always wondered if that was the kid's mother, if she'd been trying to get to him in those last few seconds."

"I remember that picture, too. I think *The New York Post* ran it. The cop was crying."

Ben rubbed his sore neck. "Can't say I blame him."

Goldstein offered Ben a cigarette. "I hate to sound crass—not that my personality is all that sparkling to begin with—but you have other worries. I've got poeple trying to track down that partner of yours but—"

"We should leave Bill alone. He and Eunice haven't had a vacation in years."

"I know, but the mayor and the chief have been reaming my ass over not having enough qualified personnel to put on this. When I reminded them about the new budget cuts they gave me one of those 'So what?' looks." He lowered his voice. "I managed to get us thirty-six hours to come up with something before the governor calls in the FBI."

The sudden burst of a flashbulb lanced into Ben's eyes; reporters had been outside for three hours, snapping pictures, scrambling for interviews, broadcasting live from the scene for the early-bird breakfast crowd. None had yet been allowed inside the truck stop.

Goldstein glanced out the window. "I heard something about a dog?"

"It had a note in its mouth. It walked up to the first two guys on the scene and dropped it at their feet."

"Which unit?"

"Sanderson and Wagner. It went for Sanderson's throat and they had to shoot it. They left about five minutes ago. Body's in the trunk of their cruiser."

"Let me see the note."

Ben reached into his pocket and, using a pair of tweezers, took the note from its plastic evidence bag.

Goldstein fished through his own pockets, then grunted in disgust. "Shit! I don't have my glasses. D'you mind?"

"You're gonna just love this," said Ben, then began to read: "Hannibal crossed the Alps with one of the greatest armies in history. He arrived at the outer gates of Rome and Rome was in his hands. At the outer gates he stopped, then went back. What made him stop?"

"That it?"

"No. On the reverse side are the lyrics to 'Don't Get Around Much Anymore.' You haven't asked me about the bodies yet."

"How many were there?"

"That depends. The killer took the time to lay a piece of identification on each victim. The nine bodies in here matched their identification but—" he pointed to the wallets and purse "—we have no corpses for these. So the total is either nine or thirteen, depending on how you want to look at it."

"How could—?"

"That's not even the good part." Ben's hands began to shake. "No one was shot in the head. No one. The killer walked in here, sprayed the place with an AK-47, and not one person gets it in the head."

"You think it was deliberate?"

"Had to be. He didn't want to damage the faces. He *wanted* us to be able to identify the bodies quickly." He took a deep breath; when he spoke again his voice was thin and hollow and the words came out in a rapid cadence: "He tore out everyone's eyes. We couldn't find them anywhere. Then he jammed coins into the empty sockets and stapled everyone's eyelids to their foreheads. Wait until you see the pictures; all those bodies with wide silver eyes staring up at the ceiling, reflecting the light . . . ."

" . . . must've been horrible."

"It looked almost *comical!* I didn't know whether to laugh or vomit or dance a jig. Hannibal crossing the Alps. 'Don't Get Around Much Anymore.' I'm surprised he didn't ask how much wood would a woodchuck chuck if—"

"That's enough."

"Sorry." He finished his cigarette. "I never thought *we'd* see something like this."

Goldstein put a hand on Ben's arm. "I'll finish up here, talk to the reporters and such. You go home. Take a shower, rest up. One hour. I want you in my office by seven."

Ben started toward the door, then turned and said, "You know something else about that 'I'm-going-to-hunt-humans' guy? The morning after it happened, our McDonald's here had its busiest day ever. Go figure."

only seventeen hundred days this time?

you're getting unreasonable in your old age, my torturer. they died nobly.

i see.

not that nobly. so.

only seventeen hundred days this time.

your will be done.

and fuck you, too.

3

Instead of his apartment Ben went to the cemetery by the old County Home to clear his head. It was a sad, pathetic place, but he'd felt a kinship with it since his high school days when he'd worked part-time as the caretaker's assistant, helping to maintain the grounds and bury the residents or unidentified homeless whose bodies were dumped here by the county. It had been pretty once. He tried to remember that.

The home had burned down in 1970 and the cemetery fell to neglect and decay. Now the bodies were known only by the numbers sloppily engraved on their chipped, broken headstones: 107, 122, 135, and so on. There was a certain morbidity to coming here but come here he did, if only to remind himself that there were worse things than being a widower and in debt up to your ass at age thirty-five—among other things. A few solitary minutes with the nameless dead and suddenly a recurring bad dream and lonely bed didn't seem so cataclysmic.

He wandered through the weeds, used condoms, and broken beer bottles, looking at the markers.

76 . . . 85 . . . 93 . . .

There was no need for him to look, though; he knew the layout by heart, could probably even recite the numerical patterns in his sleep.

This'll be all of us someday, he thought. Sure, there would be mourners at the end, friends, family, old lovers you thought had forgotten about you, maybe a girl you had a crush on in ninth grade, and they would gather, and they would weep, and they would talk among themselves afterward and say, "I remember the way he used to . . . ." Your belongings would be divided, given away, or tossed on a fire, your picture moved to the back of a dusty photo album, and, eventually, those left behind would die too, and no one would be left to remember your face, your middle name, even the location of your grave. The seasons would change, the elements would set to work, rain and heat and cold and snow would smooth away the inscription on the headstone until it was no longer legible and then, later—days, weeks, decades—someone who happened by would glance down, see the faded words and dates, mutter "I wonder who's buried here," then go on about their business. No one would be left to say that this man was important, or this woman was kind, or that anything they strove for was worthwhile.

He thought then of Cheryl, his wife, and the lovely spot in Cedar Hill Cemetery where her grave was. He swallowed twice, very hard, not wanting to remember the night she and their son had died. Ben had been thirty-two and just promoted to detective. It should have been the beginning of a better life for them.

Should have been.

He wondered how many of the forgotten dead surrounding him had built their life on the unstable foundation of what Should Have Been.

A few feet away, perched on the jagged remains of a headstone, was a black butterfly. It wasn't its color that attracted Ben's gaze but its stillness; its wings did not so much as flutter in the breeze. As he knelt down to get a better look (Cheryl had loved butterflies) Ben saw that it wasn't entirely black; a thin strip of white encircled its body at an area just below the antennae. It almost looked like—he chuckled under his breath at the absurdity of the thought—a very tiny animal collar.

He froze a moment. Something about this butterfly was familiar.

His left eye twitched. He pressed on it with his finger. It stopped. He leaned closer and blew on the butterfly's wings—

—but they did not move. Not even a fraction of an inch.

He looked at the headstone:

EMILY SUE MODINE
Beloved wife of Henry Modine
Mother to William and Patricia
Born July 13, 1960   Taken Sept. 3, 1993

He stared unbelieving, blinked to make sure he wasn't seeing things, then walked the entire cemetery again.

4

Goldstein looked up from the preliminary lab report and said, "One more time?"

"There are fifteen brand new headstones out at the old County Home cemetery. I know that place by heart, I go walking out there all the time, and those things weren't there last week. The cemetery hasn't been used since the Home burned down."

"Any of the names on the headstones match those of the victims?"

"No."

"So? There are six more headstones than we have bodies and—don't look at me like that, okay? I agree it seems like more than coincidence but the mayor and the chief are going to want something more solid."

"What's the lab say?"

"There were no prints on the note, the coins, or the rifle. No serial number on the AK-47, no skin fragments, blood, saliva, nothing."

"What about the coroner?"

"Before ten, I'm told." Goldstein stood and began straightening his tie. "Let's go. Mayor wants to see us in ten minutes."

The door flew open and the desk sergeant rushed in. "Sorry, sir, but a call just came in. Two officers down."

"Jesus. Who?"

"Number 19. Sanderson and Wagner."

Ben saw Goldstein's face go pale, but when he spoke his voice was tight and steady; grace under pressure.

"I want every available unit out there."

"But—"

"Now."

"The caller said they were dead."

5

Their throats had been clawed open, their eyes torn out, their eyelids stapled to their foreheads, and Kennedy fifty-cent pieces jammed into the bloody eye sockets.

Sanderson's torso had somehow been pushed through the windshield and lay against the hood; Wagner had been pulled from behind with such force that the seat was wrenched off its track.

A large hole had been ripped thorough the back seat, enabling Ben to see into the trunk.

"Oh, Christ," he whispered. "The dog."

"What?" shouted Goldstein, trying to supervise the placing of roadblocks and barricades. It looked as if every cop in the city were there, all of them shocked, angry, and yelling at everyone or anything.

To the best of Ben's knowledge a cop in Cedar Hill had never before
been killed in the line of duty.

"The dog," he whispered again.

Goldstein said, "So where the hell is it?"

As the paramedics took the bodies away, Ben stopped a uniformed
officer and asked if he or anyone in the neighborhood had seen a large
gray dog in the past thirty minutes; the officer shook his head.

Goldstein pulled Ben aside. "Is it possible the dog wasn't dead,
only wounded? Maybe—"

A paramedic shouted, "Captain! Over here!"

They ran over to the ambulance and climbed in back.

"What is it?"

The paramedic put on latex gloves and gestured for them to do the
same, then pulled back the sheet and pointed toward the mangled glob
of meat and cartilage that had been Sanderson's throat. "Something's
been jammed in there."

Digging the tweezers from his pocket *(like you expect there to be
fingerprints this time)*, Ben retrieved the object, carefully working the
rolled note from inside the plastic bag.

"Well?"

"It says: 'I think the Hannibal question is a little beyond you, so
try this one: Why does the dogwood have three red spots? You might
ask Emily Modine that one, or even Mozart, if you can find his grave.
The city of Vienna has been looking for it for almost two centuries."

Goldstein leaned forward and put his face in his hands. "And the
other side?"

"The lyrics to 'Imagine.'"

Goldstein exhaled and sat up straight. His composure was almost
frightening. "Twenty years I've been a cop and in all that time the worst
we've ever had to deal with were those .22 calibre killings a few years
back. Took us two weeks to track down those crankheads. A turf war.
Boy, was the chief disappointed. He thought we had a bonafide serial
killer on our hands, headlines, his picture on the front page." A small
sneer appeared on his face, then just as quickly vanished. "Looks like
we got one now." He rubbed his eyes. "Sanderson and his wife were
gonna have a baby soon."

Ben closed his eyes and thought: . . . *we're gonna have a baby . . .
a baby . . . we're gonna have a baby, Ben! God, I love you . . . .*

"Okay," said Goldstein. "This is the first concrete link we've got between the killings and the headstones at the cemetery. That'll give us some weight."

"We still have four bodies missing from the truck stop."

"I can add and subtract, thank you. I'm going back to the station and see if the coroner's report is in yet. I'll send two units to search the cemetery grounds. You head out there and wait for them."

Ben reached up and massaged his neck.

he's thinking about his dream again. i know. i'm the one who sent it to him.

yes, my torturer. i found another one.

and there's not a thing you can do about it.

is there?

not without finally giving me mercy.

and you can't have that, can you?

6

Ben's radio squawked at him as soon as he climbed into his car. The dispatcher gave him a number to call and said it was an emergency.

He snatched up the car phone and punched in the number.

They answered on the first ring. "Ben? This is Monsignor Maddingly at St. Francis de Sales on Granville Street." Ben had known Maddingly for most of his life—in fact, Maddingly had baptized him. "Could you get over here right away? I know you've got your hands full right now but . . . please, Ben. Believe me, it's urgent. And don't use the siren. You won't want to draw attention to this."

Maddingly was waiting in front of the church. Ben joined him and they walked up to the large double oak doors that led inside.

"Our cleaning lady found them," said Maddingly, opening the doors.

Even from where he stood—some twenty yards away—Ben could see the two bodies hanging by their necks from beams above the altar, bookends to the solid-gold crucifix that hovered in the center.

Ben and Maddingly approached slowly, the echo of their footsteps bouncing eerily off the stained-glass windows depicting saints and prophets in solemn, multi-colored meditation.

Both bodies were naked and had evacuated their bowels on the altar; the sickening, cumulative stench of piss, excrement, and incense made Ben's stomach turn.

He stared up at the bodies and saw the deep, bloody scratch marks on their throat; frenzied marks, proof of panic, as if they'd been trying to—

"Oh God," he whispered. "They were still alive."

A soft shaft of sunlight resolved into a solid beam as it passed through the stained-glass eyes of the Virgin Mary and reflected brightly from the silver coins which replaced the eyes of both corpses.

A glob of piss-soaked excrement dropped from the leg of one body and spattered with a soft *ping!* against the rim of a silver chalice positioned in the center of the altar.

The chalice was filled to overflowing with human eyes and their still-attached stalks.

Covering his mouth and stepping to the altar, Ben saw the letters scribbled in shit on the white silk cloth which covered the marble:

DAMA

"Do you know what this means?" he asked Maddingly. "Is it part of something Latin?"

"Not that I can recall. But I'll check, I promise you." Ben was impressed by the Monsignor's outward calm. He stepped down and led Maddingly toward the sacristy. "You'll have to move all masses for at least the next couple of days."

"I figured as much. Just let me say a few more prayers over the bodies before you call this in."

Ben nodded, and for some reason felt compelled to ask: "Will you say a prayer for the soul of their killer?"

"Yes. But given my druthers I'd prefer to break his knees with a ball bat."

"That makes two of us." Ben gripped Maddingly's hand. "Thanks for calling, Monsignor. We'll assign a surveillance unit for the next forty-eight hours, just in case he tries to get to you or the cleaning lady. I'll need to talk with her before anyone else arrives."

"She's been taken to the convent."

"One more thing, Monsignor; I need to know about the legend of the dogwood."

"Is this part of the investigation? Never mind, I know—you couldn't say if it were. The legend goes like this: When Jesus was crucified some of His blood dripped onto the petals of a white flower growing at the base of His cross. The flower was so saddened by His suffering that it kept His blood on its petals to remind the world that He tried to save it from suffering. That's why when the dogwood blooms it has a red spot on each of its three petals, to symbolize where the nails went through Christ's hands and feet."

Ben finished writing it down. "Thanks. I'm going to call this in and then—"

—the growling stopped him.

Low, guttural, and wheezing, from near the altar.

Instinctively, Ben pulled out his .45 and stepped back into the church proper.

The dog from the truck stop was sitting on top of the altar from its head craned back, staring up at the bodies. Hearing Ben chamber a round from the clip, it snapped its head down and glared at him, dark eyes clouding over into bright silver. Ben could see the two large, seeping bullet holes from where it had been shot; one in its side, one in the center of its head, and he knew that it had been dead when it ripped through the back of the trunk and attacked Sanderson and Wagner, and he knew that it was *still* dead—

—*so how?*

It bared its teeth and tensed its legs to pounce as Ben readied to shoot—

—but then it stretched low, threw back its head, and released the longest, loudest, more preternaturally mournful cry Ben had ever heard; it was the cumulative wail of a million broken-hearted men shrieking their anguish into an uncaring night coupled with the screams of a million babies doused in gasoline and set aflame; a rabid, ragged cacophony of fury and despair that shook the overhead beams with such force that the golden crucifix snapped loose and crashed onto the altar. The keening grew in volume and potency until the stained-glass windows began to rupture in spiderweb patterns, casting off sections of Mary, John the Baptist, St. Francis, and even Jesus Christ.

Maddingly pressed his hands against his ears.

Ben felt as if his bones were rattling loose as he leveled the gun and took aim at the dog—

—which ceased howling, gobbled up a mouthful of eyes from the chalice, and leapt into the aisle, disappearing within the rows of pews.

Ben stepped back into the sacristy to make sure Maddingly was all right.

The pipe organ in the loft over the main entrance suddenly began playing "Don't Get Around Much Anymore."

"What the—?" said Ben. Both he and Maddingly looked up and saw a shadow move across the loft so quickly that if either of them had blinked they would have missed it.

Maddingly shouted over the deafening music: "There are twenty-five hymns programmed into the organ's memory—and that isn't one of them."

The music suddenly lowered in volume—

—the now-unseen dog howled again—

—and machine-gun fire erupted from the loft, splitting one of the beams over the altar; it cracked in half and the two bodies came slamming down.

Ben plowed three shots into the loft but the machine-gun fire didn't stop; as the bodies struck the marble base of the altar a barrage of bullets bounced them like crazy puppets jitterbugging to the music.

Maddingly, pressed against the door of the sacristy, made the sign of the cross.

The strafing veered to the side and began shattering the solemn statues.

Ben took a deep breath, said a little prayer of his own *(Just let me get to the entryway),* bolted out past the altar, and hit the aisle running toward the loft, pumping round after round toward the flash of gunfire from above.

The machine-gun fire stopped abruptly and a dark shape appeared near the loft's rail.

"Does the flapping of a butterfly's wings in Brazil set off tornadoes in Texas?" it shouted—

—then flung itself out the large window next to the organ.

Ben slammed through the double oak doors and burst into the bright sunlight.

Before he was halfway to the sidewalk he saw the two crucified bodies in the yard of the convent, each nailed to their cross with railroad spikes—one spike through each hand, another through both feet. Both were naked except for the small section of torn and blood-stained cloth tied around their waists.

Ben swung left, then right; the broken glass of the organ loft window lay scattered about but there was no sign of whoever had jumped through it.

Still holding the .45 in front of him, he walked slowly toward the crucified bodies, oblivious to the screams of passersby and the screech of tires as shocked drivers slammed on their brakes, some colliding with others; the howl of twisted metal, the belch of shattering windshield glass, cries of panic and disgust and horror.

Ben felt the tears on his face but made no move to wipe them away.

Nailed above the head of each body was a piece of wood into which letters had been burned.

The one on the left read *EL*.

The one on the right, *HAC*.

He stared up into the dead glinting coin eyes and felt the world surrender to madness. He felt helpless. Useless. It happened so fast, too damn fast and there wasn't a thing he could do about it so what the hell good was he anymore—

—so Ben Littlejohn stood there, screaming inside.

7

He had been like this once before, three years ago.

Cheryl was in her seventh month of pregnancy. Both she and Ben had been anxious since the beginning; their two previous attempts had ended in miscarriage. But, as difficult as this third pregnancy was, it looked as if it might happen this time.

He'd come home from work to celebrate his promotion and found the downstairs lights turned off.

"Cheryl?" he called.

And was answered by a low, pained groan from overhead.

He took the steps three at a time, calling her name all the way.

Cheryl was flopped onto the floor. Her color was hideous and she was sweating and shaking. She looked at him and coughed up a small spray of blood and mucus that slopped across her cheek. Ben ran over and knelt down, trying to be gentle as he began to move her but she shook her head and placed a trembling hand against his chest, her eyes moving to indicate the phone receiver swinging back and forth from the bedside table and he asked, "Did you already call?" and she nodded, wincing from the pain as he touched her face, felt how *cold* it was, then kissed her forehead and began to lift her back onto the bed but he didn't have the balance, the angle was all wrong and he slipped and both of them tumbled to the floor and Cheryl threw back her head to scream but couldn't, the pain was that intense, and as the sound of approaching sirens sliced through the night Ben stared helplessly at his wife's straining vocal cords and thought: *If she can just scream then she'll be all right* but no sound would come as Cheryl hitched, spasmed, spit up more blood and lost consciousness and then the paramedics came out of nowhere and shoved Ben away, two of them going to work on Cheryl while another readied the gurney.

The emergency room was a storm of rushing white lab coats as doctors and nurses rolled Cheryl into an exam room. Her EKG was erratic as hell and Ben felt less than useless as he watched the team go at his wife with stunning speed and efficiency, then before he knew what was happening a keening noise erupted and was quickly muted by a nurse as the doctor in the middle of the group grabbed a defibrillator—"Clear!"—and Ben pressed his hands against his mouth to squelch his cry as the electricity shot through Cheryl's body, causing it to convulse.

"Flat-line."

The doctor applied the paddles again—nothing. Ben felt a scream rising in his throat and choked it back, watching numb and horrified as a scalpel appeared in someone's hand and swooped down like a buzzard, the incision made, the blood flowing, and suddenly the doctor had his hand inside Cheryl's chest, massaging her heart, and Ben caught a glimpse of white vein beneath membrane—

—"Oh, *Jesus,*" someone said—

—and he looked down to see something ooze from between Cheryl's legs, a sickening glop of purplish-black meat trapped in a crawling flow of blood, water, and something that looked like cottage cheese. He glimpsed part of a tiny face—

—the doctor shook his head and pulled his hands from Cheryl's chest—

—the silhouette of a nose, a section of chin—

—the EKG was snapped off—

— her body began to deflate, it seemed, like a carnival balloon—

—the room spun—

—and Ben pushed through the doctors toward his wife and child.

He saw his son's impossibly blue-black face, the strangling power of the umbilical cord around the neck, and something inside of him snapped, loosening fear and dragging wire hooks against the inside of his skin; he felt his knees start to buckle and fought to stay standing but the sensation was overpowering, he was nothing against it—

—looming overhead, something huge, something dark and vast and bigger than the whole goddamn planet, they were all buried in its shadow as it plummeted toward them and he wanted to look up but his body wouldn't move and he couldn't breathe because in moments he would be lying crushed on the ground, the thing about to slam on top of him like a meteor—

—he felt something brush his cheek then, the smallest of breezes, like a fly buzzing past—

—the fear passed, replaced by sudden, thundering grief.

He wept quietly for all the holidays he and Cheryl would never celebrate, for every disappointment she'd ever experienced, every joy that was dampened, every hope that was tainted, all the things she wanted to do but never did and now never would. He cried for all of it, screaming inside.

Later, as he sat in his car in the parking lot, Ben saw something that looked like a black butterfly on the windowshield. Cheryl had always loved butterflies. He stared at it, saw the small white strip around the upper portion of its body that looked too much like the umbilical cord around his dead son's neck, and laid his head against the steering wheel, the sobs wracking his body.

It wasn't until the rampage in Cedar Hill was finally over that Ben remembered having seen the butterfly the night of his family's dying.

For all the good it did.

that, my torturer, was the night i first became aware of him.
i wasn't sure that he would do.
but that was just you trying to confuse me, wasn't it?
he'll do nicely.

8

As Ben and Goldstein approached the mayor's office the secretary looked up from his desk, buzzed open the office door, and shook his head in pity.

They entered.

The Honorable Rachel S. Moore was sitting behind her desk, one hand supporting her bowed head, the other holding a telephone receiver to her ear.

"Yessir, I understand. Tomorrow." She hung up and gestured for Ben and Goldstein to sit down. "That was the governor. He's decided that you two couldn't find your butts with both hands and a search party, so he's calling the Feds at noon tomorrow—and the *only* reason he agreed to wait that long is because I begged him. I hate to beg, so I'm in a lousy mood, which means you'd better have something for me."

Ben and Goldstein alternated their recitation of the events since the massacre at the truck stop. When they finished, Mayor Moore shook her head and asked Goldstein for a cigarette. "I don't give a shit if this *is* a smoke-free building." She produced an ashtray from her desk and the three of them lit up.

She looked at Ben and said, "How long were you in the church?"

"Not more than seven or eight minutes. I have no idea where the crosses and bodies were hidden or how he could've gotten them up so quickly without being seen. When he jumped through the window I couldn't have been more than five seconds behind him but he was gone and the crosses were up. I've been trying to figure it out and it's just not possible. Granville Street is the most traveled in the city."

"No chance the bodies could have already been there and you—"

"No way."

"I didn't think so. I don't have to tell you how pissed the governor is, what with this being an election year. He doesn't want to call in the Feds any more than the rest of us but this has to be taken care of fast or he'll look bad. I guess he took pity on my begging—did I mention that I hate to beg?—and he agreed to make all facilities and personnel at his disposal available to us, including state troopers and National Guard units." She leaned forward and gave both men a hard, unblinking stare.

"One of the people crucified outside the convent was Esther Simms. That grand old woman practically raised me after my mother died." She rubbed her eyes and tried to smile. "I hope that if you get the chance to shoot this psycho you'll have the decency to fire an extra round into him for me."

Ben and Goldstein remained silent.

"What about the lab report and the coroner's office? Anything there?"

Ben cleared his throat. "We got a detailed report from the lab before we came over here. The coins in the eye sockets of all the victims . . . the minting dates coincide with the birth year of whoever they were . . . attached to."

"Jesus," said Mayor Moore. "How in hell could the killer know that?"

Goldstein said, "We wondered if the minting dates might also coincide with the dates of death on the new headstones in the old County Home cemetery, but they didn't."

"We've got three units stationed out there," added Ben. "They made a thorough search of the grounds but didn't find anything. Those headstones are heavy. He has to store them somewhere nearby."

Moore said, "You do have positive ID on all the victims, right?"

Ben exchanged a worried look with Goldstein, then said, "Sort of."

"What's that mean?"

"All bodies matched their identification and were positively identified by either friends or relatives, but the coroner followed routine and fingerprinted the bodies and . . . ." He exhaled and cracked his knuckles.

"If you want my attention, you've got it, but my patience is getting a bit strained."

"According to the fingerprints the first half-dozen victims were Richard Speck, Theodore Bundy, Edward Gein, Charles Whitman, Herbert Mullen, and Juan Corona. Those're the only names I can recall without looking in the files, but every set of fingerprints identifies one of the victims as a dead mass murderer. He had to have gotten into the system somehow, because as soon as the prints were run through a second time the whole thing shut down."

Rachel Moore lit another cigarette. "So he's a Sneaker. Wonderful. Anything else?"

"Just that the coins are whole silver and not sandwiched."

"Come again?"

Ben took a quarter from his pocket and showed it to her as he explained. "The U.S. Mint manufactures what are called 'sandwiched' coins for mass circulation. They stopped making whole silver coins before WWII. The majority of coins today are made of nickel and copper." He pointed to the copper strip around the circumference of the quarter. "The coins attached to the victims were whole silver."

"Any ideas on that?"

"None."

The phone bleeped. Rachel Moore pushed the intercom button. "What is it, Steve?"

"The station manager from WLCB radio is on the line for Captain Goldstein. He says it's an emergency."

She punched the line.

Goldstein listened for a moment, then said, "And this was how long ago? Can you run the tape for us? Yes, *now.*" He looked at Moore. "We need the speaker. The killer phoned them about ten minutes ago. The DJ recorded the call."

A crackle of static came over the speaker, followed by a hiss, then the sound of Guy Donovan, Cedar Hill's favorite morning DJ: "WLCB request line. This is Donovan. What would you—"

"This is the person who visited the Buckeye Lake Truck Stop this morning, then left an offering at the Saint Francis de Sales Church."

"That was all on the news," said the mayor.

The killer: "I have a question for the police: Does the flapping of a butterfly's wings in Brazil set off tornadoes in Texas?"

"That wasn't," whispered Ben.

The killer continued, his words edged with a profound weariness, even sadness: "There are one hundred and fifty-seven bodies buried in the old County Home Cemetery. I have placed headstones on fifteen of their graves for you, one in exchange for each person killed. I am willing to give you some time before I kill anyone else so Captain Goldstein and Detective Littlejohn can piece things together, but if anyone tries to take them off the case I will not hesitate to kill the remaining one hundred and forty-two people that are needed for . . . balance.

"I believe that Detective Littlejohn took physics for a little while when he went to college, so he might understand about the flapping of a butterfly's wings in Brazil; a theory of chaos math, fractals and such, with just a touch of Markov's Chain of Disintegration. It'll come back to him soon enough.

"As for the letters found in the church and on the crosses, they spell 'Haceldama.' It's Hebrew, as I'm sure Captain Goldstein can tell you, and means 'The Field of Blood.'

"I'm sorry about the people I've killed. And I'm sorry about the people I'm going to have to kill. I've spent an eternity being sorry, but for some, 'sorry' just doesn't cut it. Try apologizing to a baby being eaten away by cancer, or to an old woman whose family dumps her in a nursing home to die; try saying 'I'm sorry' to a country filled with starving people or a homeless man who freezes to death on a park bench. You may offer your sympathies to the lonely and broken-hearted people who shamble through the ruined places of this world but, in the end, you'll walk away. Apologize, then walk away, and feel no responsibility whatsoever.

"That is part of the seed from which the black butterfly was born. And that is why you have to deal with me.

"You cannot protect yourselves.

"Ever.

"Only I can do that."

Click.

Rachel Moore looked first at Ben, then Goldstein, asking respectively: "What the hell does he mean about butterfly wings? And Haceldama?"

"Physics was a long time ago," said Ben. "I flunked out of the course after one semester."

Goldstein raised his hands, palms out. "Don't ask me about anything Judaism. I fell away from the faith when I was sixteen."

She considered all this for a moment. "All right. I'll need a copy of that tape for the governor. Is anyone checking the records at the new County Home? If there's some way we can identify the rest of those bodies—"

"—already doing it," said Ben. "We've got people at the Home, the courthouse, the county land office, and checking the burial register of every parish. A record has to exist somewhere."

"Providing someone thought to make copies and transfer them before the old Home burned down," said Goldstein.

"Yeah," said Ben, absent-mindedly massaging his throat.

✦　　✦

you feel it, don't you, benjamin? The memory of your dream?

you're running through a dead field with tears in your eyes. Your arms ache because you're carrying something heavy. Your chest is crackling with anger, sorrow, confusion, and guilt. you want to be rid of it all.

then you see the tree, you wake up choking . . .

. . . and remember the way your son looked.

9

While Goldstein was inside getting the tape from the station manager, Ben sat in his car outside WLCB radio and tried not to surrender to depression; now that Cheryl was gone these all-too-frequent bouts were more than he could handle.

He reached into his pocket and removed the picture of her that he always carried with him. It had been taken on their wedding day. God, she'd been so beautiful. Her gaze held everything for him: promise, possibility, passion. Ben found himself remembering every past nuance about the moment the picture was taken: the scent of her perfume, the slant of light, the bead of sweat that ran down his spine, the aroma of the flowers on the altar, the way she held his hand and squeezed it—not one long squeeze but a series of them, as if in rhythm with her heart, now his as well: squeeze *(I Cheryl take thee Benjamin to be my wedded Husband),* release, squeeze *(. . . to love and to cherish till death . . .),* release, the two of them exchanging themselves with every pulse, every breath, each willingly bestowing something to the other until, at the moment the photograph was taken, they were no longer Ben and Cheryl but a one beyond Oneness. This day; this time; this breath; this love: Immortal.

Three years and it still ached.

To think about what Should Have Been.

His vision blurred for a second and he realized he was crying.

"God, honey," he whispered so low it was almost a prayer. "I miss you so much. Still."

Christ! He had to stop this.

Call in and see if there's any word on the burial records.

He put the picture away, then reached toward the radio—

—as the killer's voice sliced through the static.

"She was quite lovely, Ben. You're right to miss her so much."

"What the—"

"After you wake up from your dream, what happens?"

He snatched up the microphone. "How did you get on this frequency?"

"The rope burn that's around your neck for just a second. Remember? You have to be familiar with the term 'stigmata.'"

"What do you *want?*"

"Oro, fiat illud, quod tam sitio; Ut te revelata cernens facie. Visu sim beatus tuae gloriae. Amen."

A great pressure coiled around Ben's neck. He fell forward, gasping, his lungs screaming for air as the pressure intensified, crushing his larynx—

His world spiraled downward into darkness where—

—a man named Herbert Mullin killed thirteen people as a sacrifice to the gods, claiming the deaths would prevent earthquakes in California; during police questioning he hinted that the deaths had been "preventing other things" as well—

—into darkness where—

—Juan Corona took a machete and slaughtered sixteen migrant workers on his farm and claimed that the murders were "an act of holy preservation"—

—where—

—William "Theo" Durant strangled and mutilated four women of his parish in 1895, then dragged their bodies to the tower of Emanuel Baptist Church and hanged them by their necks, claiming their corpses would serve as "a reminder of God's anger against humanity for turning away from its fellow men."

Ben became Mullin and Corona and Durant, as well as Bundy and Gein and Whitman and others like them in the past, the present, and the future. He raped and mutilated, he flayed and cannibalized, he stared at victims from the scope of a rifle and bathed in their blood and clothed himself in their dead flesh—

—and every savage act was filled with release and redemption, for even though part of him knew the acts were unspeakably depraved, a deeper, stronger part sensed that the butchery was somehow preventing a final act of even greater violence and destruction.

Dum vista est, spes est: Where there is life, there is hope.

A motto for the smorgasbord of slaughter.

✦   ✦

He clutched the steering wheel so tightly his knuckles began turning white. Staring ahead with the intensity of a man being led into the gas chamber, Ben remembered the voice of the killer over the radio, remembered looking at Cheryl's picture, remembered the pain that twisted through him before he'd black out—

—but he didn't remember coming to, or driving away, or even where he was going.

He was dressed differently—

—his hands looked so old—

—and his head felt so heavy—

—and this wasn't his car—

—so what in the . . . ?

He pulled into the parking lot of a public cafeteria. There were six cars, plus three semis, one of them hauling gasoline. He reached into his shoulder holster and removed a Colt Commander 9mm Perabellum with a nine-round magazine and special silencer attachment. He jacked open the chamber and inserted a tenth round, then shoved it back into his shoulder holster and put an extra clip in his pocket.

Pulling four sticks of dynamite from under the front seat and stuffing them into the lining of his coat, he wondered: *What the hell am I doing?*

Buying time, came the answer. He looked in the rearview mirror. He didn't recognize his face.

Inside, the overhead lights were far too bright, giving the place a cavernous feel, accentuated by the pinging echo of silverware clattering through a dishwasher.

Three large men were sitting in a room at the far end marked TRUCKERS ONLY.

He took a seat at the counter. The waitress was a big old friendly gal named Margie who smiled through slightly discolored teeth and never stopped talking to the cook—a short, nervous-looking young man wearing a silver skull earring.

Two other waitresses were sitting at a far table. Probably on break.

A well-dressed man came out of the restroom and sat at a booth near Ben.

A small office window near the trucker's room revealed a stooped bookkeeper within.

Six vehicles, six people.

He turned and spoke (with the killer's voice) to the well-dressed man. "I've been thinking about Edward N. Lorenz, the mathematician-turned-meteorologist who opened up the field of chaos math. He applied certain convection equations to the short-term prediction of weather and watched them degenerate into insanity. He wrote: 'Does the flapping of a butterfly's wings in Brazil set off tornadoes in Texas?' Yes—Because that seemingly harmless movement creates a small yet potent change in atmospheric pressure which interacts with other minute changes, and these combine with still more unpredictable variables that come down through the exo- iono- and stratosphere to mingle with the cumulative 'butterfly effects' in the troposphere, and before you know it—WHAM!—you've got thirty people dead in a trailerpark while hundreds more stand weeping among the ruins of their homes. And this can happen in *seconds*. Think about that. A monarch flutters its wings, and in less than a minute chaos can come crashing down on your world and reduce it to smithereens."

"I don't know what you're talking about," said the man, "but I'm minding my own business, so why don't you—"

With a *snick!* from the Colt his face peeled back and slapped against the window, hanging in place for a moment before slithering down.

Margie came next, a shriek barely having time to escape her throat before the round punched through her chest, lifted her off her feet, and sent her walloping backward into a row of metal shelves that groaned and buckled as their contents plunged to the floor with her in a bloody smack of shatterglass shower.

Cook Silver Skull hurtled sideways as the bullet demolished a quarter of his head, landing on top of the grill and convulsing as his blood sizzled and his flesh scorched and his body spasmed before he shit his pants and rolled onto the floor oozing and smoking.

Eight seconds had elapsed.

The two waitresses screamed and vaulted toward the doors but two quick snicks decorated the tables with squirming bits of their skulls and gray matter.

At fifteen seconds and counting the truckers were on their feet, one of them pulling an eight-inch Bowie knife and rushing full-force, screaming, "YOU PSYCHO-FUCK SON-OF-A—" A round *snick!*ed through his throat but he kept coming, arms pinwheeling as he spewed blood and tried to ram the knife home as he collided with Ben and they fell, the knife skittering under a chair.

Ben pumped another round, this one at a vicious angle, flipping up through the trucker's stomach and blowing out just above the tailbone dragging a gummy white loop of lower intestine with it.

Twenty-nine seconds.

The other two truckers had armed themselves with knives snatched from place-settings.

Snick!—one lost his balls and collapsed, screaming at the top of his lungs and clutching the soggy-meat hole between his legs.

The other one dove behind the counter, skidded in a puddle of Margie, and smashed through the kitchen door. Ben pulped his knees with two shots. The trucker hit the side of his face against a stove knob on the way down, tearing a thick gash from cheek to temple.

Ben grabbed him by the hair, dragged him to his feet, ejected and replaced the empty clip, put a fresh round through his chest and shoved him against the deep-fat fryer, ramming his face into the bubbling oil. The trucker managed to get his face out of the oil for a moment, its skin sloughing off like wax melting down a candle before Ben plowed two more shots through his back and he slumped forward, head submerging into the scalding pit as dozens of blackened french fries writhed around his skull.

Catapulting himself out the kitchen door with such force he wrenched the hinges out of the frame, Ben lunged toward the small office and blasted the window into a puking supernova of fractureburst fragments. Someone inside tried to choke back a moan as Ben kicked away the remaining shards of glass and climbed inside.

An old woman with palsied, liver-spotted hands was lying face-down on an adding machine behind a small metal desk, a phone receiver clutched against her chest.

Heart attack.

Ben held the receiver to his car and heard ". . . aine County Sheriff's Department, is this an emergency? Hello?"

Jerking the phone cord out of the wall, he spun around and clamped the old woman's head between his hands, snapping it sideways and shattering her neck.

Back in the restaurant the last trucker was still screaming and clutching at the raw, gushing chasm where his nuts used to be but Ben walked past him and toward the entrance; one of the waitresses was still alive.

He grabbed the Bowie knife, flipped the girl onto her back, and rammed the knife into her forehead. To the hilt.

He crossed the gore-slicked floor and straddled the last trucker's waist, pressing the gun into his cheek.

Fifty-eight seconds.

Chaos rules.

"Getting back to the 'butterfly effect.' Human behavior is a lot like that—determined by pre-existing yet uncontrollable events which, when considered in the context of inviolable laws of momentum, completely account for all subsequent events. So what causes behavior to suddenly veer toward the self-destructive? The butterfly effect."

"P-p-please m-mister," choked the bleeding man beneath him. ". . . it . . . ohjesusgod . . . it hurts so . . . so m-much . . . please d-don't . . . kill me . . . . " He closed his eyes and began to whimper, then weep, fear and hysteria burrowing inward to a place beyond fear.

". . . don't wanna . . . die . . . I got k-kids who . . . ohgod . . . ."

Ben continued speaking in the killer's voice. "Imagine the butterfly is the embodiment of everything that causes us to ignore or add to the suffering of others, and the flapping of its wings is the force of our apathy spilling outward. In less than a second it combines with the myriad emotions we expel—anger, lust, happiness, despair, whatever—until they become a single entity. Multiply that by however many times a day a person turns away from the suffering of others, then multiply that by the number of people in the world, then multiply *that* by the seconds in a week, a month, a year or a decade, and pretty soon you've got one hell of a charge building up. After the point of maximum tension is reached the combined forces rupture outward and target who or whatever is closest at the time. Gives a whole new meaning to 'shit happens.'"

"OHGODPLEASEMISTER—"

Snick!

Blowing out its pilot light, he shoved two sticks of dynamite under the gas stove and lit their extended fuses. Outside, he shoved a stick halfway into the tank of the gasoline truck, another under the semi next to it.

Two minutes later, when he was almost six miles down the road, the cafeteria went up in a titanic mushroom-cloud blast that roared two hundred feet into the air and sent shockwaves rippling over one-third of the county. Debris rose so high it took almost ninety seconds to come back down.

Staring in the rearview mirror, Ben saw the cloud assume a very appropriate shape.

A blink and a breath, then he said: "Two thousand days more."

And was answered by an echo:

that was nebraska. September of 1977. look it up if you want. just a snapshot from the scrapbook of my memory. hope you appreciated it.

With a sick feeling in the pit of his stomach, Ben realized that he had.

10

He awoke to pain, bright light, and the sound of many people running by.

He was on a bed behind a plastic green curtain.

A hospital emergency room.

Monsignor Maddingly: "Are you all right? Al said you had some kind of seizure."

Ben swallowed once—it hurt; twice—a little less; three time—still uncomfortable but he could live with it. "How long was I—"

"A little over two hours."

"Where's the Captain?"

"Called away on some kind of emergency. Said he'd try to get back."

Ben sat up and pressed his hand against his head to stop the dizziness. "W-what're . . . what are you doing here?'

"I was administering extreme unction to a patient when you were brought in. Al told me about the tape and it triggered a synapse in this old brain. Let me ask you something—did all of the bodies have coins in place of their eyes? Silver coins?"

". . . yeah . . . ?"

"Fifteen bodies?"

"Yes."

Maddingly nodded his head.

"What?" said Ben.

"You were baptized in the Catholic Church. Think about it: fifteen bodies, two coins each—"

"—thirty pieces of silver." Ben touched his still-tender neck.

"Judas Iscariot," said Maddingly.

"Then, the Field of Blood—"

"Haceldama. The potter's field in Israel where Judas was buried in an unmarked pauper's grave. To this day no one knows the exact location of that field. Thousands of bodies buried there, and nothing to mark the spot."

The curtain was yanked back and Goldstein stepped through, looking as if he hadn't slept in a week. "The dead have arisen."

Ben asked, "Where did you go? What happened?"

"All fifteen bodies disappeared from the morgue. Right in the middle of the autopsies, There was a blackout, some kind of small boiler explosion, the building was evacuated, and by the time the coroner's team went back inside the bodies were gone. The building was empty in less than twenty minutes."

"What did you do?"

"Christ!—sorry, Monsignor—what *could* I do? I had Moore phone the governor and request some help. Every available cop is on the street and this guy is playing 'Ring Around the Rosey' with us. There is no doubt in my mind now that he's capable of killing as many people as he claims. And that scares the hell out of me. So the National Guard comes in and Cedar Hill goes under curfew." He ran a hand through his hair and looked out at the doctors and nurses and the suffering patients with wounded souls.

"Al?" said Maddingly. "What is it?"

"Just tired, I guess. Thinking about . . . things."

"Like what?"

Goldstein turned toward Ben. "I never told you how sorry I was about Cheryl, did I? But I was. I am. She was a fine woman."

". . . thanks . . ." whispered Ben, wondering what the hell was on his captain's mind.

Goldstein watched a woman holding a towel against her bleeding face roll by on a gurney, then sighed. "I used to listen to my father tell stories about the camps. He saw his parents die at Gunskirchen Lager in Lambach. I got so sick of him going over and over the details, as if the only reason he was allowed to survive was so he could become this living memorial tape loop. The only time he ever really acknowledged

my existence was when he needed an audience for his perpetual eulogy.
One day I screamed, 'I'm sorry I wasn't there. I'm sorry you had to see
it. I'm sorry I haven't suffered and died like they did so you'd love me,
too.' He never spoke about it again, but the ghosts stayed with him.
That's why I fell away from the faith and left home: I couldn't stomach
the sight of what his faith had done to him. He wasn't my father, he
was a repository for phantoms. Every time I saw those ghosts in his
gaze I felt diminished. So I walked away. I didn't even go back for his
funeral.

"The thing is," he said, turning to face Maddingly and Ben,
"sometimes I look in a mirror and catch a glimpse of his ghost in my
own eyes, and I wonder if we're not all just walking graveyards, our
memories serving as coffins for all those we've seen die, and the people
they saw die, and the people they saw die. I'm six months away from
retirement and I just"—his voice cracked—"can't . . . *look* at it anymore.
It feels like this guy . . . this *thing,* has beaten us. And if he has . . . if
he has . . . "

A nurse stepped in and said she had a call for Ben at the desk and
the caller had said it was an emergency.

Ben stumbled his way to the desk and lifted the receiver.

"How was Nebraska?" said the killer. "Figure anything out yet? I
hope so—"

"—wait a second, I—"

"—because your time's up. Meet me at the cemetery in fifteen
minutes. Come alone."

"There're cops stationed there, you know."

"They've been called away on an emergency."

"What do you—"

Just as the line went dead a patrolman rushed to the desk, trying
not to shout as he said, "A call just came in from downtown, sir. We
got a sniper."

*so, my tortuurer, here we are again. will you divinely intervene,
or will this end the same way as all the times before?*

*like benjamin and his captain, i, too, have been thinking about
things.*

*the caterpillar that crawled into my mouth as i hung there. how it
slipped down my throat and made its cocoon inside me.*

*caiaphas had his servants cut down my body and bury it along with
the coins of my so-called betrayal. then, as the season changed, the
traditor papilio emerged from me.*

how terribly clever of you to stigmatize it.
your son's blood marked the dogwood with holiness.
my death marked the black butterfly with disgrace.
and the rest of it . . .
you really outdid yourself
have you ever asked yourself if they really deserve this?
i didn't think so.
time is short. dum vista est, spes est.

11

The storm clouds were already gathering by the time Ben got there.
Low rumbles of thunder were accentuated by vivid flashes of silent
lightning that dazzled his eyes and seemed to dance across a nearby
pond, turning it into a sheet of fire before everything pitched into
darkness. A blink and a breath, then his gaze recovered from the
preceding flash, enabling him to see the tendrils of mist rising from the
graves, twisting and coiling.

The .45 gripped tightly in his left hand, he climbed out of the car
and ascended the small hill that led to the cemetery proper. Goldstein
hadn't been crazy about Ben coming out here alone but the situation
downtown was serious; eight people had already been wounded—but
none, thank God, had yet been killed.

"Why didn't it ever occur to us that there might be two of them?"
he'd asked as Ben started the car.

"Damned if I know."

"Thirty minutes," said Goldstein. "If I don't hear from you by then,
sniper or no sniper I'll come to get your ass and bring three units with
me."

"You'll hear from me."

Goldstein had grabbed Ben's arm then, and said, "You be careful.
Don't fuck with him. I hate heroes, got it? They're mostly all dead."

Ben had nodded then driven away as Goldstein and Monsignor
Maddingly (who insisted he go to the scene, perhaps he could talk the
sniper down) climbed into a squad car.

Ben checked his watch.

He had nineteen minutes.

At the far end of the grounds, near a foot trail that had once led all the way around the place, a lone mercury vapor lamp came on, its murky light coming downward to illuminate a thin figure hunched over a shattered headstone.

Ben jacked a round into the chamber and moved slowly forward. His breath was staggered and heavy and he couldn't shake the feeling that he and this figure weren't alone.

Another burst of lightning spiderwebbed across the sky and Ben had to bite his lip to keep from crying out.

Suspended from various trees surrounding the cemetery, some hanging by their necks, others by their ankles, still others impaled on the ends of jagged branches, the bodies stolen from the morgue dangled, pale, naked, gutted angels. Their opened, empty chest cavities looked like the gaping maws of giant insects. Flesh flaps swayed in the rising wind; faces no longer capable of further expression were frozen into grisly smirks; and arms devoid of conscious impulses swung witlessly back and forth as if beckoning him forward.

Ben took a deep breath and strode onward.

The figure rose to its feet.

Ben froze mid-stride and almost choked. "... *oh God* ..."

"Hello, my love," said Cheryl.

One thousand days of cumulative grief, loneliness, anger, and confusion instantaneously welled up in Ben's chest, shaking him within and without. He lowered the gun and tried to move but couldn't, part of his mind screaming that this wasn't happening, it couldn't be true, and as he worked his mouth and jaw to form words that refused to be articulated his wife moved toward him, her smile filled with Spring, her arms parted for his embrace, and Ben Littlejohn suddenly didn't give a damn about the killer, all that mattered was Cheryl, who was here, who was real, who was his life and reason and oh God she was so close, he could smell the scent of her skin, tender and sensual as the horror of the last eleven hours faded, the taste of one thousand days of bitter longing withered, and the chaos that had so long been the core of his existence turned in on itself and hinted at order.

He lurched toward her, tripped over a section of headstone, and dropped to one knee, then, through a veil of near-blinding tears, wrapped his arms around her waist and buried his face in the center of her torso as the sobs exploded.

" . . . ohjesus baby I've missed you so much so much ohgod I love you I missed you I need you so much . . ."

"Shhh, there, there," she said, stroking the back of his head. "It's almost over now."

" . . . love you so much . . ."

He began to stand, blinking the tears from his eyes—

—she was gone.

And there, at his feet, at the corner of the headstone, was the black butterfly he'd seen this morning.

The killer's voice echoed: "When Hannibal arrived at the gates of Rome he saw the black butterfly resting there, and knew his victory would be futile. What good is it, after all, conquering a city that would fall to flames anyway?"

Taking in a deep breath filled with steel, rage, and snot, Ben snapped up the gun and clenched his teeth.

"Where are you?" he whispered.

"Turn around," said the killer.

He was much smaller than Ben had imagined but it was easy to see, even through the shabby clothes he wore, that his body was tight and powerful; layers of sinewy muscles rippled whenever he moved.

His eyes, so clear and startlingly blue, nailed Ben to the spot; they were the most haunted he'd ever seen, brimming with ghosts. So many, many ghosts.

"Hello, Ben."

"What did you do with Cheryl? Goddamnit, where's my wife?"

"Nearby. Don't worry, you'll see her again."

Ben raised the gun, pointing directly between the killer's eyes.

"Shoot if you want, but it won't do any good. I've tried it so many times it's almost funny."

"Who are you?"

"I'd have thought that was obvious by now." He smiled then, a wistful, tired expression that turned his wind-burnt face into a mask of lattice-work lines. "So, are you going to use that thing, or what? Nice gun, by the way. "

Ben glanced quickly and saw the .45 shimmer in his hand, then turn into the Colt 9mm Perabellum he'd held in the Nebraska dream.

It was a testament to his professional composure that he did not throw it down.

The killer shook his head and walked past Ben, kneeling down by the headstone and extending his hand. The butterfly moved toward it on dozens of tiny insect legs until it nestled securely in the center of the killer's palm.

"If you want Cheryl back, Ben, you won't pull that trigger."

"Who's your partner?"

"My what?"

"Your partner. Who's the sniper?"

"Oh, right. His name's Randy Perry. He's a mechanic from Heath who's been getting treated for depression. He'll manage to shoot seven more people before the SWAT team takes him down. They'll check into his background and find enough evidence to link him to the truck stop killings. Case closed. Another chapter for the *Time-Life* Serial Killers books.

"How do you know that?"

The killer stood, cradling the butterfly in his hands.

"Have you ever said or done anything that you later regretted, Ben? Of course you have, who hasn't? You wish you could take it back but you can't. A loss of control in a moment of confusion or weakness or anger and suddenly you've contributed to the damage in the world. It's out there, it's done, and you can't change it.

"When you were attending Catholic school, did anyone ever ask your religion teachers that classic smartass question: 'Can God create a rock so big that even He can't lift it?' Well, He can.

"On the day Christ died God's rage was so overwhelming that He lost His mind for a moment, and in that moment he created a day when the world would end. He spit out that day and sent it flying into the universe where it still waits. And He can't take back that day, He's tried. So there you have that 'rock' so big even God can't lift it.

"From my corner of purgatory I screamed at Him not to punish the world for the wrong I had committed. 'The sin is mine!' I cried. 'Let the suffering be mine, also. Torture me, not them.'

"So He sent me back. It took a long time but eventually I realized the nature of my punishment. Do you remember thinking 'two thousand days more' after the killings in Nebraska. That's how much time those deaths bought. By killing those nine people I put two thousand days between us and the end of the world."

Ben, repelled yet fascinated, asked, "Was there a cemetery near that place?"

"Half a mile away in a farmer's field were nine hoboes who'd been beaten to death by railroad men in 1931 and buried without being identified. There was nothing to mark their grave. No one knew they were there. Still don't, as a matter of fact."

"So for each person who dies and is buried without a name or anything to mark their grave—"

"—I have to kill a person whose death will be noticed, whose grave will bear their name, whose friends will weep and whose family will remember them. It helps to restore the balance of pain and thus postpones the . . . end of everything."

The storm clouds dropped lower, churning and thundering and flashing jagged lightning as Judas Iscariot parted his arms toward the cemetery. "There are hundreds of thousands of places like Haceldama, like this place, all over the world, with new ones being dug every hour. It didn't take long to understand there was no possible way I could maintain the balance of pain on my own.

"So I begat Bundy and Whitman and Corona and Gein; Cowan and Gacy and Berkowitz and Haarman; Gilles de Rais and Starkweather and Rojas and Speck and countless others, some of whom won't even be born for another fifty years. Their tallies add to the time the world has left."

"How do you know?" shouted Ben. "What proof do you have?"

Judas tensed his jaw, his eyes narrowing as his voice became a deep, grieving, deadly whisper. "Do you see this?" He held out his hand to show the black butterfly. "A species of *lepidoptera* so rare it has been classified as extinct for over a hundred years. Its Latin name is *traditor papilio*—'betrayer butterfly'. Also called the 'Judas Moth' because of its white strip, symbolizing the rope burn around my neck after I used the cattle-halter to end my wretched life. There are only thirty of them in existence, one for each piece of silver I accepted. They can only be found on unmarked graves—they were born in one, so they are drawn to the same. They move by crawling. They never flap their wings. They are indestructible but capable of unbounded destruction."

"The 'butterfly effect'?" asked Ben.

"Taken to a hideous extreme. The day will eventually come when all thirty of them will go back to the place of their birth. Once gathered upon my grave they will simultaneously flap their wings, and next will be Nothing. Unimaginable Nothing. Vengeance, as the saying goes, will be the Lord's."

The gun held limply at his side, Ben whispered, "Why me?"

Judas shook his head. "Can't answer that one. I don't do the choosing. The butterflies do. I simply . . . beget."

"Why the theatrics, then?"

"I have found, over the centuries, that chaos helps to speed up the . . . I guess you'd call it the recruiting process. And, as terrible as it sounds, it amuses me to watch how people react. If that sounds cold-blooded I won't apologize. After ten thousand years I'll take my enjoyment when and however I can get it. You simply cannot think of them as people, merely a means to an end."

Ben stared at the spot where his wife had stood just a few minutes ago, trying to deny all of it.

"You have more of a conscience than most," said Judas. "But, being a policeman, you will also have more opportunity and freedom." He stood next to Ben, his long gray hair blowing backward, and placed a hand on his shoulder. "So I will promise you this: for every death at your hands you will be given one hour with your wife and son."

"*. . . son?*"

"Your son. As he would have been had he lived."

The first spattering of rain began to fall on their heads. The sky was fracturing.

"Come on, Ben," said Judas, looking toward the sky. "There is no more time for you. You can't help Al or Maddingly or anyone else now. What's done is done. This is why you were born.

"Your wife and son, Ben. And the continued stillness of butterfly wings."

12

Ten days later most of the Midwest was still talking about the tornado that all but leveled Cedar Hill. One hundred and twelve people were dead, and the count was expected to be higher once the clean-up was finished.

Such was the subject under discussion by Phil Dardis of Cedar Rapids, Iowa as he and his wife packed themselves and their three kids into their station wagon, pulled out of their clean suburban driveway, and drove toward their big family reunion picnic twenty-two miles away.

Fifteen minutes later, right smack the hell in the middle of a country road lined on both sides with dense trees, they came upon a young, good-looking priest whose car had died on him. Despite his wife's protests, Phil, a good Catholic all his life, pulled over to give the priest some help.

"Is there something I can do for you, Father?"

"Reverend, actually, and yes. I'm afraid my fan belt snapped. Could you do me the kindness of driving me to the nearest phone?"

"Of course. There should be one at the park. That's where we're heading."

"Lovely family."

"Thank you. Here, let me help you with that. Don't wanna leave your bag out here where someone could grab it. Lucky for you we came along. Not many folks drive this road, too out-of-the-way. Whoa—this bag's pretty heavy, Fath—uh, I mean, Reverend."

"Church decorations. I'll take it if you can't—"

"Shit! Oops, sorry. Darn thing came open and—what the hell?"

"I'll take that."

"Jesus, wait a second! You ain't no—hold it JESUS GODDAMN CHRIST LUCY GET OUT OF—!"

It was a few hours later before he saw them standing by the side of the road. Ben pulled over and flung open the door. Cheryl climbed in first, then Jimmy. They had to fumble around the guns and rifles and other weapons, but that was okay, they were finally reunited. There was a lot of crying and kissing and hugging and rejoicing.

Cheryl told Ben that if he wanted to make love they'd have to find a place soon, they only had five hours and oh by the way the Dardis family bought another ninety-eight days and where did you get that big gray dog in the back seat Jimmy just loves it.

Ben nodded his head and said the dog's name was Caiaphas and it was a gift from a friend. Then he stared out at the road and thought five hours with his family wasn't enough.

Forty minutes down the road they picked up a couple of hitchhikers before getting on the interstate—New-Agers with crystals around their necks and one of those ersatz-Native American backpack things to carry their baby in.

Ben smiled later as he tossed their heads into a rest area Dumpster.

It was all worth it; and it was good.

Here, with his family; to have the time.

"Look," said Cheryl, pointing at a patch of flowers. "What a beautiful butterfly."

THE PIG MAN

Augustine Bruins Funnell

The memory remains, like a scar on the soul.

I was nine that spring, yearning for summer vacation so I could run free through the fields and hills surrounding the farm, or spend lazy August afternoons reading comics with Gene. Vacation loomed like a reward, and the closer the middle of June came, the more I looked forward to it.

I came home from school the last Friday in May, and found that my father had hired someone to help with the chores and the haying. He was introduced to me as Mr. Spafford, but the minute I saw him he received the sort of name only a child could give: the pig man. He had a prominent nose, protruding and blunt at the end, with squinting eyes set close to either side; the way his chin rose made his mouth seem to start just beneath the nose. The thick jowls of his cheeks were covered with coarse beard stubble, and only added to the porcine image. First sight of him made me nervous, but when he spoke in a gentle voice and held out a thick hand as if I were already grown-up, my uncertainty softened.

At supper he told us interesting little stories, not a one of which I could remember afterward. But it didn't matter; I liked the sound of his voice and the way he strung words together. When he complimented my mother on the meal and made appreciative noises over the dessert — lemon meringue pie — it was like watching the glow of firelight off my grandfather's silver watchchain: smooth and warm. But he still resembled a pig to me, and even though I respectfully called him "Mr.

Spafford" whenever I addressed him, I was thinking "Mr. Pig Man" every time.

After supper my father and our new hired hand went to the barn to finish the chores, and I busied myself helping my mother clear the table.

"So what do you think of Mr. Spafford?" my mother asked.

"He looks like a pig," I said, snickering.

Her look was disapproving, but a smile crinkled the corners of her mouth. "He does, a little," she agreed, "but we don't judge people by their looks, Artie. We judge them by what they say and do."

I couldn't find anything to argue with in that. "He talks nice," I said, and her smile told me I'd atoned for my uncomplimentary remark. "And he sure liked your pie." Her smile widened, and when I left to start my homework she was humming contentedly.

About half an hour before I went to bed the pig man knocked softly on my door and came into my room for a few minutes. We talked about how I was doing in school, what I wanted to be when I grew up, and half a dozen other things. His voice was hypnotic, and twice when he asked me things about my mother I didn't catch the questions the first time, and he had to repeat them. When he left he said we could go into town someday and see a movie if my parents didn't object, and the wink he gave me suggested it was all but settled.

It wasn't until after he'd gone that I realized he smelled funny. Not anything disagreeable, but unusual. As unusual and unexpected as the smooth silver voice flowing out of that ugly face. But it didn't matter; I liked him.

"Worth every penny," I heard my father tell my mother a week later while he washed up for supper. Through the window I could see the pig man just leaving the barn and latching the door behind him. He stood for a moment, peering at the western sky while my father continued, "As a matter of fact, if he gets a better offer I'll match it."

My mother smiled, nodding.

"Damn good man," my father finished, and took his place at the table.

When the pig man came in to clean up he winked at me, and told my mother the smell of supper was even better than the last smell of supper. She beamed and made an embarrassed noise, then began humming to herself as she brought food to the table.

After supper my father went back to the barn, and the pig man came upstairs with me to offer five minutes of help with my arithmetic. When he went downstairs I heard muted conversation between him and my mother, then my mother's tinkling laughter just before he went out to the barn.

"Damn good man," I whispered, echoing my father with a delicious twinge of excitement at the feel of the curseword rolling off my tongue. I hurried through my homework, then raced outside to the barn to help. I watched surreptitiously as the pig man fed the pigs, amused in my childish way at the resemblance between human and animal. What made the similarity even more amusing was the way the animals responded to him. They were much less zealous in their gluttonous pursuit of room at the trough, managing an almost patient half-scramble. Even our gravid brood sow sequestered by herself in a corner pen, always belligerent and as willing to chomp fingers and legs as corn or barley or oats, approached her trough with restraint remarkable for a pig, and ate quietly. The cows didn't kick at him when he milked them, even when he performed the job on the side opposite to which they were accustomed. The cats curled around his legs, purring expectantly every time he emptied milk from its pail into the larger can, and although he didn't overdo it, he seldom disappointed them.

Of all the farm animals, only Buster, our mongrel-collie dog, didn't take a shine to the pig man. He didn't growl or bark or threaten, but whenever the pig man got near, old Buster — half-blind and not long for the world — would get laboriously to his feet and pad away into the shadows. If the pig man's chores took him there, Buster would again struggle to his feet and pad away. I figured the dog only wanted a quiet corner all to himself. He was old and dying, after all, and I didn't begrudge him the solitude.

Summer vacation. I had my chores, of course, but I also had plenty of free time to wander through the hills behind our house, playing at the dozens of roles my child's imagination created, not one of them having anything to do with Grade Five. I also had Gene's place to bike to, a couple of miles up the road, and his hills to wander through. We seemed to spend every other day together, either playing or reading comics, or, sometimes, making up our own comics. They were good days, and I thought the warmth and freedom and contentment of summer would last forever.

I was wrong.

It was a Saturday, and for a change, Gene was to bike to my place, bringing with him a stack of new comics we hadn't seen yet, which we planned to carry into the attic to read and copy in the dim light there. I met him half way and we biked back together, chattering about all the important stuff boys chatter about, and when we went through the kitchen I had my first intimation that there were things beyond the world of boyhood, things which couldn't be put behind me with the arrival of the newest *X-Men* or *Avengers* comic.

My mother sat alone in the kitchen, early afternoon sunlight streaming through the windows and bathing her like one of the saints I'd seen in our family Bible. When she looked at our entrance it was as if she'd just awakened from a deep sleep, and she looked at us for a full ten seconds before the film over her eyes finally lifted and she recognized us. She spoke, but the words were dreamy and disconnected, and I couldn't be sure of what she'd said. I knew something was wrong, and a cool tingle danced along my spine. When she hugged herself as if for warmth, the tingle got very cold indeed.

Gene didn't notice, or if he did he must have thought she'd been asleep. But she was *my* mother, and I saw in her eyes something I couldn't explain, didn't understand, and which frightened me terribly. Why? Because the person looking out of those eyes *wasn't* my mother at all; it was someone else with her face and her body wearing her clothes, but it wasn't her.

Then, abruptly, it *was* her again, and she smiled and got up and hugged me and asked if we were going into the attic to read comics. We told her we were, and she smiled again and told us to have fun. Then, humming, she busied herself at the sink.

When we climbed the stairs I should have noticed the scent, but my mind was still trying to deal with the unexplainable feelings I'd had in the kitchen. So I missed it. But Gene didn't.

"What's that smell?" he asked me.

It took no more than that to focus my attention on the scent, and I recognized it at once: the scent of the pig man. Not the barn smell or the hayfield smell, but his own unique human smell, the one I'd noticed that first time he came to my room. It still wasn't disagreeable, just stronger. And as we walked past my parents' bedroom toward the second flight of stairs I realized it was coming from inside. Closed doors were not inviolate in our family in those years, so I pushed it open and stood staring dumbly at the room. Sunlight splashed across the floorboards and the unmade bed, and my mother's bottles of perfume and such rested on the bureau as sedately as ever. But the scent of the pig man, like something between peppermint and brandy (I realize now) was overpowering. Fainter at other times, it had been indescribable to me, but here in such concentration it was unmistakable.

The sound of my mother's arrival sent slivers of guilt through me, and when I turned to face her I caught fear dancing through her eyes. For what seemed forever but couldn't have been more than a couple of seconds we stared at each other, mother and child sharing something that one understood all too well, and the other not at all.

I was saved by Gene's, "Boy, that's a nice smell. What is it?"

My mother smiled at him. "Probably just my perfume," she said. "You boys scoot now; I've got housework to do."

And that gave substance to the unease I'd felt since we entered the kitchen, because I couldn't remember my parents' bed ever going unmade. My mother made it as soon as she got up, often as soon as she donned her housecoat. Yet here it was afternoon, and she was just making the bed. But I was a child, nine years old, and I didn't understand. I knew there was something unusual about the situation, but that was all. In the attic the scent of the pig man reached us only faintly, and after a while I was able to forget it entirely. But later, when I heard the clank and rattle of my father's truck returning from town where he'd gone earlier in the day, I couldn't suppress my fear and guilt. When I peered through the dusty window as he got out of the vehicle, alone, and traipsed toward the house I was afraid, and I didn't know why.

At four o'clock, Gene had to start home, and I rode with him half way. On the ride back I peddled slowly, stopping several times to listen to the birds, check out water gurgling slowly through a culvert, or peer through the trees to see squirrels and chipmunks. Anything to keep from getting home too soon.

Suppertime found me without an appetite, which worried my mother, but I stayed in my room anyway, and when she left to serve my father and the pig man their suppers I crept slowly down the hallway to my parents' bedroom. I opened the door softly and entered, and was not at all surprised to find the window open and the curtains blowing gently in the breeze. The scent of the pig man was still there, faint to be sure, but definitely still there. It didn't smell anything at all like my mother's perfume.

When I crept back to my room I felt as guilty as I had earlier, but I hadn't matured any that afternoon: I was still only nine years old, and I didn't understand.

After supper my mother came to check on me, but I couldn't meet her eyes. I heard something in her voice I'd never heard before, but I kept my attention riveted to the *Sgt. Fury and His Howling Commandoes* comic I was pretending to read, and I answered her questions with grunts and monosyllables. She was a different woman now, and I was afraid.

Later, the pig man came, but there was nothing different about him at all. He smiled and joked that he sure appreciated my not feeling well enough to eat, because that extra piece of chocolate cake sure had been good. Then he produced a piece of it from behind his back and set it on my study table. The scent of brandy and peppermint was faint, but it seemed overpowering to me at that moment.

I wanted him to go, but he sat on the bed and took my shoulders in his hands. When that voice of liquid silver told me to look into his eyes I was powerless to resist, but I felt no fear, no menace. As he kept talking I felt far away, different, no longer Artie hiding in his room because he was afraid and guilty without knowing why, but another kid somewhere else, content with the world and his place in it. It felt strange, but good, too. Very, very good. It made me feel important and happy, for no reason I could get clear in my mind, and when he left, it took me a long time to readjust to the bed and table and walls and posters. For a little while, there, everything had been perfect.

The week before school started, the sow produced a litter of pigs, and I went to the barn a dozen times a day to check on them and watch them and listen to their squeals. They were so much cuter than the adult versions that I asked my father if I could have one for a pet. He explained that pigs weren't the same as dogs, and no matter how much attention and affection I gave one, it wouldn't grow up to be like Buster. Since Buster was only slightly more pet-like than the average fence post these days, I took precious little consolation from that, and I sulked for two days.

Until the pig man woke me one morning as the sun cracked the eastern horizon, and thrust into my arms a soft, hyperactive ball of fur that seemed intent on licking the skin off my face. Later that day Buster died, but I didn't care: He'd been my father's dog anyway, and I had one of my own now.

Exactly when my father began to suspect, I don't know. It simply dawned on me one day that the lines in his forehead had deepened, and the tightness around his eyes was so severe that he seemed to regard the world through a perpetual squint. After I noticed that I discovered he and the pig man no longer spoke, that amusing stories at the supper table were non-existent, and my parents seemed to argue an awful lot. While these arguments exacted a terrible toll on my father, they seemed to affect my mother hardly at all. She still hummed as she worked, told me stories, cooked fabulous meals, and smiled when the pig man paid her a compliment. Which was often.

In the barn I felt the strong tension between the men, but most of it seemed to originate with my father. The pig man remained oblivious to Father's hardened expression and surly attitude, and after a while I began to ignore it myself . . . because the pig man touched me often, clamped his thick hands around my shoulders and stared into my eyes and let me feel better and happier than I was. I began to wonder why my father didn't avail himself of this magical feeling; still nine, I didn't understand the intensity of that other magical feeling, the one that brings men and women together, and far too often drives them apart.

My father began to drink that winter. The pup and I found him at suppertime one evening in January, sitting on a bale of hay and staring at the concrete floor of the barn, a bottle of some foul-smelling liquid warmed by his huge hands. When he saw me two distinct emotions flickered through his eyes: hurt and resentment. They scared me, but fortunately they disappeared almost at once.

"C'mere," he said with a jerk of his head, and although I didn't want to go, I went. He moved over and I sat beside him, noticing the smell of days-old sweat and too-long uncleaned barn clothes.

"It's suppertime," I told him.

He nodded, but said, "I ain't eatin'. Ain't goin' in." The words were slurred. He took a long drink, and wiped the back of a dirty hand across his mouth, then fixed me with a narrow gaze. "Bet you can't wait to get back in there, eh?"

I was beginning to get scared. I shrugged. My pup got bored with the conversation and padded toward one of the stalls to investigate the actions of a couple of the cats. When I called him back he bounced across the straw-strewn concrete and wagged his tail furiously until I picked him up and cradled him in my arms. He was getting close to being too big for that sort of treatment, but at that moment I felt a lot more secure with him in my lap . . . after all, the pig man had given him to me, and the pig man could make me feel perfect.

"I would'a got you a goddamn dog," my father said, and his eyes narrowed even further. When he looked from it to me all the resentment was gone, but the hurt that had overcome it was complete. "And we could'a got a kid to adopt too . . . Christ knows there's enough of 'em nobody wants." He took another drink. "Whaddaya think it'll be, Artie? Boy or a girl?"

I didn't know what he was talking about, and the longer I thought, the more curious it became. At that instant I didn't want to ever grow up; the world of adults was a lace far too mysterious for the likes of me. I couldn't think of anything to say, so I shrugged.

"A pig, maybe," my father said. "A horny old boar. Or twins. A horny old boar and a horny old sow." He took another drink, then looked again at the pup, squirming to be free of my grasp. "I would'a got you a goddamn dog," he said softly.

To his eternal credit he reached over then and patted my dog, then rested his hand on my head and stroked my hair. To my eternal damnation, I flinched. Drunk as he was, he caught it, and there flashed through his eyes something I hope I never see again.

Fathers are bulwarks; they stand invincible against the vagaries of the world, and they absorb the best shots fate can deliver. They do not cry. It cost him, but my father maintained the fiction. At least long enough to tell me, "You better get inside; you'll miss your supper."

Relieved and glad to be away from him, I left at once. The dog and I raced along the path through the snow, and when we got to the house I found my cooling supper on the table in an empty kitchen. The scent of peppermint and brandy was strong.

It was late that evening that my mother, her eyes alive and her face aglow, told me I would have a sibling.

Whether he was determined not to be driven off his own farm, or there was a streak of emotional masochism in him, my father did not leave. Nor, curiously, did he fire the pig man. Perhaps he knew the pig man wouldn't go. Or if he did, my mother would go with him. It was the natural course of events as I passed my tenth birthday, and no cause for wonderment at all. The strain between the various elements of adulthood on the farm *was* a cause for wonderment, though, and not just mine. Gene wondered aloud one cold Saturday afternoon why my father slept out in the barn and why he never spoke, and I began to feel the first touches of humiliation visited upon those related to people who do not measure up to the norm. "Man, he's weird," Gene told me when I explained that my father simply preferred to sleep in the barn, and he looked at me as if I too might soon begin acting oddly. But I didn't take the opportunity to tell him about the pig man. We'd been pals for a couple of years, ever since his family had moved into the old MacDonald house up the road, and we had shared everything. But not the pig man and his magical ability; I kept that to myself, held it tight to my heart like a special possession.

We'd never had many visitors anyway, but when word got around that the hired hand was sleeping in the house and the husband was bunking out in the barn, the trickle dried completely. Sometimes at school I was the butt of jokes from the other kids, but it was usually the older ones who initiated the teasing, and I could ignore them because more often than not I didn't understand what they were talking about. I understood the derision though, and when the kids my own age picked it up there was more than one bloodied nose. Unfortunately, the other one was usually mine. Gene did a precarious balancing act between support and laughter, depending upon which of his other friends was teasing me at the time. It was good to know there were some kids he liked less than me, but disappointing to realize I wasn't at the top of his list in the same way he was at the top of mine.

To this day I don't know how my father managed to get through the winter months of that new year. He refused to enter the house if either my mother or the pig man were inside, but once they left he would go in, eat, and sometimes wander through the rooms like a lost child. Gene and I came upon him once as we descended the stairs from the attic, and the look he turned on me made me want to cry. He was standing in the doorway of the bedroom he'd shared with my mother, but he seemed unable to step inside. Perhaps the scent of the pig man, mildly all-pervasive now, kept him out.

Sometimes when he returned to the barn he'd take a loaf of bread and a jar of cheese spread or peanut butter, and occasionally when I played there or helped with the chores I'd find him sitting in the corner where he slept on pallets softened with straw, eating quietly and carefully. He hadn't shaved since I'd found him drinking that night the previous August, and crumbs would lodge in his thick beard, making him look slovenly and mean.

For all that the situation took out of him, it could not rip loose his love of the land and the farm he'd built on it. He worked tirelessly, mending fences, repairing the barn, measuring feed to the animals as diligently as he always had, and all without ever a glance or word to the pig man. Those jobs which required two men were performed by two men, one sullenly oblivious to the other, the second whistling and occasionally asking questions which went unanswered, or making conversation which went unheeded. It always made me uneasy, but the pig man could remedy that simply by taking my shoulders in his big hands and talking to me and staring into my eyes for a mere two minutes. I'd go away happy, another boy in another world, and the peculiarities of life at the farm would seem as natural as dirt, unchanged and eternal.

The horror came at the end of April. My mother's belly had swollen monstrously, and I was hard-pressed not to think of her as resembling the fat-bellied brood sow in the barn, also gravid once more. Had she not seemed happy and excited I would have been afraid for her. But these were adult mysteries, and I trusted her ability to cope with them.

We were sitting at the supper table, my mother, the pig man and I, when a sudden pain shot through my mother's eyes. She gasped, dropped her fork, and activity blossomed around me. The pig man helped her to her feet, told me to stay where I was and finish supper, then gently guided my mother out of the kitchen and through the living room. I heard their steps on the stairs, and a muffled reassurance from the pig man every time my mother gasped.

My nervous excitement wouldn't let me eat. I paced through the kitchen with the still-unnamed dog following mindlessly, then stole quietly into the living room; but waiting at the bottom of the stairs only heightened my excitement, and almost without realizing what I was doing I began climbing the stairs, slowly, softly. As if he understood, the dog made no noise behind me.

At the landing I had to stop to breathe; all the way up I'd held my breath, and my lungs were ready to explode. In the stillness of the hallway the exhalation seemed inordinately loud, but it was drowned almost immediately by a cry of pain from my mother.

The scent of peppermint and brandy was strong and getting stronger as I crept down the darkened hallway toward the bedroom, but I barely noticed it. A sliver of light showed under the door, and when I stepped into it I was so scared I thought I'd drop dead on the spot.

My mother wasn't making any noises now, but the pig man was speaking softly to her, words I couldn't decipher. His liquid silver voice went on and on for a long time, and when I could take it no longer I turned the doorknob and opened the door a crack.

My mother rested on the bed, her eyes closed and a soft smile playing about her lips. More than ever she resembled one of those martyred saints in the Bible, even with the sheen of perspiration across her forehead and trickling down her cheeks. Her dress was bunched up around her thighs, the almost obscene mound of flesh just above it rising and falling gently with each measured breath. The pig man sat on the edge of the bed with his back three-quarters to me, still speaking softly. His hands were on my mother's shoulders, kneading gently in rhythm to the cadence of his voice. The scent of peppermint and brandy was overpowering, but I forced myself to stand there, my heart thudding like a hammer on stone. When the pig man's hands gradually began to move from my mother's shoulders to her collarbones, then down further toward her breasts, I turned like the child I was to flee the dark mysteries of the adult world.

Half an hour later the pig man found me in the kitchen, toying with what remained of my supper while the dog waited patiently for such scraps as I deigned to give. He smiled at me in such a way that I knew. He knew I'd disobeyed and gone upstairs, but also in such a way that I

knew he wasn't going to punish me. He pulled his chair across the floor
and placed it beside mine, and I knew what was coming.

He said nothing at first as his hands clamped around my shoulders
very close to the throat, then he began speaking in that unique way, and
in seconds Artie disappeared from the face of the planet, replaced by
another boy who understood everything and was happy and content and
liked and loved.

When it was over he told me, "Your mother's fine, Artie; she's
going to have a baby soon," I thought it the most natural news in the
world, and could not conceive of any objection anyone anywhere might
have.

"Will you be okay down here?"

I nodded, because I was absolutely certain I would be, that I would
live a thousand years and never know anxiety or fear or loneliness, but
if I did I could handle them all perfectly.

"Good." He clapped me gently on the shoulder. "I'm going back
upstairs now, but I'll call you later. Okay?"

I nodded and smiled, and when he patted the dog and scratched its
ears it seemed to me the dog nodded and smiled too. He left, but the
scent of peppermint and brandy remained, a reassuring fragrance in that
house of uncertainties.

Exactly when I heard the first of my mother's cries I'm not sure,
but it must have been a couple of hours at least. I hadn't moved from
the chair, my contemplations of the universe and my place in it so
thoroughly absorbing that little but her cries *could* have intruded. The
euphoria dissipated a little more when my mother cried again, a piteous
sound that made me squirm. Her outbursts continued for a while, then
there was complete silence and I waited desperately for the pig man to
call me.

He didn't. Instead, I heard a sharp slap and a sudden high-pitched
wail, and even I knew what had happened. I hopped out of the chair,
certain I could go up now without waiting for a summons, too excited
to wait in any event.

I hadn't even gotten to the living room doorway when the kitchen
door burst open and my father, raged and dirty and wild-eyed, charged
through like some huge, mad dog. His glazed eyes riveted me to the
floor almost in mid-step, and when he took his first rapid stride toward
me I thought he was going to kill me. But he brushed past without a

word, the breeze of his passing foul with days-unwashed perspiration and the myriad smells of the barn. It was then that I noticed the axe he was carrying, newly-honed and glittering in the warm kitchen light.

Rabid, he charged through the living room and up the stairs. I knew something horrible was about to happen, but my rising excitement and morbid fascination at the expected violence would not let me stay downstairs. My father in miniature, I charged up the stairs too, the dog yipping with excitement.

My father was just disappearing through the bedroom doorway when I reached the landing. He roared something I couldn't decipher, and I heard the liquid voice of the pig man, containing urgency for the first time I could remember, reply . . . but that was lost when my mother screamed.

By the time I reached the doorway my father had axed the pig man at least once, and was making sure of his handiwork with a second or third blow. A serenity far inside me evaporated with the sickening sound of the blade demolishing flesh and bone, and I turned from the carnage with a hopelessly lost feeling inside.

When the sounds of savagery stopped I turned back, but I didn't focus on the grisly remains of the pig man. I watched my father instead as he dropped the axe and advanced on the bed, infinite hurt and sorrow and rage virtually pouring out of him. My mother's eyes were wide with shock, and she barely resisted as my father ripped from her arms the blanket containing the new-born infant. Then reality registered, and she struggled to regain the baby.

Too late. My father shoved her, hard, and after her ordeal she crumpled like a rag. A corner of the blanket fell away, and I stared open-mouthed at a tiny pink version of the pig man, identical except for beard stubble.

When my mother made no further move to interfere, my father turned to look at the child in his arms. He saw its features, and a strangled gasp of horror and revulsion bubbled through his lips. I think that until that moment he'd harboured the desperate, secret hope that it might after all be his. The hard lines in his face deepened. He forced himself to stare at it long and hard, and for one terrible instant I thought he would dash it to the floor.

"Pig!" he hissed. "It's a goddamn pig." He moved quickly then, was by me and out of the room before I could say anything. I started after him, then stopped when my mother's sobbing finally cut through the lingering internal echoes of the axe striking the pig man. But there was nothing I could do for her, and my morbid fascination with the final product of my father's humiliation forced me from the room and after him.

Even in the darkened hallway I could see the bloody footprints, and at a breathless clip I followed them to the landing and down the stairs, then through the living room and into the kitchen where, finally, they disappeared. But the kitchen door was open, and coatless I rushed into the April night, the dog bounding excitedly behind. My father was almost to the barn, already bathed in light streaming through its dusty windows. I yelled at him, but if he heard he paid no heed. I sped over the path, reaching the barn just a handful of seconds after he disappeared. I darted through the door, but he was already where he wanted to be, and there was no power on this tortured earth that could have stopped him.

He hurled the blanketed bundle into the brood sow's pen, and when I heard the beast's grunts and squeals as it scurried toward the squalling infant I turned and bolted back toward the house. Half-way there I threw up, and a few seconds later I passed out.

My mother was never the same after that, and perhaps it was just as well. She spent a week in the hospital and I stayed at Gene's, but when she came back she looked at me without recognition, and often I'd find her wandering about the yard, sniffing, looking under the steps, searching the bushes, all the while humming softly to herself.

My father spent a couple of weeks in jail awaiting trial, but obviously crazy, they locked him up somewhere far away, and no one would ever take me to see him. By the time I was old enough to go myself he was a long time dead and buried.

My mother's brother quit his job in the city and came to look after the farm and us. He brought with him his wife and three children, and after a while I was able to sleep at night without dreaming of Father charging through the house with an axe in his hands, then charging back out with a blanket. But now thirty-four, I still can't sleep without that other dream snaking its way into my mind, night after night after night. No matter how hard I try I can't forget the sight of the brood sow a month later as she nursed her litter of seven squalling piglets, each with its hairy pink body and the pig man's features, all smelling of peppermint and brandy.

The memory remains, like a scar on the soul.

MOBIUS

Richard Christian Matheson

Heat blistering. Head leaned, grinning at the sun. About forty. Swollen, staring eyes. The man in the tie stared at him. Spoke calmly. Smoked.

"Ready to talk?"

"I want some Coke or somethin' . . . I'm thirsty."

"Later."

"I'm thirsty."

Words thick. Hard to understand. Lips rising, falling, chalk dry.

"Let's answer some questions first. How many people have you killed?"

"Isn't there nothin' around here to drink?"

"Seventy-three, that's a lot, Jimmy. You're a vicious man."

"That how many?"

"You don't remember killing them?"

"Hey, man . . . I'm fucking *thirsty*."

"Ever been to L.A.?"

"'I Love L.A..' Know Randy Newman? Fuckin' incredible. He's famous, you know. Randy Newman . . . fuckin' incredible."

"Ever heard of the 'Offramp Slasher'? Dumps his victims next to freeway offramps, in the bushes . . . Hollywood?"

"Heard of what he did. I was at this topless bar. Saw it on the TV. He cuts off peoples' . . . (smiles) . . . cuts off everything, right?"

"How'd you know what he did? Wasn't ever printed in the paper. Wasn't on the news either. Only the killer would know that. How'd you know, Jimmy?"

Silence. Toying with a hole in greasy jeans, tearing it like a cut in skin.

"Let's talk about Debbie Salerno."

"I'm thirsty. You said I could have a Coke."

"Debbie Salerno was found next to the Vine Street offramp and she'd been sexually . . . torn apart. Blonde, fifteen years old."

The greasy jeans tore more, fat white threads taut. Snapping. Eyes closed. Thin veins puffing at the temples. Brown teeth grinning stupidly, diseased and soft.

"We talked about her yesterday. Remember, Jimmy? You gouged her eyes out while you raped her. You remember doing that? Remember how it felt?"

Pulling on upper lip. Shrug.

"It was okay. Somethin' to do."

"So tell me more."

"How many you say you killed? Thousand?"

"You can do better than that. How many was it, Jimmy?"

"I'm gonna be famous. Like Jack the Ripper. Randy Newman."

"Seventy-three. You killed 'em all. How tall was Debbie?"

"Debbie who?"

"*Salerno.*"

"Never heard of her."

"Don't fuck with me, Jimmy, I'm running out of patience. You confessing or jerking me off?"

"Okay . . . She was five-three, five-two. I don't know. She was screamin' . . . what'd'm I supposed to do, measure her?"

"How'd you meet her?"

"You tell me."

"Alright, you sick fuck, I'll tell you . . . here's exactly how it went down: you were in your van, cruising Sunset and you were shooting garbage. Maybe a couple hundred in your arm. You were cranked and you got that little urge you get. And then you saw her. Her hood was up. Starting to remember yet? She needed help . . . you pulled over. What'd you say to her, Jimmy?"

A big smile. Cracked lips stretching.

"I said, 'Hey . . . pretty lady . . . need a lift, or did you lose somethin' in there?' She thought that was funny. She got in and we drove."

"Where'd you do it, Jimmy?"

"Somewhere . . . lots of lights. A view."

"Hollywood hills? Above the strip?"

"I guess. Hey man, it's hot in here."

"Answer the question. Hollywood hills?"

"Okay, man! Hollywood hills! You happy? Get off my ass!"

"We're not done yet."

"*I'm* done! You're driving me fuckin' crazy with all your questions."

Biting skin off bottom lip. Tasting blood.

"Tell me more."

"Whattya mean more? Whattya want . . . you wanna hear about all of 'em one more time?"

"Yeah."

"Like who?"

"Anybody you want. You got a big list, remember?"

"So whattya want? Guys? Fags? Kids?"

"I know all this shit! I know how it went down! I know what it looked like and smelled like. I saw the faces . . . heard the begging. So fuck off!"

"I'm here to find out if you really did it, Jimmy. That's why we've been doing this stuff for three weeks and you know it. You tired? So am I. So, you give me details . . . we can get this over with and you're in a nice quiet cell."

"Fuck you, man! I answer no more. I know all this shit. I'm tired. I need sleep. We've been through this. I know every name, every offramp, what they were wearing, how they were found! How many pieces I cut 'em into. You can't mess with my head. I *know*. Now give me my fuckin' Coke!"

"How did you kill Thomas Dremmond?"

"Senior or junior? I killed 'em both, remember? Nice try. Told you about it day before yesterday."

Knuckles rubbed into bloodshot eyes.

"How'd you do it?"

"Fire. Torched him. Like I told you. I'm tired."

"How about Donald Belli?"

"Cut everything out."

"Which way was he facing?"

"Oh, fuck you! Toward Highland Ave, okay? We've been through this!"

"Maria Vera. How?"

"Coathanger. Body left sitting up. Get me a fuckin' Coke!"

"Not easy being famous is it?"

The man in the tie looked at him. Stared. Thought.

"Alright . . . I'm convinced. Get out."

The needle arm reached back and grabbed a torn duffel filled with bloody clothes. The rotted smile looked at the man with the tie.

"Tell them what you told me, you'll be famous. Keep it exact. Here's change for a drink."

The brown teeth grinned and the retarded young man with the duffel got out and walked toward the police station, mind bloated with hideous facts that were now mesmorized; now his.

The man in the tie watched him enter, then pulled away and drove on toward Texas, almost getting the urge when a Cadillac cut him off.

THE RENDERING MAN

Douglas Clegg

1

"We're gonna die someday," Thalia said, "all of us. Mama and Daddy and then you and then me. I wonder if anyone's gonna care enough to think about Thalia Inez Canty, or if I'll just be dust under their feet." She stood in the doorway, still holding the ladle that dripped with potato chowder.

Her brother was raking dried grass over the manure in the yard. "What the heck kind of thing's that supposed to mean?"

"Something died last night," Thalia sniffed the air. "I can smell it. Out in the sty. Smelt it all night long, whatever it is. Always me that's first to smell the dead. 'Member the cat, the one by the thresher? I know when things's dead. I can smell something new that's dead, just like that. Made me think of how everything ends."

"We'll check your stink out later. All you need to think about right now is getting your little bottom back inside that house to stir the soup so's we'll have something decent come suppertime." Her brother returned to his work; and she to hers. She hoped that one day she would have a real job and be able to get away from this corner of low sky and deadland.

The year was 1934, and there weren't too many jobs in Moncure County, when Thalia Canty was eleven, so her father went off to Dowery, eighty miles to the northeast, to work in an accountant's office, and her mother kept the books at the Bowand Motel on Fourth Street, night shift. Daddy was home on weekends, and Mama slept through the day, got up at noon, was out the door by four, and back in bed come three a.m. It was up to Thalia's brother, Lucius, to run the house, and make sure the two of them fed the pigs and chickens, and kept the doors bolted so the winds—they'd come up suddenly in March—didn't pull them off their hinges. There was school, too, but it seemed a tiny part of the day, at least to Thalia, for the work of the house seemed to slow the hours down until the gray Oklahoma sky was like an hour-glass that never emptied of sand. Lucius was a hard-worker, and since he was fifteen, he did most of the heavy moving, but she was always with him, cleaning, tossing feed to the chickens, picking persimmons from the neighbor's yard (out back by the stable where no one could see) to bake in a pie. And it was on the occasion of going to check on the old sow, that Thalia and her brother eventually came face to face with the Rendering Man.

The pig was dead, and already drawing flies. Evening was coming on strong and windy, a southern wind which meant the smell of the animal would come right in through the cracks in the walls. Lucius said, "She been dead a good long time. Look at her snout."

"Toldja I smelled her last night." Thalia peeked around him; scrunched back, wanting to hide in his lengthening shadow. The snout had been torn at—blood caked around the mouth. "Musta been them yaller dogs," she said, imitating her father's strong southern accent, "cain't even leave her alone when she's dead."

The pig was enormous, and although Lucius thrust planks beneath her to try and move her a ways, she wouldn't budge. "Won't be taking her to the butcher, I reckon," he said.

Thalia smirked. "Worthless yaller dogs."

"Didn't like bacon, anyways."

"Me, too. Or ham."

"Or sausage with biscuits and grease."

"Chitlins. Hated chitlins. Hated knuckles. Couldn't chaw a knuckle to save my life."

"Ribs. Made me sick, thought a ribs all drownin' in molasses and chili, drippin' over the barbeque pit," Lucius said, and then drew his hat down, practically making the sign of the cross on his chest. "Oh, Lord, what I wouldn't give for some of her."

Thalia whispered, "Just a piece of skin fried up in the skillet."

"All hairy and crisp, greasy and smelly."

"Yes," Thalia sighed. "Praise the Lord, yes. Like to melt in my mouth right now. I'd even eat her all rotten like that. Maybe not."

The old sow lay there, flies making haloes around her face.

Thalia felt the familiar hunger come on; it wasn't that they didn't have food regularly, it was that they rarely ate the meat they raised—they'd sold the cows off, and the pigs were always for the butcher and the local price so that they could afford other things. Usually they had beans and rice or eggs and griddle cakes. The only meat they ever seemed to eat was chicken, and Thalia could smell chicken in her dreams sometimes, and didn't think she'd ever get the sour taste out of her throat.

She wanted to eat that pig. Cut it up, hocks, head, ribs, all of it. She would've liked to take a chaw on the knuckle.

"She ain't worth a nickel now," Thalia said, then, brightening, "you sure we can't eat her?"

Lucius shook his head. "For all we know she's been out here six, seven hours. Look at those flies. Already laid eggs in her ears. Even the dogs didn't go much into her—look, see? They left off. Somethin' was wrong." He shuffled over to his sister and dropped his arm around her shoulder. She pressed her head into the warmth of his side. Sometimes he was like a mama and daddy, both, to her.

"She was old. I guess. Even pigs die when they get old." Thalia didn't want to believe that Death, which had come for Granny three years before, could possibly want a pig unless it had been properly slaughtered and divvied up.

"Maybe it died natural. Or maybe," and her brother looked down the road to the Leavon place. There was a wind that came down from the sloping hillside, sometimes, and coughed dust across the road between their place and the old widow's. "Could be she was poisoned."

Thalia glanced down to the old gray house with its flag in front, still out from Armistice Day, year before last. A witch lived in that house, they called her the Grass Widow because she entertained men like she was running a roadhouse; she lived alone, though, with her eighteen cats as company. Thalia knew that the Grass Widow had wanted to buy the old sow for the past two years, but her parents had refused because she wasn't offering enough money and the Cantys were raising her to be the biggest, most expensive hog in the county. And now, what was the purpose? The sow was fly-ridden and rotting.

Worthless. Didn't matter if the Grass Widow killed it or not. It recalled for her a saying her daddy often said in moments like this:

"How the mighty are fallen." Even among the kingdom of pigs.

Lucius pulled her closer to him, and leaned down a bit to whisper in her ear. "I ain't sayin' anything, Thay, but the Widow wanted that sow and she knew Daddy wasn't never gonna sell it to her. I heard she hexed the Horleich's cows so they dried up."

"Ain't no witches," Thalia said, disturbed by her brother's suspicions. "Just fairy tales, that's what Mama says."

"And the Bible says there is. And since the Bible's the only book ever written with truth in it, you better believe there's witches, and they're just like her, mean and vengeful and working hexes on anything they covet." Lucius put his hand across his sister's shoulder, and hugged her in close to him again. He kissed her gently on her forehead, right above her small red birthmark. "Don't you be scared of her, though, Thay, we're God-fearin' people, and she can't hurt us 'less we shut out our lights under bushels."

Thalia knew her brother well enough to know he never lied. So, the old Grass Widow was a witch. She looked at her brother, then back to the pig. "We gonna bury her?"

"The sow? Naw, too much work. Let's get it in the wheelbarrow and take it around near the coops. Stinks so bad, nobody's gonna notice a dead pig, and then when Mama gets home in the mornin', I'll take the truck. We can drive the sow out to the renderin' man." This seemed a good plan, because Thalia knew that the Rendering Man could give them something in exchange for the carcass—if not money, then some other service or work. The Rendering Man had come by some time back for the old horse, Dinah, sick on her feet and worthless. He took Dinah into his factory, and gave Thalia's father three dollars and two smoked hams. She was aware that the Rendering Man had a great love for animals, both dead and alive, for he paid money for them regardless. He was a tall, thin man with a pot belly, and a grin like walrus, two teeth thrusting down on either side of his lip. He always had red cheeks, like Santa Claus, and told her he knew magic. She had asked him (when she was younger), "What kind of magic?"

He had said, "The kind where you give me something, and I turn it into something else." Then he showed her his wallet. She felt it. He'd said, "It used to be a snake." She drew her hand back; looked at the wallet; at the Rendering Man; at the wallet; at her hand. She'd only been six or seven then, but she knew that the Rendering Man was someone powerful.

If anyone could help with the dead sow, he could.

✦   ✦

The next morning was cool and the sky was fretted with strips of clouds. Thalia had to tear off her apron as she raced from the house to climb up beside Lucius in the truck. "I didn't know you's gonna take off so quick," she panted, slamming the truck door shut beside her, "I barely got the dishes done."

"Got to get the old sow to the Rendering Man, or we may as well just open a bottle-neck fly circus out back."

Thalia glanced in the back; the sow lay there peacefully, so different than its brutal, nasty dumb animal life when it would attack anything that came in its pen. It was much nicer dead. "What's it anyways?" she asked.

"Thay, honey?"

"Renderin'."

"Oh," Lucius laughed, turning down the Post Road, "it's taking animals and things and turning them into something else."

"Witchcraft's like that."

"Naw, not like that. This is natural. You take the pig, say, and you put it in a big pot of boiling water, and the bones, see, they go over here, and the skin goes over there, and then, over there's the fat. Why you think they call a football a pigskin?"

Thalia's eyes widened. "Oh my goodness."

"And hog bristle brushes—they get those from renderin'. And what else? Maybe the fat can be used for greasing something, maybe . . ."

"Goodness sakes," Thalia said, imitating her mother's voice. "I had no idea. And he pays good money for this, does he?"

"Any money on a dead sow's been eaten by maggots's good money, Thay."

It struck her, what happened to the old horse. "He kill Dinah, too? Dinah got turned into fat and bones and skin and guts even whilst she was alive? Somebody use her fat to grease up their wheels?"

Lucius said nothing; he whistled faintly.

She felt tears threatening to bust out of her eyes. She held them back. She had loved that old horse, had seen it as a friend. Her father had lied to her about what happened to Dinah; he had said that she just went to retire in greener pastures out behind the Rendering Man's place.

She took a swallow of air. "I wished somebody'd told me so I coulda said a proper goodbye."

"My strong, brave little sister," Lucius said, and brought the truck to an abrupt stop. "Here we are." Then, he turned to her, cupping her chin in his hand the way her father did whenever she needed talking to. "Death ain't bad for those that die, remember, it's only bad for the rest of us. We got to suffer and carry on. The Dead, they get to be at peace in the arms of the Lord. Don't ever cry for the Dead, Thay, better let them cry for us." He brought his hand back down to his side. "See, the Rendering Man's just sort of a part of Nature. He takes all God's creatures and makes sure their suffering is over, but makes them useful, even so."

"I don't care about the sow," she said. "Rendering Man can do what he likes with it. I just wish we coulda et it." She tried to hide her tears; sniffed them back; it wasn't just her horse Dinah, or the sow, but something about her own flesh that bothered her, as if she and the sow could be in the same spot one day, rendered, and she didn't like that idea.

The Rendering Man's place was made of stone, and was like a fruit crate turned upside down—flat on top, with slits for windows. There were two big smoke stacks rising up from behind it like insect feelers; yellow-black smoke rose up from one of them discoloring the sky and making a stink in the general vicinity. Somebody's old mule was tied to a skinny tree in the front yard. Soon to be rendered, Thalia thought. Poor thing. She got out of the truck and walked around to pet it. The mule was old; its face was almost white, and made her think of her granny, all white of hair and skin at the end of her life.

The Rendering Man had a wife with yellow hair like summer wheat; she stood in the front doorway with a large apron that had once been white, now filthy, covering her enormous German thighs tight as skin across a drum. "Guten tag," the lady said, and she came out and scooped Thalia into her arms like she was a tin angel, smothered her scalp with kisses. "Ach, mein leibchen. You are grown so tall. Last I saw you, you was barely over with the cradle."

Just guessing as to what might be smeared on the woman's apron made Thalia slip through her arms again so that no dead animal bits would touch her. "Hello, ma'am," she said in her most formal voice.

The lady looked at her brother. "Herr Lucius, you are very grown. How is your mutter?"

"Just fine, ma'am," Lucius said, "we got the old sow in the back." He rapped on the side of the truck. "Just went last night. No good eating. Thought you might be interested."

"Ach, da, yes, of naturally we are," she said, "come in, come in, children, Father is still at the table mit breakfast. You will have some ham? Fresh milk and butter, too. Little Thalia, you are so thin, we must put some fat on those bones," and the Rendering Man's wife led them down the narrow hall to the kitchen. The kitchen table was small, which made its crowded plates seem all the more enormous: fried eggs on one, on another long fat sausages tied with ribbon at the end, then there were dishes of bread and jam and butter. Thalia's eyes were about to burst just taking it all in—slices of fat-laced ham, jewels of sweets in a brightly painted plate, and two pitchers, one full of thick milk, and the other, orange juice.

The Rendering Man sat in a chair, a napkin tucked into his collar. He had a scar on the left side of his face, as if an animal had scratched him deeply there. Grease had dripped down his chin and along his neck. He had his usual grin and sparkle to his eyes. "Well, my young friends. You've brought me something, have you?"

His wife put her hand over her left breast like she was about to faint, her eyes rolling to the back of her head, "Ach, a great pig, shotzi. They will want more than just the usual payment for that one."

Thalia asked, "Can I have a piece of ham please?"

The Rendering Man patted the place beside him. "Sit with me, both of you, yes, Eva, bring another chair. We will talk business over a good meal, won't we, Lucius? And you, sweet little bird, you must try my wife's elegant pastries. She learned how to make them in her home country, they are so light and delicate, like the sun-dried skin of a dove, but I scare you, my little bird, it is not a dove, it is bread and sugar and butter!"

After she'd eaten her fill, ignoring the conversation between her brother and the Rendering Man, Thalia asked, "How come you pay good money for dead animals, Mister?"

He drank from a large mug of coffee, wiped his lips, glanced at her brother, then at her. "Even dead, we are worth something, little bird."

"I know that. Lucius told me about the fat and bones and whiskers. But folks'd dump those animals for free. Why you pay money for them?"

The Rendering Man looked at his wife, and they both laughed. "Maybe I'm a terrible businessman," he said, shaking his head. "But," he calmed, "you see, my pet, I can sell these things for more money than I pay. I am not the only man capable of rendering. There is competition in this world. If I pay you two dollars today for your dead pig, and send you home with sweets, you will bring me more business later on, am I right?"

"I s'pose."

"So, by paying you, I keep you coming to me. And I get more skins and fat and bones to sell to places that make soap and dog-food and other things. I would be lying if I didn't tell you that I make more money off your pig than you do. But it is a service, little bird."

"I see," Thalia nodded, finishing off the last of the bacon. "It seems like a terrible thing to do."

"Thay, now, apologize for that," Lucius reached over and pinched her shoulder.

She shrugged him off.

The Rendering Man said, "It is most terrible. But it is part of how we all must live life. Someone must do the rendering. If not, everything would go to waste and we would have dead pigs rotting with flies on the side of the road, and the smell."

"But you're like a buzzard or something."

The man held his index finger up and shook it like a teacher about to give a lesson. "If I saw myself as a buzzard or jackal I could not look in the mirror. But others have said this to my face, little bird, and it never hurts to hear it. I see myself as a man who takes the weak and weary and useless, empty shells of our animal brethren and breathes new life into them, makes them go on in some other fashion. I see it as a noble profession. It is only a pity that we do not render ourselves, for what a tragedy it is to be buried and left for useless, for worm fodder, when we could be brushing a beautiful woman's hair, or adorning her purse, or even, perhaps, providing shade from the glare of a lamp so that she might read her book and not harm her eyes. It is a way to soften the blow of death, you see, for it brings forth new life. And one other thing, sweet," he brought his face closer to hers until she could smell his breath of sausage and ham, "we each have a purpose in life, and our destiny is to seek it out, whatever the cost, and make ourselves one with it. It is like brown eyes or blond hair or short and tall, it is there in us, and will come out no matter how much we try to hide it. I did not choose this life; it chose me. I think you understand, little bird, yes. You and I know."

Thalia thought about what he'd said all the way home. She tried not to imagine the old sow being tossed in a vat and stirred up in the boiling water until it started to separate into its different parts. Lucius scolded her for trying to take the Rendering Man to task, but she ignored him. She felt like a whole new world had been opened to her, a way of seeing things that she had not thought of before, and when she stepped out of the truck, at her home, she heard the crunch of the grass beneath her feet differently, the chirping of crickets, too, a lovely song, and a flock of starlings shot from the side of the barn just as she tramped across the muddy expanse that led to the chicken coops—the starlings were her sign from the world that there was no end to life, for they flew in a pattern, which seemed to her to approximate the scar on the left hand side of the Rendering Man's face.

It was like destiny.

She climbed up on the fence-post and looked down the road. A dust-wind was blowing across to the Grass Widow's house, and she heard the cats, all of them, yowling as if in heat, and she wondered if that old witch had really poisoned the pig.

2

Thalia was almost twenty-nine, and on a train in Europe, when she thought she recognized the man sitting across from her. She was now calling herself just Lia, and had not lived in Oklahoma since she left for New York in 1939 to work as a secretary—she'd taught herself short-hand and typing at the motel where her mother had worked. Then, during the war, Lucius died fighting in France, and her mother and father, whom she'd never developed much of a relationship with, called her back to the old farm. Instead, she took up with a rich and spoiled playboy who had managed to get out of serving in the military because of flat-feet, and went to live with him at his house overlooking the Hudson River. She went through a period of grief for the loss of her brother; after which, she married the playboy in question.   Then, whether out of guilt or general self-destruction, her husband managed to get involved in the war, ended up in a labor camp, and had died there not two weeks before liberation. She had inherited quite a bit of money after an initial fight with one of her husband's illegitimate children. It was 1952, and she wanted to see Germany now, to see what had happened, and where her husband of just a few months had died; she had been to Paris already to see the Hotel where her brother supposedly breathed his last, suffering at the hands of the Nazis but dying a patriot, unwilling to divulge secret information. She was fascinated by the whole thing: the war, Paris, labor camps, and Nazis.

She had grown lovely over the years; she was tall like her father and brother had been, but had her mother's eyes, and had learned, somewhere between Oklahoma and New York, to project great beauty without having inherited much.

The man across from her, on the train, had a scar on the left-hand side of his face.

It sparked a series of memories for her, like lightning flashing behind her eyes. The stone house on the Post Road, the smokestacks, the mule in the front yard, an enormous breakfast which still made her feel fat and well-fed whenever she thought of it.

It was the Rendering Man from home.

On this train. Traveling through Germany from France. Now, what are the chances, she wondered, of that happening? Particularly, after what happened when she was eleven.

Not possible, she thought.

He's a phantom. I'm hallucinating. Granny hallucinated that she saw her son Toby back from the First World War walking towards her even without his legs.

She closed her eyes; opened them. He was still there. Something so ordinary about him that she knew he was actually sitting there and not just an image conjured from her inner psyche.

He spoke first, "I know you, don't I?"

She pretended, out of politeness, that he must not be talking to her. There was a large German woman sitting beside her, with a little boy on the other side. The German woman nodded politely to her, but didn't acknowledge the man across from them. Her little boy had a card trick that he was trying to show his mother, but she paid no attention.

"Miss? Excuse me?" he said.

Then, it struck her: he spoke English perfectly, and yet he looked very German.

He grinned when she glanced back at him. "See? I knew I knew you, when I saw you in the station. I said to myself, you have met that girl somewhere before. Where are you from, if I may ask?"

"New York," she lied, curious as to whether this really could possibly be the Rendering Man. How could it? He would have to be, what? Sixty? This man didn't seem that old, although he was not young by any stretch. "I'm a reporter."

He wagged his finger at her, like a father scolding his child. "You are not a reporter, miss, I think. I am not saying you are a liar, I am only saying that that is not true. Where is your notebook? Even a pencil? You are American, and your accent is New York, but I detect a southern influence. Yes, I think so. I hope you don't mind my little game. I enjoy guessing about people and their origins."

She felt uncomfortable, but nodded, "I enjoy games, too, to pass the time."

She glanced at the German woman who was bringing out a picnic for her son. Bread and soup, but no meat. There was not a lot of meat to go around even six years after the war.

The man said, "You are a woman of fortune, I think. Lovely jewelry, and your dress is quite expensive, at least here in Europe. And I heard you talking with the conductor—your French is not so good, I think, and your German is worse. You drew out a brand of cigarettes from a gold case, both very expensive. So, you are on the Grand Tour of Europe, and like all Americans with time on their hands, you want to see the Monster Germany, the Fallen."

"Very perceptive," she said. She brought her cigarette case out and offered him one of its contents.

He shook his head. "I think these are bad for the skin and the breathing, don't you?"

She shrugged. "It all goes someday."

He grinned. "Yes, it does. The sooner we accept that, the better for the world. And I know your name now, my dear, my little bird, you are the little Thalia Canty from Moncure County Oklahoma."

She shivered, took a smoke, coughed, stubbed the cigarette out. She had white gloves on her hands; she looked at them. She remembered the German wife's apron, smeared with dark brown stains. She didn't look up for a few minutes.

"I would say this is some coincidence, little bird," the Rendering Man said, "but it is not, not really. The real coincidence happened in the Alsace, when you got off the train for lunch. I was speaking with a butcher who is a friend of mine, and I saw you go into the cafe. I wouldn't have recognized you at all, for I have not seen you since you were a child, but you made a lasting impression on me that morning we had breakfast together. I saw it in you, growing, just as it had grown in me. Once that happens, it is like a halo around you. It's still there; perhaps someone might say it is a play of light, the aurora borealis of the flesh, but I can recognize it. I followed you back to the train, got my ticket, and found where you were seated. But still I wasn't positive it was you, until just a moment ago. It was the way you looked at my face. The scar. It was a souvenir from a large cat which gouged me quite deeply. No ordinary cat, of course, but a tiger, sick, from the circus. The tiger haunts me to this day, by way of the scar. Do you believe in haunting? Ah, I think not, you are no doubt a good Disciple of Christ and do not believe that a circus cat could haunt a man. Yet, I see it sometimes in my dreams, its eyes, and teeth, and the paw reaching up to drag at my flesh. I wake my wife up, at night, just so she will stay up with me and make sure there is no tiger there. I know it is dead, but I have learned in life that sometimes these angels, as I call them (yes, dear, even the tiger is an angel for it had some message for me), do not stay dead too long. Perhaps I am your angel, little bird; you must admit it is strange to meet someone from just around the bend on the other side of the world."

She looked at him again, but tried not to see him in focus because she felt the pressing need to avoid this man at all costs. "I'm sorry, sir. You do have me pegged, but I can't for the life of me place you."

He smiled, his cheeks red. He wore a dark navy coat, and beneath it, a gray shirt. When he spoke again, it was as if he had paid no attention to her denial. "My wife, Eva, she is in Cologne, where we live, and where I should be going now. We came to Germany in 1935, because Eva's parents were ill and because, well, you must remember the unfortunate circumstance. I was only too glad to leave Oklahoma, since I didn't seem to get along with too many people there, and Germany seemed to be a place I could settle into. I found odd-jobs, as well as established a successful rendering business again. And then, well," he spread his hands out as if it were enough to excuse what happened to Germany. "But I knew you and I would meet again, little bird, it was there on your face. Your fascination and repulsion—is that not what magnets do to each other, pull and push? Yet, they are meant to be together. Destiny. You see, I saw your brother before he died, and I told him what was to come."

She dropped all pretense now. "What kind of game are you playing?"

"No game, Thalia Canty."

"Lia Fallon. Thalia Canty died in Oklahoma in the '30s."

"Names change through the years, even faces, but you are the little bird."

"And you are the Rendering Man."

He gasped with pleasure. "Yes, that would be how you know me. Tell me, did you run because of what you did?"

She didn't answer. "What about Lucius?"

The Rendering Man looked out the dark window as a town flew by. Rain sprinkled across the glass. "First, you must tell me."

"All right. I forgave myself for that a long time ago. I was only eleven, and you were partly responsible."

"Did I use the knife?"

She squinted her eyes. Wished she was not sitting there. "I didn't know what I was doing, not really."

"Seventeen cats must've put up quite a howl."

"I told you. I didn't know what I was really doing."

"Yes you did. How long after before you ran?"

"I ran away four times before I turned seventeen. Only made it as far as St. Louis most of the time."

"That's a long way from home for a little girl."

"I had an aunt there. She let me stay a month at a time. She understood."

"But not your mama and daddy," he said with some contempt in his voice. "A woman's murdered, we all called her the Grass Widow. Remember? Those Okies all thought she was a witch. All she was was sad and lonely. Then, all she was was dead. She and her cats, chopped up and boiled."

"Rendered," she said.

"Rendered. So they come for me, and thank god I was able to get my wife out of the house safely before the whole town burned it down."

"How was I to know they'd come after you?"

He was silent, but glaring.

"I didn't mean for you to get in trouble."

"Do you know what they did to me?" he asked.

She nodded.

He continued, "I still have a limp. That's my way of joking; they broke no bones. Bruises and cuts, my hearing was not good until 1937, and I lost the good vision in my right eye—it's just shadows and light on that side. Pain in memory brings few spasms to the flesh. It is the past. Little bird, but you think I am only angry at you. All those years, you are terrified you will run into me, so when you can, you get out for good. I was sure that little town was going to make another Bruno Hauptmann out of me. Killing a sad widow and her pets and boiling them for bones and fat. But even so, I was not upset with you, not too much. Not really. Because I knew you had it in you, I saw it that day, that we were cut from the same cloth, only you had not had the angel cross your path and tell you of your calling. It is not evil or dark, my sweet, it is the one calling that gives meaning to our short, idiotic lives; we are the gardeners of the infinite, you and I."

"Tell me about my brother," she pleaded softly. The German woman next to her seemed to sense the strangeness of the conversation, and took her son by the hand and led him out of the cabin.

"He did not die bravely," the Rendering Man said, "if that's what you're after. He was hit in the leg, and when I found him, he had been in a hotel with some French girl, and was a scandal for bleeding on the sheets. I was called in by my commander, and went about my business."

"You worked with the French?"

He shook his head. "I told you, I continued my successful rendering business in Germany, and expanded to a factory outside of Paris in '43. Usually the men were dead, but sometimes, as was the case with your brother, little bird, I had to stop their hearts. Your brother did not recognize me, and I only recognized him when I saw his identification. As he died, do you know what he told me? He told me that he was paying for the sins that his sister had committed in her lifetime. He cried like a little baby. It was most embarrassing. To think, I once paid him two dollars and a good sausage for a dead pig."

Lia stood up. "You are dreadful," she said. "You are the most dreadful human being who has ever existed upon the face of the earth."

"I am, if you insist. But I am your tiger; your angel," the Rendering Man said. He reached deep into the pocket of his coat and withdrew something small. He handed it to her.

She didn't want to take it, but grabbed it anyway.

"It is his. He would've wanted you to have it."

She thought, at first, it was a joke, because the small leather coin purse didn't seem to be the kind of thing Lucius would have.

When she realized what it was, she left the cabin and walked down the slender hall, all the way to the end of the train. She wanted to throw herself off, but, instead, stood and shivered in the cold wet rain of Germany, and did not return to the cabin again.

She could not get over the feeling that the part of the coin purse that drew shut resembled wrinkled human lips.

3

"He's here," the old woman said.

She heard the squeaking wheels of the orderly's cart down the corridor.

"He's here. I know he's here. Oh, dear God, he's here."

"Will you shut up, lady?" the old man in the wheelchair said.

An orderly came by and moved the man's chair on down the hall.

The old woman could not sit up well in bed. She looked at the green ceiling. The window was open. She felt a breeze. It was spring. It always seemed to be spring. A newspaper lay across her stomach. She lifted it up. Had she just been reading it? Where were her glasses?

Oh, there. She put them on. Looked at the newspaper. It was *The New York Times.*

March 23, 1994.

She called out for help, and soon an orderly (the handsome one with the bright smile) was there, like a genie summoned from a lamp. "I thought I saw a man in this room," she said.

"Mrs. Ehrlich, nobody's in here."

"I want you to check that closet. I think he's there."

The orderly went good-naturedly to the closet. He opened the door, and moved some of the clothes around. He turned to smile at her.

"I'm sure I saw him there . . . Waiting. Crouching," she said. "But he may have slipped beneath the bed."

Again, a check beneath the bed. The orderly sat down in the chair beside the bed. "He's not here."

"How old am I? I'm not very old, really, I'm not losing my wits yet, am I? Dear God in heaven, am I?"

"No, Mrs. Ehrlich. You're seventy-one going on eleven."

"Why'd you say that?"

"What?"

"Going on eleven. Why eleven? Is there a conspiracy here?"

"No, ma'am."

"You know him don't you? You know him and you're just not saying."

"Are you missing Mr. Ehrlich again?"

"Mr. Ehrlich, Mr. Vane, Mr. Fallon, one husband after another, young man, nobody can miss them because nobody can remember them. Are you sure I haven't had an unannounced visitor?"

The orderly shook his head.

She closed her eyes, and when she opened them, the orderly was gone. It had grown dark. *Where is my mind?* she thought. *Where has it gone? Why am I here at seventy-one when all my friends are still out in the world living, why, my granny was eighty-eight before senility befell her, how dare life play with me so unfairly.*

She reached for her glass of water, and took a sip.

Still, she thought she sensed his presence in the room with her, and could not sleep the rest of the night. Before dawn, she became convinced that the Rendering Man was somewhere nearby lurking; she tried to dress, but the illness had taken over her arms to such a great extent that she could not even get her bra on.

She sat up, half-naked, on her bed, the light from the hallway like a spotlight for the throbbing in her skull.

"I have led a wicked life," Thalia whispered to the morning. She found the strength at five-thirty to get her dressing gown around her shoulders, and to walk down the hall, sure that she would see him at every step.

The door to Minnie Cheever's door was open, which was odd, and she stepped into it. "Minnie?" Her friend was nearly ninety-three, and was not in bed. Thalia looked around, and finally found Minnie lying on the floor, on her way to the bathroom. Thalia checked her pulse; she was alive, but barely. Thalia's limbs hurt, but she used Minnie's wheelchair to get Minnie down the hallway, onto the elevator, and down to the basement, where the endless kitchen began.

✦   ✦

They found her there, two cooks and one orderly, like that, caught at last, Thalia Canty, all of seventy-one and going on eleven, chopping Minnie Cheever up into small pieces, and dropping each piece into one of several large pots, boiling with water, on the stove.

She turned, when she heard their footsteps, and smiled, "I knew you were here, we're like destiny, you and me, Mister Rendering Man, but you'll never have me, will you?" She held her arms out for them to see, "I scraped off all the fat and skin I could, Mister Rendering Man, you can have all these others, but you ain't never gonna get my hide and fat and bones to keep useful in this damned world. You hear me? You ain't never gonna render Thalia, and this I swear!" She tried to laugh, but it sounded like a saw scraping metal. The joke was on the Rendering Man, after all, for she would never, ever, render herself up to him.

It took two men to hold her down, and in a short time, her heart gave out. She was dead; when her body was taken to the morgue, it was discovered that she'd been scraping herself raw, almost to within an eighth of an inch of her internal organs.

It was a young girl, a candy-striper named Nancy, going through Thalia's closet to help clean it out, who found the dried skins beneath a pile of filthy clothing. The skins were presumably from Thalia's own body, sewn together, crudely representing a man. Thalia had drawn magic-marker eyes and lips and a nose on the face; and a scar.

Those who found Thalia Canty, as well as the candy-striper who fainted at the sight of the skin, later thought they saw her sometimes, in their bedrooms, or in traffic, or just over their shoulders, clutching a knife.

She would live in their hearts forever.

An angel.

A tiger.

WEIGHT

Dominick Cancilla

Scraps had been a loving and faithful companion for more than six years, and as Alex knelt on the fire escape holding a gun to the dog's head, he shook with revulsion.

The dog had been a birthday gift for Melissa, Alex's youngest. She'd picked it out herself from a dozen or so spaniel pups at the pet store, and Alex had invested a tidy sum in dog food and veterinary visits since that time.

Scraps was like part of the family, but she had gained a pound and a quarter over the last month and could no longer be trusted.

Alex steeled his nerves and pulled the trigger.

The dog's body shivered and collapsed. The .38 was powerful enough to kill the animal instantly at such close range, and the blast sent shards of bone and blobs of grey matter flying off in all directions, leaving a thin red mist floating in the air behind them. Blood and flesh sprayed up the barrel of the gun and over Alex's hands and rubber apron.

Alex was covered by more of the mess than he was used to, probably because he had been so close to the dog when he fired, and the sudden backwash of red caused him to stand and jump back, dropping the gun to the fire escape's grilled floor. His gloved hands moved quickly through the redness on his chest, hoping to find nothing more than dog remains.

The blood ran down the front of Alex's apron and nothing more. Only blood.

A blush of emotion washed over Alex as he realized his stupidity. If the animal had been further along, if the blood had been intermingled with more than brains and matter hair . . .

Alex looked down at Scraps, lying beside the revolver with blood coming from her nose and mouth. One emotionless brown eye stared up at him. The scent of gunpowder floated in the air.

Scraps had fallen with the damaged side of her head down, and Alex allowed himself to imagine that she was whole, despite the evidence splattered across the fire escape railing.

With loving care, Alex picked up his daughter's pet and lay her in the mouth of the propane barbecue which stood behind him. He scrubbed the gun and fire escape with alcohol, and put the dirty rags alongside Scraps, followed by his gloves and apron.

After a silent prayer, he lit the barbecue.

Alex cleaned off his overshoes with alcohol and a scrub brush before going back into the apartment. He was tired, emotionally drained, and being alone only made his emotions more intense. He knew it was necessary to send Ann and the girls to the McPhearson's for a few hours while he did what he had to do, but that knowledge was no consolation to him now.

He dropped into the easy chair he loved most and pulled a magazine from the ragged pile of aging periodicals on the floor beside him. *Time's* cover story "Life Only For The Thin?" was old news. Alex had read it a dozen times, always hoping to find some new bit of information, and always being disappointed. *Time* offered nothing but rumor, innuendo and pleas for patience and restraint.

Restraint could lead to death and tragedy, Alex knew. It was a thing of the past.

The smell of burning hair and flesh oozed into the apartment, interrupting Alex's self-depreciating musings. The stench made Alex feel dirty, and kept the memory of what he had done fresh in his mind. The grainy pictures of dry, hole-riddled people and overweight women being executed suddenly became too real for comfort. Alex dropped the magazine, got up from his recliner and headed for the bathroom where relaxation could be found in the form of a hot bath.

The plumbing was still working, and Alex watched with pleasure as the bathtub filled with hot water. He undressed slowly, luxuriously, laying his clothes across the toilet seat. The air filled with steam from the bath, clearing Alex's head.

Standing naked, Alex poured two cups of vinegar into the filling bathtub to take care of anything which was not killed by the heat.

Alex decided to get a quick shave in before bathing, all the better to feel clean afterwards. He got his razor and a bar of soap from the drawer in the sink cabinet, and used a forearm to brush a clear spot in the bathroom mirror.

When Alex's face appeared in the reflective surface, he dropped the shaving supplies to the floor and shivered with horror.

Alex had never been a handsome man. He had tried to distract attention from premature baldness and a face pockmarked by acne during high-school with a full beard, but it was not well cared for. His nose had been broken twice and there was a small scar through his right eyebrow. The blood which dotted his face, and the few clots of Scraps' tissue which hung from his beard did nothing to improve the picture.

His eyes wide with fear, Alex ran to the fire escape for the alcohol. When he pulled open the sliding door, his eyes and nose were assaulted by thick, black smoke, driven into the apartment by a summer updraft. Ignoring these as best he could, Alex scrubbed his face and chest with the alcohol, pouring it into his nose, rinsing out his mouth, and dousing his ears. He stopped only when the bottle was empty.

What a fool he had been! He should have worn the welder's mask, should have put on more clothing, should have shot the dog from a distance like he usually did.

When he killed other creatures, Alex killed them where they stood and let their owners, or family, clean up after them. He didn't want to be near a potentially infested animal long enough to take it to a neutral area. For this reason, he never even thought to take Scraps into one of the abandoned apartments or to some other location, someplace where he wouldn't have to worry about people picking up a living egg.

More doubts went through Alex's mind. Had he scrubbed every surface? Was there some infested piece of the dog waiting for him, hiding in some corner?

Scraps had been so like a member of the family that Alex, deep in his soul, had not been convinced that the animal could be a danger. He had touched it, gotten close to it, even after he knew that it might be a carrier. That was a mistake, one that he swore he would never make again.

The wind changed, pulling the smoke away from the building. Alex stood naked on the fire escape, his eyes tearing, his legs and arms shaking with fear.

Orange flames swirled about a charred jumble of bones in the barbecue, but Alex could see only a blur. On unsure feet, he felt his way back into the apartment and collapsed into his easy chair. With his face in his hands, Alex sobbed.

✦   ✦

While Alex wept, the bathtub overflowed. He managed to catch it before the water did any real damage, but it was enough to completely ruin an otherwise horrible day. By the time he had recovered from his shock, cleaned up the bathroom and gotten dressed, there was barely time to shovel what remained of Scraps into a Hefty bag before Ann and the kids got home.

With the windows and doors all open, the acrid smell began to fade and Alex found some measure of composure. He stood on the fire escape, staring at the street below, trying to remember how things had been before.

There had been a time when Sixth was one of the busiest streets downtown and one had to wait months, if not years, to get an apartment anywhere in the area. Now only a few cars crawled by below, and only a handful of the two hundred apartments in Alex's building were occupied.

Most of the apartments visible from Alex's balcony were dark both day and night, and signs of life were few. Across the street and three stories down a man in a blue bathrobe stood cooking what looked like hamburgers on his own balcony barbecue. Alex had seen thick, oily smoke from that same barbecue on more than one occasion. He hardly even noticed such things anymore.

The whole business had seemed like nothing more than an interesting bit of world news at first. The damage seemed to be limited to derelicts and transients, all in faraway parts of the country. Nobody cared. It had been easy to say that cool heads should prevail. Charity organizations jumped on the bandwagon, the President was asked to provide research funds, there were marches, and telethons, and concerts.

Everyone patted themselves on the back for being socially conscious, and made sure to cross the street when a homeless person approached.

Then a few shelters were wiped out completely, social workers and volunteers started to be affected. Then nurses, doctors, police officers, even people who just jogged through the park on weekday mornings were dying, and taking their families with them. When white, middle-class Americans started to be affected, tolerance fell by the wayside and panic set in.

It was open season on poor people, and the police turned a blind eye as nameless hundreds were murdered in the name of public good.

Then more details of the condition came to light and things went from bad to worse. Anyone with a weight problem was suddenly in danger. Homicide rates skyrocketed, the city went berserk.

Never one to believe the popular press, Alex had written the whole thing off as hysteria. He could believe that the poor, the unwashed, the uneducated were being affected, but not regular, healthy people like him, not families like his. By the time he got it through his head that the city was unsafe, it was too late. He'd lost his job, the company credit union had folded, his car had been stolen during the August Exodus, there was nothing left. If he wanted to leave, he'd have to do it on foot, and that meant putting his family at the mercy of a city full of unclean and unknown surfaces. They wouldn't last a week.

In all the world, the only place that Alex truly trusted was his own apartment. He knew every inch of floor space, every nook and cranny, and all of it was spotlessly clean. The same could be said of the McPhearson's place down the hall, and of the floor and walls which connected the two apartments.

The only time that Alex ever left the safe, clean areas was when he, Ann and Angus McPhearson went on their weekly "shopping" trips. He always felt silly walking through the downtown area dressed with gloves, thick clothing and his old welder's helmet protecting every inch of skin from potential human contact, but he'd learned long ago that it was far better to feel foolish now than to die later.

A key turned in the front door, telling Alex that his family was home. Ann stuck her head to see if the coast was clear before letting the children in, and was reassured by her husband's smiling face as he came to greet her.

The children came close behind their mother, and made sure that the door was closed and bolted behind them.

Alex opened his arms for a communal hug. "How was it at the McPhearson's?" he asked, hoping to sound cheerful. There was no reason to include his kids in the gloom which had overtaken him.

Melissa, the youngest, spoke first. "It was neat, Dad. They have cartoon videos and Lisa had a cold but we made popcorn in the microwave all by ourselves!"

"Wow, that's great," said Alex. Melissa seemed oblivious to what had been going on in her absence and that pleased him. Ann had been calm when the dog's weight started to rise, and did not mention it to the girls. Small weight fluctuations happened all the time, particularly in animals, and there was no need to make a fuss before it was necessary. When they realized that the dog's weight was not going to go back down, they decided to pretend that the dog had simply died. Gone to Dog Heaven and all that. They would wait as long as possible to tell the tale.

Melissa would be saddened by the news, of course. She would wonder about the dog, and cry when she realized it was gone forever, but these were relatively small hurdles. The important thing was that she believe the little lie, and Melissa was too young to think of doubting her parents.

Katie was another story.

When Alex looked at his oldest daughter, he saw hatred. She was only seven years old, but there was a lifetime of betrayal in her eyes. Alex didn't know how much she knew, or whether she really understood what had happened, but he knew that, in time, the girls would come to understand what he had done.

That night as Alex lay in bed, his wife snoring softly beside him and the children long ago weighed and tucked in, he found sleep elusive. He had seen and done more horrible, distasteful things in the last few months than he cared to remember, and they were finally starting to sink in.

Before the market turned sour, Alex had been a construction foreman. He was strong, both physically and emotionally, which made up for his rather average intelligence. It was these characteristics coupled with his generosity and confidence that brought people to him when the time came for unsafe loved ones to be put to rest.

Back when the building was fully occupied, the apartment across the hall had been occupied by the Lenowskis, Mike and Julia. Alex had known Mike from college, and had dated Julia a few times before meeting Ann. They were wonderful neighbors, just as the McPhearsons were. The six of them used to get together to play pinochle every month; these days it was bridge.

Just as the first few downtown-area bums were starting to die, Mike and Julia had a child. It was a beautiful baby, round and active with a thin head of blonde hair and piercing blue eyes. Ann's maternal instincts had been aroused and endless hours of cooing over the infant followed.

When the baby was a few weeks old, Mike started to get nervous. He stopped eating regularly and worked a lot of late hours at the office. Julia confided to Ann that she thought her husband was having an affair, but Alex knew differently. Mike was worried about the baby.

Babies, all children in fact, had been a problem from the first. They sometimes grew fast naturally, and sometimes they didn't, making it hard for a parent to judge. The rumor mill was full of paranoid stories which told in graphic detail of fat infants bursting in the night, killing their parents, their siblings, their neighbors.

The baby was ten weeks old when Mike finally cracked.

"I love my wife, Alex," Mike had said, standing in the doorway with two days beard and a new revolver held loosely in his hand. "I love her more than anything and I can't let anything happen to her." His hands were raw from constant rubbing, and his speech punctuated by long pauses. "We can have another child. Soon. I love my son. I just . . . I love my wife more."

Fat tears rolled down Mike's cheeks and his voice hitched. "I can't stand the thought of Julia dying that way. I just can't. And the baby, the baby's getting so big."

Silence hung heavy in the air while Mike tried to compose himself. "I can't do it myself, Alex, and you're the only person we can trust. Julia . . . " He'd broken off there, overwhelmed by emotion. Mike pressed the gun into Alex's hand and started dragging him out of the apartment, toward the half open apartment door across the hall.

Alex hadn't known what to do. The best plan he could formulate was to take the baby away, say he was going to get rid of it and give it to a church or something. Mike was too far gone to be trusted around the child any more.

The Lenowski's apartment was a mess. Books, glasses, clothing were strewn about the floor; the couch had been pulled away from the wall; a portable radio stuck out of a jagged hole in the picture tube of Mike's new television. Julia was nowhere to be seen, but Alex thought he could see a formless something lying still on the floor in the darkened bedroom down the hall. He did not investigate further.

Only the baby's crib seemed to be untouched by whatever storm had hit the room.

Lying in its bassinet, surrounded by padded blue fabric and ruffles, the baby looked completely innocent. It smiled up at Alex, cooing and drooling. The child wasn't even strong enough to roll over, and here was its father crying for it to die.

Nobody knew how to tell true fat from the outside, they still don't. It was possible, even probable, that there was nothing wrong with the baby, but as Alex looked down he found himself in an emotional struggle. He wanted to save the blameless child from the hysteria overtaking its parents, but what if he did and turned out to be wrong? What if the child really was infested? A child's hands go everywhere; there might already be eggs clinging to its skin, its hair, its crib, its toys. If Alex picked it up, he could be infested himself. And then his family.

Alex thought of how Ann would look, her face bulging, her slim frame covered with fat, her swollen tongue holding her mouth open. The gun rose and fired before Alex had a chance to stop it.

The bassinet jumped and rolled backwards on casters, the frilly cloth on one side melting from pink to red. Mike screamed and ran to pick up the child. "What have you done!" he screamed as the last beats of a dying heart poured a red stain across his chest and face.

Alex dropped the gun, turned and left without saying anything.

That night Alex was woken from a fitful sleep by a loud report from across the hall. He never saw his neighbors again, and he never ventured into their apartment.

A cold shiver ran through Alex's body as he lay in bed, recounting these events. Since that time he'd done a score of dogs and cats, a few birds, even goldfish. On one occasion he put away a senile old woman, and on another a five-year-old child.

It was never easy, killing a living thing, but not knowing was the worst part. Alex could never be sure that the thing he killed was really infested. He'd heard that you can cut someone open and look to see if they were, but such tests would fail if you looked in the wrong places or if the eggs had not yet begun to hatch, and with medical help so hard to get, the person being checked was just as likely to die of an infection as anything. It was easier just to kill outright and try to forget about it, if you could.

Like Mike's baby, Scraps had probably just gained weight naturally for some reason or another. The dog had been cooped up in the apartment for a long time and couldn't be coaxed to exercise with the rest of the family, and it certainly ate enough. Scraps may or may not have been infested, and Alex would spend the rest of his life wondering.

There was silence within Alex for a few moments, and then he asked himself a question: if Scraps had been infected, how had she gotten to be? There was no sure answer for that question, either.

Nobody was certain where the parasites came from originally, but once in a host they could be transmitted through blood when they were still eggs or through direct contact when fully grown; this was certain. There were rumors that the eggs could be inhaled, or deposited in a drop of sweat, even though scientists in government employ denied it. People tended to avoid physical contact completely these days, and only fools used public toilets or walked barefoot any more.

Adult worms were supposed to be very thin and nearly transparent. They were invisible in a glass of water or on a heavily patterned surface. Their incubation period was uncertain, so Scraps may have picked one up when she was still taken on her twice-daily walks and carried it around with her ever since. If so, had a breeder of parasites been living among them for six months? Perhaps the dog had actually been losing weight at the same time the infestation was gaining? It could have been passing out eggs, or even adults, in its stools for weeks.

The girls took turns cleaning up after the dog.

Alex imagined himself standing with Katie on the balcony, her body bloated, her chin doubled, and her eyes staring up at him with hatred. He could see her head jerk back in slow motion when the gun went off, one of her pigtails torn free, spiraling down toward the street. He could imagine the smell of her burning body as she lay half in and half out of the barbecue with rosy flames dancing through her Sunday dress.

The same thoughts ran over and over through his mind for hours.

It was almost three in the morning when Alex's painful imaginings were interrupted by a pounding on the front door. He had still not slept a wink, and the sheets were caked to his naked body with sweat.

Ann woke up while Alex was putting on a robe, and lights flicked on in the girls' room.

"I'll see what it is," Alex said to his wife, "tell the girls that everything's all right."

Alex finished tying his bathrobe belt on the way to the front door. The pounding didn't stop until he began to undo the latches.

Light from the hallway surprised Alex with its brightness, causing him to squint, but even under these conditions he could see that it was Angus McPhearson standing outside his door.

The look on Angus' face was one of horror. There was no color in his cheeks, and his jaw hung loose. The words which came out of him were whispered and strained. "It's Lisa, Alex. You've got to help her. She's sick."

A hundred thoughts rushed through Alex's mind. Lisa had been sick when Ann and the girls visited earlier; she'd stayed out of sight. In fact, they'd had to cancel their bridge night that week, and the week before. It didn't take a genius to see that something might be very wrong with Lisa, the woman who took care of Scraps and the girls when Alex and his wife were away.

Fear and lack of sleep pushed Alex toward a hasty decision and stripped him of his inhibitions. Deep in his gut Alex knew that Lisa had more than a bad case of the flu or a nasty virus. He half ran to the desk where his gun was hidden.

At the end of the hallway, the McPhearson's apartment door stood open, and Alex ran toward it with Angus close behind him crying, "You don't need the gun, Alex. She's just sick. Just sick!"

When Alex bounded into the apartment, he saw that this was not the case at all.

Aside from Alex and his family, the McPhearson's were the only people on the floor who had not left town since the worms arrived. They'd been good neighbors, and good friends, for many, many years, but the Lisa McPhearson who stood before Alex now was someone he hardly knew.

Lisa had propped herself up in the bedroom doorway across from Alex, wearing nothing. Only a few weeks before she'd been a slim, athletic woman, but now she was bloated from neck to ankle. The skin on Lisa's legs, arms and stomach was pulled taut and striped with stretch marks; it looked almost as if she could be burst with a pin.

"I didn't know it was going to get like this, Alex," Angus' voice cried from the hallway. "I just thought she was sick, you know. Just sick."

Angus pushed past Alex into the room. "You don't need the gun, Alex," he said. "She just needs medical attention. I thought, you know, that maybe we could put her on a special diet or start doing those exercises you guys do."

A bizarre husky laugh erupted from Lisa. Her mouth spread into a toothy grin and her body shook with hysterics. Alex could see that the skin on her stomach had started to move with more than laughter. He raised the gun.

A convulsion wracked Lisa's body, and another, each followed by a yell and more deep, maniacal laughter. Then rain started to fall from between her legs.

At first Alex thought that Lisa was wetting herself, and then, as the pile below her grew, he saw he was wrong.

It was worms. Hundreds. Thousands. Thin and clear, they poured from between Lisa's legs as she laughed. The worms writhed and began to spread across the floor.

Alex fired.

The bullet ripped through Lisa's breast and pushed her back against the door jamb. A flap of skin hung loose on her chest, and Alex thought that he could see her heart beating through frosted glass. The worms tumbled out through the flap and down her stomach.

A second bullet stopped Lisa's heart, and a third tore through her neck.

With a scream, Angus ran to his fallen wife.

"No, no!" he cried, taking the deformed, bloody sack of a woman in his arms.

The worms wasted no time in squirming up Angus's pants legs, over his hands and arms. His screams of pain and anguish were intermixed as the creatures began to suck liquid from his body.

Alex could only stand and stare, frozen with grotesque curiosity, until he felt a prickling sensation against his feet.

The worms almost covered the floor. They had moved quickly, more quickly than Alex would have thought possible, and were now burrowing their way into his bare feet. Alex looked down to see half a dozen of them disappear into him through thin red tunnels.

Back in his apartment there was more alcohol and vinegar. He could burn and cauterize the wounds, perhaps kill the things before they lay their eggs or drink the fluid in his body.

Alex turned to run but his legs betrayed him. He fell to the floor and was immediately struck by a wave of parasites, tearing at his flesh, his face. The worms made quick work of the large man, and began to make their way down through cracks in the floor, hoping to find further nourishment on the floors below.

Katie slept soundly in her bed. The noise down the hall was muffled, and did not bother her. Even the pounding she heard earlier did nothing more than make her stir.

In her dreams, Katie played ball with Scraps in the park like they used to, before it was dangerous to be around other living things. They rolled around in the grass and ran among the trees, without a care in the world. But these simple pleasures had a sour taste to them; Katie knew that she would never see her dog again, and even in her dreams she cried.

Katie was filled with a sadness which threatened to consume her. As she slept, a thin tear creeped from the corner of her eye, dropped to the floor, and wriggled out of sight.

LAYOVER

Ed Gorman

In the darkness, the girl said, "Are you all right?"

"Huh?"

"I woke you up because you sounded so bad. You must have been having a nightmare."

"Oh. Yeah. Right." I tried to laugh but the sound just came out strangled and harsh.

Cold midnight. Deep midwest. A Greyhound bus filled with old folks and runaway kids and derelicts of every kind. Anybody can afford a Greyhound ticket these days, that's why you find so many geeks and freaks aboard. I was probably the only guy on the bus who had a real purpose in life. And if I needed a reminder of that purpose, all I had to do was shove my hand into the pocket of my P-coat and touch the chill blue metal of the .38. I had a purpose all right.

The girl had gotten on a day before, during a dinner stop. She wasn't what you'd call pretty but then neither was I. We talked of course, the way you do when you travel; dull grinding social chatter at first, but eventually you get more honest. She told me she'd just been dumped by a guy named Mike, a used car salesman at Belaski Motors in a little town named Burnside. She was headed to Chicago where she'd find a job and show Mike that she was capable of going on without him. Come to think of it, I guess Polly here had a goal, too, and in a certain way our goals were similar. We both wanted to pay people back for hurting us.

Sometime around ten, when the driver turned off the tiny overhead lights and people started falling asleep, I heard her start crying. It wasn't loud and it wasn't hard but it was genuine. There was a lot of pain there.

I don't know why—I'm not the type of guy to get involved—but I put my hand on her lap. She took it in both of her hands and held it tightly. "Thanks," she said and leaned over and kissed me with wet cheeks and a trembling hot little mouth.

"You're welcome," I said, and that's when I drifted off to sleep, the wheels of the Greyhound thrumming down the highway, the dark coffin inside filled with people snoring, coughing and whispering.

According to the luminous hands on my wrist watch, it was forty-five minutes later when Polly woke me up to tell me I'd been having a nightmare.

The lights were still off overhead. The only lumination was the soft silver of moonlight through the tinted window. We were in the back seat on the left hand side of the back aisle. The only thing behind us was the john, which almost nobody seemed to use. The seats across from us were empty.

After telling me about how sorry she felt for me having nightmares like that, she leaned over and whispered, "Who's Kenny?"

"Kenny?"

"That's the name you kept saying in your nightmare."

"Oh."

"You're not going to tell me, huh?"

"Doesn't matter. Really."

I leaned back and closed my eyes. There was just darkness and the turning of the wheels and the winter air whistling through the windows. You could smell the faint exhaust.

"You know what I keep thinking?" she said.

"No. What?" I didn't open my eyes.

"I keep thinking we're the only two people in the world, you and I, and we're on this fabulous boat and we're journeying to someplace beautiful."

I had to laugh at that. She sounded so naive yet desperate too. "Someplace beautiful, huh?"

"Just the two of us."

And she gave my hand a little squeeze. "I'm sorry I'm so corny," she said.

And that's when it happened. I started to turn around in my seat and felt something fall out of my pocket and hit the floor, going *thunk*. I didn't have to wonder what it was.

Before I could reach it, she bent over, her long blonde hair silver in the moonlight, and got it for me.

She looked at it in her hand and said, "Why would you carry a gun?"

"Long story."

She looked as if she wanted to take the gun and throw it out the window. She shook her head. "You're going to do something with this, aren't you?"

I sighed and reached over and took the gun from her. "I'd like to try and catch a little nap if you don't mind."

"But—"

And I promptly turned over so that three-fourths of my body was pressed against the chill wall of the bus. I pretended to go to sleep, resting there and smelling diesel fuel and feeling the vibration of the motor.

The bus roared on into the night. It wouldn't be long before I'd be seeing Dawn and Kenny again. I touched the .38 in my pocket. No, not long at all.

If you've taken many Greyhounds, then you know about layovers. You spend an hour-and-a-half gulping down greasy food and going to the bathroom in a john that reeks like a city dump on a hot day and staring at people in the waiting area who seem to be deformed in some way. Or that's how they look at 2:26 A.M., anyway.

This layover was going to be different. At least for me. I had plans.

As the bus pulled into a small brick depot that looked as if it had been built back during the Depression, Polly said, "You're going to do it here, aren't you?"

"Do what?"

"Shoot somebody."

"Why would you say that?"

"I've just got a feeling is all. My mom always says I have ESP."

She started to say something else but then the driver lifted the microphone and gave us his spiel about how the layover would be a full hour and how there was good food to be had in the restaurant and how he'd enjoyed serving us. There'd be a new driver for the next six hours of our journey, he said.

There weren't many lights on in the depot. Passengers stood outside for a while stretching and letting the cold air wake them up.

I followed Polly off the bus and immediately started walking away. An hour wasn't a long time.

Before I got two steps, she snagged my arm. "I was hoping we could be friends. You know, I mean, we're a lot alike." In the shadowy light of the depot, she looked younger than ever. Young and well-scrubbed and sad. "I don't want you to get into trouble. Whatever it is, you've got your whole life ahead of you. It won't be worth it. Honest."

"Take care of yourself," I said, and leaned over and kissed her.

She grabbed me again and pulled me close and said, "I got in a little trouble once myself. It's no fun. Believe me."

I touched her cheek gently and then I set off walking quickly into the darkness.

Armstrong was a pretty typical midwestern town, four blocks of retail area, a fading brick grade school and junior high, a small public library with a white stone edifice, a court house, a Chevrolet dealership and many blocks of small white frame houses that all looked pretty much the same in the early morning gloom. You could see frost rimmed on the windows and lonely gray smoke twisting up from the chimneys. As I walked, my heels crunched ice. Faint streetlight threw everything into deep shadow. My breath was silver.

A dog joined me for a few blocks and then fell away. Then I spotted a police cruiser moving slowly down the block. I jumped behind a huge oak tree, flattening myself against the rough bark so the cops couldn't see me. They drove right on past, not even glancing in my direction.

The address I wanted was a ranch house that sprawled over the west end of a cul-de-sac. A sweet little red BMW was parked in front of the two-stall garage and a huge satellite dish antenna was discreetly hidden behind some fir trees. No lights shone anywhere.

I went around back and worked on the door. It didn't take me long to figure out that Kenny had gotten himself one of those infra-red security devices. I tugged on my gloves, cut a fist-size hole in the back door window, reached in and unlocked the deadbolt, and then pushed the door open. I could see one of the small round infra-red sensors pointing down from the ceiling. Most fool burglars wouldn't even think to look for it and they'd pass right through the beam and the alarm would go off instantly.

I got down on my haunches and half-crawled until I was well past the eye of the infra-red. No alarm had sounded. I went up three steps and into the house.

The dark kitchen smelled of spices, paprika and cinnamon and thyme. Dawn had always been a good and careful cook.

The rest of the house was about what I'd expect. Nice but not expensive furnishing, lots of records and videotapes, and even a small bumper pool table in a spare room that doubled as a den. Nice, sure, but nothing that would attract attention. Nothing that would appear to have been financed by six hundred thousand dollars in bank robbery money.

And then the lights came on.

At first I didn't recognize the woman. She stood at the head of a dark narrow hallway wearing a loose cotton robe designed to conceal her weight.

The flowing dark hair is what misled me. Dawn had always been a blonde. But dye and a gain of maybe fifteen pounds had changed her appearance considerably. And so had time. It hadn't been a friend to her.

She said, "I knew you'd show up someday, Chet."

"Where's Kenny?"

"You want some coffee?"

"You didn't answer my question."

She smiled her slow, sly smile. "You didn't answer mine, either."

She led us into the kitchen where a pot of black stuff stayed warm in a Mr. Coffee. She poured two cups and handed me one of them.

"You came here to kill us, didn't you?" she said.

"You were my wife. And we were supposed to split everything three ways. But Kenny got everything—you and all the dough. And I did six years in the slam."

"You could have turned us in."

I shook my head, "I have my own way of settling things."

She stared at me. "You look great, Chet. Prison must have agreed with you."

"I just kept thinking of this night. Waiting."

Her mouth tightened and for the first time her blue eyes showed traces of fear. Softly, she said, "Why don't we go in the living room and talk about it."

I glanced at my wristwatch. "I want to see Kenny."

"You will. Come on now."

So I followed her into the living room. I had a lot ahead of me. I wanted to kill them and then get back on the bus. While I'd be eating up the miles on a Greyhound, the local cops would be looking for a local killer. If only my gun hadn't dropped out and Polly seen it. But I'd have to worry about that later.

We sat on the couch. I started to say something but then she took my cup from me and set it on the glass table and came into my arms.

She opened her mouth and kissed me dramatically.

But good sense overtook me. I held her away and said, "So while we're making out, Kenny walks in and shoots me. Is that it?"

"Don't worry about Kenny. Believe me."

And then we were kissing again. I was embracing ghosts, ancient words whispered in the back seats of cars when we were in high school, tender promises made just before I left for Nam. Loving this woman had always been punishment because you could never believe her, never trust her, but I'd loved her anyway.

I'd just started to pull away when I heard the floor creak behind me and I saw Kenny. Even given how much I hated this man—and how many long nights I'd laid on my prison bunk dreaming of vengeance—I had to feel embarrassed. If Kenny had been his old self, I would have relished the moment. But Kenny was different now. He was in a wheelchair and his entire body was twisted and crippled up like a cerebral palsy victim. A small plaid blanket was thrown across his legs.

He surprised me by smiling. "Don't worry, Chet. I've seen Dawn entertain a lot of men out here in the living room before."

"Spare him the details," she said. "And spare me, too, while you're at it."

"Bitch," he whispered loud enough for us to hear.

He wheeled himself into the living room. The chair's electric motor whirred faintly as he angled over to the fireplace. On his way, he said, "You didn't wait long, Chet. You've only been out two weeks. You never did have much patience."

You could see the pain in his face when he moved.

I tried to say something but I just kept staring at this man who was now a cripple. I didn't know what to say.

"Nice set-up, huh?" Kenny said as he struck a stick match on the stone of the fireplace. With his hands twisted and gimped the way they were, it wasn't easy. He got his smoke going and said, "She tell you what happened to me?"

I looked at Dawn. She dropped her gaze. "No," I said.

He snorted. The sound was bitter. "She was doin' it to me just the way she did it to you. Right, bitch?"

She sighed then lighted her own cigarette. "About six months after we ran out on you with all the money, I grabbed the strongbox and took off."

Kenny smirked. "She met a sailor. A fucking sailor, if you can believe it."

"His name was Fred," she said. "Anyway, me and Fred had all the bank robbery cash—there was still a couple hundred thousand left—when Kenny here came after us in that red Corvette he always wanted. He got right up behind us but it was pouring rain and he skidded out of control and slammed into a tree."

He finished the story for me. "There was just one problem, right, bitch? You had the strongbox but you didn't know what was inside. Her and the sailor were going to have somebody use tools on the lock I'd put on it. They saw me pile up my 'vette but they kept on going. But later that night when they blew open the strongbox and found out that I'd stuffed it with old newspapers, the sailor beat her up and threw her out. So she came back to me 'cause she just couldn't stand to be away from 'our' money. And this is where she's been all the time you were in the slam. Right here waitin' for poor pitiful me to finally tell her where I hid the loot. Or die. They don't give me much longer. That's what keeps her here."

"Pretty pathetic story, huh?" she said. She got up and went over to the small wet bar. She poured three drinks of pure Jim Beam and brought them over to us. She gunned hers in a single gulp and went right back for another.

"So she invites half the town in so she can have her fun while I vegetate in my wheelchair." Now it was his turn to down his whiskey. He hurled the glass into the fireplace. A long, uneasy silence followed.

I tried to remember the easy friendship the three of us had enjoyed back when we were in high school, before Kenny and I'd been in Nam, and before the three of us had taken up bank robbery for a living. Hard to believe we'd ever liked each other at all.

Kenny's head dropped down then. At first I thought he might have passed out but then the choking sound of dry tears filled the room and I realized he was crying.

"You're such a wimp," she said.

And then it was her turn to smash her glass into the fireplace.

I'd never heard two people go at each other this way. It was degrading.

He looked up at me. "You stick around here long enough, Chet, she'll make a deal with you. She'll give you half the money if you beat me up and make me tell you where it is."

I looked over at her. I knew what he said was true.

"She doesn't look as good as she used to—she's kind of a used car now instead of a brand-new Caddy—but she's still got some miles left on her. You should hear her and some of her boyfriends out here on the couch when they get goin'."

She started to say something but then she heard me start to laugh.

"What the hell's so funny?"

I stood up and looked at my watch. I had only ten minutes left to get back to the depot.

Kenny glanced up from his wheelchair. "Yeah, Chet, what's so funny?"

I looked at them both and just shook my head. "It'll come to you. One of these days. Believe me."

And with that, I left.

She made a play for my arm and Kenny sat there glowering at me but I just kept on walking. I had to hurry.

The cold, clean air not only revived me, it seemed to purify me in some way. I felt good again, whole and happy now that I was outdoors.

The bus was dark and warm. Polly had brought a bag of popcorn along. "You almost didn't make it," she said as the bus pulled away from the depot.

In five minutes we were rolling into countryside again. In farmhouses lights were coming on. In another hour, it would be dawn.

"You took it, didn't you?" I said.

"Huh?"

"You took it. My gun."

"Oh. Yes. I guess I did. I didn't want you to do anything foolish."

Back there at Kenny's I'd reached into my jacket pocket for the .38 and found it gone. "How'd you do it? You were pretty slick."

"Remember I told you I'd gotten into a little trouble? Well, an uncle of mine taught me how to be a pickpocket and so for a few months I followed in his footsteps. Till Sheriff Baines arrested me one day."

"I'm glad you took it."

She looked over at me in the darkness of the bus and grinned. She looked like a kid. "You really didn't want to do it, did you?"

"No," I said, staring out the window at the midwestern night. I thought of them back there in the house, in a prison cell they wouldn't escape till death. No, I hadn't wanted to shoot anybody at all. And, as things had turned out, I hadn't had to either. Their punishment was each other.

"We're really lucky we met each other, Chet."

"Yeah," I said, thinking of Dawn and Kenny again. "You don't know how lucky we are."

JOHNNY HALLOWEEN

Norman Partridge

I should have never been there.

Number one: I was off duty. Number two: even though I'm the sheriff, I believe in letting my people earn their pay. In other words, I don't follow them around with a big roll of toilet paper waiting to wipe their asses for them, even when it comes to murder cases. And number three: I'm a very sound sleeper—generally speaking, you've got a better chance of finding Elvis Presley alive than you've got of waking me between midnight and six.

But it was Halloween, and the kids next door were having a loud party, and I couldn't sleep. Sure, I could have broken up the party, but I didn't. I'm a good neighbor. I like to hear the sound of kids having fun, even if I think the music we listened to back in the fifties was a lot easier on the ears. So I'm not sour on teenagers, like some cops. Probably has something to do with the fact that Helen and I never had any kids of our own.

It just didn't work out for us, is all. When Helen had the abortion, we were young and stupid and we figured we'd have plenty of chances later on. That wasn't the way it worked out, though. I guess timing is everything. The moment passes, things change, and the life you thought you'd have isn't there when you catch up to it.

What it is, is you get older. You change and you don't even notice it. You think you're making the decisions, but mostly life is making them for you. You're just along for the ride. Reacting, not acting. Most of the time you're just trying to make it through another day.

That's how most cops see it. Like my deputies say: shit happens. And then we come along and clean up the mess.

I guess maybe I do carry around that big roll of toilet paper, after all.

So, anyway, Helen had asked me to get another six-pack and some chips. She does like her Doritos. It was hot, especially for late October, and a few more beers sounded like a good idea. I worry about Helen drinking so much, but it's like the kid thing. We just don't talk about it anymore. What I usually do is drink right along with her, and then I don't feel so bad.

So I was headed up Canyon, fully intending to go to the Ralphs Supermarket on Arroyo, when I observed some suspicious activity at the old liquor store on the corner of Orchard and Canyon (if you want it in cop-ese).

Suspicious isn't the word for it. A couple of Mexican girls were coming out of the place. One was balancing a stack of cigarette cartons that was so high she couldn't see over it. The other had a couple of plastic sacks that looked to be filled with liquor bottles.

I pulled into the lot, tires squealing. The girl with the liquor bottles had pretty good instincts, because she dropped them and rabbited. The strong smell of tequila and rum hit me as I jumped out of the truck—a less sober-hearted man would have thought he'd died and gone to heaven. Me, I had other things on my mind. The girl with the cigarettes hadn't gotten too far. She didn't want to give up her booty. Cartons were slipping and sliding and she looked like a drunken trapeze artist about to take the big dive, but she was holding tough.

Tackling her didn't seem like the best idea, but I sure didn't want to let her work up any steam. I'm not as fast as I used to be. So what I did was I grabbed for her hair, which was long enough to brush her ass when she wasn't running and it wasn't streaming out behind her. I got a good grip first try; her feet went out from under her, she shrieked like a starlet in a horror movie who's about to taste chainsaw, the smokes went flying every which way, and it was just damn lucky for me that she wasn't wearing a wig.

"It wasn't me!" she said, trying to fight. "I didn't do it! It was some guy wearing a mask!"

"Yeah, right. And you've got a receipt for these cigarettes in your back pocket. Sorry . . . got you red-handed, little miss."

I hustled her across the lot, stomping cigarette cartons as I went. That gave me a kick. God, I hate smokers. We went inside the store, and that's when I saw what she'd meant when she said she hadn't done anything.

The kid was no more than twenty, and—like the old saying goes—he'd never see twenty-one. He lay on the floor, a pool of dark blood around the hole in his head.

"We saw the guy who did it," the girl said, eager to please, real eager to get my fingers out of her hair. "He cleaned out the register. He was wearing a mask . . . . "

Dead eyes stared up at me. My right boot toed the shore of a sea of blood. Already drying, going from red to a hard black on the yellow linoleum. Going down, the clerk had tripped over a stack of newspapers, and they were scattered everywhere. My face was on the front page of every paper, ten or twenty little faces, most of them splattered with blood.

" . . . a Halloween mask," she continued. "A pumpkin with a big black grin. We weren't with him. We pulled in after it was over, but we saw him leaving. I think he was driving an El Camino. It was silver, and it had those tires that have the chrome spokes. We were gonna call you before we left, honest. We figured the clerk was already dead, and that we'd just take what we wanted and— "

"Let it lay." I finished it for her, and she had the common decency to keep her mouth shut.

I just stood there for a minute, looking at the dead kid. It was like looking at myself thirty years ago. Like that poem about roads not taken. I almost envied him. Then I couldn't see him anymore—I saw myself at eighteen, so I looked away.

At the papers, at my smiling face.

At the headline: HERO RESCUES BABY FROM WELL.

Some hero. A grinning idiot with blood on his face.

The Mexican girl couldn't wait anymore. She'd run out of common decency and was starting to worry about herself again.

She opened her mouth.

I slapped her before she could say anything stupid.

My fingers striking hard against her tattooed tears.

"The other girl got away," I said. "I'll bet she had the gun. Long black hair, about five-six, maybe a hundred pounds. Maybe a little more . . . it's hard to tell with those baggy jackets they wear. Anyway, she probably tossed the weapon. We'll beat the bushes on Orchard. That can wait until tomorrow, though."

Kat Gonzalez nodded, scribbling furiously. She was one of ten deputies who worked under me, and she was the best of the lot.

"I'm leaving this in your hands, Kat. I mean to tell you, I'm all out." I wanted to take a six-pack from the cooler, but I resisted the temptation. "I'm going home."

Kat stopped me with a hand on my shoulder. "Sheriff . . . Hell, Dutch, I know what happened here when you were a kid. This must feel pretty weird. But don't let it eat at you. Don't— "

I waved her off before she could get started. "I know."

"If you need to talk— "

"Thanks." I said it with my back to her, and the only reason it came out okay was that I was already out the door.

I stomped a few more cigarette cartons getting to my truck, but it didn't make me feel any better. The night air was still heavy with the aroma of tequila and rum, only now it was mixed with other less appealing parking lot odors.

Burnt motor oil. Dirt. Piss.

Even so, it didn't smell bad, and that didn't do me any good.

Because it made me want something a hell of a lot stronger than beer.

I drove to Ralphs and bought the biggest bottle of tequila they had.

I was eighteen years old when I shot my first man.

Well, he wasn't a man, exactly. He was seventeen. And he was my brother.

Willie died on Halloween night in 1959. He was wearing a rubber skull mask that glowed in the dark, and "Endless Sleep" was playing on the radio when I shot him. He'd shown up at the store on the corner of Canyon and Orchard—it was a little mom-and-pop joint back then. With him was another boy, Johnny Halowenski, also wearing a mask.

A pumpkin face with a big black grin.

They showed up on that warm night in 1959 wanting money. The store had been robbed three times in the last two months, each time during my shift. The boss had said I'd lose my job if it happened again. I'd hidden my dad's .38 under the counter, and the two bandits didn't know about it.

Skullface asked for the money. I shot him instead. I didn't kill him, though. Not at first. He had enough spit left in him to come over the counter after me. I had to shoot him two more times before he dropped.

By then Pumpkinface had gotten away. I came out of the store just in time to see his Chevy burning rubber down Orchard, heading for the outskirts of town. There wasn't any question about who he was. No question at all. I got off a couple more shots, but none of them were lucky.

I went inside and peeled off the dead bandit's skull mask. I sat there stroking my brother's hair, hating myself, crying.

Then I got myself together and called the sheriff's office.

When the deputies arrived, I told them about Johnny Halowenski. I didn't know what else to do. They recognized the name. L.A. juvie had warned them about him. Johnny had steered clear of trouble since moving to our town, and the deputies had been willing to go along with that and give him a break.

But trouble had caught up with Johnny Halowenski in a big way.

I knew that, and I laid it on. My dad had been a deputy before he got too friendly with the whiskey bottle, and I knew it was important to get things right, to make sure that Halowenski wouldn't be able to get away with anything if the cops caught up to him.

I told the deputies that Halowenski was armed and dangerous.

I told the deputies that Halowenski took off his mask when he got in the Chevy, that there could be no mistake about his identity.

Everything I said ended up in the papers. There were headlines from Los Angeles to San Francisco about the Halloween murder/robbery at a liquor store near the border and the ensuing manhunt.

One paper mentioned that the suspect's nickname was Johnny Halloween. After that I never saw it any other way. Almost every year I'd see it a few times. On FBI wanted posters. In cheap magazines that ran stories about unsolved crimes. And, on Halloween, I could always count on it turning up in the local papers.

Johnny Halloween. I leaned back against my brother's granite tombstone and stared up at the night sky, trying to pick out the name in the bright stars above.

Drinking tequila, thinking how I'd never seen that name where I wanted to.

On a tombstone.

◆   ◆

I knew he'd show up sooner or later, because we always met in the cemetery after the robberies.

Johnny came across the grass slow and easy, his pistol tucked under his belt, like the last thing in the world he wanted to do was startle me. I tossed him the bottle when he got near enough. "Let's drink it down to the worm," I said.

He didn't take a drink, though. He would have had to lift his mask, and he didn't seem to want to do that, either.

"Miss me?" he asked, laughing, and his laughter was bottled up inside the mask, like it couldn't quite find its way out of him.

"It's been a while," I said. "But not long enough to suit me."

He tossed me a thin bundle of bills. "Here's your cut. It's the usual third. I don't figure you've still got my dough from the last job. If I could collect interest on it, it might amount to something."

I didn't say anything to that. I didn't want to rise to the bait.

"Well, hell . . . it's good to see you too, Dutch. The old town hasn't changed all that much in thirty years. I went by my daddy's house, and damned if he isn't still driving that same old truck. Babyshit brown Ford with tires just as bald as he is. Seventy-five years old and still drives like a bat out of hell, I'll bet. How about your daddy? He still alive?"

I pointed two graves over.

"Yeah, well . . . I bet you didn't shed too many tears. The way he used to beat hell out of you and Willie, I'm here to tell you. Man could have earned money, throwin' punches like those— "

That hit a nerve. "Just why are you here, Johnny?"

Again, the bottled-up laugh. "Johnny? Hell, that's a kid's name, Dutch. Nobody's called me that in twenty-five years. These days I go by Jack."

"Okay, Jack. I'll stick with the same question, though."

"Man, you're still one cold-hearted son of a bitch. And I thought you'd gone and mellowed. Become a humanitarian. Do you know that your picture made the Mexico City dailies? Sheriff rescues baby from well. That took some kind of big brass cojones, I bet."

My face had gone red, and I didn't like it. "There wasn't anything to it," I said. "I found the baby. I'm the sheriff. What was I supposed to do?"

We were both quiet for a moment.

"Look, Johnny—Jack—I'm tired. I don't mind telling you that the years have worn on me, and I don't have much patience anymore. Why don't you start by giving me your gun. I'm going to need it for evidence. I've already got one suspect in custody—nobody will ever connect what happened tonight to you. So you can figure you got your revenge, and you can tell me how much money you want, and we can get on with our lives."

"You know," he said, "I hadn't thought about you for years and years. And then I saw that picture in the paper, and damned if I wasn't surprised that you'd actually gone and become a cop. Man oh man, that idea took some getting used to. So I said to myself, Jack, now you've just got to go see old Dutch before you die, don't you?"

He knelt before me, his blue eyes floating in the black triangles of that orange mask. "See, I wanted to thank you," he said. "Going to Mexico was the best thing that ever happened to me. I made some money down there. Had a ball. They got lots of pretty boys down there, and I like 'em young and dark. Slim, too—you know, before all those frijoles and tortillas catch up to 'em. You never knew that about me, did you, Dutch? Your brother did, you know. I had a real hard-on for his young ass, but he only liked pussy. You remember how he liked his pussy? Man, how he used to talk about it. Non-fucking-stop! Truth be told, I think he maybe liked the talkin' better than the doin'. And you so shy and all. Now that was funny. You two takin' your squirts under the same skirt."

"You got a point in here somewhere, or are you just trying to piss me off?"

"Yeah. I got a point, Dutch."

Johnny Halloween took off the pumpkin mask, and suddenly I had the crazy idea that he was wearing Willie's skull mask beneath it. His blue eyes were the same and his wild grin was the same, but the rest of his face was stripped down, as if someone had sucked all the juice out of him.

"It's what you get when you play rough with pretty boys and don't bother to wear a raincoat," he said. "AIDS. The doctors say it ain't even bad yet. I don't want it to get bad, y'see."

I stared at him. I couldn't even blink.

He gave me the gun. "You ready to use it now?"

I shook my head. "I'm sorry," I said, and I was surprised to find that I really meant it.

"Let me help you out, Dutch." That wild grin welded on Death's own face. "See, there's a reason it took me so long to get here. I had to swing past your place and talk to Helen. Did a little trick-or-treating and got me some Snickers. Nothing more, nothing less. And when I'd had my fill, I told her everything."

There was nothing I could say . . .

"Now, I want you to do it right the first time, Dutch. Don't drag it out."

. . . so I obliged him.

It took two hours to get things done. First I heaved up as much tequila as I could. Then I drove ten miles into the desert and dumped Johnny Halloween's corpse. Next I headed back to the cemetery, got in Johnny's El Camino, and drove two miles north to a highway rest stop. There were four or five illegals standing around who looked like they had no place to go and no way to get there. I left the windows down and the keys in the ignition and I walked back to the cemetery, hoping for the best.

On the way home, I swung down Orchard and tossed Johnny's pistol into some oleander bushes three houses up from the liquor store.

My house was quiet. The lights were out. That was fine with me. I found Helen in the kitchen and untied her. I left the tape over her mouth until I said my piece.

I didn't get through the whole thing, though. Toward the end I ran out of steam. I told her that Johnny and Willie and me had pulled the robberies because we hated being so damn poor. That it seemed easier to take the money than not to take it, with me being the clerk and such a good liar besides. I explained that the Halloween job was going to be my last. That I'd been saving those little scraps of money so we could elope, so our baby wouldn't have to come into the world a bastard.

It hurt me, saying that word. I never have liked it. Just saying it in front of Helen is what made me start to crack.

My voice trembled with rage and I couldn't control it anymore. "Johnny took me over to his house that day," I said. "All the time laughing through that wild grin. He had me peek in the window . . . and I saw Willie on top of you. . . and I saw you smiling. . . "

I slapped Helen then, just the way I'd slapped the Mexican girl at the liquor store, like she didn't mean anything to me at all.

"I was crazy." I clenched my fists, fighting for control. "You know how I get . . . Everything happened too damn fast. They came to the store that night, and I was still boiling. I planned to kill them both and say I hadn't known it was them because of the masks, but it didn't work out that way. Sure, I shot Willie. But I had to shoot him three times before he died. I wanted to kill Johnny, too, but he got away. So I changed the story I'd planned. I hid Willie's skull mask, and I hid the gun and the money, and I said that Willie had been visiting me at the store when a lone bandit came in. That bandit was Johnny Halloween, and he'd done the shooting. And all the time that I was lying, I was praying that the cops wouldn't catch him."

I blew my nose, got control of myself. Helen's eyes were wide in the dark, and there was a welt on her cheek, and she wasn't moving. "I was young, Helen," I told her. "I didn't know what to do. It didn't seem right—getting married, bringing a baby into the world when I couldn't be sure that I was the father. I wanted everything to be just right, you know? It seemed like a good idea to use the money for an abortion instead of a wedding. I figured we'd just go down to Mexico, get things taken care of. I figured we'd have plenty of time for kids later on."

That's when I ran out of words. I took the tape off of Helen's mouth, but she didn't say anything. She just sat there.

I hadn't said so much to Helen in years.

I handed her the tequila bottle. There was a lot left in it.

Her hands shook as she took it. The clear, clean liquor swirled. The worm did a little dance. I turned away and quit the room, but not fast enough to miss the gentle slosh as she tipped back the bottle.

I knew that worm didn't stand a chance.

I don't know why I went out to the garage. I had to go somewhere, and I guess that's where a lot of men go when they want to be alone.

I shuffled some stuff around in my toolbox. Cleaned up the workbench. Changed the oil in the truck. Knowing that I should get rid of the pumpkin mask, but just puttering around instead.

All the time thinking. Questions spinning around in my head.

Wondering if Helen would talk.

Wondering if I'd really be able to pin the clerk's murder on the Mexican girls. Not only if the charges would stick, but if I had enough left in me to go through with it.

Wondering if my deputies would find Johnny's corpse, or his El Camino, or if he'd left any other surprises for me that I didn't know about.

They were the kind of questions that had been eating at me for thirty years, and I was full up with them.

My breaths were coming hard and fast. I leaned against the workbench, staring down at the pumpkin mask. Didn't even know I was crying until my tears fell on oily rubber.

It took me a while to settle down.

I got a .45 out of my toolchest. The silencer was in another drawer. I cleaned the gun, loaded it, and attached the silencer.

I stared at the door that led to the kitchen, and Helen. Those same old questions started spinning again. I closed my eyes and shut them out.

And suddenly I pictured Johnny Halloween down in Mexico, imagined all the fun he'd had over the years with his pretty boys and his money. Not my kind of fun, sure. But it must have been something.

I guess the other guy's life always seems easier.

Sometimes I think even Willie's life was easier.

I didn't want to start thinking that way with a gun in my hands.

I opened my eyes.

I unwrapped a Snickers bar, opened the garage door. The air held the sweet night like a sponge. The sky was going from black to purple, and soon it would be blue. The world smelled clean and the streets were empty. The chocolate tasted good.

I unscrewed the silencer.   Put it and the gun in the glove compartment along with the three hundred and fifteen bucks Johnny Halloween had stolen from the liquor store.

Covered all of it with the pumpkin mask.

I felt a little better, a little safer, just knowing it was there.

HOPE

Steve Bevan

A man can always hope, can't he? Sure he can. But what he hopes for, now that's another question altogether. You spend enough time alone, you begin to hope for things you'd always taken for granted. Like the sight of a human face, for one thing. Or the sound of a human voice, the soft touch of a woman's hand. You might do anything for these simple gifts.

It was just last night that I was standing outside the grass and dirt walls of my one-room soddie and staring across the Dakota prairie. I think God was tired on the day he made the prairie. There's just mile after mile of emptiness. Nothing. The sight of all that grass stretching to the sky is downright terrifying to some, if you're not used to it. I've heard of folks driven mad by too much open sky.

I was watching the clouds. The sun was going down and they started to blow in from the north, swollen things that made me think of black blood boiling in the sky. Mottie — that's my ox — started to wailing in the barn. It was going to be a bad storm, so I made sure the barn doors were closed up good and tight. Then I loaded the wheelbarrow with buffalo chips for the fire. As I pushed the barrow across the yard back to the soddie, a cold wind began blowing. At first, it made a low moan, like the sound of someone crying from far away. Sometimes I swear I can hear voices on that bitter wind.

Before I had even closed and barred the door, the first of the rain started falling and it pounded the sod roof like hundreds of fists. I sat in my rocker by the stove and turned up the lantern. Aside from a table for eating, a bed in the back corner, and a bench by the stove for cooking, my home was empty. That's pretty much the way I felt — empty. I had just started reading my verses in the book of Numbers when I heard the knocking on the door.

Now that was strange. I'd seen no one headed my way, no one for miles in any direction. On the prairie a man can look out into those grasses that roll like swells on the ocean and see farther than he cares to see. Sometimes you figure you'd be better off not knowing who or what's coming your way. I've often wondered if I'll see, on the day I die, the grim reaper plodding along the horizon half an hour before he calls for me. I reckon I could've missed a man on horseback in the storm. But my eyes are sharp and I reckon it would be just as likely for a man to have sprung up out of the dirt.

I'm not one to turn away a traveler, especially in the midst of a storm. And like I said, loneliness takes its toll. I unbarred the door and let the wind push it open. Night had painted the prairie as black as the heart of the devil. The icy rain slapped against my cheeks, stinging my skin. I held the lantern out in front of me. There was no one there. All I could see was the light bouncing off the sheets of rain, the rain turning the earth to mud. And I could hear and feel the bite of the cold wind, its roar carrying those whispering voices that rose and fell like a distant crowd.

"Who's out there?" I yelled over the howling storm.

No one answered. I started wondering if I should have brought my rifle to the door.

"Last chance! Anyone out there?"

After a few long seconds I turned back inside to set down the lantern and bar the door. But something about the walls of my soddie stopped me. I swear in God's name I saw those dried sod walls that're twenty inches thick and had seen two Dakota winters and more rain and tornadoes than any wooden house could withstand, turning to mud before my eyes. What's worse is, the mud was moving, like it was filled with living things, squirming and sliding just below the surface of the muck.

"Hello?" a female voice called out.

I spun around, nearly dropping my lantern. A woman and a small child were huddled together out in the rain.

"Can you help us?" the woman asked, wiping the rain from her eyes. "It's just my daughter and me. We were caught in the storm."

It had been so long since I'd heard a woman's voice, I don't think I've ever heard a sweeter sound. I stood there like an idiot, gaping at the two of them. It didn't occur to me at the time why a woman and her child were traveling alone, without so much as a blanket between them. I was thankful for the company.

"Come on in," I said. "Dry yourselves."

As they passed through my door, I could smell the dirt of the prairie on their dresses and in their hair. It was the same scent I'd smelled on myself last spring when I'd been digging the well. I closed and barred the door.

I'd forgotten about the walls, you understand. When I looked this time, they were as dry as dust. I scratched my head. It must have been the lantern, I figured. Lantern light's strange sometimes, makes shadows do odd things.

Looking back now I think about the odd things the mind can do, the things you make yourself believe. It's a sad state when you can't trust yourself. It makes you feel like your mind is just an old, broken wagon being led in circles by a blind horse. What's a man if he's lost his mind?

"My name's John Christian," I said, smoothing my tangled hair.

"I'm Ella," the woman said. Her face was plain but pretty, the kind of woman a man might take for his wife. She wore a simple gray dress that was well suited for farm work. "This is my daughter Daisy."

"Pleased to know you, Miss Ella. How are you Daisy?"

The child looked up at me with huge, dark eyes. Both women were dripping wet and skinny to the point of death. I could tell they'd seen hard times. That's not unusual on the Dakota prairie, but it still tugs at your heart to see a child and her mother go hungry.

I strung a rope in the corner where the bed is and hung a sheet from it to give the ladies some privacy while they changed. I gave them a couple of my old nightshirts to put on until their dresses dried. Meanwhile, I dropped a few more chips into the stove to beat back the cold. I wished I could've cleaned myself up; there's something about having a woman around that makes a man suddenly realize he hasn't had a bath in a couple of weeks. Before too long we were sitting in front of the fireplace, me on the packed earth floor, Miss Ella in the rocker, and the child on a stool between us.

"You live alone, do you, Mr. Christian?" Miss Ella asked.

"Please, call me John. Can I offer you two some dinner? I've just some stew. It's not much, but the meat is fresh and it's hot and filling."

"We've already eaten, haven't we Daisy?"

The child nodded solemnly.

"Yeah, I live alone," I said to answer her question. "Came out here two years ago this June. Water's scarce but the land is good."

"You've a fine home, John," she said. "Solid walls and a dry floor. My husband built such a place and it's a comfort in a storm."

"Where is your husband, Miss Ella, if you don't mind my asking?"

A shadow passed over her face. Or it could have been the flicker of the flame in the lantern. Lantern light is tricky, as I've said.

"He's an evil man," she said. "Pray you don't cross his path. If he's not dead already, he should be. Shouldn't he, Daisy?"

"Why?" I asked. "What did he do? Gambling? Drink too much?"

"Nothing quite so harmless," she said in a low voice. "It was this past winter. The snow was heavy. I don't have to tell you that. Do I, John?"

I shook my head. The snow had been terribly heavy during the two winters I'd spent in this part of Dakota.

"Food was scarce. We first had to slay the milk cow for the meat. And— "

Just then the little girl, Daisy, started to cry. It wasn't a loud cry, like healthy children are known to make to get attention. It was just a few quiet sniffles and a whole lot of tears. And somehow that made her crying all the worse.

"You'll have to excuse Daisy," the mother said, making no move to comfort her daughter. "The memory is still fresh and it hurts her to remember."

"I understand. No need to go on."

Just then, I heard the wind pick up outside. It made a hollow cry as it whipped around the house. It sounded almost like a train whistle you might hear from miles away, a lonely sound that leaves you a little cold inside.

I was glad to have company on such a terrible night. And I was eager for more conversation. But I could see in the deep lines on Miss Ella's face that rest was what she wanted and needed. I let them bundle up together on the only bed in the rear corner. It was big enough for three, but I knew it wouldn't be proper. So, I wrapped myself with a blanket and curled up in front of the fading fire in the stove. Sleep came quickly and I remember drifting off to the haunting sound of the wind howling, an almost human sound that held hints of whispered words.

I don't know what it was that woke me. There's something about being stared at that just doesn't sit right with most folks, and that includes me. I remember sitting up straight. The soddie was filled with a reddish glow from the dying embers in the stove, a light that was just dim enough to fill the shadows with more shadows and make you see more than was actually there. I turned around to look in the direction of the bed and that's when my heart started thudding in my chest.

Miss Ella and the child were standing by the foot of the bed. They were holding each other's hands and looking at me. It was their faces that set my heart to racing. Their skin was as white and smooth as bleached bones and they just stared at me. I don't know how else to say it, but that they stared. It was horrible. All I wanted was for their faces to be gone from my sight, to be free from their relentless and accusing eyes.

And then they started moving. Still staring at me, they reached down and began lifting their nightshirts. What I saw were deathly white bones where their flesh should have been. Bits of tendon and dried blood stained the perfect whiteness of their skeletons and I could see where a heavy knife had scarred the bone while cleaving away the muscle.

I think I screamed then. I'm not sure. As I said, the mind is not always a perfect thing. It doesn't always remember events exactly as they happened, if you know what I mean.

What I remember next are the sounds in the walls, the sound of mud stirring, of earth moving. I looked just in time to see the figures of Ella and Daisy disappear into the sheet of churning mud, returning back to the same earth that spawned their likenesses. Or perhaps they returned back to the corner of my mind that created them. I don't know anymore. I only know they are gone, if indeed they ever were here.

I found the knife this morning. It was buried under the bed, beneath a few inches of dirt. The blood is still on the blade. The meat that has kept me alive these past few weeks is no longer fresh. Like my brain, the worms have done their work and the rotting has progressed too far for it to be of any use.

What's left of my wife and daughter are buried back behind the barn. I can almost remember having a wife and a daughter. But it's hard to know anymore. I'm not sure what's real and what's dreamed.

I know it gets cold in the Dakota winters, and a man can get hungry. Maybe I had to kill them. Maybe.

A man can always hope. My hope is to be with my Ella and my daughter Daisy before this night is through. I'm ready to face the Lord and account for what I've done. What else is there for a man, except to admit what he's done and ask for forgiveness? Is there forgiveness for what I've done?

The wind is blowing now. Can you hear it? It's the sound of the wind whistling through the bones of the dead. And I can hear the whispers carried on that wind and they're telling me that they are coming. Soon the slithering noises in the walls will begin, the sound of bodies moving in the mud, the sound of the earth coming to greet me.

A man can always hope.

THE MAILMAN

Bentley Little

If Jack had known that the mailman was a dwarf he never would have moved into the house. It was as simple as that. Yes, the neighborhood was nice. And he'd gotten a fantastic deal on the place — the owner had been transferred to New York by the company he worked for and had had to sell as quickly as possible. But that was beside the point.

The mailman was a dwarf.

Jack got the cold sweats just thinking about it. He had moved in that morning and had been innocently unpacking lawn furniture, setting up the redwood picnic table under the pine tree, when he had seen the blue postal cap bobbing just above the top of the small front fence. A kid, he thought. A kid playing games.

Then the mailman had walked through the gate and Jack had seen the man's small body and oversized head, his fat little fingers clutching a stack of letters. And he had run as fast as he could in the other direction, away from the dwarf, aware that the movers and neighbors were staring at him but not caring. The mailman dropped the letters in the mailslot of the door and moved on to the next house while Jack stood alone at the far end of the yard, facing the opposite direction, trying to suppress the panic that was welling within him.

The dwarf jumped out from somewhere hidden and grabbed Jack's arm. "You got a quarter? Gimmee a quarter!" He held out a fat tiny hand no larger than Jack's.

The young boy looked around, confused, searching for Baker, for his father for anyone. His glance met, for a second, that of the dwarf, and he saw an adult's face at his child's level, old eyes peering cruelly into his young ones. A hard experienced mouth was strung in a straight line across a field of five o'clock shadow. Jack looked immediately away.

"Gimmee a quarter!" The dwarf pulled him across the sawdust to a booth, where he pointed to a pyramid of stacked multi-colored glass ashtrays. "You'll win a prize! Gimmee a quarter!"

Jack's mouth opened to call for help, but it would not open all the way and no sound came out. His eyes, confused, frantic, now darting everywhere, searching in vain for a familiar face in the carnival crowd. He put one sweaty hand into the right pocket of his short pants and held tight to the two quarters his father had given him.

"I know you have a quarter! Give it to me!" The dwarf was starting to look angry.

Jack felt a firm strong hand grab the back of his neck, and he swung his head around.

"Come on, Jack. Let's go." His father smiled down at him, safety, reassurance, order in that smile.

Jack relaxed his grip on the coins in his pocket and looked up gratefully at his father. He grabbed his father's arm and the two of them started to walk down the midway toward the funhouse, where Baker was waiting. As he walked, he turned back to look at the dwarf.

The little man was scowling at him. "I'll get you, you little son-of-a-bitch." His voice was a low rough growl.

Frightened, Jack looked up. But his father, ears at a higher level, hearing different sounds, was unaware of the threat. Jack gripped his father's hairy arm tighter and stared straight ahead, toward Baker, making a conscious effort not to look back. Beneath his windbreaker and t-shirt, his heart was thumping wildly. He knew the dwarf was staring at him, waiting for him to turn around again. He could feel the hot hatred of the little man's eyes on his back.

"I'll get you," the dwarf said again.

Jack sorted through the mail in his hand. The envelopes were ordinary — junk, forwarded bills, a couple of letters — but they felt tainted, looked soiled to his eyes, and when he thought of those stubby fat fingers touching them, he dropped the envelopes onto the table.

Maybe he could sell the house. Or call the post office and get the mailman transferred.

He had to do something.

The fear was once again building within him, and he picked up the remote control and switched on the TV. *The Wizard of Oz* was on, a munchkin urging Dorothy to "follow the yellow-brick road!" He switched off the TV, his hands shaking. The house seemed suddenly darker, the unpacked boxes throwing strange shadows on the walls of the room. He got up and flipped on all the lights on the first floor.

It would be a long time before he'd be able to fall asleep.

Jack unpacked in the morning but spent the afternoon shopping, staying far away from the house. He noticed two mailmen on the way to the mall, but they were both normal sized.

Why hadn't he checked?

How could he be so stupid?

He arrived home at five-thirty, long after the mailman was supposed to have come and gone. Was *supposed* to have. For there he was in his absurd blue uniform, lurching ever so slightly to the right and to the left, not quite balanced on his stumpy legs, three houses up from his own.

Jack jumped out of the car and ran into the house, shutting and locking the door behind him, hurriedly closing the drapes. He crouched down behind the couch, out of view from any window, closing his eyes tightly, his hands balled into tense fists of fear. He heard the light footsteps on the porch, heard the metal clack of the mailslot opening and closing, heard the small feet retreat.

Safe.

He waited several minutes before standing up, until he was certain the dwarf was gone. He was sweating, and he realized his hands were shaking.

"*Gimmee a quarter.*"

His experience with the dwarf at the carnival had been scary, but though he'd never forgotten the rough voice and small cruel face, it would not have been enough to terrify him so thoroughly and utterly that he now shuddered in fear when he saw a man under four feet tall. No, it was Vietnam that did that. It was the camp. For it was there that he saw the dwarf again, that he realized the little man really was after him and had not simply been making empty threats, that he learned of the dwarf's power.

The guards were kind to him at first; or as kind as could be expected under the circumstances. He was fed twice a day, the food was adequate, he was allowed weekly exercise, he was not beaten. But one day the food stopped coming. And it was three more days before he was given a cupful of dirty water and a small dollop of nasty tasting gruel served on a square of old plywood. He ate hungrily, drank instantly, and promptly threw up, his starved system unable to take the sudden shock. He jumped up, pounding on the door, demanding more food, delirious and half-crazy. But the only thing he got for his trouble was a beating with wooden batons which left welts on his arms and legs and which he was sure had broken at least one rib.

Sometime later — it could have been hours, it could have been days — two guards he had never seen before entered his cell. "Kwo ta?" one of them demanded angrily.

"English," he tried to explain through cracked and swollen lips. "I only speak —"

He was clubbed on the back of the neck and fell face down on the floor, a bolt of pain shooting through his shoulders and side.

"Kwo ta?" the man demanded again.

He nodded, hoping that was what they were looking for, not sure to what he was agreeing. The men nodded, satisfied, and left. Another man returned an hour or so later with a small cupful of brown water and a few crusts of hard bread smeared with some sort of rice porridge. He ate slowly this time, drank sparingly and kept it down.

He was taken outside the next day, and though the brightness of the sun burned his light-sensitive eyes, he was grateful to be out of the cell. Hands manacled, he was shoved against a bamboo wall with several other silent emaciated prisoners. He glanced around the camp and saw a group of obviously high-ranking officers nearby. One of the men shuffled his feet, moving a little to the right, and, in a moment he would never forget, he saw the dwarf.

He was suddenly cold, and he felt the fear rise within him. It couldn't be possible. It couldn't be real. But it was possible. It was real. The dwarf was wearing a North Vietnamese army uniform. He was darker than before and had vaguely Oriental eyes. But it was the same man. Jack felt a sinking feeling in the pit of his stomach.

Kwo ta

Quarter.

The Vietnamese guards had been trying to say "quarter."

The dwarf smiled at him, and he saw tiny white babyteeth. The small man said something to another officer, and the other officer strode over, pushing his face to within an inch of his own. "Gi meea kwo ta," the man said in a thick musical accent.

And Jack began to scream.

He spent the rest of his incarceration in solitary, where he was beaten regularly and fed occasionally, and when he was finally released he weighed less than 90 pounds and was albino white, with bruises and welts and running sores all over his body. He saw several guards on his way to the airstrip, but though he searched desperately before stepping onto the plane, he saw no sign of the dwarf.

The dwarf was waiting for him when he arrived at Vandenberg, however, disguised as a cheering onlooker. Jack saw the horrible face, the oversized head on its undersized body, between the legs of another POW's family. He had in his hand a small American flag which he was waving enthusiastically. He was no longer Vietnamese — his hair was blonde, his light skin red with sunburn — but it was without a doubt the same man.

Then the face faded back into the crowd as friends and family of the newly released men rushed forward onto the tarmac.

He had avoided dwarves and midgets ever since and had been pretty successful at it. Occasionally, he had seen the back of a small man in a mall or supermarket, but he had always been able to get away without being seen.

He had had no problem until now.

He picked up the mail from where it had fallen through the slot, but the envelopes felt cold to his touch, and he dropped them on the table without looking at them.

The next day he left the house before noon and did not return until after dark. He was afraid of seeing the dwarf at night, afraid the small man would come slinking up the steps in the darkness to deliver the mail, but the mail had already been delivered by the time he returned home.

He returned the next night a little earlier and saw the dwarf three houses up from his own, in the exact spot he'd seen him before, and he quickly ran inside and locked the door and closed the curtains, hiding behind the couch.

Jack was gone the next three afternoons, but he realized he could not be gone every day. It was not practical. He only had three more weeks until he started teaching, and there was still a lot of unpacking to do, a lot of things he had to work on around the house. He could not spend each and every afternoon wandering through shopping centers far away from his home in order to avoid the mailman.

So he stayed home the next day, keeping an eye out for the mailman, and by the end of the week he had settled into a routine. He would hide in the house when the mailman came by, shutting the curtains and locking the doors. Often he would turn on the stereo or turn up the television so he would not be able to hear the mail drop into the slot, but he would inevitably turn all sound off before the mailman arrived and sit quietly on the floor, not wanting the dwarf to know he was home.

And he would hear the rhythmic *tap tap tapping* of the little feet walking up the wooden porch steps, a pause as the mailman sorted through his letters, then the dreaded sound of metal against metal as those stubby fingers forced open the mailslot and pushed in the envelopes. He would be sweating by then, and he would remain unbreathing, afraid to move, until he heard the tiny feet descend the steps.

Once there was silence after the mail had been delivered, and Jack realized that though he had heard the mailslot open, he had not heard it fall shut. The dwarf was looking through the slit into the house! He could almost see the horrid little eyes scanning the front room through the limited viewspace offered by the slot. He was about to scream when he heard the slot clack shut and heard the light footsteps retreat.

Then the inevitable happened.

He waited silently behind the couch until the mailman had left and then gathered up his mail. Amidst the large white envelopes was a small blue envelope, thicker than the rest, with the seal of the postal service on the front. He knew what that envelope was — he'd gotten them several times before.

Postage Due.

Heart pounding, he looked at the "AMOUNT" line, knowing already how much he owed. Twenty-five cents.

A quarter.

And he stood there unmoving while the shadows lengthened around him and the room grew dark, and he wondered where the dwarf went after work.

The next morning Jack went to the main branch of the post office. The line was long, filled with businessmen who needed to send important packages and women who wanted to buy the latest stamps, but he waited patiently. When it was his turn, he walked up to the front counter and asked the clerk if he could talk to the postmaster. He was not as brave as he'd planned to be, and he was aware that his voice quavered slightly.

The postmaster came out, a burly man on the high side of fifty, wearing horn-rimmed glasses and a fixed placating smile. "How may I help you, sir?"

Now that he was here, Jack was not sure he could go through with it. His head hurt, and he could feel the blood pulsing in his temples. He was about to make something up, something meaningless and inconsequential, but he thought of the dwarf's cruel little face, thought of the demand on the postage due envelope. "I'm here to complain about one of your mailmen," he said.

The postmaster's eyebrows shot up in surprise. "One of my mail carriers?"

Jack nodded.

"Where do you live, sir?"

"Glenoaks. Twelve hundred Glenoaks."

The postmaster frowned. "That's Charlie's route. He's one of our best employees." He turned around. "Charlie!" he called.

Jack's hands became sweaty.

"He's right in the back there," the postmaster explained. "I'll have him come out here, and we'll get this mess straightened out."

Jack wanted to run, wanted to dash through the door the way he had come, to hop in the car and escape. But he remained rooted in place. The post office was crowded. Nothing could happen to him here. He was safe.

A man in a blue uniform rounded the corner.

A normal-sized man.

"This is Charlie," the postmaster said. "Your mail carrier."

Jack shook his head. "No, the man I'm talking about is . . . short. He's about three feet high."

"We have no one here who fits that description."

"He delivers my mail every day. He delivers my neighbors' mail."

"Where do you live?" Charlie asked.

"Twelve hundred Glenoaks."

"Impossible. I deliver there."

"I've never seen you before in my life!" Jack looked from one man to the other. He was sweating, and he smelled his own perspiration. His mouth was dry, and he tried unsuccessfully to generate some saliva. "Something weird's going on here."

"We'll help you in any way we can, sir," the postmaster said.

Jack shook his head. "Forget it," he said. He turned and strode toward the door. "Forget I even came by."

The next day he received no mail at all, though, looking out the window, he saw the dwarf happily walking down the other side of the street, delivering to other homes. Then the next day, the same thing. Jack stayed on the porch the following afternoon, and before he knew it the little man was walking up his sidewalk, whistling, holding a fistful of letters, a cheerful expression on his cruel hard face. Jack ran inside the house, locked the door and dashed into the back bathroom. He sat down on the toilet and remained there for over an hour, until he was sure that the dwarf was gone.

Finally, he washed his face, opened the bathroom door and walked down the hallway to the living room.

The mailslot suddenly opened, two letters fell through, and the slot closed. He heard a low rough laugh and the quick steps of the dwarf running off the porch.

The gun felt good in his hands. It had been a long time. He had not held a pistol since Vietnam, but using firearms was like riding a bike and he had forgotten nothing. He liked the weight against his palm, liked the smooth way the trigger felt against his finger. His aim was probably not as good as it had been — after all, he had not practiced for almost twenty years — but it would not need to be that good at the close range at which he planned to use it.

He waited behind the partially open curtains for the mailman.

And Charlie stepped up the walk.

Jack shoved the pistol in his waistband and yanked opened the door. "Where is he?" he demanded. "Where's the goddamned dwarf?"

The mailman shook his head, confused. "I'm sorry, sir. I don't know what you're talking about."

"The dwarf! The little guy who usually delivers the mail!"

"I'm the mailman on —"

Jack pulled the gun. "Where is he, goddamn it?"

"I-I-I-d-don't know, sir." The mailman's voice was shaking with fear. He dropped the letters in his hand and they fluttered to the walk. "P-please don't shoot me."

Jack ran down the porch steps, shoving his way past the mailman, and hopped into his car. With the pistol on the seat beside him, where he could easily reach it, he drove up and down the streets of the neighborhood, looking for the small man in the tiny blue postal uniform. He had been driving for nearly ten minutes and had almost given up, the lure of the pistol fading, when he saw the dwarf crossing the street a block and a half ahead. He floored the gas pedal.

And was broadsided by a pickup as he sped through the closest intersection, ignoring the stop sign.

The door crumpled in on him, a single jagged shard of metal piercing his arm. The windshield and windows shattered, harmless safety glass showering down on him, but the steering wheel was forced loose and pushed through his chest. In an instant that lasted forever, he felt his bones snap, his organs rupture, and he knew that the accident was fatal. He did not scream, however. For some strange reason, he did not scream.

From far off, he heard sirens, and some part of his brain told him that Charlie the mailman had called the police on him, though he knew they would be too late to do any good. Nothing could save him now.

He moved his head, the only part of his body still mobile, and saw another man staggering dazedly toward the sidewalk.

And then the dwarf appeared. He was wearing street clothes, not a postal uniform, but he still had on a mailman's hat. There was a look of concern on his face, but it was a false expression, and Jack could sense the glee behind the mask.

"I'll call the paramedics," the dwarf said, and his voice was not low and rough but high and breathless. He patted his pockets, and Jack suddenly knew what was coming next. He wanted to scream but could not. "Do you have a quarter for the phone?"

Jack wanted to grab the pistol but could not move his hands. He tried to twist away, but his muscles would not work.

The dwarf smiled as he dug through Jack's pockets. A moment later, he pulled his hand away from the pocket. He held up a silver coin dulled by a streak of wet blood.

Jack closed his eyes against the pain for what seemed like hours, but heard nothing. He opened his eyes.

The dwarf laughed cruelly. He put the quarter in his pocket, tipped his hat, and walked down the street, whistling happily, as the sirens drew closer.

SILHOUETTE

Stephen Mark Rainey

It's true, I swore that I'd never go back to that house. But of course I went back; how could I not? Being sent to Chicago on business wasn't something I'd foreseen when I'd beat such a hasty retreat from that city almost ten years before. Certainly, when my company informed me that in order to research a major software vendor up north I'd have to spend a week on the Gold Coast, my first impulse was to demur. But then, anyone who works for MICROWORLD Magazine knows better than to demur when the boss hands out an assignment.

And rationalization came easy; even easier when my cab from O'Hare embarked down the Kennedy Expressway toward the Loop. After ten years, here I was thinking how familiar everything seemed, though lots of new buildings had sprouted along the skyline and daytime traffic, even at off-hours, had gotten heavier. No, it wasn't a return to Chicago itself that I had forsworn; merely a return to a particular house.

But from my hotel I could reach that house in a matter of minutes by taxi — or if I gave myself a little more time, by walking. And that is what I ended up doing, on this May evening after I'd concluded my day's business. The allure was too strong to resist, for in ten years fear subsides. Wounds heal. The intellect rationalizes.

On my walk beneath the streetlamps now firing to life amid the twilight, I didn't know what to expect, or what I would do once I reached my destination. For all I knew the house could have been torn down years ago. But suddenly, there it was, standing agelessly behind the short, black iron-rung fence that surrounded the narrow grassy lot. It was a typical brownstone set among dozens of similarly designed dwellings, camouflaged in normality to anyone not searching specifically for ghosts. Hiding on a relatively quiet residential street between Lincoln and Clark beneath a canopy of brooding maple trees, it might have escaped my own notice but for the broad front porch and circular stained glass window just above it; little features that distinguished the house to perhaps no one other than myself, and those who'd shared at least a few of my experiences here.

And then I saw it. *The head*! In the small, warmly glowing window next to the porch, that unnaturally elongated silhouette, the shape of something inhuman. It was still there.

I shivered. Behind the window, I knew, stood a two foot tall crucifix, the body of Christ backlit by a small lamp, casting its shadow upon the translucent shade to give the impression of a weirdly distorted figure looking out upon the night. I had been similarly struck by its suggestion of the grotesque when at age twenty-one I glimpsed it for the first time, and I had certainly never forgotten about its effect.

That the effect persisted almost certainly meant that my friends still lived in this house, a fact I confirmed by stepping up to the front porch and finding the name "Breheim" still adorning the rusty black mailbox beside the door. I lingered on the porch for several minutes, foolishly intimidated by the prospect of knocking.

Finally, I lifted my hand and rapped soundly on the door, half-hoping I'd hear no stirring inside, no boards groaning to signal the approach of the building's inhabitant. But those noises came shortly: a soft, tentative creaking, a momentary scrabbling at the lock. And the door swung open to reveal a dim figure, who reached to flip on the porch light. And when we gazed at each other, she sighed and nodded slightly, her suspicion that I would one day break my vow now fulfilled.

"There have been changes made since you stayed here," she said softly.

She turned away and I followed her inside, drinking in the smell of the place which remained exactly as I remembered it: a slightly musty, sweet scent mingled with the not unpleasant whiff of mothballs that seems to pervade old houses. The furniture was different, though. No longer the old second-hand relics, these were mostly new pieces of expensive design. The walls, once papered with a mildew-tinged flower pattern, were now bare, painted pale beige with ivory molding. Above, a dim chandelier conjured a comfortably warm atmosphere in the living room, its light barely spilling into the dining area through an archway at the room's far end.

Nina wore a tasteful suit of black and tan, her auburn hair impeccable as always, her fingers decorated with many glittering rings. Still very attractive after ten years, I thought; yet she looked . . .old. Weather-beaten. The creases at the corners of her eyes were deep. Her walk, once so deliberate and assured, seemed unsteady, almost faltering. She was over forty years old now; but she bore a weariness laid upon her by more than just time.

"Walter is in the den," she said, her voice low and edged with the roughness of a heavy smoker. "He will be happy you've come."

"I see your financial situation is no longer grim," I said with a chuckle. When I'd lived in the upstairs apartment, Walter and Nina Breheim were barely surviving week to week. My monthly rent payment essentially kept them afloat. But over time, I'd become more than just a tenant; we were good friends.

She led me back to the small parlor, which had always been Walter's sanctuary. I knew I'd find him in front of his music machines: in the old days a tower built of amplifiers, receivers, cassette decks, turntables and speakers twice as powerful as the building's plaster — or the neighbors — could bear. Now, his modernized system was just as powerful but occupied only a fraction of the space, with speakers only a few inches high. The shelves of record albums still reached the ceiling, though, and had been joined on all sides by almost as many compact discs. And in his same old battered rocking chair, headphones covering his ears, Walter sat with his back to me, seemingly unaware he had a visitor. His hair, once jet black and moppish, was now close-cropped and iron gray.

"Walter," Nina said softly, touching his shoulder, and he turned. His cool green eyes had grown even colder, and peered out from sockets that seemed to have been drilled much deeper since I'd last seen him. But those eyes flashed with surprise and pleasure, and I found myself smiling like a fool, ridiculously pleased I'd seen fit to bury my old pledge.

"David!" he cried and stood up so fast that his headphones slipped off and clattered to the floor. "David Isley! I don't believe it!" He grasped my outstretched hand, his grip still painfully firm, firmer than I could match. Like Nina, though, he seemed to have aged more than I would have expected in ten years. He was probably forty-five. He looked sixty.

"You need a drink," Nina said. "Still gin and tonic?"

"Tanqueray."

She smiled. "Sit down. Back in a moment."

I took a seat on the rose-colored loveseat that occupied the corner adjacent to the sound system. The parlor, though updated, felt like the same place it always had been.

"What on earth brings you back here?" Walter asked.

I gave him a brief rundown of my assignment, citing the proximity of my hotel as the reason for my visit. Nina returned momentarily with drinks for all of us and sat down across from me, studying me intently with her deep green eyes. She lit a cigarette and I noticed the slightest trembling of her fingers.

"So you couldn't resist coming to see us," Walter said. "I always thought you might. I'm glad you were able to overcome your, uh, objections."

At that, we all fell quiet for several moments. Walter gazed pensively at me.

"So," I said at last. "Is it truly gone?"

"Yes," Walter said. "It is gone."

Nina nodded in agreement. "Since that night, we've slept well."

It was to their credit that my friends had been able to remain in this house after everything that happened, after what we'd discovered. And I believed them, that the house was clean; certainly it must be, since here they sat, sharing drinks with me. Still, I knew that Walter and Nina had been fundamentally changed. The house might no longer be haunted, but these people were.

"Let me take you upstairs," Nina said. "We no longer rent the apartment. It's strictly for guests. We would love to have you stay with us rather than at the hotel."

I shrugged. "I'll have to think about that."

Nina and Walter both rose and ushered me through the living room to the entry foyer and the steep stairwell to the upstairs apartment. I must admit to feeling a little apprehensive at the idea of returning to the very rooms where I had once lived, where so many of the things that prompted me to flee the city had taken place.

"You won't recognize the place," Walter said. "We have made changes."

I stopped then, just as I was about to set foot on the stairs. I was facing the alcove whose window overlooked the sidewalk. A short lamp with a crystal base provided warm, golden light, and a large, ornately framed mirror hung upon the wall.

The crucifix wasn't there. No body of Christ casting its shadow on the translucent window shade. But I had *seen* . . . *!*

With a hoarse gasp, I slipped into the past.

◆ ◆

Nina Breheim had inherited the crucifix from her parents, and seemed to find it attractive in its place. I didn't care for it, not after seeing the way it looked at night, silhouetted eerily against the window like some twisted denizen of the grave who, if indeed risen, had come forth with purely evil intent. Nina and Walter had befriended me so readily, though, that I could never bring myself to offend them over anything so trivial.

But in all other matters there was honesty between us. I settled in with them shortly after arriving in Chicago fresh out of Beckham College, hoping to pursue a career in journalism. They offered the upstairs apartment for relatively low rent, and having virtually no savings to draw upon, I could hardly be particular in my choice of lodging. But it was a fine place for a young single man to live, with one bedroom, a bath, kitchenette and small living area. The Breheims had just bought the house at quite a reasonable price, but had still exhausted most of their money in the process. They needed a good tenant.

They cheerfully helped me move my few belongings into the apartment, and invited me to share any and all meals with them, as long as I chipped in on the food. They were a few years older than me, but as they apparently had few friends in the area, they seemed to desire my companionship as much as my money.

Our first dinner together became a drunken party.

"Back in Nova Scotia, my Grandad was a judge, you know," Walter told me, tossing back what must have been his fifth gin. "In those days, in Breton Cove, there weren't but two judges. And hardly anybody had cars back then, but both of them did. Now wouldn't you know that the two of them ended up getting the first two speeding tickets in Breton Cove! Of course, since they were the town's only judges, they had to sentence each other. Well, Grandad figures that he'll show due

professional consideration, and fines the other judge a dollar. Then they
switch robes, and our other judge says, 'Now that we have cars in this
town, it's up to us to set a good example. But two tickets in one day?
Suddenly speeding has become a trend!' So he fines Grandad
twenty-five dollars."

Nina and I laughed, though I knew she must have heard that story
countless times. I later learned, in fact, that Walter always told that story
when he first got to know someone. She'd heard it on their first date.
And sure enough it worked; he'd hooked her.

I lived in the house for over a month without experiencing the first
hint of any disturbance, thinking I'd be happy to stay as long as the
Breheims would have me. I found work in the circulation department
of *The Sun Times*, an admittedly lowly job, but lucrative enough to keep
me in my room and with plenty of food and drink. I even went out to
nightclubs most weekends, sometimes accompanied by Walter and
Nina, though they had grown staid enough to prefer their own living
room most evenings.

It began on a cool September night, the kind I most enjoyed: just
right for sleeping with the windows open and bundling up in the covers.
Traffic after midnight was generally light, and the trees and houses
muffled the noises from nearby Clark Street. When I awoke, it was just
past two a.m.; I thought some of the neighbors must have taken their
baby out and it wasn't happy to be roused at such an hour. The crying
started low and weak, but escalated steadily into a mournful wail. I first
felt pity for the child, then anger at the parents for allowing it to continue
for so long. Then I began to wonder if perhaps the child had been
abandoned on the street.

I rose from bed and went to the window, only to find that the sound
did not come from the street after all. The wailing seemed to echo from
the hall beyond my closed bedroom door. None of the other windows
were open that I knew of, and surely, neither Nina nor Walter would
have admitted company with a child at this hour! Opening the door
slowly, I looked out into the hall, dark but for a circle of multi-colored
light cast from the stained glass window.

The sound definitely came from below; perhaps one of the
downstairs windows was open and the crying was echoing through a
nearby alley. But I didn't intend to go exploring, and, muttering
something one shouldn't mutter about children, I turned to go back to

bed. But then the door to the stairwell opened and Walter appeared, silhouetted against the light from the foyer.

"Oh, you're up," he said quietly. "You hear that crying?"

"God, yes."

"It seems to be inside the house."

"What?"

"Yes. Come down."

I joined him in the living room, where the crying grew louder.

"I've checked everywhere. It sounds like it's coming from the basement."

He led me to the kitchen and the door that opened to the unfinished basement which they used only for storage. Yes — now the sound seemed very close at hand. But then, even as we stood there, the crying began to trail away, falling completely silent when Walter opened the door. Flipping on the light, he took a few tentative steps down, shaking his head as if realizing this was a futile quest. He turned back before reaching the bottom.

"Had to have come from the alley outside," he said. "Tomorrow I'll see if there are any windows open or broken. The furnace is in the basement; maybe somehow the sound was echoing through the conduits."

We agreed to leave further suppositions till morning, then bid each other a second goodnight and returned to our respective bedrooms. As I headed up the stairs, I found myself stepping gingerly, furtively, almost as if my softest footfall intruded too loudly upon the darkness. I realized then that I was quite nervous, far moreso than one should expect after hearing something so basically frivolous as an unidentified crying. Before slipping back into bed, I closed the hall door and locked it, as well as my window, feeling that open portals left me somehow exposed. And sleep eluded me for a long time after I'd turned out all the lights, for every little sound I heard startled me into canny wakefulness.

The next morning, the sun was a welcome arrival, despite my intense fatigue from such a poor night's sleep.

Walter, it turned out, ended up having to work that day, a Saturday. He was a pharmacist's assistant at a nearby drug store, on-call almost around the clock. So we did not see each other that morning at all; in fact, he did not return home until after dark. Nina, however, had breakfast with me, and told me that she too had heard the crying but hadn't bothered getting out of bed. For some reason, the noise had not affected her the way it had Walter and myself.

"He was like you," she said, sipping her coffee. "Seemed nervous and restless when he came back to bed. I can't imagine why you were so upset by the crying of a baby."

"It's not so much the crying itself," I told her, "it's just that the conditions seem so strange."

She shrugged. "This is a very old house, and the other houses nearby, the alleys, they trap noises. When I was a little girl, we lived on the south side of the city in an old place not much different than this one. Sometimes at night I could clearly hear people talking from way down the block. The wind would echo through the nearby alleys and through our chimney, creating a weird harmony, almost like something alive. Yet it was a comforting sound to me."

"Interesting," I said. "I suppose it takes a while to get used to the noises when you move into a place."

"Exactly. I'm sure it's nothing to be concerned about," she said with a wry smile I interpreted as a dismissal.

Without further words on the matter, we finished our breakfasts. Nina had errands to run, and I intended to call some of my friends from work so we could make plans for another night on the town. Yes, I drank too much in those days, but my drinking was happy, almost carefree. Drinking in the years thereafter had less innocent implications.

I did go out that night, and came home to a good night's sleep. Indeed, by then I'd virtually forgotten the uncomfortable incident of the night before. Walter and I never discussed it again, even when he made his own thorough check of the basement to make sure none of the lower windows were open or broken.

But the following night, I found myself again feeling unaccountably nervous. At first I could not even trace this uneasiness back to the sound of the baby crying. I knew only that my body felt tense and my mind would not succumb to the allure of sleep. At one a.m., I was still awake and fidgeting.

Nothing happened, though. Not one unusual noise, not a single unidentifiable movement. Eventually, fatigue overcame my anxiety, but when it did, the dreams that flooded my unconscious made me later wish I'd remained awake after all.

✦   ✦

I was in the Breheim's house, but it seemed to be another period in time. The furniture was all different, even older than the second-hand pieces that now occupied the rooms. Two people sat in chairs in the living room: grotesquely old, *twisted*-looking people, I thought. A man and a woman, hair thin and completely white, faces withered and wrinkled so that the features themselves were almost unidentifiable. I seemed to be peeking into the room from a concealed place, perhaps the dining area, in hopes of avoiding their notice. For reasons I did not understand, I did not want them to see me.

Then, the sounds! Beginning softly, then rising: a chorus of insane, gibbering voices, forming meaningless syllables that overlapped and harmonized, argued discordantly. When I looked at the old woman, her eyes were closed, her mouth open, her face raised to the ceiling as if all her attention was directed to the sounds. The man seemed to listen just as intently, but his eyes were open, now focused on the front door.

The Breheims' crucifix was there, in the alcove — an incongruity that somehow upset me even more than the noises and the strange couple that occupied the dream room.

Then the wailing began: the same child's mournful crying I had heard the night before while I was wide awake — that Walter and Nina had heard as clearly as I.

And finally came the thumping. Rhythmic, hollow; like giant footsteps approaching from a distance. It grew louder, providing a cadence for the ethereal voices. It came from behind me, from the direction of the kitchen.

From beyond the door to the basement stairs.

As the thumping drew nearer, the two ancient faces turned towards my hiding place, and two pairs of eyes fell upon me, widening horribly as they registered my presence. The old woman stood up, and I saw that she wore a shapeless, dust-colored smock that fell over what must have been an emaciated body. The man rose as well, clad identically to her. And two pairs of bare feet left the floor, and their bodies hovered in mid-air before me, their eyes now radiating an awful heat that seemed to sweep over and through me.

A childish giggle came out of the air.

And behind me, the door to the basement crashed open.

I sat up in my bed with a cry, bathed in cold sweat. The window was open.

But it had been closed when I went to bed! I had not opened it again since the night I'd heard the crying.

I got up and lowered the sash, only to freeze in my place as a deep drumbeat echoed from downstairs. My heart raced into overdrive, and I held my breath, anticipating a repetition of the noise.

It came again seconds later: a heavy *thump* somewhere below —very likely from the basement stairs, I thought; just like that in my dream. And then came another sound that surprised me as much as the other had terrified me.

It sounded like madrigal music; delicate vocal harmonies drifting softly up the stairwell, and I thought Walter must be playing music in his parlor. Perhaps, I considered with some relief, the thumping had just been something on a record.

But I realized I was mistaken when moments later I recognized the voices as belonging to Walter and Nina. They were intoning "Holy, holy . . . holy," in lovely harmony, their voices muted into chamber music by the depths of the house. I could only listen, hypnotized.

After a time, they fell silent. And I realized that the thumping had also subsided some time earlier. Their familiar voices had actually been soothing after the intense terror of my nightmare. I debated going downstairs to confront them, to find out exactly what was going on. But in the end, disinclined by the uncomfortable chill in the air and the silence that now prevailed in the house, I crawled back under my covers instead.

At last I was able to drift to sleep, despite being troubled by so many disturbing questions — not the least of which was the extent to which the Breheims were involved in something that now seemed not just inexplicable — but strangely sinister.

"No, I don't recall being awake at all," Nina said, sitting across from me at the breakfast table. "I never heard anything. Did you, Walter?"

He looked uneasy. "I — I remember having bad dreams. But nothing else."

Nina looked at me so curiously I could not believe she was telling me anything but the truth. And Walter obviously appeared fatigued, as if he hadn't slept any better than I.

"What were your dreams?" I asked. "Can you remember?"

He shook his head. "Not distinctly. I think I remember music."

"Music, yes," I said. "There was very strange music, if it could actually be called that. Haunting."

Nina's eyes took on a far away look. "Wait. I seem to recall dreaming of . . . sounds, if not music. Heavy sounds. Like a heartbeat."

"It wasn't a heartbeat," I said. "I think it was footsteps."

"Something was coming," Walter said softly. "Yes. Something terrible."

"Then I heard you," I said. "I heard you both. Singing. Or chanting, really. 'Holy, holy . . . holy.' Quite lovely — yet frightening in context."

Nina smiled weakly. "I don't think either of us are known for our vocal prowess."

"Don't be modest, Nina," Walter said. "We both sang in the church choir, David. But that was years ago."

"I see," I replied, nodding. "So is it possible the both of you were singing in your sleep?"

Walter chuckled. "I don't see how. We haven't practiced."

At that, I had to laugh. But now, even our nonchalant Nina seemed to fall into quiet contemplation, a dark shadow settling upon her face. "I would be lying," she said, "if I told you this didn't sort of freak me out."

"Likewise," Walter said. "David, you say your window was open but you did not open it. And I can assure you, neither of us has been to your rooms and no one else has been in the house — at least no one invited. Most likely you opened it in your sleep. Have you ever sleepwalked?"

"No, not that I know of. No more than the two of you perform concerts for somnambulants."

Nina's face brightened and Walter chuckled aloud. "Touche, monsieur," he said. "If it were past noon I'd buy you a drink. As it is, you'll have to settle for another cup of coffee."

I smiled and handed him my cup. He poured, and we finished our breakfast mostly in silence, each of us puzzled — but worse, for the first time since we'd met, uncomfortable with each other. I don't think any of us were prepared for that, or willing to allow it to continue.

The question was, what did one do about unexplained sounds and unsettling dreams? Especially when there seemed to be no pattern to them . . . .

Oftentimes, we could go days, occasionally weeks without a single restless night. Other times — usually when any of us was alone in the house — the sound of a baby's crying would begin soft and low, always beginning in the basement, only to become a whirlwind of miserable wailing that seemed to echo from *behind* the walls. But as soon as the basement door was opened, the crying would quickly fade.

One evening I came home late from work to be greeted by the sound of bitter weeping. This was no mystifying child's cry, but a mature, adult voice, wracked with heavy sobs.

It was Nina. She knelt on the living room floor, leaning against the sofa, her face buried in her hands, chest heaving as she cried. At first she didn't see me come in, but when I went to her side, she looked up with tear-jewelled eyes.

"They killed it," she whispered. "It was just a baby, and my God they killed it."

"What did you see, Nina?"

"I was resting on the couch," she said, struggling to catch her breath. "I heard it begin to cry. And those voices started. Christ, David, the room changed. Everything was old. I could see things — vaguely, like shadows. They were beating it, two old people. They beat it and threw it down the stairs. Then they went after it. Oh God, the voices. You should have heard the voices."

I touched her hand; it was icy. "Everything's all right now," I said, though I felt my own heart quailing. "Nothing's changed here."

"I know," she said, wiping her eyes. "It all seems to be fading. Almost like a dream. But David, I didn't dream it. I was awake. I swear to you, I was awake."

"I believe you," I said, truthfully. "Let's get you a drink."

She accepted my hand and I helped her to her feet, where she managed to stand shakily on her own. She slowly headed toward the kitchen, and I followed a couple of steps behind. "Where's Walter?" I asked.

"He called and said he had to work late."

It was now almost nine. I made a gin and tonic for Nina, and as an afterthought made one for myself. As she sipped it, her nerves slowly settled. But I could feel something in the house. An atmosphere of tension; of expectation.

"I won't leave this house," she said firmly, as if anticipating my suggestion. "This is ours, we bought it." She even worked up a little smile and said, "No squalling shadows pay the mortgage here. We do."

I smiled too, but suddenly a movement from the direction of the dimly lit living room caught my eye. A shadow seemed to be creeping across the floor, a movement so subtle I wasn't sure at first that I was really seeing it. I didn't say anything, for fear of upsetting Nina further. But as I watched, the shadow took on the distinct form of a very small person, shuffling slowly forward — stopping just short of the open door.

Ever so slowly, a pale globe slid into view around the side of the door, like the face of a featureless moon. It stopped before fully revealing itself, as if an eavesdropping child had carelessly stepped a hair too far into the open.

I felt goosebumps on the back of my neck. But unwilling to give in to fear, I instead dashed through the dining room into the living room, ready to confront whatever apparition dared invoke my wrath.

Of course, there was nothing and no one in the living room. We were alone in the house.

"David," called Nina. "David, what is it? Did you see something?"

I sheepishly returned to the kitchen and laid my hands on Nina's shoulders. "I thought I did. Just a trick of the eye, I guess. Maybe the lights from a passing car. Now you've gotten my nerves on edge. That's very bad of you."

She reached up and squeezed my hand, and all my fear dissipated beneath a rush of affection for her — no, nothing adulterous — and my previous suspicion that the Breheims could be somehow responsible for the things happening here vanished completely.

But regardless of the complete innocence of my feelings for her, when Walter opened the front door a minute later, I drew my hand away quickly and felt myself blushing. Fortunately, Nina was quickly up to greet him and by the time he came in to say hello to me I was completely back to normal, such as it was.

✦   ✦

On my way up to bed that night, I could feel an uncustomary chill in the stairwell, and what seemed like an electrical charge building in the air, like the tangible atmospheric ionization before a thunderstorm. Still, there's something inside the rational man that leads us to carry on with our normal routines, regardless of the evidence of our senses, as if the clinging to familiar dogma is an amulet to counter any unknown.

I went through my nightly ablutions, prepared for bed as always, picked up a book, and settled beneath the covers — leaving not only the bedside lamp on, but the lights in the kitchenette and bathroom. It was Thursday night, and I had to go to work as usual in the morning. I very much wanted to get a good night's sleep, and strange as it seems, even after the episode with Nina and the apparition I *thought* I'd seen, I managed to relax somewhat.

Not only that, after reading until my eyelids couldn't prop themselves open any longer, I drifted into an uneasy, but undisturbed sleep — at least until I heard a heavy thump sometime much later in the night.

I woke up surrounded by darkness. All the lights had been extinguished. The digital clock read just past three a.m. And the baby was crying.

"Oh God," I muttered aloud, sitting up and rubbing my eyes, having reached the point where I was more angered than frightened by the unwelcome disruption. But when another thump sounded from beyond my door, a little shiver passed up my spine, for it was louder and heavier — and seemingly closer — than any I had heard previously. This seemed to be coming from the stairwell right outside my apartment door. And it was drawing nearer. A jarring *thump . . . thump . . . .* that clearly meant something was on the steps, moving closer with each repetition.

I have never had a victim's mentality; I was not prepared to wait placidly for a potentially dangerous visitation. So, turning on all the lights, I hurried straight to the kitchenette and grabbed the biggest butcher knife from the cutlery drawer. And with only the briefest hesitation to half-heartedly pray for my own deliverance from evil, I stalked straight to the stairwell door, stopped and grabbed for the handle.

Thump. It was close. Whatever *it* was.

Drawing in a steadying breath, bracing myself for the sight of something I might not completely comprehend, I pulled the door open.

But even this mental preparation could not prevent me from gasping in shock when I realized what I was seeing. Illuminated only by the hall light shining down through my open door, a rigid figure was *bouncing* up the stairs on one blunt end: the crucifix from the downstairs window, Christ's head thrown back and mouth gaping in unutterable agony. The wooden eyes, lit with the unmistakable fire of life, glared at me in terror, as if the force animating it was powerful enough to dethrone God himself. In the background, the baby's screaming rose higher and higher, finally drowning even the thumping on the stairs.

When this travesty was one step from the top, I slammed the door shut and pressed myself against it, wondering what such a thing might do to me if it did manage to break through. Even if it didn't do *anything*, its very presence threatened to shatter my remaining sanity. In retrospect, I've sometimes wondered if that was not the intent of its motivating force all along.

But nothing came. In fact, moments later, the crying, the pounding on the stairs, all had fallen silent — except the frantic pounding of my heart. But no! Far below, something began clanging sharply, like iron against stone. Over and over again, stronger, more determinedly, and I knew in my soul that this was something different, something of human design. It was in the basement.

I opened the door and — of course — found the stairway clear. I hustled down, made my way through the dark living room to the kitchen, where a light now burned and the basement door gaped darkly at me, emitting the sharp, furious clanging.

Indeed, I now saw that the single bulb below was lit, and I could hear a deep gasping for breath between the iron pounding. Bolstered by this sign of human activity, I rushed down to find Walter with a pick axe in hand, drawn back to strike at the brick wall at the far northern corner of the house. He saw me, but did not pause. Only after he'd swung several more times, shattering brick and spraying red dust into his face, did he speak to me.

"It's here, David. By God, I followed it and I found where it comes from. Here. Back here."

I leaned close and saw that he'd knocked out a portion of wall roughly a foot in diameter — and beyond lay a chamber of darkness of unknown depth. Barely giving me time to move away, Walter drew back and smashed away another section of bricks with the pick, this time tugging a few of the fragments toward him. And from this chasm now spilled the single most appalling sight ever beheld by these eyes:

A pile of old bones, gray and brittle with age, coated with red brick dust, some obviously broken by Walter's pick axe.

A skull rolled from the opening. Just a small thing, about the size of the half-seen moonface that had peered around the door the afternoon before.

I barely glanced up when a moment later I heard Nina's footsteps on the stairs, followed momentarily by a succession of short, hysterical screams.

The much older-looking Walter now stared at me with an expression of concern. Nina looked on with an air of trepidation, as if all the fears of the past might somehow intrude upon the peace they had known for better than a decade.

"Are you all right?" she asked.

I just shrugged. "I don't know. Sometimes it doesn't seem like I've ever been away, that it could ever really be over. I mean, how do we *know* it's over? After what we saw?"

Walter nodded thoughtfully. "I know, my friend. I still have dreams. *It* had to come from somewhere, right? That's what haunts us. Where it came from."

"But by staying here, we've managed to achieve some kind of closure," Nina said. "There's never been any evidence that it could ever happen again."

I wanted so badly to tell them about having seen the crucifix in the window on my approach, but I knew it would only upset them uselessly. They had learned to live with their memories. I had not. I didn't want to undermine the foundation they'd built by revealing what could still conceivably be written off as a delusion on my part.

Not that I believed that, of course. If anything, I was sure now that some residue of that ancient force remained in this house, and my own presence had perhaps momentarily catalyzed it. But only for that moment, I told myself.

"Well," Walter said. "Let's go upstairs."

I followed them up, remembering the horror of that thing bouncing on its end up the stairs, the face of the crucified, wooden savior reflecting such hellish agony. Maybe my coming back was not a good idea after all.

But no. The joy of seeing my friends again could not be overpowered even by the reminders of that old terror.

Sure enough, the upstairs apartment was very different than during my stay. Once gloomy with age, it now seemed bright and new, with fresh wallpapering and paint, contemporary furnishings, new light fixtures and lamps — so great a change, in fact, that I could not picture anything ominous or menacing daring to trespass here.

"It's lovely," I said. "You made a wise decision."

"Would you like to stay? We certainly would love to have you, David."

I had to shake my head. "I appreciate that. But . . . I can't. I just can't."

"I understand," Nina said. "I can't blame you. But promise us this. If you come to town again, do not hesitate to come again. Please?"

"I will," I promised. "I will come again."

We returned downstairs and I had one more drink before I had to start back to my hotel. As we stood facing each other by the front door, I said to Walter, "You know, that night when I heard you singing — do you really have no memory of that?"

"None," he said. "But Nina and I spoke of it at great length. You know, there was something very powerful in this house. Something we don't have all the answers to, and never will. But even though we were not aware of it at the time, I believe our own spirits were reacting. And counteracting. I think perhaps they preserved our bodies independent of our will. Think about that, David."

"Indeed," I said. "Well. You have no idea how good it was to see you."

Both of them came forward to embrace me. Then I left the house with a brief look back, noting that the window where the crucifix had been was now properly empty; but I couldn't suppress the chill from knowing that, for the briefest moment, on this very night, *something* from the past had paid us an unwelcome visit.

And then I heard it. Behind me, rising lightly in the night, barely discernible. Softened by the distance, mingled with a low breeze, the lovely, haunting harmony drifted to me, and my quick glance back revealed two silhouettes on the porch, standing rigidly side by side, a faint luminescence in their eyes — a reflection from streetlights, I told myself. Merely a reflection.

"Holy, holy . . . holy . . . ."

I ran. I ran until I reached Clark and on and on, chased by the music long after it should have been smothered by the sounds of traffic and jets and el trains and nearby pedestrians. But it rang in my ears and my skin felt cold, for the air around me still held a charge like the one I'd felt in the stairwell on that final night. I knew that my coming back had activated it, but I prayed it was only temporary and that by tomorrow morning, all would have returned to normal.

No, it wasn't just that a baby had been beaten in that house and bricked up while still alive. Murder is a human act, and however atrocious, nothing a human being can conceive or do is shocking. Nothing. Only something inhuman, something beyond our comprehension, something that serves to remind us of just what our place is in this world can shock the soul the way the Breheims and I were shocked.

Those bones — I'll never forget the weird angles of those tiny bones, the single gaping eye socket in the little, horn-studded skull. That the thing was ever born, that it once lived and was killed in a house in which I spent months of my life — *that* is a fact that haunts and shocks me, and Walter and Nina Breheim.

That, and my soul's inevitable conjectures of the thing's unknown, unspeakable lineage.

ROADKILL

Tom Elliott

Bill straightened and leaned against his shovel; he passed a bare arm across his forehead, and was surprised at the prodigious amount of sweat that clung to the soft blond hairs of his forearm. Far in the distance, Abilene floated in the morning heat like some wavering, enchanted kingdom in the sky. He glanced over at Johnny. "What'd you say?" he asked.

"Fucking assholes," Johnny repeated, then kicked at the drying animal carcass glued to the pavement of Texas Highway 351.

"Who?"

"Cops. I hate 'em. Fuck 'em all."

"Better not let *him* hear you." Bill nodded at the cop sitting behind the wheel of the pickup truck parked a few dozen yards down the road. The cop was stoically smoking a cigarette while he pondered the Saturday funnies.

"Fuck him, too," Johnny said, but with less conviction. "I shoulda took traffic school again."

Bill pried at the edge of the armadillo with his shovel, and it came away from the pavement with a soft slurping sound. He scooped it up and dumped it atop the other stiff bodies already covering the pickup's bed.

"I thought you already took traffic school three times."

Johnny stopped and stared at Bill; he looked indignant, though Bill wasn't sure why. "Yeah," Johnny said finally, "but this—" he indicated the bit of fluff at his feet that had once been a jack rabbit "—this is what they call cruel and unusual punishment." He shoveled it up and dumped it in the pickup.

Bill stared off into the distance. "It's not so bad," he said. "A couple of hours in the fresh air beats hell out of some boring lecture."

"I never liked fresh air," Johnny confessed. "And they give you doughnuts in traffic school." He hesitated, then added, "And the classroom doesn't smell like rotten meat."

Bill nodded. "Got me there."

Together they sat on the lowered tailgate and without a word the cop started the engine and drove slowly down the road's shoulder. Just as they were beginning to enjoy the soft flow of air against their faces, the truck stopped, and Johnny and Bill dismounted with twin sighs of resignation.

"You want the coyote, or the whatever-it-is?"

Johnny considered his choice a moment too long, and Bill headed for the whatever-it-was.

"I'll get the coyote," Johnny said belatedly.

"Right," Bill said, poking at the large flattened whatever-it-was, dried now to the stiff consistency of beef jerky. "Must have been a big dog," he muttered.

The head of the whatever-it-was showed both eye sockets (its eyes long gone) close together, like that halibut Bill had caught once off the Gulf Coast. It was so flat Bill could not picture what it had looked like alive.

His shovel made a metallic scraping sound against the pavement as he edged it under one of the animal's legs. He lifted it a few inches, then froze.

"Johnny," he said breathlessly. "Johnny! Come here!"

Bill inched away from the whatever-it-was. The hairs prickled on the back of his neck.

"Yeah?"

Bill pointed at his discovery, and Johnny looked down.

Folded under the end of the leg Bill had pried up was an even flatter hand, and now it hung limply from the end of the shattered wrist. One of its fingers still retained some of its original plumpness, owing somewhat to the fact that the leg had protected it from further flattening, but more so because of the gold ring.

Johnny crossed himself nervously, mumbling something in Spanish. "Somebody ran over a *kid*, man," he said.

"I don't think so," Bill said, and Johnny's eyes jerked up to stare into his.

"What you mean, man? It sure ain't a dog. Dogs don't wear fucking rings, man. That's a *human bean*, man."

"I don't think so," Bill repeated. "Count the fingers."

He waited while Johnny counted.

"The others must be around here someplace," Johnny said weakly.

"I don't think so."

"Would you stop *saying* that?! *Hijo de la chingada*! I don't think so! I don't think so! I don't think—"

Bill punched Johnny in the arm. "Shut the fuck up, asshole. You want him to hear us?"

Together they looked over at the pickup; the cop had abandoned the funnies and now seemed completely absorbed with the possibility that a foreign object might have lodged in one of his nostrils.

Johnny rubbed at his shoulder. "Don't go hittin' me, man," he warned.

Bill carefully slid the blade of his shovel under the bulk of the whatever-it-was and levered it over.

They both gasped. Johnny crossed himself again.

A second, smaller head, flattened like the first, peered out of a slot in what appeared to be the thing's belly. The features of this smaller head, however, had been protected by the animal's body from the insults of tire tread, and Bill was able to picture what the thing had looked like in life.

"A baby," Johnny whispered, echoing Bill's thoughts. "It was carrying a baby. In a pouch, like one of them kangaroos or something."

Bill squatted next to the thing and put a trembling hand against the tiny crushed face.

Johnny shoved ineffectually at Bill's shoulder. He looked horrified. "Don't *touch* it, man!" he cried.

Bill adjusted his feet for better balance, and gingerly tugged at the tiny head. For a moment there was some resistance, then the body of the baby emerged with a wet sucking noise.

"I think I'm gonna throw-up, man," Johnny whispered, but Bill ignored him.

The baby had four pencil-thin arms, and three of its hands were crossed almost reverentially across its tiny chest. Clutched between the delicate fingers of the fourth was a small bit of something that looked like a scrap of cardboard.

Bill pinched the bit of cardboard between his fingers and pulled. It came away with the tiny hand still connected to it.

"Eeeuuuu," Johnny said, looking away.

It was a book, about the size of a Crackerjack prize. Bill used a fingernail to open its covers; inside were tiny silvery images of alien scenes and a few odd-looking characters scattered about the pages. Its purpose was clear. *I bet I'm holding the alien equivalent of* Horton Hears a Who, *Bill thought*.

Without a word, he slipped the tiny book into his shirt pocket. He glanced up at Johnny; the action was bound to elicit a comment from the man, but Johnny remained silent, his face very pale, his lips quivering.

Bill leaned over and slid his hand fully into the pouch-slit of the mother-thing. The inside of the pouch felt warm and slick, and Bill was reminded of a vagina. Then his fingers brushed against the edge of something hard and circular. He pulled it out.

It was a gold metallic disk, about the size of a CD, on its center was printed very clearly "Greetings from the People of Planet Earth."

"Oh Jesus," Bill said.

"Wha—?" Johnny said; he looked like he might cry. "Don't show me no more, man. I can't take it. I really can't."

Bill held the disk up. "Do you know what this is?"

"Yeah," Johnny said. "The Space Cadets cover of 'Purple People Eater.' How the fuck should I know, man?"

"You know those rockets they send up every few years, the ones that are supposed to send pictures back of Saturn and shit like that?"

Johnny nodded uncertainly.

"I read *Penthouse* or somewhere that they put a recording on those rockets. Recordings in all sorts of languages saying 'Greetings from Planet Earth.'" Bill waved the disk in the air, and the Texas sun flickered across Johnny's eyes.

"That's what this is, Johnny. It's one of those disks. From a rocket we shot into space."

"Sounds like bullshit you're making up to me."

"I'm telling you, man. I *read* it somewhere."

They stared at the disk in Bill's hand for a long moment, then together they looked down at the mother-thing, and at the remains of its child.

"We should tell him," Johnny said, indicating the truck.

Bill shook his head. "You think that asshole's gonna know what to do? I thought you hated cops."

"Sure, but hey, man, this is some serious shit."

"You think this is gonna get us off road-kill detail? Man, if we tell him, he's just gonna tell his boss, who'll tell his boss, and then the CIA and the FBI and all kinds of government spooks are gonna come down here and turn this into a real circle-jerk."

"And you'n me, man, we'll be *famous*!"

"We'll be shit," Bill said. "I read an article once about a guy who discovered a spaceship in Arizona a couple of years ago."

"You read too much, man."

"Maybe," Bill said. "Anyway, right after he reported it, he disappeared. Poof. Into thin air." Bill snapped his fingers.

"Maybe the guy owed money and—"

"Maybe shit!" Bill said. "Maybe the CIA and FBI boys decided they needed to talk to this guy *at length* — you now what I mean? Maybe this guy didn't disappear; maybe he's still alive, sitting in a little room where the CIA and FBI boys can shoot the breeze with him whenever they like."

"No way, man," Johnny said, but Bill thought that the man's eyes were as wide open as they could get. He was getting through.

"Or maybe," Bill continued, "maybe the guy did disappear. Maybe he's buried in some Arizona cemetery, with somebody else's headstone over his grave."

"That's fuckin' crazy, man," Johnny said, but his swarthy face was pale.

Bill stood up and — after a moment's thought — flung the disk out into the vast expanse of Texas plain. He gave Johnny a warning look, then gripped the handle of his shovel. "Maybe it is," he said, and then he scooped up the mother-thing and its baby, walked over and dumped the load into the back of the pickup.

The dull thud roused the driver from his nasal investigation; he wiped his fingers on his pant-leg and cranked up the engine. "Took you guys long enough," he called back over his shoulder.

"This heat is gluin' the fuckers to the freeway, man," Bill said. He sat on the tailgate and stared pointedly at Johnny, who still stood beside the already-drying spot on the road.

After a moment, Johnny came over and sat beside him with a resigned sigh. "Man, I hate cops," he said. He was silent for a moment. "Hey!" he suddenly called out to the driver. "When we gonna stop for lunch?"

But the driver's response was drowned by the grinding of gears, and the pickup jerked into motion. Grumbling, it moved on down the line.

THE RIFLE

Jack Ketchum

She found the rifle standing on its stock in the back of his cluttered closet.

Unexpected as a snake in there.

Not that he'd made very much attempt to hide it. It was leaning in the corner behind the twenty-pound fiberglass bow and the quiver of target arrows his father had bought him for Christmas — over her objections. His winter jacket hung in front of it. She'd moved the jacket aside. And there it was.

He'd complained in the past about her going in his closet and for a long time she'd obliged him. Privacy, she knew, was important to a ten-year-old — it was especially important to Danny. But when you noticed dustballs rolling out from under the door *somebody* was going to have to get in there and clean and obviously it wasn't going to be him.

She was only planning to vacuum.

Now this.

She reached around behind her and turned off the Electrolux. For a moment she just knelt there staring at the rifle in the heavy summer silence.

A slim black barrel lurking in the shadows.

A secret, she thought.

Yet another.

She reached inside and grasped the cool metal. Drew it out into the light.

The rifle was an old bolt-action .22. Her brother had owned one very much like it when he was fifteen — took it down to the VFW target range on Saturdays for a while. Then he discovered girls.

Danny was only ten.

Where in god's name had he got it?

Richard wouldn't have bought it for him. Not even her ex-husband was fool enough to think for one minute that she'd allow a weapon in the house. No, it had to be . . .

. . . her father's.

Which meant that Danny had also stolen it.

They'd visited his farm the weekend before last. She was struck again by how empty the house seemed now that her mother was gone and had sat in the kitchen with her father drinking cup after cup of black coffee, knowing how starved for conversation he was now. So that Danny was on his own most of the day. Through the big bay window she saw him go into the barn where her father kept his two remaining horses. A little later noticed him walking through the field of long dry grass toward the woods and stream beyond. And then she'd forgotten all about him until what must have been over an hour had passed and he came slamming in through the screen door with a big box turtle in his hand, Danny all excited until she told him to put it back by the stream where he'd found it, that they weren't taking a turtle all the way back to Connecticut with them and that was that.

Her father kept his newer guns behind glass on a rack in the living room.

The older ones, the ones he never used anymore, were stacked in the workshop of the cellar.

She examined the stock. It was scratched and pitted. Her sinuses were giving her hell this summer and she could barely smell a thing but she sniffed it anyway. It smelled of earth and mold. It was her father's, all right. She sniffed again, the scent of old gun oil on her hands. Probably he hadn't used it in years.

It would be months before her father noticed it was missing. If then.

She threw the bolt. Inside a brass shell casing gleamed.

She felt a sudden mix of shock and fury.

My god.

He'd *loaded* the goddamn thing.

Her father would *never* have left it loaded. That meant that Danny had searched around the basement for shells as well. And found some. *How many more did he have? Where were they?*

She resisted the urge to go tearing through his drawers, rummaging through his closet.

That could wait.

What she needed to do now was find him and confront him. One more confrontation. More and more as he got older.

She wondered how he'd explain *this* away.

It was not going to be like stealing Milky Ways from the Pathmark Store.

It was not going to be like the fire he and Billy Berendt had set, yet denied they'd set, in the field behind the Catholic Church last year.

He couldn't lie his goddamn way out of this one.

Couldn't say that he'd meant to pay for the candy bars but didn't because he got to looking at the comic books and forgot they were in his pocket. He couldn't claim that the two eyewitnesses — kids from the rougher part of town who'd seen Billy and Danny go into the field and then come out running and laughing just before smoke appeared on the horizon — had it in for him.

The rifle was concrete. The bullet even more so.

They did not lend themselves to easy explanation.

It was not going to be like the jackknife from Nowhere or the brand-new Sega-Genesis computer game from Nowhere or the Bic cigarette lighters that kept cropping up which he'd always *found on the street*. What a lucky kid.

She was angry. She was scared.

Angry and scared enough so that her hands were shaking as she removed the shell from the breech and put it in her jeans pocket. She felt a by-now all-too-familiar access of what could only be called grief, a feeling that even though her son was only ten she'd already lost him somehow, as though there were something in him she could no longer touch or speak to and for which mourning was easily as justifiable and as appropriate as her father's grief over the loss of her mother.

She knew it was important to push that feeling aside. To let the anger flow freely instead. She needed the anger. Otherwise too much love and loss, too much sympathy and — *let's face it* — too much plain old-fashioned self-pity would only weaken her.

Tough love, she thought. That's what's left.

She'd tried the shrinks. Tried the counsellors. She'd tried to understand him.

Taking things away from him, privileges — the computer, TV, the movies — was the only thing that seemed to work anymore.

Not even that sometimes.

Well, they're all going out the window today. Everything.

She slid the black bolt of the rifle back into position and marched on out of the room. She knew where to find him.

At the clubhouse.

The grass in her back yard tickled her ankles. It was time to cut the lawn again. Humidity made the stock of the rifle feel sticky in her hand. She slid between the two pine trees in back of the lawn out onto the well-worn path into the woods.

The path belonged to the boys. Billy Berendt, Danny, Charlie Haas and the others. She never came back this way. Hardly ever. Only when she was calling him for supper and he was late and didn't answer — even then she rarely had to venture this far. The path was only two feet wide at most through thick, waist-high brush, dry brown grass and briars as tall as she was. A path the width of a boy's body — not the width of her's. She was glad of the jeans — already studded with burrs — and unhappy with the short-sleeve blouse. A thorn bush scored two thin lines of blood along her upper arm. She used the barrel of the rifle to part another.

She heard the stream rushing over its rocky bed through a line of trees to her left. The path split ahead of her. She took it to the right, away from the stream.

All these woods would one day be developed, bulldozed into oblivion. But in the three years they'd lived here that hadn't happened yet — and Danny was getting to the age where soon it wouldn't matter. In the meantime the woods and stream were part of the reason she'd wanted the place for him.

Nature, she believed, was a teacher. She'd grown up on a farm and thought that most of what she knew about life she'd glimpsed there first and then had come to understand more fully later. Birth, death, sex, the renewal of the land, its fragility and its power, the chaos inside the order, the changes in people that came with the change of seasons. The impacability of the natural world and how important it was simply to accept that.

She wanted all this for Danny.

What she'd had. And what now sustained her.

She knew that many women would have been bitter about a broken marriage that they hadn't chosen to end. But she wasn't. Not really. Unhappy, yes, of course — but there had never really been any bitterness. Love, she thought, was a contract you signed knowing that someday the signatures might fade. Richard had fallen out of love with her and in love with someone else. A simple change of seasons. Hard as winter, but bearable and somehow even understandable. It was no longer necessary to the scheme of things that people mate for life. Reality was what it was and couldn't be changed by her own distress in the face of it. She thought Richard's choice of second partners was one he someday might live to regret. But that was his affair. She'd let him go.

And she might have been bitter about Danny too. Instead she simply kept plugging away. Though the boy was far from easy. He'd *never* been easy. But since the breakup four years ago he always seemed, if not actually *in* trouble, always on the verge of it. Sliding grades. Clowning, fighting in class. Bad language around the girls at school. Once he'd been caught throwing stones at Charlie Haas on the playground. And of course there were the stealing and brushfire incidents.

Beyond paying child-support his father was no help at all. Richard thought it was all typical boy behavior. It would pass, he said. She'd never been a boy and it was possible he was right.

But Richard didn't have to live with him.

Didn't have to endure the tantrums when he didn't get his way or the hostile silences.

She felt exhausted by him sometimes.

What more could a kid get into?

He could get into firearms, obviously.

At age ten.

Great. Just great.

She wondered how he'd smuggled it home in the first place and then remembered the blanket she kept in back of the station wagon. He could have hidden a box of dynamite back there and she'd never have known it.

Very cute, Danny. Very sneaky. Very neat.

Her arms felt sticky with sweat, itchy from the pollen and dust in the air and the warm brush of leaves. She could barely breathe for all the damn pollen.

But she was nearly there now.

She could see its location in the distance to the right of the path, up a hill through a tall thin stand of birch.

His clubhouse. His personal sanctuary.

Aside from the occasional visit from Billy Berendt, inviolate to the world.

Until today.

Once, perhaps a hundred years ago, there had been a house here but it had long since burned to the ground — leaving only the root cellar — and whoever the owners were they'd never rebuilt it. He'd taken her up to look at it, all excited, shortly after they moved in and he first discovered it. At that time it was nothing but a hole in the ground five feet by eight feet wide and four feet deep, overgrown with weeds. But he'd cleared the weeds to expose the fieldstone walls and raw earth floor within and, with her permission, begged a pair of old double doors from her father's barn, and he and Richard had spent one uncommonly ambitious afternoon painting the two doors green and sinking hinges into the walls and then attaching the doors so that they covered the hole and could be secured together by a combination padlock from the outside and a simple hook and eye from the inside.

Total privacy.

He called it his clubhouse.

His private little gathering of one.

She had always thought it was kind of sad. Possibly not even good for him.

But Danny had always been a loner. She guessed that was his nature. He always seemed to tolerate the other neighborhood boys more than he actually befriended them — though for some reason they all seemed to like him well enough and were eager to get him out to play even though they were excluded from the clubhouse and were probably jealous that Danny'd discovered it first. For some reason that didn't seem to matter. Maybe the place imparted status of some kind. She didn't know. Boys, she thought.

All she knew was that he spent a lot of time here. More than she'd have liked.

She'd bought him a battery-powered lantern. Not much light got
in through the doors, he said. A step-ladder for going up and down.
Toys and books and games would disappear and then reappear in his
room as well as mason jars from the kitchen and hammers and boxes of
nails from the toolbox so she knew he was bringing them out here and
then returning them according to some private agenda.

She never pried.

But now she was going to have to take all this away from him too
for a while.

She leaned on the rifle, catching her breath before starting in on the
remaining trek up the slope of the hill. She heard bees buzzing in the
grass beside her.

Her sinuses were killing her.

Warm wind ruffled her hair. She steeled herself for what was to
come and headed on.

The doors had weathered considerably since last she'd seen them.
They could seriously use another paint job. She saw that the
combination lock was gone. That meant he had it with him. He was
inside.

"Danny."

No answer. She listened. No movement either.

"Danny. I know you're in there."

She reached down for the doorhandles and rattled the doors.

"Come out here. Now."

She was starting to get seriously angry again. *Good,* she thought.
You damn well *should* be angry.

"I said now. Did you hear me?"

"You're not supposed to be here."

"What?"

"I said you're not supposed to be here. You never come out here."

"Well that's too bad because I'm here now. Do I have to kick these
doors apart or what?"

She heard a click and the rattle of glass and then steps on the ladder.
She heard him unfasten the hook and the door creaked open.

He slid through the doors, out of the dark below, and let the doors
fall shut behind him. There was something furtive about him.
Something she didn't like. He knelt and took the padlock out of his
pocket.

"Leave it," she said. "Stand up. Look at me."

He did as he was told. And saw the rifle. Glanced at it once and then turned away.

"Where did you get this?"

He didn't answer. He just kept staring down the hill, arms folded across his skinny chest.

"It's your grampa's, isn't it."

No answer to that one either.

"You stole it, didn't you."

"I was going to put it back," he said. *Sullen. Caught.* "Next time we went there."

"Oh really? Were you going to put this back too?"

She took the bullet from her pocket and held it out to him.

"Or were you planning to use it?"

He sighed, staring down the hill.

"You have more of these?"

He nodded.

"Where?"

"My drawer."

She looked at him. Her son. Her son who wouldn't meet her eyes.

"You're in big trouble. You know that, don't you."

He sighed again and then bent down with the padlock in his hand to secure the double doors.

She remembered the way he'd opened them, just wide enough to slide through and no further.

"Leave it," she said. "What's down there?"

"Just my stuff."

"What stuff. You have some more surprises for me?"

"No."

"Open it up. I want to see."

"Mom . . . it's *my* stuff."

"As of today you don't *have* any stuff. Not until I say you do. Do you understand me? Now open it."

"Mom!"

"Open it!"

He stood there. *He isn't going to move,* she thought.

Why you little sonova . . .

"God dammit!"

She reached down and threw open one door and then the other and the first thing that hit her was the smell even with her sinus problem, the smell was rank and old and horrible beyond belief, and the second thing was the incredible clutter of rags and jars and buckets on the floor and the third was what she saw on the walls, hanging there from masonry nails pounded into the fieldstone, hung like decorations, like trophies, like the galleries she'd seen in castles in Scotland and England on her honeymoon and which were hunter's galleries. A boy's awful parody of that.

His stuff.

She gagged and put her hand to her mouth and dropped the bullet. She stooped reflexively to pick it up again.

She looked at him, hoping that her knees wouldn't buckle.

Hoping crazily in a way that he wouldn't even be there.

He was staring directly at her. The first time since he'd climbed out of the root cellar. The expression on his face was neutral but the look in his eyes was not. The eyes were examining her coldly, intent on her reaction.

As perhaps they had examined coldly what was down below.

Adult eyes. But not the eyes of any adult she'd ever seen or ever dreamt to see.

Was this her son?

For a moment she felt a stunning terror of him. Of this little boy who didn't even weigh ninety pounds yet. Who still balked at showering every day and washing his hair on schedule. It was a terror that skittered suddenly inside her and seemed to awaken all her memories of him at once, memories like claps of thunder — the stealing, the stone-throwing, the fire, the dark half-hidden glances, the bullying tantrums — terror that suddenly gave pattern to all this, all the interstices of understanding and *seeing* suddenly closing together for her to compose a black seamless wall of events and behavior which defined him.

And *she knew.*

She looked into his eyes and saw what he was.

And knew what he would become.

She reeled under the weight of it. Ten years of life.

When had it begun? At the breast?

In the womb?

She needed to know the whole of it, needed to embrace the horror of this as she had always needed his embrace. However cold. However distant.

She had always needed to embrace her son.

"You have a light . . . down there?" she murmured.

He nodded.

Her voice faltered.   Then, *"Go turn it on,"* she said.

He preceeded her down the ladder and switched on the lantern. The room was suddenly very bright.

She stood in his chamber and looked at the walls.

The box turtle — *had he smuggled it here from her father's house too or was this a different one and how many others? what about before he found the clubhouse? what about . . . ?* The turtle was nailed to the wall by its feet. Its shriveled head lolled back onto its greying shell. The frogs were impaled by a single nail through roughly the center of their bodies and there were six of them. Some belly-up, some not. She saw a pair of withered garter snakes, three crayfish. And a salamander.

Like the turtle the cats were nailed through all fours. He had eviscerated both of them and looped their entrails around them and nailed the entrails to the wall at intervals so that the cats were at the center of a kind of crude bulls'eye. She saw that he had strangled them with some sort of rope or twine. He had nearly taken off the head of the larger one in doing so. Its black-and-white fur was caked with old dried blood.

The other was just a kitten.

A tabby.

She was aware of him watching her.

She was aware too of the tears in her eyes and knew what he didn't know — that the tears were for her. Not for him. Not this time. She wiped them away.

She had heard of people like this. Read about them. Saw them on the evening news. It seemed they were everywhere these days.

She knew what they were. And what they were not.

She had not expected her son to be one of them.

Her son was ten. Only ten. She saw all the years of his life ahead of him. So many years.

So much death to come.

Treatment, she thought. He needs treatment. He needs help.

But they did not respond to treatment.

"I'm going back up," she murmured. Her voice sounded flat and strange to her and she wondered if it did to him and then wondered if it was the fieldstone walls and earthen floor that made her voice sound the way it did or if it was something inside her, some sea-change in her that was expressing itself now in this new strange voice.

She thought, *implacable*.

She moved up the step ladder and stepped out into the field and heard him snap off the lantern below as she threw the bolt on the rifle and inserted the bullet into the chamber. He looked up at her once just as he was near the top and she saw that no, there was nothing to save in his nature and she fired into his left eye and he fell back into the root cellar. She closed the double doors.

She would have to return the rifle to her father's. She would have to distract him somehow and put it back in his workshop where it belonged.

And then she would call . . . whoever.

Another missing boy.

Sooner or later they'd find him, the combination padlock in his pocket and they'd wonder. Who would do such a thing?

Such things.

Those things on the walls.

My god.

How had it happened?

It was a question she would ask herself, she thought, for a great many seasons after, as spring plunged into sweltering summer, as fall turned to winter again and the coldness of heart and mind set in for its long terrible duration.

PIECES

Ray Garton

I've been coming to pieces lately.

It seems that the more things come together in my mind, the more I come to pieces.

I've been in therapy for a long time, but it really hasn't seemed to help. Oh, sure, it's made me break down and cry a few times — something that men, in our society, aren't really supposed to do, no matter *what* Phil Donahue says — but it hasn't improved things any. I wasn't even sure why I was there in the first place, except that something just seemed ... wrong.

Just a few days ago, it hit me. It was like a lightning strike, like a sixties acid flashback or some sort of memory flash a Vietnam vet would have. My father hovering over me in bed in the dark of one rainy night, telling me that we were just playing a game, that's all, but a secret game, a *secret* game that no one else could know about, so I would have to keep it a secret, a deep dark secret, and tell nobody, *nobody*. But the game hurt. It hurt bad.

It came to me while I was sitting alone one night on the sofa in only my underwear reading a magazine article about child abuse, and it seemed to come out of that part of my brain that was only black, with nothing in it, like a blind spot in my eye. In fact, it *exploded* from that part of my brain and, at the same time, the fourth and fifth toes dropped off my left foot, which was dangling loosely from my knee and fell to the carpet with soft little tapping sounds.

Of course, that wasn't my only problem at the time. My wife had just left me because, as she put it, "You are un-understandable. There's something about you that is unreachable and untouchable and it seems to make you just as angry as it makes me sad. I can't take it anymore."

So she left. A few hours later, my right earlobe broke away and peeled off like a piece of dead skin.

But I guess that's getting off the subject, isn't it? Back to the secret games. I'm not sure when they happened or how long they went on. I'd never brought it up with my therapist. I'd stopped therapy some time ago because I figured I could sit home and cry for a hell of a lot less money, and the memory flashes did not start until my appointments stopped.

I had six weeks of vacation coming at work — I'm a shift manager at a power plant — and after my wife left me, I decided to take them all at once. I had nothing in mind, just . . . rest. A relief, I guess.

I remember something my wife told me. She said, "There's something inside you that you know nothing about and you have *got* to take a break, just take a vacation from your life and find out *what it is*!"

That wasn't my reason for taking the vacation. I was just tired. I mean, your wife leaves you, you get hit with some memory you hadn't conjured up since you were a kid . . . you deserve a vacation, right? So I took it.

To tell you the truth, I wasn't that concerned about my earlobe or my toes. I tossed them into the trash. No big deal, really. It hadn't hurt, there was no bleeding and I didn't even have a limp. But I admit I was surprised by the suddenness of their departure. But so what, right? A couple toes? An earlobe? Big deal.

So, I took the vacation. I had nothing in mind but to sit around the house and relax, do nothing. Watch TV. Watch movies on the VCR. Read. Sleep. Relax.

Then I got broad-sided by that memory, that . . . *thing*.

I put it out of my head, went out of the house and browsed through a video store and picked up half a dozen movies to watch. The video store was in a mall and, to pass the time, I decided to do some window-shopping.

It was outside a store called Art 2 Go that the next memory hit me. In the window, I saw a painting of a little boy who looked so innocent . . . and yet, there was something in his eyes that seemed so *adult*, so grown up and mature, and so very, very haunted.

My mind suddenly filled with the memory of my father holding me down on his lap, and I remembered the hard, throbbing thing beneath me.

My left hand dropped to the floor.

I stared at it as if it were an ice cream cone dropped by a child.

A fat woman with red-dyed hair and carrying a brown paper bag began to scream. She screamed and pointed at the hand and dropped her bag.

I swung the plastic bag of videos under my left arm, picked up the hand, and hurried away, hoping no one else had noticed. The woman's screams faded behind me.

I took it home with me, that hand, and put it on the coffee table, staring at it as I sat on the sofa. Suddenly, I didn't want to watch any of the videos I'd gotten.

But I put one in anyway. Just for the noise. I sat on the sofa, mostly staring at my hand on the coffee table. Occasionally, I looked up at the movie. At one point, I saw a screaming little child being chased down a hallway by a man whose big hands reached out like mitts to clutch the child's hair and—

—I suddenly remembered the time my father had done the same to me. The memory had come from nowhere, slamming into my face like a slab of concrete.

My right arm disconnected itself from my body and slid out of my shirt sleeve, falling to the floor with a *thunk*.

The child on television screamed, and was dragged backward to the bedroom.

My eyes widened until they were bulging.

My left arm plunked to the floor.

I began to cry uncontrollably. I couldn't help myself. The tears flowed and my body — what was left of it — quaked with sobs.

My father had done that very thing to me. He had done many *other* things to me, things that pranced around at the edge of my memory. I wanted to remember them, to bring them up . . . and yet, I did not, because they were horrible, far too horrible to hold up before my mind's eye for inspection.

I looked at the coffee table and saw my hand. I thought of my earlobe and toes. I looked down at the floor and saw my pale, disembodied arms.

And suddenly I felt sick.

I rushed, armless, to the bathroom and vomited for awhile, then hurried into the bedroom, assuming I had little time left.

In the bedroom, I had an electric typewriter set up on a small table. I managed to place a piece of paper firmly in the carriage with my mouth, then lean down and use my mouth to reel the paper in. Then, I began to type this with my nose. It has taken a long time.

But in that time, my mind has been working frantically with the memories that have been conjured up like bloated corpses from the bottom of a bog. In fact, just a few minutes ago, I remembered my father saying to me once, "Just pretend it's a popsicle, that's all . . . just a popsicle . . . suck on it like it's a popsicle." And then my right leg, from the knee down, slid out of my pantleg like a snake and thunked to the bedroom floor.

I've been trying not to think about it, trying to concentrate on what I'm doing, typing this as fast as I can with my nose, to tell whoever finds me what happened.

But another memory comes to mind, this one far worse than all the others, more painful, and

For Andrew Vachss: one of the last true heroes

RUSTLE

Peter Crowther

"Okay, where do we start?"

The man shrugged. "You tell me."

"Why don't you try to tell me what it's like."

"Tell you what it's like?"

"Yes."

"What what's like?"

"This other room."

"Well . . . it's a room. It's just . . . a room."

"You say it's just a room: what kind of room?"

"Kind of room?"

"Yes, is it a bedroom? Is it a—"

"No, it's not a bedroom. Not exactly."

"Not exactly? What do you mean by 'not exactly'?"

"There's no bed in it."

"Right. No bed. But you said 'not exactly'. Why?"

"There are things in there."

"Things?"

"Yeah, sleeping things."

"There are sleeping things in the other room?"

He nodded.

"What . . . like pajamas? Sheets? What?"

"No." A trace of exasperation. "Things!"

"Tell me what kind of things."

"I don't know what kind of things. I've not seen them. I've told you, I don't go in there."

"So how do you know there are things in there?"

"I've heard them."

"Doing what? Talking?"

The man giggled. "No, not talking."

"What then?"

"Sleeping."

"You've heard them sleeping?"

Another nod.

"What . . . like breathing? Snoring?"

"Yeah. Well . . . breathing, you know, breathing heavy . . . like you do when you're asleep."

The doctor looked over at the policeman. The policeman shrugged. The man between them rocked slowly, back and forth, his hands clasped between his knees.

"So when do you hear them, these things?"

He hesitated and then said, "When I take them a girl."

Doctor Malloy scribbled something on his pad.

"How many girls have you taken them, Edward?" The man sitting at the back of the room uncrossed and re-crossed his legs, the material of his uniform rustling in the stillness of the interview room.

The doctor looked up and leaned to the side, shaking his head. "I would rather you just let me talk to Edward, Inspector."

The policeman sighed and settled back on his chair.

"Can you answer that, Edward? Can you answer the Inspector's question? Can you tell me how many girls you've taken into the room?"

He sighed. "I've told you, I don't—"

"I know, I know . . . you don't go in the room."

"Right."

"So, how many girls have you taken into your room?"

"Eleven."

"Eleven girls?"

"Yeah. Eleven."

"You sound very sure."

"I am. I keep count."

The doctor made a note of Edward's use of the present tense and said, "When do you take them?"

"When? Like what time?"

"No, I mean how often."

"It varies."

"Why does it vary, Edward?"

"It varies because it depends on when they want another one."

" 'They' being the sleeping things, the things you haven't seen?"

"Yeah."

"They let you know when they want another one?"

The man nodded and looked around the room.

"How do they let you know that?"

"The room appears."

Doctor Malloy removed his glasses and pulled a handkerchief out of his trouser pocket, started to clean the lenses. "The whole room—just appears?"

"No, just the door."

"A door appears? All by itself?"

"Yeah."

"Where does it appear, this door? What is it like?"

"It's just a door. It's purple. A purple door. And it appears in different places. Sometimes it appears in the sitting room, sometimes in my bedroom. One time it appeared in the kitchen while I was cooking."

"The door just appears by itself? No walls attached to it?"

"Yeah, by itself." He chuckled. "You can walk right around it, right around the back." His face suddenly lit up and he chuckled again. "Like . . . like Doctor Who's telephone box."

"Is there anything around the other side?"

"No, there's just the door."

Doctor Malloy replaced his glasses and then tore a sheet of paper from his pad. He held out the sheet of paper to the man. The man accepted the sheet and looked questioningly. "I want you to draw me the door."

"Why?"

The question came back so fast that it surprised him. "Just draw me the door, Edward."

"I don't have a pencil."

The policeman rose to his feet slowly and removed a button-topped Biro pen from his jacket pocket. "He can have this," he said. The doctor nodded and Edward turned around to accept the pen.

As the man began to sketch, Doctor Malloy said, "Over how long have you been taking the girls?"

"Mmmm . . . ? About two months. Maybe three."

"Where do you get them?"

"From outside. From the streets. Nobody misses them."

"You persuade them to go back to your apartment?"

The man nodded without looking up. "Yeah."

"Do you take them back to have sex?"

The man stopped drawing and stared at the paper.

"I said—"

"I heard you."

"Well?"

"I suppose that's what they think we're going to do."

"And do you?"

"No!"

"Where are the girls now, Edward?"

"I told you, they're in the room. Behind the door." He threw the paper across at Doctor Malloy and tossed the pen over his shoulder at the policeman. "There!"

Doctor Malloy picked up the paper and looked at the carefully drawn door. It was like any door, a round handle, beading surrounding four inlaid panels, and a number between the two upper panels. The number was 17.

"This is very good, Edward."

The man did not respond.

"What's the number?"

"Seventeen."

"Yes, I can see that it's seventeen. What does it mean?"

"Mean?"

"Did you ever live in a house that had the number seventeen?"

The man thought for a minute and then shook his head.

"You're sure? When you were a child, maybe?"

"I'm sure."

Doctor Malloy slid the sheet into his pad. "So, you take the girls back to your room and then what?"

The man clenched his lips like a little boy trying to hold his breath.

"Do they see the door?"

"Of course they see the door!"

"And you open it and send them in?"

"Yeah."

"Do they go—do they struggle? Do you have to push them?"

"No. They just step inside."

"Don't they think that it's strange, you asking them to step through a door that's just standing in the middle of the apartment?"

He shrugged. "They haven't said so. I think maybe they've had stranger requests."

"What is it like inside the other room?"

"I—I haven't been all the way in."

"But you told us that you took girls into the room, Edward."

"I meant I took them up to the room. Not inside, just up to it."

"Have you never been inside at all?"

"Once."

"Is it different than the part of your own room that's around the other side of the door?"

The man nodded enthusiastically.

"So it's kind of like a magician's door?"

"Yeah, like a magician's door. That's just what it's like, yeah."

"How far did you go inside?"

The man's eyes opened wide and his bottom lip began to tremble slightly. "Nuhvurfah," he mumbled through clenched teeth.

"I'm sorry, I didn't catch that."

"I said, not very far."

"What's it like in there?"

"Dark. It's very dark. And big."

"Big? How big?"

"I don't know how big. But it is big. It stretches into the distance. And it smells."

"What of? What does it smell of, Edward?"

The man stared at the doctor. His eyes seemed faraway, lost in thought. "Dirt," he said at last. "It smells of dirt—you know . . . . " He waved his hands around and then clasped them tightly together. "And it smells of . . . of blood and warmth."

"Blood, you say. What does the blood smell like?"

"It smells like blood. How else—"

"No, I mean do you think it smells of blood because you know that there's blood in there?"

He shook his head emphatically. "No, I told you. I've only been in there once and I couldn't really see much."

"But you could see something?"

"Yeah."

"What could you see?"

"Shapes. Moving around."

"You saw these shapes when you went into the room by yourself?"

"Yeah."

"Do you see them when you put the girls into the room?"

He shook his head.

"Do the girls see the shapes?"

He shrugged. "They don't say anything if they do."

"You put them inside the door and then what happens?"

"The door closes."

"Do you close the door?"

"No."

"The girls?"

He narrowed his eyes and considered. "No, I don't think so."

"Do the shapes close the door?"

"They must."

"These shapes: what exactly are they like?"

The man shuddered involuntarily.

"Don't—Don't worry, now. Just take your time. Try to describe them to me."

"Heaps." It sounded like hiccups.

"Heaps?"

"Piles of clothes . . . washing."

"So, just blobs of . . . of material?"

He nodded. And then pointed quickly to a point on the floor behind where the doctor was sitting. "There," he said, "like that."

For a second, Doctor Malloy felt completely disorientated, so that, when he turned around, the grey and lifeless bundle on the floor some four or five feet to his side looked for all the world like one of the sentient and malevolent entities that the man had described. The thing seemed to hug the ground as if reluctant to leave . . . or, maybe, preparing to pounce.

But it wasn't a blob or a creeping thing. It was the crumpled raincoat that he had dropped across the chair behind the door on his way in. He swivelled around and looked at the door. There was the chair. There was nothing on it.

He looked back to the coat. It was some eight or ten feet from the door. He was sure he hadn't just dropped it on the floor. It was most unlike him if he had.

"Did you move my coat?" he said, turning his attention to the policeman at the back of the room.

The policeman frowned and jabbed a finger at himself. "Me? No, Doctor. Not guilty I'm afraid."

He looked at Edward. "Did you move my coat, Edward?"

The man shook his head fiercely.

Doctor Malloy shrugged.

The air conditioning gave the slightest rustling sound, like a cloth being pulled across something, being pulled away to reveal . . . .

"And then what happens?"

"What happens when?" The man seemed puzzled by the sudden question.

"When the girl has gone through the door." His voice was slightly louder now, drowning out the air conditioning.

"The door goes."

"It goes?"

"Yeah, goes. Disappears. Vanishes."

"And then what."

"I tidy up the flat."

"In what way do you tidy up?"

"Their clothes. I put their clothes into a cardboard box."

The doctor watched the man carefully, weighing up his words before he spoke. "Edward, where do the clothes come from?"

Edward frowned and jerked his head as if trying to fathom out a difficult problem. "From the girls."

"From the girls?"

He nodded.

"Do you have them take off their clothes when they get into your apartment?"

Edward shook his head.

"So they go into—they go through the door with their clothes still on?"

"Yes. With their clothes on."

He leaned forward slightly and lowered his voice. "Then where do they come from, Edward?"

"Come from?"

"The clothes. If you send the girls into the room fully clothed and, as you've already told me, you don't go inside the room, then how do you get the clothes back on your side of the door?"

"They . . . they're left outside the door."

"So how does it work? The door opens and something drops the clothes out on your side?"

"N—no."

"Do you go through the door and get the clothes?"

"I told you, I don't—"

"Then how do the clothes appear?"

Edward crinkled up his mouth tightly and stared into some unfathomable distance just over the doctor's shoulder.

"Edward, I want to help you. Do you believe that? Do you believe I want to help you?"

He nodded. "Yes."

"Then we must be truthful with each other, yes?"

"Yes, truthful."

"Okay. Do you kill the girls, Edward?"

Edward shook his head.

"Do you have the girls take off their—"

"No."

"—take off their clothes and then—"

"No!"

"—and then you kill them and you cut them up—"

"No!" He turned around to the policeman who watched him impassively. "Tell him . . . tell him I don't kill them . . . I—"

"—and then cut them up and get rid of all the pieces. Except for the clothes."

Edward was snivelling. "I never killed anybody. Really. I take them in there because the things want me to."

The doctor sighed and leaned aback on his chair. He waited for what must have been two full minutes and, when the man's sobbing had subsided, said, "And they just dump the clothes outside the door, right?"

Edward nodded and breathed in with a shudder.

"They leave the clothes and they go." He phrased it so that it wasn't a question. Edward did not respond. "Where? Where do they go? Where does the door go to when it leaves your apartment?"

"I—I don't know. I've never seen it."

"Why not? Doesn't that strike you as strange? This door keeps appearing and disappearing in your house and you never see it either arrive or leave? Can you understand how difficult it is for me to believe you, Edward?"

"Yes. I can see that. But it's all true."

The doctor scribbled something on his paper.

"I'm always asleep," Edward said.

The doctor stopped writing and looked up.

"I'm always so tired when . . . when the girls have gone through the door." He sighed heavily. "And I go lie down, sleep. When I wake up the door has gone and the clothes are left behind. I gather up the clothes and put them in a cardboard box."

"Is that the box we found, Edward?"

"Yes."

"Inspector, what clothes were in Edward's box?"

The man turned around and stared at the policeman. Unperturbed, the policeman read from a notebook lying open on his lap. "Nine pairs of women's underpants—G-strings, panties and the like—four brassieres, four suspender belts, six pairs of tights, six individual stockings, two headscarves, one beret, five sweaters, five blouses or shirts, two waistcoats, one dress, four skirts, five pairs of trousers—three are blue denim, one bright yellow, plus a pair of ski-pants—four coats, two zip-up jackets, six handbags, three pairs of baseball boots, one pair of sandals and seven pairs of shoes, two flat-heeled and five high-." He closed the notebook and nodded to the wall by his side. "There. All present and correct," he added.

Doctor Malloy looked to the wall. There was the box, brown cardboard, its leaves standing at angles to the sides. Draped over the front leaf was a pair of blue, lace-edged panties.

The policeman stood up, tutted and walked across to the box. As he nudged the panties back into the box, the air conditioning gave out a low thrum.

"And how many women did you estimate that to represent, Inspector?"

"We worked it out to at least eleven, working on the footwear," he said as he regained his seat.

The man had turned around again and was now watching the doctor. Doctor Malloy felt tense.

"Edward, when we came into your flat there was no door anywhere."

"No."

"But you had the girl with you."

"She was a policewoman."

"Yes, I know she was a policewoman, but you didn't, did you? You didn't know that."

"No."

"And we were listening to you talk to the policewoman. That's why we broke into the flat. Let's hear that tape now." He nodded to the policeman. "Inspector?"

The policeman got to his feet again, sighing, and walked across the holding room to turn on the cassette player.

"We've forwarded it to the part where you both reach the flat," Doctor Malloy said.

There was hissing and crackling, the sound of the material of the policewoman's sweater rubbing on the microphone, and the distinct rap of footsteps.

"God . . . is it much further?"

"Nearly there."

"I should bloody hope so."

"Yeah, nearly there."

"Twenty, you said, yeah? Twenty quid?"

"Yeah, I'll give you twenty pounds."

"And no funny business, right?"

"No funny business."

The sound of a key being placed in a lock and turned. Elsewhere in the room, the pipes surged and a sharp but soft breath came from the cassette player.

"What was that?"

"What was what?" the policeman said.

Doctor Malloy pointed at the machine. "That! A . . . a sigh or something."

"I didn't hear anything," came the response.

Doctor Malloy reached over and pressed STOP.

The machine stopped.

They listened.

Nothing.

Just the air conditioning rubbing and pulling, twisting and turning itself, like stretched fabric.

"Wind it back."

The policeman walked across to the table and rewound the tape. To Doctor Malloy, the high-pitched gabble sounded like the noise that came from his spin-drier as it tumbled his shirts around and around and . . . .

The policeman pressed PLAY.

" . . . there."

"I should bloody hope so."

"Yeah, nearly there."

"Twenty, you said, yeah? Twenty quid?"

"Yeah, I'll give you twenty pounds."

"And no funny business, right?"

"No funny business."

The sound of the key again, entering the lock, turning. But this time there was nothing else. Doctor Malloy settled back and listened. When he looked down at his hands, he saw they were white, grasping his pencil so hard that, as he released his grip, a sharp pain washed through his finger ends.

"I don't do funny business," the woman's voice said.

"I don't want you to."

"What do you want then?"

"I'll tell you when we get inside."

"No, I want to know now."

A handle being turned.

"No, I'll tell you inside. Look, the door's open. It's safe for you to come in."

Footsteps.

When the man's voice starts again, it sounds further away. "Look, nothing to be afraid of. Come in."

Slow footsteps. They stop and start, stop and start.

The woman breathes out and her sweater rubs the mike. "Look, I'm not sure about this."

More footsteps. "What aren't you sure about? Look, there's nothing here. Noth—It's gone!"

"What's go—"

A door slams and cuts off the last word.

"—king door. It's gone."

Hurried footsteps move away. The man's voice is distant again. "It's not here!"

The woman's voice is faint and urgent now, the feigned roughness completely replaced by a soft and insistent fear. "I think you'd better come up," she says amidst rustling noise.

"She's talking straight into the mike there," the policeman pointed out.

"Where was it?" Doctor Malloy asked. "The microphone?"

The policeman tapped his armpit. "There, nestled into her bra, just underneath her arm."

The doctor nodded.

"Now, please!" the policewoman's voice begs.

The man's voice comes back again, louder now. "It's not anywhere."

"What's not anywhere, love? Look, I told you no funny stuff, didn't I?"

Somewhere in the distance more footsteps sound, several sets, running, growing louder.

"Where is it?"

"Where's wh—"

"Where is it? Did you see it?"

Footsteps getting louder.

"Did I see wha—"

"Where is—"

The sound of thumping and breaking, splintering.

Footsteps now very loud. Several new voices. The sound of scuffling. Was it scuffling . . . that noise, that sibilant crumpling sound?

"I think you know the rest," the policeman said as he turned off the cassette player. He walked back across the room and sat down.

The man stared at his hands, rocking gently. "They knew," he said softly.

"What's that, Edward?" Doctor Malloy said. "They knew?"

"The things. They knew she was a policewoman. That's why they moved the door. They knew even before I did."

"So where is it now?"

"Wherever it goes when it's not in my flat."

"And where's that?"

"I don't know."

The air conditioning wheezed and fell silent.

✦ ✦

Frowning, Doctor Malloy watched two uniformed policemen accompany Edward Clegg down the corridor towards the cells.

Behind him, in the holding room, Inspector Andrews picked up a brassiere that had fallen out of the box. He must have knocked it out earlier. "Problem?" he asked.

"I don't know. Something . . . there's something about what he said."

"Like what?" The Inspector came out into the corridor pulling a packet of Gold Leaf cigarettes from his pocket and put one in his mouth.

"He didn't know his pick-up was a policewoman."

"So?"

"So why didn't he carry on the way he had done with all the others?"

Andrews blew out a plume of smoke and grunted.

"And where are the women?"

"He's got rid of them."

"Yes, but where? No signs of any struggles. No signs of any blood. And no sign of any bodies, despite the entire force combing the area for the past three weeks."

"So what are you saying?"

"Oh, I don't know."

"You're not telling me you believe him are you? That what he's telling us is true?"

"That's two questions. The answer to the first is yes, I do believe him. But, to the second, of course I don't believe his story is true. Only that he believes it is."

A shrill sound rang out and Inspector Andrews switched off the bleeper on his lapel. "Trouble," he said as he started to run along the corridor in the direction that Clegg had just gone. Doctor Malloy followed.

Just around the corner they reached the steps leading down to the cells. Two flights down, Clegg was sprawled on the floor, crying and fighting with his escort.

"I'll go down," Doctor Malloy said.

When he reached the men he said, "What's the problem, Edward?"

"I . . . I didn't tell you everything."

"Do you want to tell me now?"

Clegg sniffed and nodded.

"What is it that you want to tell me?"

"The things . . . when I wouldn't tell you how I knew they wanted the girls?"

"Yes."

"They whispered it to me."

"Now?"

"No, back at the flat."

The two constables looked at each other and raised their eyes.

"They whispered through the door?"

"No. The first time. The first time I found the door, I went through it."

"So the time you told us about was the first time that the door appeared?"

"Yeah."

"And you haven't been in there since?"

"No way!"

"Why?"

"Because of what they whispered. And that's why you can't put me down there." He nodded his head in the direction of the dimly lit corridor of cells now just one flight below where they were standing. In one corner, the corner where the overhead light was at its dimmest, a pile of towels lay jumbled against the wall.

"What did they say to you, Edward?"

"They asked me to bring them women. Told me if I didn't they would come and get me. They said they'd seen me now and so they knew what I looked like. They said I had to give them women and that if I didn't then they'd come and get them themselves."

Doctor Malloy waited.

Clegg looked at the impassive faces of the constables.

Doctor Malloy said, "And what else did they say?"

"They . . . they told me that they'd take me as well."

"Take you where, Edward?"

"Wherever it is . . . behind the door. They said they'd get me."

"They can't get you here, Edward."

The man looked up at the doctor and shook his head. "Yes they can," he said.

The constables led him away.

✦ ✦

"You think you should do this?"

"Yes. There must be something there that could tell us what he's doing with the women." Doctor Malloy pulled on his overcoat and wrapped it tightly around himself.

"But we've been through the place from top to bottom. There isn't anything."

The doctor shrugged. "I think I should take a look."

"You want me to have someone go with you?" Inspector Andrews handed a pair of keys on a ring to the doctor.

"No, I'll go by myself." He dropped the keys into his pocket and walked towards the exit.

Inspector Andrews was lighting another cigarette when the call came through. He listened to the voice on the other end of the line, frowning. He grunted an acknowledgement, replaced the receiver and stubbed out the cigarette.

When he got down to the cells the constables had cut the body down from the hot water pipes that threaded across the cell's ceiling.

"How?"

One of the constables held up a pink brassiere.

"Jesus Christ. You'd only just brought him down here," he said in exasperation.

The constable nodded and shuffled his weight from one foot to the other. "Nothing we could do, sir. You didn't ask us to stay with him. I asked him if he wanted a cup of tea or anything and he said yes. Few minutes later I brought the tea and there he was."

They all looked down at the body and then up at the pipes.

"Doesn't seem possible, does it?" the second constable said to nobody in particular.

The inspector shook his head.

The first constable was turning the brassiere over and over in his hands. "Funny," he said.

"Funny? I don't think it's fu—"

"No, not him, this!" and he held out the brassiere. "No make."

The inspector took it from him. "No make?"

"And no size details, either. There's nothing on it."

"Is it one of the items from the box?"

"I think so, yes. Where else would it have come from?"

"That's a very good question, Constable," he said. "More to the point, how the hell did it get down here?" He turned the brassiere in his hands and checked along the back straps. The constable was right. There were no manufacturer details on the garment at all. He looked up and said, "The other clothes still upstairs?"

The constables looked at each other. "We haven't moved anything," said the one who had made the discovery of the tagless brassiere.

Inspector Andrews stuffed the garment into his pocket and turned sharply around.

Doctor Malloy turned up his coat collar against the cold wind and ran from his car to Edward's apartment building. He went through the main doors, up the stairs two at a time and then stood outside Edward's door. The key felt strange in his hand. He inserted it into the lock, turned and pushed the door.

Walking inside, he was aware of something different.

The place was completely black. No light anywhere.

He turned to the wall at his side and flicked the light switch. As the room burst into brightness, he half-expected to see the door waiting for him. But the room was empty.

Doctor Malloy kicked the door closed behind him and put the key back in his pocket. The answer was here, he was sure.

Something was here, whatever it was. He could feel it.

He walked across the room to the kitchen and pushed open the door. Empty.

He felt his heart beating.

Get out, a tiny voice said deep in his brain. He ignored it and walked back across the room, stamping his feet on the floor and listening for any change in the sound.

Suddenly a telephone started ringing.

He looked around for the telephone, trying to pin-point the sound, but couldn't see one. Then he realized it was coming from the room opposite the kitchen. The bedroom. He walked across and pushed open the door.

Even in the small amount of light thrown in from the main room, he could see that the place was a mess. There were clothes everywhere.

The ringing was louder now and he saw the telephone. It was next to a lamp sitting on a small cabinet beside a bed which was strewn with shirts and trousers, socks and ties. He shook his head and flicked the light switch on the wall beside him. It didn't work.

He walked across the bedroom and lifted the receiver. He placed it by his ear but didn't speak.

The familiar voice of Inspector Andrews said, "Malloy?"

"Yes?" He stood with his back to the door and stared at the wall watching the line of light cast by the door shimmer on the wallpaper.

"Listen." The Inspector sighed. "Our man's topped himself."

"What? How?"

"Hanged himself with a bra."

"Oh, wonderful!" He pushed his hand into his trouser pocket and flicked his fingers against the key.

"But get this. None of the clothing has any manufacturers' labels."

"Huh?"

"Not one. None of the underclothes, none of the blouses or the jeans, not even any of the shoes."

Doctor Malloy watched the line on the wallpaper, the thin boundary between light and darkness, slowly move to his right. The door was closing.

He reached out and flicked the switch on the bedside lamp. The close light made him feel better. Safer, somehow.

"Malloy?"

"I'm still here." He pushed a pile of clothes onto the floor and sat on the cleared edge of the bed. "I'll tell you this . . . your boys ought to clean up after they check a place."

"Clean up? How do you mean?"

"Edward's bedroom. It's a mess. Clothes everywhere. Anyway—"

"Clothes everywhere? I'm not with you. The place was neat as a new pin when we left. And there weren't any clothes."

The door finally drifted shut with a soft click.

Doctor Malloy frowned. "No clothes? None at all?" He reached down and picked up a shirt. It felt faintly warm to the touch. He fumbled one-handed until he exposed the back of the collar. There was no label.

He turned his head to look at the door and felt something slip inside his chest. There were two doors.

One of them was the door that Doctor Malloy had come through when he entered the bedroom: the other was completely unattached to anything, standing a few inches away from the wall. It was purple and had the number 17 boldly emblazoned between two inlaid panels.

"It's here," he said into the receiver. But even as the words left his mouth he knew that the Inspector wouldn't respond. He leaned forward and looked under the table. The telephone wire had been torn apart. Several pieces of clothing were gathered around the two pieces of wire, and others—Malloy saw a striped regimental-style tie and a pair of green boxer shorts slide over the lamp socket—were slowly making their way towards his feet.

In front of the purple door, a pile of sheets was gathering—they were almost as high as the door handle.

He stood up and dropped the receiver.

There was a sharp tearing sound and the light went out.

Then, in the blackness, there was only the soft click of a door opening—though no new light was introduced into the room—and a flurry of insistent, excited rustling.

WHEN THE SILENCE GETS TOO LOUD

Brian Hodge

My name is Greg, son of Jerry, who was son of Luther, son of Jefferson . . .

Ho.

Sounds like a laugh now, and I guess that's appropriate. The joke's on us, the new patriarchs. That's what we were going to be. Reclaiming what we'd lost, what we were so eager to blame the well-meaning women in our lives for civilizing out of us.

But reclamation of any kind is too far beyond us now. All I have left is this testimony to the elemental man within, who must be quite amused by now, and to my own soul. At this point I can finally afford the honesty—it's cheap enough.

My name is Greg, father of Kyle.

In all honesty I can say I don't hate him.

Not yet, at least.

Give me another hour, once the cords have cut into me a little deeper, and then we'll see how I feel.

September weekend in the Minnesota woods: they had chosen the dates as if possessed by the foresight of visionaries. The days bright, the weather fair, the nights dry. Roughing it had never been quite so pleasant.

Eight fathers and eleven sons, daughters left behind to tend hearth and home. Leave them to kitchens with their mothers, while men and man-children communed with the timeless, to discover the unifying ancient within them all. Better they seek it now, at the threshold of puberty and younger, than to find themselves wandering emasculated through the ripening fields of young adulthood.

It was the least fathers could do: steer their sons from the missteps that had so handicapped themselves. The revisionist bibles of these patriarchs were newer tomes: *Iron John* and *Fire in the Belly,* read and reread aloud to one another during weekly groups held in basements like tribal councils, and if a passage of great personal relevance brought a lump to the throat, or tear to the eye, that was well and good. Better still, a blessing. For they were men, and they were there for one another.

Minnesota woodland beckoned cool and pure, and they rolled behind the wheels of 4x4s and Suburbans. The rowdy youngsters, all between six and eleven, were gangly raw bundles of energy and nerves, tipped with burning fuses of caffeinated sodas and their healthy love of sanctioned mischief and a break in routine: their fathers had pulled them out of half a schoolday of Friday classes.

Greg Fischer walked among the newly-disembarked sons with a canvas bag held open wide. "Okay, that's it, turn 'em off. No more Gameboys until we head back Sunday evening. Drop 'em right here, that's it."

The order was at best grudgingly accepted, as if to merely contemplate the severance brought on symptoms of withdrawal. Kyle, ten, surrendered his most willingly, looking at his father and the bag with nonchalance that approached defiance. Saying, as it were, *See Dad, it doesn't hurt.* The boy had been like that all his life. After spankings, even. A kindergartner at stiff attention, glaring through brave tears like some proud five-year-old POW, announcing that it hadn't hurt, because he'd tightened up his bottom.

Supplies were unloaded, and tents pitched beneath pines that towered with the stately dignity of those who can afford to be so utterly indifferent to time. So lofty over men and boys and their air of the moment, breathe it quickly or it's stale.

Evening was quick upon their heels, then a night whose depth they never saw from their front doors. Theirs was a view fit to be witnessed from the mouth of a cave, the forest gripped by a deeper chill, dry and crisp, lit by the cool suns of other worlds, while nightbirds called and nocturnal paws were heard, never seen. They were surrounded, and it was holy, and they knew themselves to be its masters. Dominant males, naturally.

They dined on steaks, grilled over an open fire and foil-wrapped potatoes thrust into the glowing embers. Sodas for the kids, beer for the fathers, and if the boys begged for a taste of the brew — forbidden at home by their mothers — out here it was okay. Out here there were no rules but instinct. Fitfully they drank, then tore the cans away from grins wide or hesitant, and seemed more proud of the resultant watery belches than anything.

"All right, guys, listen up," said Charlie Draper. "This next part is one of the most important rituals we'll be doing this weekend." In the workaday world Charlie tested eyes and fitted contact lenses. "We call this . . . The Naming of the Lineage. Because I tell you this, guys, if you don't know where you've come from, you can't ever really know who you are."

"And if you don't know who you are," added Zack Deitz, "then how you gonna know where you're *going?* Am I right?"

They ringed the fire with their bodies. Some standing, some squatting, some sitting on camp stools or lawn chairs brought from home. The fire and its steady crackle a beacon for their hearts, souls. Fathers' eyes wide as they beheld it like a pagan oracle, and so mesmerized, they began:

"My name is Charlie, son of Mitchell, son of Dean," said Draper.

"Ho!" cried the rest, a deep bark of masculine approval, and then Charlie lay a soft hand on his nine-year-old's shoulder, nodded down to him.

"My name is Chris, son of Charlie . . . son of Mitchell, um, son of Dean."

"Ho!"

Turning back to his father, then, both of them beaming from myopic eyes. On around the circle:

"My name is Greg, son of Jerry, son of Luther, son of Jefferson." The names became arcane words from a conjuring spell, spoken amongst the assembly with a reverence that gave them their power. While they had always meant something to Greg, something bordering on the sacred, there was no denying that out here under trees and night they meant far more.

"Ho!"

The pride became a living entity; he could feel it in his chest, his throat. Even before he had identified this longing, all he'd ever *really* hungered for, of lasting significance, was to pass down his heritage to a succeeding generation.

He had sired well — this seed before him, grown so tall. Made so like him in his own image. And then again, so not.

Greg nodded.

"My name is Kyle, son of Greg, son of Jerry, son of Luther, son of Jefferson."

"Ho!"

On around the assembly it went, names pealing like the chimes of bells, in voices high and low. Once the patriarchal roads that had brought them all to this night had been named, several of the fathers went to the vehicles to retrieve the drums. And bring them round the fire.

Cheaply made, most of them. Inferior hide stretched taut over inferior hollows, and lashed firm with rawhide. Men who, in their family lives, were more at home in offices and stockrooms, garages and boardrooms, sat joyfully in the dirt, bellies full of warm meat and cold drink, and haphazardly pounded out simple rhythms in celebration of themselves and the night.

Greg looked up from his drumming to grin at Kyle, who rolled his eyes as he watched his father leap up. Thrusting the cudgel at his son, passing the torch, then sitting him at the drum to carry on, while Greg massaged kinks from his lower back, then hurled himself toward the fire. Arms and legs in abandon, to tread a shuffling path around the blaze with the bolder of the others.

He found dance a language beyond race, beyond time. So very human, on fundamental levels best left open to hear the whispers and roars of the divine.

Greg just hoped his knees would hold out.

For tomorrow would be grand.

Tomorrow they would hunt.

It comes upon you when you're out like this, away from the city, or even the smallest of towns: the sense of walking through something ageless, that you'll never understand. And in its eyes you're no more than a maggot, squirming in the home you've made in the carcass of what used to be more wilderness, and has since become pavement and tract housing.

I suppose, as fathers go, I'd been lax about exposing Kyle to this other world. Always figured there'd be time. Sure, we'd driven past it, and I'd turn around and chew him out from behind the wheel if he pitched trash out the window. Sure, he'd seen it on TV, in movies. But never first-hand.

So I have to wonder if maybe. After ten years, the first time a kid comes face-to-face with unspoiled wilderness he isn't hit a lot harder than his old man.

And, since there's less wilderness each passing year, if whatever spirit it is in the forest that makes us feel so humble gets a little more concentrated for every acre it's forced to retract in upon itself.

It's a theory.

Morning found grumpy risers among fathers and sons alike. Coffee was passed around with a value higher than gold. Bacon and eggs sizzled in skillets while, hunters all, they dressed for the day.

Zack Deitz was the unofficial leader of Saturday's hunt. He owned the most guns.

"We're going after a deer or two today," he called out for the benefit of the boys. "And I bet cash money not a one of you fellows has ever stalked a deer before. Am I right? Lemme see the hands of my experienced hunters."

None were raised.

"Do squirrels count?" asked one boy, finally.

Zack grinned, fist over heart. "You bet they do. But a deer's different. Squirrels, they don't look at you with big brown eyes, and I don't want any mama's boy crying about Bambi, you hear me? Used to, the man was the *hunter* of the family. If the man didn't go out and bring back the meat, the family went hungry. Now we can buy it all nice and bled clean for us, cut and wrapped in plastic and kept nice and cool . . . but it's not the same. Boys, I tell you . . . getting so I can't even bring myself to eat a package of meat my wife brings home from the supermarket. Just doesn't *taste* right anymore . . .

"'Cause nothing tastes better than your own kill. That's why we're here. So we can remember what's it's like to be hunters."

One tentative hand was raised. "Sir?"

"Yeah, Bobby?"

"Deer season doesn't start for another few weeks."

Zack Deitz grinned with wicked arched eyebrows, patted the stock of his Remington. "The deer doesn't know that. The rifle doesn't either." He shook his head, spat tobacco juice over one shoulder. Getting deadly serious again. "You think the Indians used to care if it was deer season or not? The hunters that used to live in caves, you think they cared about some rule called deer season? That's the problem today, too many rules about things that got *no* business having rules made about 'em. You can't put a rule on hunger. Can't put rules on eating. It's not natural. We're here because we obey a law that runs a whole lot deeper than any rule some game warden says."

They were off in a quarter-hour, some with rifles, others unarmed and tramping along merely for the thrill of the hunt. It was a miracle that this platoon did not drive away all wildlife well in advance of its own footfalls. But at last:

The sighting of the white bobtail flashing through the trees, strong thin legs bounding with a grace bestowed only by nature . . . and taken with speed so remotely fierce it could only belong to man. Heavy recoil of rifles into shoulders, rolling crack of the shots and the powder smell thick in their nostrils, gunsmoke wreathing heads like victory laurels.

The sanctified hush of life in the forest come to an abrupt standstill as the deer paused, stunned into insensibility, wounded above the front shoulder. It staggered forward, once, twice, its hesitant attempts to walk reminiscent of a fawn's, then buckled onto its side with twitching legs. Its bowels jetted mortality and the deer fell still. The hunters gathered, holy mass in a green cathedral.

Zack Deitz slit the animal's throat with a heavy knife, pulled the triangular head back to widen the slash, and the blood spilled rich and hot.

As one by one, the boys lined up to have him trace a bold streak of red along each cheek.

Victors, they returned to camp with the field-dressed deer lashed to a stout greenwood branch, borne on shoulders. Men and boys alike stepped jauntier than hours before, little weariness left considering their hours of tramping through the woods.

"Dad?" said Kyle, walking alongside. While the deer was being gutted he'd amused himself by borrowing a knife to sharpen a branch into a crude spear, and now carried it back to camp. Point up, but there would be no chastisements. *Don't carry it that way, you'll fall and put an eye out* were words left at home.

"Yeah?" said Greg.

"Did the deer hurt much?" He spoke with a ten-year-old's near-clinical fascination with mortality. Kids could so often distance themselves at that age.

"Some. But not for long. It was over quick."

"Do you think it minds that we'll eat it?"

Greg smiled, his sense of fatherhood warming over an entirely new fire, too rarely stoked: he, a mentor whose wisdom was sought to make sense of a world where there were but two classes; victor and vanquished. "It doesn't think that way, like we do, Kyle. Out here almost everything's food for something else. There's a simple beauty in that. and if that's the fate an animal meets, well, most of the time it'll give up. Instinct tells it to accept."

Walking side by side, Kyle turned this over in his mind. Then: "Do I have to wash the blood off my face when I get home?"

Greg nodded. "I think your mom would appreciate that, don't you?"

"How come? If I bring something home from school — a paper or like that? — she sticks it on the refrigerator. How come this is different?"

Greg laughed. At Kyle's age they all had a concept of logic and justice that was so simple. Wonderful in theory, essentially unworkable in its purity; too bad. "It just is. Moms don't understand things like getting blooded after your first hunt."

"So . . . if we don't get to *look* any different when we go home . . . what's the good of coming out here at all?"

Greg patted him on the chest, then had to look twice at him. Such a change, the addition of two streaks of red on his cheeks. Above them Kyle's eyes were an older boy's, and, surprisingly, it was not such a welcome sight after all. The first true foretaste Greg had had of someday being handed his walking papers.

How bitter, how sweet. To do your job right meant to strive for your own eventual obsolescence.

He patted Kyle's chest again. "So you can feel it in here. Where it really counts."

Kyle nodded, reluctant, anything but convinced. He found a scattering of fallen leaves, kicked them with petulance. "Sucks," he said quietly.

Greg found a certain wisdom in that, too.

The camp was split that evening when dusk claimed the forest for its own. Two fires blazed in rings of stone; the boys had wanted one for themselves, and their fathers heartily agreed it was a fine idea. Men in the making, were they not?

Kyle watched his father and the others, some thirty feet away. Boisterous and frequently roaring with hilarity, all of them hoisting beers and indulging in back-slapping intimacy. Talking of the closing baseball season, the coming football season. Women on TV and in the movies. Prostate glands.

Kyle turned back to their own fire, smaller . . . yet somehow a more thoughtful fire. Chad Deitz tended and fed it with devotion that bordered on the religious. They gazed quietly into its depths, muted orange light reflecting from solemn faces. The hard glint of eyes, the dried maroon rite of passage still streaking every cheek, lifeblood of an animal which had forfeited itself to feed their bodies for a night, their spirits forever.

"What do you think Hell's like?" Kyle asked.

The other ten looked at him. Some quizzical, some surprised. A couple of the youngest with hesitant awe: he had said a word they were not allowed to speak at home.

"In Hell I bet you have to stay after school every day," said Chris Draper.

"The weather's always your least favorite season," this from Bobby Reinsert.

"They make you eat seconds on vegetables," Chad Deitz said, then his brother Matt shoved his shoulder and said, "No, all they serve is Brussel sprouts!" And one and all were repulsed.

Adam Golding made his bangs cockeyed with his fingers. "If you get a dumb haircut, it never grows out again."

"Then *you're* in Hell *already!*" his older brother Coy said.

"And they never let you see the end of your favorite TV shows," came another voice from the outer circle, and this thought seemed to wound them as none other. Then they all laughed, at first skittishly, then with more assurance. Self-awareness.

A small shift in wind sent woodsmoke drifting toward Kyle's face, and he shut his eyes. Breathed it, did not cough. Like his lungs were *made* for it, drew something from it that older lungs could never strain.

How warm would it be tomorrow? Just once he would like to strip away his clothes, cover himself head to toe with mud, crouch still and silent beside quiet waters and see what his reflection looked like. The woods did that to you, he figured. Made you think of things you'd never even consider at home. Like a song you could never hear as long as a roof hung over your head.

Out here you were forced to listen . . . which was okay, because you *wanted* to. Not like school, where you had no choice and some days that made you want to throw some teacher down the stairs for it, just for underestimating you. Treating you like a baby.

The darker it got, the louder that song played. And these wusses got shook up by the thought of missing the end of their favorite shows?

"I think in Hell," said Kyle, very slowly, and even the two eleven-year-olds in their circle quieted and paid attention, as if the right to speak had always been his, "you have to grow up and listen to a million people telling you what you should be like, no matter how stupid it sounds. And you can tell just by looking at them they don't know what they're talking about."

Silence; just the feeding fire and the loud wet laughter from thirty feet away.

Kyle hitched a thumb over his shoulder, and the others looked at their fathers, who they were. Illuminated by the fresh light of old wisdom and young eyes.

"They're full of shit, you know."

And the other boys shrugged, then gave sheepish nods, one at a time, even the littlest ones, as if, yes, they'd known that all along.

When I was in college, in my fraternity, we used to have very concrete ideas on what separated men from boys. Most of them involved alcohol, and the number of pubic scalps you claimed to dangle from your belt, belonging to members of our sister sorority or women we met at parties or the Greek bars.

We were wrong. I recognized that in time. But I miss those days, if not for their ideals, at least for their simplicity. We had an outlook and we stuck with it. It was only when I was out in the real world that it all got so confusing.

Trying to find out what it meant to be a man, what answer would satisfy everybody. Going through life, then, attempting to become the epitome of the sensitive male, and wondering why so many women still seemed attracted to the abusers and reprobates. Becoming one on those for a while, and wondering why I felt so lousy about myself. Starting a family, finally, and wondering why I woke up one day and realized I never truly knew what I was.

But realizing I wasn't alone. A lot of others out there were just as confused as I was. For so long we'd been told who and what we were, what the women in our lives wanted us to be . . . was it any wonder we eventually turned to one another? We all sought that elemental male, that primal hairy man, buried inside each of us and who had been stilled for so long that we'd come to find his silence deafening.

How sure we were of ourselves, that we knew how to recapture the elusive bastard. Through shared memories and celebration of our fathers and grandfathers, through ceremony and ritual.

Ho ho ho.

We were as lost as we ever were. Worse, I think. Because we didn't know it. The idiot with the wrong map is usually worse off than the idiot with none.

How clear that must have been to our sons.

Who saw, instead of patriarchs, pretenders.

And how clear that must have been to the primal man, buried so deep, beyond the reach of neurosis. The primal hairy man who looked out from within us all and recognized only in whose hearts he would find the warmest caves.

Dawn brought perplexity, confusion, and finally panic.

Fathers awakened to discover that their sons were missing, all of them, from the oldest to the youngest. Sleeping bags still conformed to the earlier shape of their bodies, but no longer held their warmth.

Amid the mounting babble of fathers' voices — some charged with grave annoyance, others worry — Greg tried his best to remain a center of calm. There was a reason for this, all they need do was look for hints as to what the boys might have done.

Had they gone hunting on their own? someone asked. Unlikely. No guns had been taken. Gone off somewhere for a more private breakfast, a continuance of their own solitary little powwows from last night? Again, unlikely; the food supply was unpilfered.

Someone suggested wolves, and even though it was a perfectly ludicrous explanation, it nevertheless gave them a moment's taste of supreme terror. Minnesota's woods were home to well over a thousand, and they could be heard at night this far north, their cries from the very heart of desolation. Only after that initial grip of unease was the ridicule heaped, but the moment was enough: the damage had been done to their nerves.

"Hey. Look. What's with the drums?" Charlie Draper was over by one of the Suburbans, fists on hips, looking down in confusion.

Their tribal drums lay in an unceremonious jumble. Hollows open top and bottom, the stiff hides beside them like a pile of discarded tissues.

"The lacings," someone said. "They took the rawhide lacings."

Zack Deitz swore. Boys will be boys, they all knew that, all cherished that. But desecrating the drums, now that was just too much to tolerate.

Fathers' voices took to the air, calling for their sons, then waiting, calling again. Never a reply. The boys were either out of earshot or were refusing to answer, and Greg passed the next hour with urgently mounting distress as they fixed their breakfast eggs and sausages and coffee while waiting for their sons to return. Perhaps the scent of food would lure them back.

An hour, though, was quite enough, by unanimous quorum. This had ceased to be cute. Or funny. Or dismissed as the serendipity of youth. This was rude and disrespectful, and any kid thinking it would be tolerated had another thing coming.

They would go out and find their sons, bring them back like men, fugitives to face their crimes. They needed someone to linger back at the camp, though, in case the wayfarers slipped past their fathers and returned unseen. Someone would have to keep them here. Brent Piercy was chosen, since he had bunions, and blisters from yesterday's hunt. He seemed relieved.

The other seven laced their boots and began a northerly trek, back into that deeper woodland walked yesterday. There was much talk of what to do once the boys were found. Cutting the weekend short with most of Sunday before them would suit the crime, if they were here primarily for the boys' sake . . . but what a shame to penalize themselves that way. Hell, this was God's country.

Make the boys sit out the rest of the day in the vehicles, then. Time out, like a penalty box. Without their damn Nintendos.

On they walked, north, driven almost by instinctive impulse, some deep-rooted knowledge that this was the direction their sons had gone. As if they could smell the passage lingering in the air, a scent trail left by bodies they had seen grow from tiny babies, small enough to be seated in a cupped pair of father's hands.

So much forest, so much. Greg found it easy to liken it to the imponderables of deep space. The slippery chore of trying to grasp the idea of space going on forever, without containment. No wall or boundary ahead to mark its end, the beginning of something new. Just more of the same, eternally. Like these trees, coaxed ever higher by the pull of decades and centuries, and the forest floor, rich with the rot of forever.

Greg felt the pendulum swing, a slow passage of hours marked by the shortening of the trees' shadows, until they were but dark puddles beneath a noonday sun. Then they began to lengthen again, in the opposite direction. Shadows reaching for the cusp of night, and the longer they got, the more it seemed that everyone out here was a babe in the woods.

The fathers began to find the clothes in late afternoon — a shoe tossed here, a shirt dropped there—and the growing catalogue of punishments began giving way to a hunger to simply clutch their sons again. Hold them close, smell them, rub in the reassurance of their existence.

"This is Chad's," said Zack Deitz, of a small blue sweatshirt held in both hands. Looking up, then, at the others, so much unsaid, but then, where was the need? They were all feeling the same things. "Getting late, we better split up . . ."

Greg went wherever Deitz pointed him; Deitz was the hunter, Dietz should know. The wisdom of fatherhood, to Greg, seemed in this moment very much an inflated concept. His son was missing and he could not take charge, wishing only for someone more skilled than he to tell him where to look, what to do. Wanting a stronger back than his to bear this terrible apprehension.

Walking. Walking. Feet crunching leaves, twigs, the shadows straining before him even as he watched. Daylight didn't just die in woods this deep—it was murdered, and bled black. Hearing, near and far, voices of fathers calling for sons. Supplanted, though, by the more distant howls of some wolfpack. A chorus shrill and mournful fit to chill the spinal fluid of any two-footed listener, overlapping into a tapestry of savage eloquence, and a nobility which these seekers of the primitive could never hope to touch.

He was going in circles. Snagging himself on thorns and underbrush, staring at trees whose spread of branches looked familiar. Had he passed them just five minutes ago, ten? Made different now, though, by waning light? New shadows came to fill the void? While even the voices of his brethern dwindled.

He turned his head. Off to his right, a sound, faint. The tender whimper of a child, frightened by evening and crouching in guilt? Greg broke his hesitant stride, tore past trees and ferns and rotting logs, and the sound grew louder, he was homing in with unerring accuracy—

And found him. Charlie Draper, the optometrist nearly blind without his glasses. Tied against a tree, back-first, so tightly he might as well have been moss. Blinking madly, and words were beyond him, Greg could see that now. A rawhide strip had been lashed so tightly across the corners of his mouth that his lips were skinned back over his teeth in a painfully grotesque rictus.

Impulses were many and conflicting: To help, to run, to seek out the others. But in the wild, Greg dimly understood, such a moment of hesitation often becomes the terminator line between victor and vanquished.

And just before they blindsided him, to make swift work of his skull and knees with their crude bludgeons, he at least caught glimpses: flashes of their young bodies, quick and lithe, thickly caked with mud. And their eyes, crazed by some hunger that went deeper than bellies.

When he awoke, Greg realized he was in the same predicament as Charlie Draper had been. Made a part of some tree, tied around the torso and legs with vines; arms stretched around back, wrists lashed together on the far side of the trunk. The rawhide lacing around his wrists and face and neck had been tied while wet, very tight, and Greg sobbed. As it dried, it would begin to shrink, and tighten even more. Painful? Excruciating would be no exaggeration before long. Where had the boys learned that trick? Had it just come to them? Had they tilted their heads to the night and trees, and listened?

Then he remembered: Someone had, when they were making their drums, said the finished instruments would be far more resonant if the rawhide heads and lashings were soaking wet when tied over the frames.

The suggestion had been voted down—too much time before they'd be able to start pounding them.

Greg was guessing he and the rest had been tied far from one another, for better isolation. He remembered seeing the boys passing through the trees, once, before he'd come fully conscious again. Retaining this image of them, thin and spindly-legged, somehow more powerful in their nudity, total or near, than they had ever appeared when he'd seen them in Little League uniforms. Smeared with mud, they looked to be from another culture entirely, and a few carried torches made from branches and leaves, and rags that might once have been clothing.

And of course, they gave deference to a chieftain.

My Kyle.

What we, as fathers, had hoped to find out here, maybe it came effortlessly to our sons. As much as it hurts to admit it, maybe we were too far gone.

Or maybe what we'd hoped to find is more sentient than I ever gave it credit, and by force or stealth it took our sons, mind and heart and soul. Whispering to them in the night, in their dreams.

Or maybe we just drove them crazy ourselves, with our sad games.

Whatever happened to them, should I hate our sons because they fulfilled our purpose the only way that made sense to them? Isn't mythology full of elders usurped by their sons?

Maybe it's best this way, that they start by making a clean break, claiming their heritage by force. And leaving us, their sacrificed fathers, to rot on our trees, our bones like primitive totems to remind them where they'd come from.

And so I wait. Strangulation and dehydration will claim us long before any searchers will find us.

And so. I wait. Still unable to hate my son.

Hoping only that, before I die, I can at least manage to find that long-lost child inside myself. Turn him loose, set him free.

Because it's never too late to learn.

THE RABBIT

Jack Pavey

I've been living under this bridge for awhile now, or at least I do when no one bigger than me shows up. It's not that bad. I've got a couple of blankets I found, and with a few bottles of cheap port wine, I can manage the dreamless sleep I need to keep sane. I can't say how long I've been here, because the last time I looked at a calendar and saw how long it had been since it all happened, it scared me into a two-week drunk that put me in the charity ward. Mirrors are starting to bother me too. When you no longer recognize the face staring back at you from a mirror, it's time to go to the liquor store by the bus station, and get a couple more bottles of Dr. Port's Forget-It-Fluid. It works most of the time, except for the memory I've been trying to kill the most — Benjy and the rabbit.

It stays with me, this memory; a hard, steel ball centered in my brain. It pulses with heat, enough to pop my eyes and ears open, and unless I blur my vision and dull my senses, it will play it all out, starting with the final scene.

I'm standing outside our house, trying to make sense of what just happened, somewhat hypnotized by the spinning funhouse shadows created by the flashing red lights of the police cars and ambulances in the street. I hear the muffled thump of a gunshot from inside the house, and I feel like I'm moving in slow motion as I run up the porch, down the hall and burst into Benjy's room. He's lying there, crumpled on the floor, with a genuine death-grip on the old Colt .45 pistol his uncle gave him. On one temple, he wears a small, black hole about the size of a

nickel, and it's breathing tiny wisps of charcoal smoke. The contents
of his skull are caked on the adjacent wall like so much neon offal, the
shape and shade of a melting stop sign.

Earlier that summer, Benjy and I had rented a small, battered house
in an old residential area near downtown. The ink was barely dry on
our college diplomas, but we lucked out and found some fairly good
paying jobs right away; his in programming, mine in sales. We had just
moved in the last stick of furniture, a thrashed thrift-store sofa, when
Mrs. Randall paid us her first visit.

"Hello?" She was standing on her tiptoes, outside the screen door,
like she was looking over a wall, or couldn't see us for some reason.
"Hello?" she said.

We dropped the couch, and Benjy, being closer to the door, turned
to greet her. "Hi, I'm Ben." He put on the toothy smile that he had
always used to placate his parents. "Won't you come in?"

"No . . . I can't . . ." she mumbled. "It's your dog . . . in our back
yard . . . it's scaring the children . . . and Mr. Wigglenose." Benjy popped
out the door and followed her off the porch.

"Don't worry about Buck, ma'am. He loves children, and I'm sure
he wouldn't hurt Mr. Wiggly." He was doing his Eddie Haskell
impersonation and made a goofy face at me as they walked by the living
room window. I went back to moving the furniture in place and a few
minutes later, Benjy, with his black labrador in tow, burst back into the
room.

"What a basket case!" He went to the fridge and pulled out a beer,
while Buck bounced around the room.

"What's wrong with her?" I asked. "She looked like the standard
housewife type."

"Well, besides being a contender for the Ms. Anorexia title, she has
these dark, sunken eyes, and she won't even look at you when you're
talkin' to her."

"Who's Mr. Wiggles?"

"Mr. Wigglenose to you, sport." Benjy took a slug of beer. "Mr.
Wigglenose is a rabbit that must have committed some heinous crime.
They've got him in a bunny jail out in their backyard." I flopped down
on the couch, laughing. Buck, who was performing a sniff search of the

house, came over and put his head on my knee, looking for a head pat. Buck was almost three years old, but he had never lost his playful, energetic puppy personality.

"How old are the kids?" I asked, treating Buck to a backscratch.

"Four or five, maybe. A boy and a girl, cute as buttons, both of 'em. I guess they're in big trouble with mommy right now."

"What for?" I asked. Benjy paused, and scratched his head.

"I don't know. Maybe because they didn't run down the street, howling like banshees when the big, nasty dog jumped the fence. The last time my folks yelled at me like that was the time I set the garage on fire. Hey! We gotta make a beer run!" He flipped his empty at the trash and missed.

"I'll buy, if you fly," I offered, digging into my pocket.

"Best offer I got all day." We trooped out the door, Benjy gripping Buck's collar. He started his old Volkswagen, and tore off down the street, Buck riding shotgun with his head out the window, his ears and tongue flapping in the wind. I turned to head back inside, and was hailed by someone's grandmother from next door, on the side opposite of the Wigglenose residence.

"Hello, young man. Did you get all moved in?" She was standing at her door; a short, rotund woman with a somewhat squashed face and a deep, maternal smile etched beneath her thick spectacles.

"Well, we got everything in, ma'am." I walked over toward her yard. "But it'll be a few days before we get everything unpacked and in order." We stood there for a few moments, smiling and nodding and sizing each other up as neighbor material. I broke first.

"My name is Dan; that was Benjy and Buck who just took off."

"Which one is the dog?" I did my best to keep from busting out laughing.

"Buck's the dog, and don't worry about him, he's just a big puppy. Doesn't bite, bark or have fleas." At that , her smile grew a little wider.

"Well, now. That's nice. My name is Nina Parker, and if there's anything I can do for you boys, why you just let me know, Dan."

"Can you tell me about the people who live over there?" I hooked my thumb towards the rabbit lady's home.

"Oh, that's the Randall house." She turned her head and gave a couple mother-hen type clucks. "Poor dear, she had to go to the hospital for a while after that stinker of a husband left her." She stared at the

Randall house, shaking her head at the sadness of it all. "He was a drinker, and ran off with some cheap hussy."

"Uh, that's too bad," I agreed. "It was nice meeting you, Mrs. Parker. I gotta finish unpacking, so I guess I'll see you later." She backed into her house, still clucking and nodding about the state of the world, what with all the drinkers and hussys about, as I headed back to the new abode. The Madams Parker and Randall were gonna just shit when Benjy got his stereo unpacked and cranked up, I thought.

The next couple of weeks flew by, and Benjy and I settled into the nine-to-five routine with alarming complacency. We kept the stereo down so low that the walls and windows barely shook and even Buck seemed to take it easy and settle into adulthood with dignity. The three of us would be sitting in the small living room, me with the contents of my jammed briefcase scattered about, trying to make sense of the forms and paperwork. Benjy would sit at his computer, tapping out the equations that would win his next paycheck, and Buck would lay between us, yawning and farting, getting up occasionally to go on canine patrol around the house.

I got home from the salt mines one afternoon to find the slightly tweaked divorcee, Mrs. Randall, waiting for me in disarray, her skin pale, her eyes dark and wild. I got out of my car slowly, approaching her with my best salesman grin.

"Good afternoon. What can I do for—"

"That dog of yours! He's back and . . . I won't have it!" she snapped, refusing to look at me, scanning the ground between us angrily.

"I'm really sorry, Mrs. Randall." She gave me a quick, sharp glance at the mention of her name. "Buck is a very gentle dog, he's never hurt anybody or anything. If you just tell him to go home, he'll obey." I was bending over, with my head tipped back, trying to maintain eye contact.

"Vicious beast! The children . . . Mr. Wigglenose . . . I'll call the police!"

"That won't be necessary, Mrs. Randall. I promise you it'll never happen again." I took a step towards the old wooden fence that sectioned off her precious back yard from the rest of the world. "Buck! Yo Buck! Come here dog!" Two furry black paws appeared on top of the fence, and with a little rattle of weathered boards, Buck scampered over.

Mrs. Randall was not appeased.

"This will not happen again," she snarled. "I will not allow that beast to terrorize my family . . . This is your last warning!" With that, she stomped off, pausing to shake her index finger at the big picture window at the front of her house. I caught a glimpse of two small children with big expressionless eyes, watching us from inside. At her gesture, they disappeared into the depths of the living room shadows. Mrs. Randall entered her house, slamming the door hard enough to quake the glass.

"Sorry!" I called after her, but my voice was just an echo on the empty street.

Buck and I went home. I rummaged through all the empty cardboard six-packs that haunted our refrigerator, and finding an intact beer, popped 'er open and took a long drink. I heard Benjy's car roar up, and a moment later, he came through the front door.

"Honey, I'm home!" he said, in his best Jack Nicholson imitation.

"In here, Benjy." He walked around the corner and squatted down next to Buck. As he administered a chin scratch and head pats, Buck thumped his tail on the floor in approval.

"Why the long face, Dan?"

I relayed the story of the naughty dog and the nutty neighbor. "Whoa, she's a strange one," he said.

"No kiddin', it's just like you said, she won't even look at you when you're talking to her. She just stares at the ground. I just wanted to shake her; 'What is it? Lose your car keys? Drop some change?' Hey, our neighbor is a couple cans short of a six-pack."

"Any suggestions?"

"We gotta keep Buck inside, with us, or chained up. It's either that, or open a line of credit at the dog pound."

"I guess you're right," Benjy sighed. "The sad part is that Buck wasn't trying to hurt the rabbit, he just likes to watch it. The first time I went over there to get Buck, he was sitting next to the cage with the kids. They were all just sitting around, looking at each other like they were old friends or something." Benjy shook his head. "Mrs. Randall started barking at her kids like a drill sergeant, for no reason. It's the kids I feel sorry for. Can you imagine growing up with a mother who's a prime candidate for a strait jacket?"

In the back yard, there was an old clothes line that stretched from a dead tree to a bolt screwed into the rear garage wall. We unknotted the rope from the tree, and shortened it so that Buck, when tethered to the garage, was stopped a good five feet before he could leap over the forbidden fence. Buck was tied up before our departure for work, and set free upon our return; a routine we all grew accustomed to over the course of a week or two.

I came home one afternoon, to find the garage door open, Benjy's car inside, and Benjy under the hood. He was cussing and sputtering, as was his habit while working on the rusty block of iron that powered his ride.

"Don't fix it too much, Benjy, or you'll end up meeting your dates at the bus stop." He stood up and swiveled his grease-streaked face towards me.

"Har, har. Did you know that insulted mechanics wielding torque wrenches are the leading cause of brain damage?"

"To themselves or others? Got a cigarette?" Benjy chuckled, and pulled a wrinkled pack of smokes from his pocket. He was shaking one loose for me when Buck came trotting up, trailing a short length of frayed rope. In his mouth, he carried a wad of dirt-soiled fur, rabbit fur.

Benjy yelped, grabbed Buck by the scruff, and dragged him into the garage. I yanked down the door, and we bumped, banged, and thrashed in the dark, until I found the switch and flipped on the lights. Buck was sitting with the Wigglenose carcass between his front paws. His head was tipped to one side, and his tail twitched in the cold concrete floor like a dancing snake.

"Well, this is just great, Benjy. What are we gonna do now?"

"Shit, I don't know. What can we do?" He held up his hands as if to surrender.

"We can get ready for a visit from the cops. She said she'd call 'em the last time Buck jumped the fence."

Benjy picked up the rabbit and examined it carefully. "Let's clean it up and put it back," he said softly.

"Uh, Benjy . . . I think you're missing a couple wrenches out of your toolbox. Don't you think they'll notice that their pet isn't eating much or moving around?"

"Check it out, Dan." He held Mr. Wigglenose up to me, and I took a step back. "No blood, no broken bones, no marks at all, except it's dirty. We brush out the dirt and put it back in the cage." Benjy took a deep breath and continued. "Hey, goldfish always end up floating in their bowl, and parakeets have been known to drop off their perch.

Small pets are constantly dying, and my guess is that's what happened here."

"What if Mrs. Randall sees you put it back?"

"Mrs. Randall left with the kids about fifteen minutes before you got home." We studied each other for a minute, intently.

"Let's do it," I said.

We went to work on Mr. Wigglenose. Attempts to brush out the dirt failed, as it was mixed with dog drool and just smeared around. Benjy dunked it in the sink and gave it a rinsing. I got the hair dryer and gave the matted pelt a good blast. When we got Mr. Wigglenose looking good, Benjy leaped the fence with the dead rabbit while I stood watch at the front door. He returned after a very long minute.

"Benjamin and Daniel: bunny morticians," Benjy deadpanned, and we both broke out into laughter. It wasn't the laughter of good humor and fellowship; it was the high-pitched, hysterical cackle of small boys who just barely escaped the school bully.

"We should have put an empty bottle of sleeping pills in there with him," I said, "and a note that reads: 'Mrs. R., can't handle your sullen attitude. I'm checking out.'" More nervous giggles. This went on for nearly an hour, until we heard a car pull up and doors slam.

The laughter stopped abruptly, and we peeked out through the curtains like a couple of perverts. It was the Randall clan alright, the missus carrying a sack of groceries and her two little charges each carrying a smaller parcel. They entered their house, and the lights came on. We continued our peeping for a bit, and when nothing happened, we took a step back from the curtain and sighed in unison.

"What's the worst that can happen if we're caught?" I asked.

"How can we get caught?" Benjy replied. "I don't think there's a rabbiticide division at the S.P.C.A., and I've never heard of anyone getting popped for giving dead bunnies a bath and a perm."

"Just the same, let's stash Buck over at your sister's place for a few days. If Mrs. Randall calls the cops or something, we'll say Buck's on vacation and won't be back for a few years—"

"And if nothing happens in a day or two, Buck comes home and everything's back to normal," Benjy finished. We nodded in agreement. "Let me take a quick shower, and we're outta here." Benjy headed for the bathroom to scrub off the car grease he was still wearing.

I wandered around the living room for awhile, first thumbing through a magazine, then snapping on the television and giving the dial a 360 degree turn, but I couldn't get interested in anything. Something was bothering me about our covert bunny-replacement program that I just couldn't identify.

When Benjy left the bathroom and shut the door behind him, it came to me like a sharp jab to the solarplexus.

"Benjy!" He turned and looked at me from down the hallway. "How did the rabbit get out of the cage?" His eyes split wide open.

"Or, how did Buck get in the cage to get the rabbit?" he countered. Buck, upon hearing his name, slowly walked down the hall towards Benjy, his tail waving back and forth in the air like a surrender flag. We stood there for a moment.

BAM! BAM! BAM!

I jumped a foot-and-a-half in the air. Someone was beating on the front door, hard enough to bust it off it's hinges. Benjy squatted down and wrapped one arm around Buck's neck, and motioned with his free hand for me to get the door. I wanted to protest, but instead I turned and wrenched it open.

It was Mrs. Randall, her face convulsing with mania.

Her drab and lifeless hair now stood straight out from her head in twisted spikes, and her dark eyes shone with a gleam that frightened me. "I have . . . a problem," she said abruptly. "The rabbit . . . died." She was breathing hard, like she just finished a five mile run.

"I'm sorry to hear that," I said quietly, "if there's anything I can do—"

"YOU DON'T UNDERSTAND!" she shrieked. "IT DIED A WEEK AGO . . . I BURIED IT IN THE BACKYARD . . . NOW IT'S BACK IN IT'S CAGE . . . ALL CLEAN . . . FLUFFY!"

She had a string of saliva hanging off one corner of her mouth and I focused on it during her tirade, as I was unable to meet her eyes. When she finished, and the impact settled in, I felt shame grip my face like a red-hued fist. I tried to talk to her; I wanted to tell her everything was alright, but only a gibbering sound, faintly resembling human speech came out. With a wail, she turned and ran home.

Benjy came up beside me and gently pushed the door shut. "Hey man, are you okay?"

I couldn't answer. I felt as if I were just subjected to a massive electrical shock. I just nodded. "C'mon Dan, let's get outta here."

Benjy picked up my car keys from the table, and after a quick reconnaissance out on the porch, he led Buck and I to my car. We dropped Buck off at Benjy's sister's and proceeded to drive around aimlessly for what seemed like hours. When the gas gauge started falling towards the empty mark, Benjy pulled over. We had drifted back towards our side of town, and were parked in front of a small neighborhood bar. We had spent the last hour or so in silence, and when Benjy cleared his throat, I felt as if I had just woke up from a bad dream.

"I don't know about you, but I sure could use a beverage right about now," he muttered.

"Sounds good, Benj." We left the car and walked inside. *Murphy's Place*, the sign outside read.

I had never been in Murphy's Place before, but it looked familiar all the same. A long, scarred bar ran the length of the room and there were a few wobbly-looking tables scattered towards the rear. The air was rank with ancient cigarette smoke and sour booze. A few old-timers were perched along the bar, hypnotized by their scotch and waters. I sat at a table in the back, and Benjy went to the bartender and returned with a pitcher of beer.

"Pretty wild, huh?" Benjy filled a couple of mugs and set the pitcher between us. "Believe me, Dan, we'll be laughin' about this once we get a little perspective on it." He attempted a chuckle, but it came out hollow and flat.

"Wrong, Benjy." We locked eyes. "We have to tell her what happened. We have to tell her now, before she loses it completely," I said quietly.

"What the hell are you talkin' about?" Benjy leaned forward. "She was ready for the rubber room long before we showed up. It's not our fault if—"

"It *is* our fault! Don't you think we have a responsibility for the way we affect the people around us?"

"What do you mean? She was already nuts! Normal people wouldn't have reacted like that, they would have scratched their head and gone back to their T.V., or called one of those goofy newspapers they sell at the supermarket, 'Alien Bunny Rises From the Grave — Marries Elvis.' If we told her what really went down, she'd come after Buck with a meat cleaver."

I shook my head. "Buck is safe at your sister's — that's not the issue." I reached into his shirt pocket and snagged his cigarettes. I pulled a bent Marlboro from the crumpled pack and lit up.

"So *what* is the issue?" he asked.

I blew out a cloud of blue smoke that wrapped around the pitcher and mugs, then dissipated. "The issue is responsibility to those around us." I picked up my mug and took a slurp. "Did you ever see that Christmas movie with Jimmy Stewart? The one where he's about to kill himself, and this angel shows him how screwed-up everything would be if he never existed? Don't you think there's a flip side to that coin?"

Benjy shrugged his shoulders and leaned back in his chair. "'It's A Wonderful Life', as screened in Hell." He paused to take a drink. "No, I just don't buy it. She was bonkers from the start, and we didn't mean any harm by putting the rabbit back. Let's just ride it out, and let whatever happens, happen." He banged his mug down on the table.

"What about the children?" I asked. He sat upright at that. "Even if you don't give a rat's ass about Mrs. Randall, her kids matter. I doubt if it was ever much fun, being a toddler in the Randall manor, but I bet it's even worse right now."

Benjy buried his face in his palms and didn't move for several minutes. I stabbed my cigarette in the ashtray and watched it smoulder. Finally, with a groan, Benjy peered out from behind his hands.

"Point taken, Dan," he said. "We'll fess up, but you do the talkin', I just can't do it."

"I'll do the talking, all I ask is that you come with me. Morale purposes only." I nodded and he nodded, and we both sat there, nodding.

"Okay, you're on," he said. "But if Mrs. Randall wigs out and comes after us with hedge clippers or something, I'll beat your ass with a canoe paddle." We traded grim half-smiles.

"If Mrs. Randall comes after us with hedge clippers, you can beat what's left of my ass with a canoe paddle," I corrected. Our half-smiles broke into full ones, and Benjy handed me my car keys as we made for the door.

I got my ride cranked up, and we headed back to the scene of the crime. Benjy slumped down in the passenger seat and lit a cigarette.

"You scared?" he asked. I slowly rocked my head affirmative. "Me too, but I'll tell you something. On retrospect, I gotta admit that you're right. I guess it's what being an adult, being a man, is all about. If you mess up, you make it right. If you screw the pooch, you answer for it. After several moments of silence, I said:

"You know, if you didn't have shit for tits, I'd ask you to marry me."

"Yeah, but what about my firm, round heinie?" We both cracked up; the best laugh we had all night.

I wanted to tell my best friend that I loved him. I wanted to tell Benjy how I hoped that our future wives would be best friends, too. I had a fantasy; our yet unborn children growing up together, our unstarted families sharing holiday feasts and picnics. At the end of this daydream, there were two gray-haired, cantankerous old men who were teasing and insulting each other; growing old, but never growing up.

I never had a chance to share it with him.

We rounded the corner that took us to our street, and were nearly blown out of the car by the shock of activity that awaited on our block.

Five police cars and two ambulances were parked at odd angles in the street in front of the Randall house. Revolving emergency lights etched shadows of shrubbery and running men on the front of houses, outlining them in flashing red. As the lights spun, so did my stomach. I glanced at Benjy and noticed his mouth was a small, tight, puckering ring.

We left the car and stumbled towards a knot of civilians that clustered in front of the action; we were intoxicated from shock and confusion. I saw someone I recognized, our next-door neighbor.

"Mrs. Parker! Nina! What happened?" She had a small hankie clutched to her face, and she lowered it as she turned to face me. Her mouth was squared up into the boo-hoo position and she spoke in choking sobs that I could not understand. She gave up for the moment, and let the tears flow.

BAM! A burly cop kicked the Randall door open from the inside. He emerged, pulling Mrs. Randall by one elbow. She had her hands cuffed behind her back, and another cop followed her out the door, gripping her other arm. The policemen looked spooked, and they held her as far away from themselves as possible, as if she were something obscene and vile.

"I JUST . . . HAD TO KNOW . . ." she shrieked, "IF IT REALLY WORKED . . ." Mrs. Randall's eyes were beaded and shining; rodent eyes caught in the glare of oncoming headlights. Her face pulsed like the hungry larva of an insect, and her plain print housedress was fouled with smeared blood. She continued to screech in a frequency that could only be duplicated by a fistful of fingernails clawing a blackboard:

"LEAVE THEM BE . . . THEY'LL COME BACK . . . LIKE MR. WIGGLENOSE . . . THEY'LL BE GOOD CHILDREN NOW . . ."

The police shoved her into a car. Nina Parker approached me, still sobbing.

"We heard the screams about two hours ago, poor dears. We called the police, but by the time they got here, she was burying them in the back yard." A grieving moan escaped her lips. "What could make her do such a thing?"

When I found Benjy, I started running and did not stop until I found this bridge.

THE FLOOD

John Maclay

. . . Floods remembered: the farm where he was born, the house in the bend of the road, the bend of the stream, the rain starting the night before, then falling steadily all day, the stream filling its banks, the water moving faster, then rushing, then creeping out over the field, the road, until the whole valley was a churning muddy river, the house and its yard a tiny island, then the water creeping farther up, up . . .

He awoke suddenly to the sound of raging wind.

"You'd better get out of bed, Jim."

Meryl's voice was pleasant but firm. He rolled over, bleary eyes passing his wife's fully-dressed image, then settling on the digital clock on the bed table. 8 (blinking colon) 05. Two hours earlier than she usually woke him, these past few years after the kids had gone and he'd taken early retirement, really become the night person he'd always tended to be. "You take the day watch," Jim's sleepy mind remembered joking to Meryl, "and I'll cover the night. That way, no burglars or rats'll come near this creaky old Maryland house." But there was a reason, he also sensed as he moved his legs over the side of the bed, sat upright, for his wife's unusual action.

Yes, he thought, fully awake, hearing it sweep through the invisibly-groaning trees outside the shaded windows, rattle the panes themselves. The wind. The hurricane.

Jim remembered, now, the night before: the soft chair in his study, the late-season Orioles game on the West Coast he'd followed on the radio from its ten-thirty start to its twelfth-inning victory four hours later. The broadcast had been punctuated by static, and interrupted several times by weather bulletins from the Baltimore station. And all the time, the wind had grown stronger.

"What's the latest?" he asked Meryl.

"Well, they still say we're going to get it. There's already a lot of rain. And that big dead limb on the maple tree, the one you were going to cut — that's down in the yard. I put the car in the garage."

"Mmmm . . . " his grunted reply; then the lights went off in the shaded bedroom. Jim got to his feet, walked over, raised the blind.

He could see right away where the wires were down; they lay sparking on the sidewalk, under a thick limb from the oak. The rest of the tall tree was bending with the wind more than he'd thought possible, and the shrubbery below was laid out almost flat to the ground. He looked across the street, could hardly see the other houses through the gray sheets of rain. But it was the street which really drew his attention. It was full of muddy water, flowing, rising . . .

Like the stream at home, he thought, suddenly wary. The flood.

An hour later, when Jim sat fully dressed with Meryl in the kitchen, finishing the breakfast she'd fixed on the old gas burner in the basement, the wind was gone. "Just caught the edge of it," the authoritative voice on the portable radio was saying. "But Hurricane Jerry's moving slowly — look for heavy rain into tomorrow."

"Well, I guess we were lucky," Meryl said. "Only some limbs down, and some bushes to tie up. You can use your new saw. And I've got plenty of candles for tonight."

"Yes." But as he glanced around the dark still room, saw the rain falling, falling beyond the curtain, flowing down the large windowpanes, he remained ill at ease. Perhaps, he thought, it was the fact that he was up early with little sleep, or that he'd eaten the unaccustomed breakfast; he'd normally have waited until lunch. Or maybe it was the low pressure, the unusual quality of the hurricane air. But more than all of these, Jim decided at length, it could have been something deep in his unconscious — the dream, the childhood memories, the water . . .

And an hour after that, his worry was palpable; real.

"Honey, come here," he called from where he stood, looking out, at the front door.

"What is it?" Meryl answered, joining him, following his eyes.

"Look . . . it's . . . out of the street. Up over the lawn."

She touched his shoulder, saw with him the brown water covering the grass, licking the bottom step of the low porch, seeming to rise inexorably even as they watched.

"I'd better check the basement," Jim said, turning away. "It's got to be in the window wells by now. I'm worried about the furnace, the hot water heater."

"Whatever you think," she replied.

But a minute later, he was back.

"Strange," he said weakly. "It's not . . . coming in. The wells are full — look like fish tanks through the glass — but it's not . . . coming in."

Meryl smiled. "Must be the new windows you put in last year. You said they'd be tight." Then she looked genuinely concerned. "But please — don't worry. You know you shouldn't, at your age, with your heart."

"All right."

He went into the living room, pulled a chair over to a window for some light, started a novel he'd picked up at the library the day before. Vonnegut — about people becoming sea creatures — about . . .

. . . And an hour later, when his waking thoughts came back to him, he wasn't worried — because he knew, somehow, that it was already too late.

"Jim . . . " It was Meryl, coming downstairs. "I was reading too, but I got up to stretch, and . . . looked outside. And . . . "

He turned his head and saw it.

The water, brownish but clear enough to see through for a distance of perhaps two feet, was above the windowsill, fully three feet above the level of the porch. And yet — he glanced instinctively at his feet — the floor of the living room, the Oriental rug, were perfectly dry.

"Not . . . " he repeated sickly, knowingly, "coming in."

"No," his wife replied, and from the look on her face, he knew it was she, now, who was concerned. "But — it must be because the windows are tight."

"No," he echoed; he just couldn't comfort her. "These are as loose as everything else on this creaky old house. Remember the heating bills? The smallest breath of air shoots right through."

Meryl shook her head . . . started to cry. "Well, then, I guess you were right, darn you with all your worry. We're finally in trouble. We're in a flood. But Jim . . . "

"Yes?" he replied, perfectly sanguine.

"Darn it, Jim, don't you see, there's something about it that's not right. Not like the stories on T.V. — where you go upstairs, wait for boats . . . "

"I do see," he answered, as if from far away; his tone made her angry now, made her throw up her hands in exasperation, walk out of the room.

Far away.

. . . His mind, as he sat there, took him back to the dream, to the floods of childhood. God, he thought, pushing himself to realize why he'd become so accepting of the weird day, the flood that didn't. . . come in.

And realizing what it was he'd accepted.

. . . Childhood memories, childhood fears, childhood myths that never leave you, that in always being there in your unconscious are much stronger, a hundred times stronger, than the daylight life, the piling up of meaningless years, and given the improbable but always possible right combination of dreaming mind, thoughts, and atypical nature, can rush back like the flood itself, the flow of your thoughts, and sweep away the years, the daylight, even the whole natural order of things, and become, as you sit in the gray, newborn, reborn mythical world of this house, watching the brown water rise to the top of the window, forever and again enclosing you in the protean, embryonic sea in which you began, will begin, can rush back and become . . .

. . . the reality . . .

And suddenly, finally, he simply didn't care; forever forgot the part-life of tree limbs and cellar windows, his daylight worries, worldly fear.

"Meryl!" he called, galvanized.

She reappeared, face composed, tears gone now; regarding him with the look that, through decades of marriage, he'd come to expect.

"I wonder . . . " She didn't say it; his mind put the words in her mouth. " . . . what you'll do next?"

She's of the daylight, he thought. And I am of the night, the flood.

" . . . The house, moving beneath the water." Jim spoke slowly, meeting his wife's eyes. And for the first time in his years with her, he simply let his words fall, also not caring whether she understood, whether he had to make her understand, at all. " . . . But the people in it . . . the little boy . . . will not drown." He smiled. "Because that's the way it is — in the dream." He paused.

"The rest . . . of the dream."

She looked at him; wondered. Then humored him — as he, Jim reflected, was determined to do with her. Because he knew exactly what she'd do.

"Honey, I tried the phone, but it's out, too. And even the radio." — Meryl, ten minutes later, returning to his chair.

"They would be," he answered dreamily.

"And the neighbors." — A few minutes after that. "I couldn't even see the other houses, for the mist. And Jim . . . "

"Yes?" There are no neighbors, he thought.

"There's the water, too. It's up to the other windows now — the second floor . . . "

"Can't get out," he mumbled, reading her mind. Even if one wanted to, his own mind added. "Drown . . . if we don't . . . keep closed." Not only the house, he thought. Our only salvation, now, is to stay inside the dream. And perhaps . . . it always was.

Defeated, she sank into a chair beside him.

The rest of the day they sat there, not speaking, watching the brown water beyond the glass. It had motion, they noticed, despite its depth; from time to time a branch would pass by, or a tangle of uprooted grass, twisting and weaving like something alive. And they sensed, too, that it was still rising — improbably, mystically, higher; above any windows, any roofs. Then slowly, imperceptibly, the water grew darker, then black, until the whole world inside and out was invisible, and Jim and Meryl could not even see each other.

It was then that he started to feel it.

"It's happening." He spoke slowly through the dark, keeping his voice even, but feeling an excitement, a wonder, he hoped she might finally share. Something he'd approached, while she slept, in the night.

"Yes," she answered. And he knew his life was complete.

He rose now, groping for her, gently raising her to her feet, embracing her. And at that moment, as her woman's soul rushed forth to him — comforting, understanding — he felt his aging heart give out.

And felt the house, at last, gently rise from its foundations . . . start its voyage, forever, beneath the protean seas . . .

Back . . . back . . . to the other house.

The one in the bend of the stream . . . where it all would begin again.

THE RIGHT THING

Gary Raisor

Downstate Illinois. August.

Something unseen was moving.

It wove in and out of the cornfield, causing the thin, brown stalks to murmur a dry protest.

Two boys, one large, the other small, stood at the edge of the field and watched expectantly.

"Jesus," the small one said, "that could be Old Man Nichol's dog, Steel, in there. What are we gonna do if he sees us?"

An odd, flat expression appeared on the larger boy's face when he looked at his brother. "We'll probably get ripped apart, and our guts'll get spread all over. Then the crows'll come and tear out our eyes and eat them." He snickered. "It'll be really disgusting."

"Tommy, you're . . . "

"I'm what?" the older boy asked. "Crazy?"

"No."

They watched the corn stalks part. A dog emerged. It wasn't Steel, it was a beagle, and there was something wrong with the animal.

It had no eyes.

The boys watched the dog stagger into the barbed-wire fence, cutting itself to the bone. The animal yelped and lurched back into the cornfield. A line of red trailed after it. After a while the corn stalks quit rustling and quiet settled in.

The older boy, Tommy Lichner, smiled, but it never reached his eyes. His younger brother Michael, who was eleven, breathed a sigh of relief and wiped the sweat from his face. "Wonder what happened to him?"

Tommy shrugged, looked away. "How would I know? Dad'll be back from town pretty soon. We'd better haul ass if we're gonna make the quarry."

"It looks like something tore his eyes out." Michael's freckled face crumpled with pain as he took a hit from his aspirator. His asthma was acting up today. It happened whenever he got too excited. This was his first trip to the quarry and his adrenalin was pumping. "Are you sure it's okay. About the quarry. Dad said he'd—" Michael's chest hitched. "—skin us alive if he ever caught us near there."

"He's not going to catch us, okay?" Tommy watched his brother struggle to breathe and he started forward. Something in Michael's eyes stopped him.

Michael took another hit from his aspirator and his breathing smoothed out, a ragged engine finally hitting on all cylinders.

"Will you come on?" Tommy touched the barbed-wire fence and his fingers came back red. "I could be doing something fun today instead of taking your scrawny little butt swimming."

"Like what?" Michael's face wrinkled up with curiosity.

"I could be over at Lisa Robinson's house."

"Oh yeah, what's so fun over there?" Michael's voice was teasing.

"None of your business, you little pervert."

"You brought it up."

"Shut up."

They walked in silence for a while, Michael eyeing his brother the way a puppy with a full bladder eyes new carpet. Finally, Michael could stand it no longer. "So you gonna tell me what you been doing over at Lisa Robinson's house?"

Tommy hesitated for a moment, trying to make up his mind about something, then plunged ahead. "I'm trying to get into her pants, okay. I've been trying all summer, but she won't let me. Are you satisfied now? Anything else?"

Michael considered his brother's words and his eyes widened. "You can't." He began laughing with manic glee.

Tommy was afraid his brother was about to have another attack. "Can't what?" Tommy finally asked.

"Get in Lisa Robinson's pants, duh."

"Michael." Tommy's voice was ominous.

"She doesn't wear any pants. I heard Stuart Grimes talking about it."

Tommy felt sudden heat building in his stomach. "How does Stuart know?"

"Cause he sits in front of her in home room. He said he's dropped his pencil so many times everyone thinks he's a spaz."

"Does anybody else in school know about this?"

"Everyone except you. There's somethin' else."

"What?" Tommy felt the heat climbing his neck.

"Stuart claims he saw her snatch." Michael saved the big news for last and he delivered it with the respect it deserved. "He says she's a real hundred percent blond."

Tommy paused to consider the mysteries of blond hair, womanhood, and the fact that Stuart Grimes knew his girlfriend didn't wear any underwear. He didn't even know that Lisa didn't wear underwear. "Stuart had better be careful about that big mouth of his. It could get him into trouble." The heat crept across Tommy's face, settled in his eyes. "Real trouble."

"You ain't mad at me are you, Tommy? I didn't tell nobody." Michael was suddenly afraid. What had started out funny had taken a wrong turn and had veered into unknown territory. His brother had a crazy, unpredictable temper.

"No, Michael, I'm not mad at you. Not at you."

They tramped on through the prickly afternoon heat.

Tommy had the oddest sensation someone was watching them. For an instant, he thought he saw a figure standing high on the hill, but he couldn't be sure because of the angle of the sun. He thought that whoever was back there was dressed in white—all in white. The idea that someone was watching them caused a chill to crawl up his back, despite the heat. When he looked again, the hill was vacant. He decided he must be seeing things. Shrugging it off, he kept walking.

Michael tagged along behind.

Tommy tasted dust in the back of his throat and spat it out. "Couple more years and I'm outta this cow fuckers' paradise." He plucked at his NORTHWESTERN T-shirt, pulling it away from his sweaty skin. "If I don't die of terminal boredom first. The only thing you can get around here is a heat rash."

"Stuart got a rash," Michael volunteered, "on his Mr. Willy. He got it from Nina Hodgkess."

"One more word about Stuart and we're going home!"

They came to another barbed-wire fence and scooted beneath its strands.

"Wait a minute." Michael spied the small white conductors nailed to the fence posts and he knew the fence was electrified. His expression became suspicious. "I thought you said we were going to the quarry? This is the wrong way, this is Mr. Nichols' farm, this is where Steel . . ."

"You're not scared, are you?" Tommy challenged.

Michael looked at his brother and squared his thin shoulders defiantly. "No, I'm not scared. It's just a stupid old dog."

"We'll only be a minute. I want to check out something, and then we'll go swimming. Okay?"

"Okay." Michael still sounded dubious.

In the far distance, past the heat waves that rose with watery undulations, a herd of Black Angus cows were crowding under the only tree in the pasture.

Michael took a few steps, changed his mind and stopped, his face going pale. "Tommy, I don't want to go any closer. This is Steel's farm. He guards those cows. You saw what he did to Stuart, bit him in the face. C'mon, Tommy, let's don't do nothing crazy."

"Are you saying I'm crazy?"

"No, Tommy." Michael tried to look away. Couldn't.

"Stuart Grimes is a big, fat pussy." Tommy had a bloodless smile painted on his face now, and his eyes had gone all hard and shiny. "Steel probably caught Stuart while he was squatting down to pee." Tommy grabbed Michael by the arm and dragged him toward the cows clustered beneath the tree. Michael's efforts to resist were useless. His older brother was too strong.

As they drew nearer the cows, Tommy started talking again, his voice flat, hard. "I heard Stuart took his old man's twelve-gauge and evened up the score with Steel."

"He shot Steel?" Michael was stunned.

"That's the rumor going round. We're going to see if it's true, or if Stuart's just blowing more hot air."

The black shapes were growing clearer in the watery heat waves, and the high sweet odor of rotting meat reached Michael. The odor grew stronger with each step. The cows lay sprawled around the tree, twisted into unnatural shapes. Looking at them, all Michael could think about was the train derailment he'd seen up in Fort Wayne, where his dad had taken him for his asthma tests. The dead cows looked just like the boxcars that had been thrown from the tracks that day.

"Whew! Man, they're getting pretty ripe." Tommy fanned the air.

"You think Stuart did this?"

"See the holes in them. They were killed with a shotgun."

Michael edged through the dead cows and something occurred to him. "What if Stuart didn't shoot Steel? What if he's still running around loose?"

Tommy's face never changed expression as he scanned the pasture. "There's Steel, over by the barn."

Following his brother's pointing finger, Michael saw the black shape that scared the shit out of every kid in town—Steel.

The hundred twenty pound Rottweiler was dead, more dead than anything Michael had ever seen in his entire life.

But the big dog hadn't died easily. He had fought to the end. His shiny dark hide was pelted with dozens of holes where the shotgun blasts had struck. There was a trail of blood and slime on the ground where he had crawled toward his attacker, even as he was dying. The last shotgun blast had been the worst, it had caught him square in the face, putting out his eyes.

Michael stared down the length of the dog, saw the Rottweiler's intestines were poking out. Dried to stiffness by the sun, they gave the dead animal a sadly festive air, sort of like pink curb feelers on an overturned, trashed black Cadillac.

"How come he's all split open?" Michael asked.

"It's the heat that causes it. Makes them swell up till they pop."

Michael didn't know how to respond to that. He tried not to look at Steel, but he couldn't help himself.

There were things feeding on Steel. Flies and crows mostly. The crows were busy tearing out chunks of pinkish gray flesh and flapping away.

With uneasy fascination, Michael watched the scavengers pick over the carcass of the dog. The boy had never thought something as big and mean as Steel would ever die. Could ever die. He yanked his arm free of Tommy's grip and threw up, his pink Berry Berry Kix spewing onto the tops of his K-Mart specials with wet, splattering sounds. When he saw his breakfast was the same color as the flesh the crows were pulling from Steel, he retched again.

Tommy examined the dog's wounds with a calm, knowing eye. "Looks like a twelve gauge to me. Man, Stuart wasn't blowing hot air, that shithead really did it. He killed Steel."

"We got to tell somebody." Michael took a hit from his aspirator. It did little to ease his cramping chest. "How come Mr. Nichols don't know about this?"

"Cause he's in South Bend at his daughter's."

Tommy was paying little attention to Michael, he only had eyes for Steel. "That bastard's gone. I can't fucking believe it." Tommy fired a dirt clod at the dead dog and it struck him on the flank, turning into a puff of dust. The crows took lazily to the air. The flies paid little attention; they kept on eating.

"He was mean." Tommy's voice was reverent. "The meanest."

"Yeah, he was the meanest," Michael agreed.

Tommy's voice was wistful. "You peed your pants the first time you saw him."

Michael grinned. He should have felt good, after all, the boogie man was dead, and he wouldn't have to be scared of him anymore. But Michael didn't feel good. An indefinable sense of loss had come over him, and when he looked over at Tommy, he knew his brother felt the same way. Some of the magic was gone from their lives. Never to return.

They started to walk away when a plaintive mewling caused them to halt.

A puppy staggered out from behind the barn, a Rottweiler. Their talking must have awakened it. The baby stared at them for a moment and tried to balance on unsteady legs. Deciding the two boys posed no threat, it managed to lurch over to where they stood.

"Where did you come from?" Michael knelt and stroked the puppy.

Tommy walked over to the corner of the barn and looked into the shadows. "That's where he came from." Tommy jerked his head at a dead female Rottweiler and her five dead puppies. All of them had been shotgunned. Some were in pieces.

The puppy staggered over to its mother and tried to nurse. Its mewling became a constant thing when it couldn't get any milk.

"The little guy's in bad shape." Tommy gently touched the pellet holes in the baby Rottweiler's skin. "I can't believe it, that asshole Stuart shot the puppies too. I wonder why didn't he finish off this one?"

"Maybe it was under the mother, and Stuart didn't see it." Michael touched the puppy's dry nose. It began sucking on his fingers. "What are we gonna do? You think Dad'll let us keep him?"

"Nah, Dad won't let us have a dog. He hates 'em." Tommy continued stroking the shiny black hide, and Michael could tell his brother was trying to make up his mind about something.

"Can't let him suffer," Tommy said, picking up the puppy. "It wouldn't be the right thing to do."

"What're you gonna do, Tommy?"

Tommy stared into the eyes of the puppy, and its tail wagged feebly while it tried to lick his face. Then it began whining and lowered its head, as though it had grown too heavy to hold up. A thin line of bloody mucus trailed from the puppy's nose, ran onto Tommy's hands, trickled into the dust. Tommy watched without expression while he stroked the tiny head with gentle fingers. "Little bastard looks just like his dad, doesn't he?"

The puppy seemed suddenly content and it snuggled up in Tommy's arms.

Michael watched wordlessly.

Tommy finally took the puppy over to the water trough where the cows drank.

"Don't do it, Tommy. Shit—"

Tommy lowered the puppy in. The baby Rottweiler's mouth opened wide as it tried desperately to breathe. Bubbles floated to the top, burst. Tommy held it under until it quit thrashing.

When Michael looked into the pink water, he saw the puppy had no eyes. Tommy had gouged them out.

Tommy wiped the sweat from his face with the back of a trembling hand. He was breathing heavily. "Come on Michael, I thought we were going swimming today." Tommy walked back to the fence in silence, his feet throwing up puffs of dust that hung in the still afternoon air like accusing eyes.

When Tommy wouldn't look back, Michael knew his older brother was crying.

Michael knew Tommy didn't like anybody to see him crying. It ruined his tough-guy act.

A little later Michael caught up, and they pushed through the bone-white sycamores, until they came to a NO TRESPASSING sign. Someone had painted three small crosses on it.

"It's the number of kids that's supposed to have drowned here," Tommy said.

"No shit?"

"Yeah, no shit."

The two boys got down on their stomachs and crawled beneath the strands of barbed wire that guarded the path to the quarry.

Michael smelled something cool and damp in the air. The quarry was close, but he didn't feel much like swimming now.

Michael stood at the rim of the abandoned rock quarry and stared down with awe. "I didn't know it was so big." The glassy surface stretched out of sight, a gash in the earth that ran for miles. Slabs of limestone, as high as a man was tall, lay along the edges of the water as though they were blocks left by some gigantic child who had been called away. The rocks were streaked with red, the color of diluted blood.

"This is where Dad used to work." Tommy spat in the water, like the words left a bad taste in his mouth.

Hundreds of cattails were clustered around the bank on the far side, and when a breeze sprang up, their heads bent together, and their soft, clicking voices whispered secrets Tommy couldn't quite decipher. He knew they were whispering about him, though.

"How come the water turns black?" Michael asked.

"Cause it's real deep." Tommy skimmed a stone.

"How deep you think it is?" Michael nervously asked, picking up a stone and trying to duplicate his brother's feat. His stone only skipped twice before being dragged down. The water looked hungry.

"Don't know. Could be a couple hundred feet, maybe more. You ain't getting scared again, are you?"

Michael dropped his gaze, stung by the accusation. "I ain't scared."

Tommy saw the hurt expression and his tone softened. "Come on, lighten up." A sudden smile crossed his face as he yanked off his T-shirt. "Last one in asks Lisa Robinson if she dyes her cunt hair."

Michael giggled.

Tommy began stripping off his jeans, hopping on one leg when they stuck to his sweaty skin. Before he could free himself, he fell into the water. When he popped to the surface, he threw his soggy jeans onto shore.

Something fell out of the pocket. It was a shotgun shell.

"I picked it up at the farm," Tommy said with an easy, guileless smile. He stroked toward deeper water where a huge, inflated innertube floated.

Michael saw the shotgun shell was unfired and something frightening occurred to him. What if Tommy had killed all those animals at Old Man Nichols' place? Michael didn't want to think about that. Because that would mean his brother really was crazy.

"You'd better hurry up if you're gonna get your scrawny, little butt wet," Tommy yelled. "We already wasted too much time on those dogs."

Michael cast a furtive glance at the quarry, scared of his brother and scared now that he had to go into the water. His hands shook when he placed his aspirator on the rocks. He walked to the water's edge, hesitated.

"Come on, dingle berry, jump. I won't do nothing to you."

"You promise?" Michael danced from foot to foot on the hot rocks, looking into Tommy's eyes, while he tried to decide whether his older brother was crazy or not. "You wouldn't ever hurt me, would you, Tommy?"

Tommy smiled.

Making up his mind, Michael leaped. The water sucked him down, closing over his head, pulling at him with flat, cold hands. He bit back a scream, clawed his way to the surface.

Tommy was watching. There was something unreadable in his eyes.

Michael waited for some comment on his bravery, but Tommy's face still held that distant expression. That meant something bad was going to happen.

"The water's freezing my nuts off," Michael said.

"You don't have any nuts. You're too little."

Michael smiled and clung to the innertube. "Hey, Tommy, they ever find the kids that drowned here?"

"No. Just their tracks at the edge of the quarry."

Michael digested this information. "You think they're still in here?"

"Yeah, what's left of them."

"What do you mean?"

"I mean there'd just be some bones, maybe a little hair, after the turtles and everything got through. No eyes though. Their eyes would be gone."

"No shit." Michael was quiet as they drifted into the shadow of the rock wall on the far side of the quarry. He looked at it and was more afraid than ever. Trickles of water oozed down the stones, thick and dark, red as blood seeping from the skin of some wounded animal. He thought of Steel's puppy and how blood had spilled from its nose before it had died. Off in the distance came the low whine of a truck pulling the grade on the Interstate. The sound reminded him of something in pain.

Michael turned to his brother. "How come you gouged out the puppy's eyes?"

"I don't know." Tommy looked away. "Maybe I didn't want him looking at me."

"Did you do it to the beagle we saw?"

"Jesus, will you knock off with all the questions. Who cares about some stupid old dog?" Anger colored Tommy's voice. "Beagles are slow and dumb, you know. Kinda like you. Maybe he was sad because he couldn't catch any rabbits. Maybe he decided to kill himself and fucked up the job. Okay?"

"Okay. Can I ask you just one more question?"

Tommy looked suddenly very tired, but he nodded. "Is it about the cows and the Rottweilers?"

"Sort of. You promise you won't get mad?" Michael asked.

"I won't get mad."

Michael took a deep breath, exhaled, and screwed up his courage. "Are you really . . . you know . . . like what the kids at school say?"

"Crazy? That's what they say, isn't it, that I'm crazy?" Tommy looked into Michael's eyes. And for a second, everything dissolved, it was like he was looking into a window of some other place, that there were people in that other place, people dressed all in white, and they were looking back at him. The teenager squeezed his eyes shut, then opened them.

And everything was okay. The people in white were gone.

"This trip's turning into a fucking drag." Tommy shaded his eyes and looked over at the rock face. "Hey, Michael, you wanna see me do something neat?"

Michael's gaze traveled up the rock wall and he realized what his brother was about to do. "No, Tommy, don't be stupid, it's too high. Don't do nothing crazy." Too late, he realized he had said the worst thing he could have said, the very worst.

"You think I'm crazy, well I'll show you crazy." Tommy swam ashore, scrambled across the rocks and disappeared into the sumac bushes. Several minutes later the teenager emerged at the top of the rock face, seventy feet above the water. Even though he flashed a wide smile, Michael could see Tommy was afraid.

"We'd better get home!" Michael cupped his hands around his mouth. "Dad's gonna be looking for us!"

"Dad can kiss my ass. I ain't scared of him." Tommy moved closer to the edge and a handful of stones rattled down, taking forever to strike the black water below. He watched them hit and it seemed like a dream. He heard Michael calling. It was all a dream.

"Wait, Tommy. I can't breathe, I can't—"

Tommy leaped into space.

Michael watched his brother descend, growing larger against the cloudless blue sky. Tommy was a good diver, but something was wrong. He must have slipped, he was flailing his arms in circles, trying to regain his balance as he plummeted downward. The distance between him and the water grew shorter. He wasn't going to get straightened out in time. Tommy's mouth opened in a wide oval, a scream that he was too terrified to utter. He smacked the water and it erupted in a violent geyser, stinging Michael.

And just like that, Tommy was gone.

Michael was too frozen to even flinch. Anxiously he waited for his brother to pop to the surface.

This had to be a joke, but Tommy didn't appear. The ripples lengthened. Died. The surface became as smooth as glass.

"Tommy, you shithead, quit it. I ain't laughing."

The seconds ticked by with agonizing slowness and still the water remained undisturbed. A dragonfly hovered, lit, sat motionless for a few seconds, and then buzzed away. Time had ceased to exist.

A faint breeze ruffled Michael's hair. He wished he had his aspirator as he listened for a sound.

There was only silence. The cattails weren't even whispering now.

This wasn't a joke; Tommy was down there in the water, way down where it was dark and cold. Where he couldn't breathe. Michael knew what that was like. He had to find Tommy. The innertube squeaked a shrill warning when Michael slid across it and fell into the watery blackness waiting below.

He groped downward, fighting back his fear.

Fighting not to breathe.

He had to find Tommy.

The quarry squeezed his chest with its soft, heavy hands when he went deeper.

Complete darkness now.

Groping.

Kicking.

Deeper, deeper, no up, no down. No Tommy. Only this empty, terrifying vastness.

Just as he was about to explode, he bumped into something.

Something cold. Hard. Whatever it was moved, wrapped around his foot, and held him fast. He kicked, trying to break free.

Fighting away panic, he started to reach down to see what held him. But the panic won out, his air was gone, and he began thrashing back and forth. Seconds passed. The tapping sound of his heart echoed in his ears, a small hard pebble skimming across the water. Clawing, his fingers raking water, he kept reaching for the surface. It remained out of reach. Whatever had hold of him wasn't letting go. He opened his mouth and screamed, and his life began spewing out in tiny silvery bubbles.

When the last bubble was gone, Michael took a breath.

Water filled his lungs and it was a sledgehammer made of ice.

He opened his mouth again, sucked more water into his lungs. It was warmer now. The cold was going away, along with his fear, along with the pain, and he wondered what he had been afraid of all this time. The water wouldn't hurt him. The water was his friend. He took another breath, and the cold was gone.

All gone.

Before the darkness came for him, Michael saw Steel. Saw the huge Rottweiler was trying to show him something. The dog was trotting down a long, brightly lit hallway, headed toward a door at the far end. The door was closed and water was oozing out from beneath. Running along the black and white linoleum.

The door flew open, and Michael saw there was someone in a bathtub, lying beneath the water. He couldn't make out the face because of a stream of bubbles that covered the surface.

The door closed. And Steel was dead, shot full of holes. And then there was only darkness.

Seconds passed. Michael breathed one last time and a few bubbles floated to the surface of the quarry, then stopped.

Everything became serene.

The dragonfly again lit, and the cattails whispered.

A ripple stirred below. Something was coming. As the insect launched itself into the still air—

Tommy appeared.

He sucked in air and flung an arm across the innertube. When he began making his way to shore, he tried not to look at the small aspirator gleaming in the sun. His face was pale and his eyes were filled with shadows. "I'm sorry, Michael, I'm sorry. It was the only way." He collapsed face down among the rocks and began gagging. Afterward, still crying, he lifted his head and wiped the bitter puke from his mouth. "I wished we could've said goodbye, but I couldn't stand you looking at me. Not you."

The sound of water lapping against the rock shore came to him, languid, peaceful, and he thought he might rest here for a moment. Just a few seconds. He was more tired than he could ever remember. Too tired to get up. The sun felt good on his icy skin. He thought about his brother and wondered if Michael was cold. Did dead people feel cold? He hoped not. His eyes grew heavy as he watched a white bird spin away from the quarry wall. He watched while it climbed higher and higher, until it finally became a speck against the cloudless blue sky. The bird was free, without guilt, and how Tommy envied it.

His eyes closed and he slept.

And while he slept, he dreamed . . . about a man and the five-year-old boy at his side.

The boy and the man stood on a creek bank, watching the turgid, green water slide by, each of them lost in his own thoughts. The heat was brutal. As the sun gazed down at them through the oaks, the boy tried to wipe away the wetness gathering in his eyes.

In the distance, heavy dark clouds inched closer, wrapping themselves around the sun, slowly smothering it. Thunder rumbled.

The boy held a burlap sack in his hands. Inside, something moved.

"Son, little things can't fend for themselves." The man's voice was patient, yet tinged with suppressed anger. "They got to have big things to take care of them, or they die." The man snapped off a piece of a branch and threw it into the water. The creek sucked it under.

The boy stared straight ahead, his face carved from stone. Only his shiny-wet eyes betrayed his desperation.

The man bent down on one knee and looked into the boy's eyes as he struggled to explain. He was a man unused to talking. "Those puppies in your sack got no mother to take care of them. They're sick and they're going to die slow. They'll suffer. You don't want that, do you?"

The boy shook his head no, scuffing bare callused feet in the dirt as he tried to swallow the lump in his throat. He felt his father's hand on his sunburned shoulder, but he didn't flinch and he didn't pull away. That would make his father angry. He didn't want to make his father angry.

"Sometimes, a man has to do things that are hard," his father explained. "That's what being a man is all about. Taking responsibility. No matter what." He lifted the oil-smudged baseball cap and wiped the sweat from his forehead. "I want you to prove to me that you're ready to be a man. You know what you got to do, don't you?"

The boy nodded, the movement almost imperceptible.

"The longer you wait, the harder it's going to be," the man said. The cap went back on and there was something final in the gesture.

"We could get them some medicine," the boy said in a small voice. "Then they wouldn't be sick."

The hand on the boy's shoulder tightened and, this time, he flinched.

"We ain't got money to buy medicine for a bunch of stray pups." The hand dug deeper into the small shoulder. The pain was intense. "They laid me off at the quarry, they said they'll call me back soon as things pick up." The seams in the tired, bitter face deepened. "That's a goddamned lie, the quarry's finished and everybody knows it."

The boy looked at his father and the boy was sure this was somehow his fault. Maybe, if just this once, he could make his father proud of him, everything would be okay. It would be back to like it was before Mom died.

The boy clutched the coarse burlap and lifted with all his strength, and yet, try as he might, he couldn't raise the bag off the ground. Whimpers of pain accompanied his struggle to drag the squirming contents nearer the water. The bag tangled in a tree root, turning the whimpers into yelps. As he kept edging nearer the creek, he thought about how small the puppies were, he thought about how they had licked his hand with their tiny, pink, sandpaper tongues when he had lowered their wriggling bodies into the bag.

He thought about how they would look

—dead.

Teetering at the edge of the creek, he looked at his father and hesitated. His eyes held a final, desperate appeal.

His father looked away.

The boy took a deep breath and pushed the bag into the water. It landed with a splash and it should have went down quickly, but it didn't, because there was an air pocket keeping it afloat. The shrill yaps of the puppies filled the boy's ears and the bag boiled as they fought to escape. He covered his ears. Then the air pocket began leaking, spewing bubbles like some childish game the boy played in the bathtub. The bag held steady for a bit, then listed to one side, then slid under. The yammering was silenced.

In a moment, the puppies were gone as though they had never existed.

But somehow one had gotten free. It swam gamely for the shore.

A second before the puppy would reach safety, the man knelt and pushed it under. The boy watched its small, pink tongue unfurl as it struggled to breathe. He watched as it died. The last thing he saw was the puppy's accusing eyes staring back at him from beneath the water. The boy stood with his own eyes fixed on the spot where the puppy had gone under, watching blankly while a last bubble floated up. It was quiet under the oaks, growing suddenly cool when the storm clouds at last wrapped themselves around the sun. A shiver passed through the boy and he wondered if he would ever be warm again. He turned away from the creek. He couldn't face his reflection.

Something was wrong with the eyes staring back at him. His eyes.

A rough hand grabbed his arm and pulled him around, made him look at the creek. "I'm proud of you," his father said, approval and regret mixed in the seamed face. "What you did might seem harsh to you now, son, but someday you'll look back on this and see you did the right thing."

The first drops of rain began falling, softly at first, then harder, distorting his reflection. But not the eyes that looked back at him. Not the eyes.

"Yes sir, I did the right thing," the boy repeated, looking into his father's eyes. He saw they were the same green as the creek, and in their depths he saw dead puppies floating, swirling around and around, staring accusingly at him with their long pink tongues lolling from their mouths.

Another voice spoke to Tommy, pulling him around. It wasn't his father's voice. "Look at me, Tommy. How many more times are we gonna do this?"

Tommy opened his sleep-heavy eyes to see his younger brother sitting on the rocks beside the quarry. "Hi, Michael, what are you doing here? I thought I killed you."

"You did." Michael frowned as he did some quick arithmetic in his head. "This makes nine hundred and eighty-three times you killed me."

"Then why do you keep coming back?"

"Because you keep bringing me back, you stupid shit. You're the one who keeps doing this over and over." The small boy was watching Tommy intently, curiosity on his face. "It's not going to change. You can't bring me back. You need to let go of me."

Tommy looked around at the quarry, saw the water was red as blood now. The sun was going down, and he realized he must have slept a long time. "I was dreaming about white rooms, Michael, endless rows of white rooms. And people with dead-white skin who keep watching me. I hear them whispering my name. What do they want?"

"They want you to let go, to get on with your life."

Tommy recoiled as their gaze locked, held. All the strength left him. "What are you talking about?"

"Letting go of the past. Don't you get it? The people you see in your dreams are doctors. You went crazy, Tommy, crazy as a shithouse rat. Now you live in a little white room where they have to watch you all the time." Michael ran a hand through his water-soaked hair and propped himself against a sycamore. "I only live in your mind. I've been dead almost three years now. I had asthma, Tommy, real bad

asthma. You took me swimming while Dad was gone to town."
Michael's gaze shifted to the sun-glinted water. "And you drowned
me." He smiled. "I guess you thought it was the right thing to do."

"It was," Tommy said softly, without conviction.

"It's not so easy doing the right thing, is it? The doctors said the
asthma might have killed me sooner or later, so maybe my drowning
was a blessing. The only problem was, you couldn't accept my death.
You kept on blaming yourself."

"You were suffering, I saw what the asthma was doing to you. I
couldn't help but see. You were always following me around like a little
. . ."

"Puppy," Michael finished. He laughed. "We know what you do
to puppies, don't we?"

Tommy flinched. In Michael's eyes he'd caught a glimpse of dead
puppies floating, swirling around and around, staring accusingly at him
with their long pink tongues lolling from their mouths.

"See something you didn't like?" Michael's grin was guileless.
"That's right, you don't like to look 'em in the eyes, do you? That must
be why you pretended your dive went wrong. So you could get me down
there where it was dark."

Tommy watched Steel come over to Michael to have his ears
scratched. "I was only doing what I thought was right."

"Well, then, don't take it so hard," Michael said with a shrug.
"Besides, it doesn't do any good. My death was for the best. You said
so yourself, you did the right thing."

"I killed three other kids, too. Brought them out here and drowned
them. They died easy, Michael, without a fight." Tommy grabbed hold
of Michael's shirt and held on. His brother's shirt was wet, cold. "I did
it because they were sick . . . I would've killed more if they hadn't caught
me."

Michael's eyes settled on Tommy's stricken face. There was only
compassion in their depths. "You're my brother," Michael said. "I
forgive you."

"But I can't forgive me. Don't you understand, I can't forgive me."

"Then you know what you gotta do? You're not scared, are you?"

Tommy smiled, and there was something fragile in the smile. "No,
I'm not scared. Not anymore." He stared at his reflection in the water,
watching it ripple beneath the hot, dry evening wind that pushed across
the quarry. Something about his image disturbed him and he couldn't

figure out what it was, not until the cattails whispered the answer to him. They had been trying to tell him all along. He nodded his understanding. His voice was filled with sadness as he began walking into the water. "I just wanted to do the right thing, Michael . . . that's all I ever wanted . . . was to do the right thing." He kept walking until the water closed over his head.

In a small white room, the last bubble floated up from the overflowing tub, and the face of Tommy Lichner appeared in the water. And it was peaceful at last. At long last. When the nurse found him, she saw he had dug his eyes from their sockets.

And was still holding them in his clenched fists.

PIG'S DINNER

Graham Masterton

David climbed tiredly out of the Land Rover, slammed the ill-fitting door, and trudged across the yard with his hands deep in the pockets of his donkey-jacket. It had stopped raining at last, but a coarse cold wind was blowing diagonally across the yard, and above his head the clouds rushed like a muddy-pelted pack of mongrel dogs.

Today had been what he and Malcolm always sardonically called "a pig of a day."

He had left the piggery at half-past five that morning, driven all the way to Chester in the teeming rain with a litter of seven Landrace piglets suffering from suspected swine erysipelas. He had waited two-and-a-half hours for a dithering young health inspector who had missed his rail connection from Coventry. Then he had lunched on steak-and-kidney pudding with a deputy bank manager whose damp suit had reeked like a spaniel, and who had felt himself unable to grant David the loan that he and Malcolm desperately needed in order to repair the roof of the old back barn.

He was wet, exhausted and demoralized. For the first time since they had taken over the piggery from their uncle four-and-a-half years ago, he could see no future for Bryce Prime Pork, even if they sold half their livestock and most of their acreage, and remortgaged their huge Edwardian house.

He had almost reached the stone steps when he noticed that the lights in the feed plant had been left burning. Damn it, he thought. Malcolm was always so careless. It was Malcolm's over-ambitious investment in new machinery and Malcolm's insistence on setting up their own slaughtering and deep-freezing facilities that had stretched their finances to breaking-point. Bryce Prime Pork had been caught between falling demand and rising costs, and David's dream of becoming a prosperous gentleman farmer had gradually unraveled all around him.

He crossed the sloping yard toward the feed plant. Bryce Prime Pork was one of the cleanest piggeries in Derbyshire, but there was still a strong smell of ammonia on the evening wind, and the soles of David's shoes slapped against the thin black slime that seemed to cover everything in wet weather. He opened the door to the feed plant and stepped inside. All the lights were on; but there was no sign of Malcolm. Nothing but sacks of fish meal, maize, potatoes, decorticated ground-nut meal, and gray plastic dustbins filled with boiled swill. They mixed their own pig-food, rather than buying proprietary brands – not only because it cost them three or four percent less, but because Malcolm had developed a mix of swill, cereal and concentrate which not only fattened the pigs more quickly, but gave them award-winning bacon.

David walked up and down the length of the feed plant. He could see his reflection in the night-blackened windows: squatter, more hunched than he imagined himself to be. As he passed the stainless-steel sides of the huge feed grinder, he thought that he looked like a Golem, or a troll, dark and disappointed. Maybe defeat did something to a man's appearance, squashed him out of shape, so that he couldn't recognize himself any longer.

He crossed to the switches by the door, and clicked them off, one after another, and all along the feed plant the fluorescent lights blinked out. Just before he clicked the last switch, however, he noticed that the main switch which isolated the feed-grinder was set to 'off.'

He hesitated, his hand an inch away from the light-switch. Neither Malcolm nor Dougal White, their foreman, had mentioned that there was anything wrong with the machinery. It was all German, made in Dusseldorf by Muller-Koch, and after some initial teething troubles with the grinder blades, it had for more than two years run with seamless efficiency.

David lifted the main switch to 'on' — and to his surprise, with a smooth metallic scissoring sound, like a carving-knife being sharpened against steel, the feeding grinder started up immediately.

In the next instant, he heard a hideously distorted shriek — a gibbering monkeylike yammering of pain and terror that shocked him into stunned paralysis — unable to understand what the shriek could be, or what he could do to stop it.

He fumbled for the 'off' switch, while all the time the screaming went on and on, growing higher and higher-pitched, racketing from one side of the building to the other, until David felt as if he had suddenly gone mad.

The feed-grinder gradually minced to a halt, and David crossed stiff-legged as a scarecrow to the huge conical stainless-steel vat. He clambered up the access ladder at the side, and while he did so the screaming died down, and gave way to a complicated mixture of gurgles and groans.

He climbed up to the lip of the feed vat, and saw to his horror that the entire shining surface was rusty-colored with fresh blood — and, down at the bottom of the vat, Malcolm was standing, staring up at him wild-eyed, his hands braced tightly against the sloping sides.

He *appeared* to be standing, but as David looked more closely, he began to realize that Malcolm had been churned into the cutting-blades of the feed grinder right up to his waist. He was surrounded by a dark glutinous pool of blood and thickly-minced bone, its surface still punctuated by occasional bubbles. His brown plaid shirt was soaked in blood, and his face was spattered like a map.

David stared at Malcolm and Malcolm stared back at David. The silent agony which both joined and fatally separated them at that instant was far more eloquent than any scream could have been.

"Oh, Christ," said David. "I didn't know."

Malcolm opened and closed his mouth, and a huge pink bubble of blood formed and burst.

David clung tightly to the lip of the feed-grinding vat and held out his hand as far as he could.

"Come on, Malcolm. I'll pull you up. Come on, you'll be all right."

But Malcolm remained as he was, staring, his arms tensed against the sides of the vat, and shook his head. Blood poured in a thick ceaseless ribbon down his chin.

"Malcolm, come on, I can pull you out! Then I'll get an ambulance!"

But again Malcolm shook his head: this time with a kind of dogged fury. It was then that David understood that there was hardly anything left of Malcolm to pull out — that it wasn't just a question of his legs being tangled in the machinery. The grinder blades had consumed him up to the hip — reducing his legs and the lower part of his body to a thick smooth paste of bone and muscle, an emulsion of human flesh that would already be dripping down into the collecting churn underneath.

"Oh God, Malcolm, I'll get somebody. Hold on, I'll call for an ambulance. Just hold on!"

"No," Malcolm told him, his voice muffled with shock.

"Just hold on, for Christ's sake!" David screamed at him.

But Malcolm repeated, "No. I want it this way."

"What?" David demanded. "What the hell do you mean?"

Malcolm's fingers squeaked against the bloody sides of the vat. David couldn't begin to imagine what he must be suffering. Yet Malcolm looked up at him now with a smile — a smile that was almost beatific.

"It's wonderful, David. It's wonderful. I never knew that pain could feel like this. It's better than anything that ever happened. Please, switch it back on. Please."

"Switch it *back on*?"

Malcolm began to shudder. "You must. I want it so much. Life, love — they don't count for anything. Not compared to this."

"No," said David. "I can't."

"David," Malcolm urged him, "I'm going to die anyway. But if you don't give me this . . . believe me, I'm never going to let you sleep for the rest of your life."

David remained at the top of the ladder for ten long indecisive seconds.

"Believe me," Malcolm nodded, in that voice that sounded as if it came straight from hell, "it's pure pleasure. Pure pleasure. Beyond pain, David, out of the other side. You can't experience it without dying. But David, David, what a way to go!"

David stayed motionless for one more moment. Then, without a word, he climbed unsteadily back down the ladder. He tried not to think of anything at all as he grasped the feed-grinder's main power switch, and clicked it to 'on.'

From the feed-grinder came a cry that made David rigid with horror, and his ill-digested lunch rose in the back of his throat in a sour, thick tide.

He was gripped by a sudden terrible compulsion that he needed to *see*. He scrambled back up the access ladder, gripped the rim of the vat, and stared down at Malcolm with a feeling that was almost like being electrocuted.

The grinding-blades scissored and chopped, and the entire vat surged with blood. Malcolm was still bracing himself at the very bottom, his torso tensed as the grinder blades turned his pelvis and his lower abdomen into a churning mixture of blood, muscle and shredded cloth.

His face was a mask of concentration and tortured ecstasy. He was enjoying it, reveling in it, relishing every second of it. The very extinction of his own life; the very destruction of his own body.

Beyond pain, he had told David. *Out of the other side.*

Malcolm held his upper body above the whirling blades as long as he could, but gradually his strength faded and his hands began to skid inch by inch down the bloody metal sides. His screams of pleasure turned into a cry like nothing that David had ever heard before — piercing, high-pitched, an ullulation of unearthly triumph.

His white stomach was sliced up; skin, fat, intestines; and he began a quivering, jerking last descent into the maw of the feed-grinder.

"David!" He screamed. "David! It's won—"

The blades locked into his ribs. He was whirled around with his arms lifted as if he were furiously dancing. Then there was nothing but his head, spinning madly in a froth of pink blood. Finally, with a noise like a sink-disposal unit chopping up chicken bones, his head was gone, too, and the grinder spun faster and faster, without any more grist for its terrible mill.

Shaking, David climbed down the ladder and switched the grinder off. There was a long, drying whine, and then silence, except for the persistent worrying of the wind.

What the hell was he going to do now? There didn't seem to be any point in calling an ambulance. Not only was it pointless — how was he going to explain that he had switched the feed-grinder back on again, with Malcolm still inside it?

The police would realize that the grinder didn't have the capacity to chop up Malcolm's entire body before David had had the opportunity to switch it off. And he doubted very much if they would understand that Malcolm had been beyond saving — or that even if he *hadn't* begged David to kill him — even if he hadn't said how ecstatic it was — finishing him off was probably the most humane thing that David could have done.

He stood alone in the shed, shivering with shock and indecision. He and Malcolm had been arguing a lot lately — everybody knew that. Only two weeks ago, they had openly shouted at each other at a livestock auction in Chester. It would only take one suggestion that he might have killed Malcolm deliberately, and he would face arrest, trial and even jail. Even if he managed to show that he was innocent, a police investigation would certainly ruin the business. Who would want to buy Bryce Pork products if they thought that the pigs had been fed from the same grinder in which one of the Bryce brothers had been ground up?

Unless, of course, nobody found out that he *had* been ground up.

Unless nobody found him at all.

He seemed to remember a story that he had read, years ago, about a chicken-farmer who had murdered his wife and fed her to the chickens, and then fed the chickens to other chickens, until no possible traces of his wife remained.

He heard a glutinous dripping noise from the feed-grinder. It wouldn't be long before Malcolm's blood would coagulate, and become almost impossible for him to wash thoroughly away. He hesitated for just one moment; then switched on the lights again, and went across to the sacks of bran, middlings and soya-bean meal.

Tired and fraught and grief-stricken as he was, tonight he was going to make a pig's dinner.

He slept badly, and woke early. He lay in bed for a long time, staring at the ceiling. He found it difficult to believe now that what had happened yesterday evening had been real. He felt almost as if it had all been a luridly-colored film. But he felt a cold and undeniable difference inside his soul that told him it had actually happened. A change in himself that would affect him for the rest of his life — what he thought, what he said, what people he could love, what risks he was prepared to take.

Just after dawn, he saw the lights in the pig-houses flicker on, and he knew that Dougal and Charlie had arrived. He dressed, and went downstairs to the kitchen, where he drank half a pint of freezing-cold milk straight out of the bottle. He brought some of it directly back up again, and had to spit it into the sink. He wiped his mouth on a damp tea-towel and went outside.

Dougal was tethering a Landrace gilt and fixing up a heater for her piglets in a "creep," a boxlike structure hanging alongside her. Piglets under four weeks needed more heat than their mother could provide. Charlie was busy in a pen further along, feeding Old Jeffries, their enormous one-eyed Large Black boar. They bred very few Large Blacks these days: the Danish Landraces were docile and prolific and gave excellent bacon. But Malcolm had insisted on keeping Old Jeffries for sentimental reasons. He had been given to them by their uncle when they took over the business, and had won them their first rosette. "Old Jeffries and I are going to be buried in the same grave," he always used to say.

"Morning, Mr. David," said Dougal. He was a sandy-haired Wiltshireman with a pudgy face and protuberant eyes.

"Morning, Dougal."

"Mr. Malcolm not about yet?"

David shook his head. "No . . . he said something about going to Chester."

"Oh . . . that's queer. We were going to divide up the weaner pool today."

"Well, I can help you do that."

"Mr. Malcolm didn't say when he'd be back?"

"No," said David. "He didn't say a word."

He walked along the rows of pens until he came to Old Jeffries' stall. Charlie had emptied a bucketful of fresh feed into Old Jeffries' trough, and the huge black boar was greedily snuffling his snout into it; although his one yellow eye remained fixed on David as he ate.

"He really likes his breakfast today," Charlie remarked. Charlie was a young curly-haired teenager from the village. He was training to be a veterinarian, but he kept himself in petrol and weekly Chinese takeaways by helping out at Bryce Pork before college.

"Yes . . ." said David. He stared in awful fascination as Old Jeffries snorted and guzzled at the dark red mixture of roughage, concentrate and meat meal that (in two horrific hours of near-madness) he had mixed last night out of Malcolm's soupy remains. "It's a new formula we've been trying."

"Mr. Malcolm sorted out that bearing on the feed-grinder, then?" asked Charlie.

"Oh . . . oh, yes," David replied. But he didn't take his eyes off Old Jeffries, grunting into his trough; and Old Jeffries didn't for one moment take his one yellow eye off David.

"What did the health inspector say?" asked Charlie.

"Nothing much. It isn't erysipelas, thank God. Just a touch of zinc deficiency. Too much dry food."

Charlie nodded. "I thought it might be that. But this new feed looks excellent. In fact, it smells so good, I tasted a little bit myself."

For the first time, David took his eyes off Old Jeffries. "You did what?"

Charlie laughed. "You shouldn't worry. You know what Malcolm says, he wouldn't feed anything to the pigs he wouldn't eat himself. I've never come across anybody who loves this livestock as much as your brother. I mean, he really puts himself into these pigs, doesn't he? Body and soul."

Old Jeffries had finished his trough, and was enthusiastically cleaning it with his long inky tongue. David couldn't help watching him in fascination as he licked the last fragments of meat meal from his whiskery cheeks.

"I'm just going to brew up some tea," he said, clapping Charlie on the back.

He left the piggery; but when he reached the door, he could still see Old Jeffries staring at him one-eyed from the confines of his pen, and for some inexplicable reason it made him shudder.

You're tired, shocked, he told himself. But as he closed the piggery door he heard Old Jeffries grunt and whuffle as if he had been dangerously roused.

The telephone rang for Malcolm all day; and a man in a badly-muddied Montego arrived at the piggery, expecting to talk to Malcolm about insurance. David fended everybody off, saying that Malcolm had gone to Chester on business and no, he didn't know when he was coming back. Am I my brother's keeper?

That night, after Dougal had left, he made his final round of the piggery, making sure that the gilts and the sows were all tethered tight, so that they didn't accidentally crush their young; checking the "creeps" and the ventilators; switching off lights.

His last visit was to Old Jeffries. The Large Black stood staring at him as he approached; and made a noise in his throat like no noise that David had ever heard a boar utter before.

"Well, old man," he said, leaning on the rail of the pen. "It looks as if Malcolm knew what he was talking about. You and he are going to be buried in the same grave."

Old Jeffries curled back his lip and grunted.

"I didn't know what else to do," David told him. "He was dying right in front of my eyes. God, he couldn't have lived more than five minutes more."

Old Jeffries grunted again. David said, "Thanks, O.J. You're a wonderful conversationalist." He reached over to pat the Large Black's bristly head.

Without any warning at all, Old Jeffries snatched at David's hand, and clamped it between his jaws. David felt his fingers being crushed, and teeth digging right through the palm of his hand. He shouted in pain, and tried to pull himself away, but Old Jeffries twisted his powerful sloped-back neck and heaved David bodily over the railings and into his ammonia-pungent straw.

David's arm was wrenched around behind him, and he felt his elbow crack. He screamed, and tried to turn himself around, but Old Jeffries' four-toed trotter dug into his ribcage, cracking his breastbone and puncturing his left lung. Old Jeffries weighed over 300 kilograms, and even though he twisted and struggled, there was nothing he could do to force the boar off him.

"Dougal!" he screamed, even though he knew that Dougal had left over twenty minutes ago. "Oh God, help me! Somebody!"

Grunting furiously, Old Jeffries trampled David and worried his bloody hand between his teeth. To his horror, David saw two of his fingers drop from Old Jeffries' jaw, and fall into the straw. The boar's bristly sides kept scorching his face: taut and coarse and pungent with the smell of pig.

He dragged himself backwards, out from under the boar's belly, and grabbed hold of the animal's back with his free hand, trying to pull himself upright. For a moment, he thought he had managed it, but then Old Jeffries let out a shrill squeal of rage, and burrowed his snout furiously and aggressively between David's thighs.

"No!" David screamed. "No! Not that! Not that!"

But he felt sharp teeth tearing through corduroy, and then half of his inside thigh being torn away from the bone, with a bloody crackle of fat and tissue. And then Old Jeffries ripped him between the legs. He felt the boar's teeth puncture his groin, he felt cords and tubes and fats being wrenched away. He threw back his head and he let out a cry of anguish, and wanted to die then, right then, with no more pain, nothing but blackness.

But Old Jeffries retreated, trotting a little way away from him with his gory prize hanging from his mouth. He stared at David with his one yellow eye as if he were daring him to take it back.

David sicked up blood. Then, letting out a long whimpering sound, he climbed up to his feet, and cautiously limped to the side of the pen. He could feel that he was losing pints of blood. It pumped warm and urgent down his trouser-leg. He knew that he was going to die. But he wasn't going to let this pig have him. He was going to go the way that Malcolm had gone. Beyond pain, out on the other side. He was going to go in the ultimate ecstasy.

He opened the pen, and hobbled along the piggery, leaving a wide wet trail of blood behind him. Old Jeffries hesitated for a few moments, and then followed him, his trotters clicking on the concrete floor.

David crossed the yard to the feed buildings. He felt cold, cold, cold — colder than he had ever felt before. The wind banged a distant door over and over again, like a flat-toned funeral drum. Old Jeffries followed him, twenty or thirty yards behind, his one eye shining yellow in the darkness.

To market, to market, to buy a fat pig.

Home again, home again, jiggety-jig.

Coughing, David opened the door of the feed building. He switched on the lights, leaning against the wall for support. Old Jeffries stepped into the doorway and watched him, huge and black, but didn't approach any closer. David switched the feed-grinder to 'on' and heard the hum of machinery and the scissoring of precision-ground blades.

It seemed to take him an age to climb the access ladder to the rim of the vat. When he reached the top, he looked down into the circular grinder, and he could see the blades flashing as they spun around.

Ecstasy, that's what Malcolm had told him. *Pleasure beyond pain.*

He swung his bloodied legs over the rim of the vat. He closed his eyes for a moment, and said a short prayer. Dear God, forgive me. Dear mother, please forgive me.

Then he released his grip, and tumble-skidded down the stainless steel sides, his feet plunging straight into the grinder blades.

He screamed in terror; and then he screamed in agony. The blades sliced relentlessly into his feet, his ankles, his shins, his knees. He watched his legs ground up in a bloody chaos of bone and muscle, and the pain was so intense that he pounded at the sides of the vat with his fists. This wasn't ecstasy. This was sheer nerve-tearing pain — made even more intense by the hideous knowledge that he was already mutilated beyond any hope of survival — that he was as good as dead already.

The blades cut into his thighs. He thought he had fainted, but he hadn't fainted, *couldn't* faint, because the pain was so fierce that it penetrated his subconscious, penetrated every part of his mind and body.

He felt his pelvis shattered, crushed, chopped into paste. He felt his insides drop out of him. Then he was caught and tangled in the same way that Malcolm had been caught and tangled, and for a split-second he felt himself whirled around, a wild Dervish dance of sheer agony. Malcolm had lied. Malcolm had lied. Beyond pain there was nothing but more pain. On the other side of pain was a blinding sensation that made pain feel like a caress.

The blades bit into his jaw. His face was obliterated. There was a brief whirl of blood and brains and then he was gone.

The feed-grinder whirred and whirred for over an hour. Then — with no feed to slow down its blades — it overheated and whined to a halt.

Blood dripped; slower and slower.

Old Jeffries remained where he was, standing in the open doorway, one-eyed, the cold night wind ruffling his bristles.

Old Jeffries knew nothing about retribution. Old Jeffries knew nothing about guilt.

But something that Old Jeffries didn't understand had penetrated the black primitive knots of his cortex — a need for revenge so powerful that it had been passed right through him.

CRASH CART

Nancy Holder

Alan sat for a long moment with his eyes closed, allowing his fatigue and disappointment to wash through him like a gray haze. Felt himself drifting and sinking; if he didn't move, he would fall asleep. He opened his eyes and picked up his soup spoon, and was shocked at the amount of fresh blood on the sleeve of his scrubs. Perhaps he should have changed into fresh ones.

Then he looked down at his bowl of cream of spinach soup, and winced: It looked just like the stuff that had backed up through the feeding tube in Elle Magnuson's stomach two hours ago as she lay dying. That crap seeping out, then the minor geyser when her son tried to fix it.

Christ, why the hell had her family done that to her in the first place? All the Enfamil had done was feed the tumor, for weeks and days and hours, and the last, awful few seconds. Code Blue, and they had yelled and screamed for him to do something, even though everyone had spoken so rationally about no extraordinary measures when she had been admitted. Her daughter shrieking at him, shouting, crying. Her son, threatening to sue. Par for the course, Anita Guzman had assured him. She'd been a nurse for twenty years, and *hombre*, she had seen it all.

Dispiritedly, he slouched in his chair. He had really liked that old lady. Her death touched him profoundly; his sorrow must show, for no one came to sit with him in the cafeteria. He looked around at the chatting groups of two's and three's. How long before he became the type of doctor for whom nobody's death moved him? Par for the long haul, years and years of feeding tubes and blood. Why had he ever thought he wanted to be a doctor?

Maybe she had been special, and they wouldn't all be this way. Maybe that's why the feeding tube and the shrieking and the threats. It was so hard to let go, of certain people especially.

He pushed the soup away, marveling that he had been stupid enough to order it in the first place. He really had no appetite for anything. Which was bad; he had hours to go until his shift was over. He didn't understand why they worked first-year residents to death like this. He never had a chance to catch up; he always felt he was doing a half-assed job because he was so tired. What if he made a mistake that cost someone their life?

What if he could have done something to save Elle Magnuson? She'd been terminal; he knew that. But still.

Alan unwrapped a packet of crackers and nibbled on one. They would settle his stomach. Maybe. If anything could. Last Tuesday, when he had asked Mrs. Magnuson how she was feeling, she had opened her bone-dry mouth and said, "I sure would love a lobster dinner." And they looked at each other—no more lobster dinners for Elle Magnuson, ever, unless they served them in the afterlife. Jesus, how had she stood it? Spiraling downward so damn fast—her other daughter hadn't made it from Sacramento in time. It had been a blessing, that last, brutal slide, but it didn't seem that way now.

He dropped the cracker onto his food tray and wiped his face with his hands.

"Oh, God, Jonesy! *God!*" It was Anita. She was bug-eyed. She flopped into the chair across from his and picked up his soup spoon. "You're not gonna believe this!"

Before he could say anything, she threw down the spoon and grabbed his forearm. "Bell's wife was brought into the ER."

"What?"

"Yeah. And he comes flying in after the ambulance, just *screaming*, 'I want my wife! Right now!'" She imitated him perfectly except for her accent. "'I want her out of here!'"

Shocked, Alan opened his mouth to speak, but Anita went on. "Then they strip her down, and she's covered with welts, Alan. Cigarette burns. Bell's absolutely ballistic. And the paramedics drag MacDonald—that new ER guy?—over to a corner, and tell him there are whips and chains on their bed and manacles on the wall, and in the corner there's a fucking *crash cart*." She gripped his arm and leaned forward, her features animated, her eyes flashing. "Do you know what I'm saying?"

He sat there, speechless. Eagerly she bobbed her head. "A crash cart," she said with emphasis. A crash cart, with the paddles that restarted your heart. A crash cart, that brought you back from the dead. In the Chief of Surgery's house.

For his wife.

He reeled. "Holy shit."

Her nails dug into him. "He would torture her so badly she'd go into cardiac arrest. Then he'd bring her back."

"With the crash cart?" His voice rose, cracked. He couldn't believe it. Bell was his mentor; Alan looked up to him like a father. Occasionally they talked about getting together to play chess. This had to be an April Fool's joke. In January.

"Believe it, *mi amor*." Anita bounced in her chair. "He's in custody." Alan stared at her. "I'm telling you the truth!"

"Bullshit" he said savagely.

"Is not! Go see for yourself. His wife's been admitted."

Numb. Scalp to sole. He ran his hand through his hair. A joke, a really stupid joke. Sure. Anita was Guatemalan and she had this very strange sense of humor. Like the time she had stuck that stuffed animal in the microwave. Now that was just sick . . .

"C'mon," she said, grabbing his wrist as she leaped to her feet. "Let's go check her out."

"*Anita.*"

"C'mon. Everyone's going up there."

He'd often wondered what Dr. Bell's wife was like; there were no photos of her in Bell's office. He had imagined her beautiful, talented, supremely happy despite the fact that she and Dr. Bell had no children.

He jerked his hand away. "No," he said hoarsely. "I don't want to see her. And I think it's gross that you—"

"Oh, lighten up. She's unconscious, you know."

"I'm surprised at you." Although in truth he had peeked in on other patients whom doctors and nurses had talked about—the crazies, the unusual diseases, even the pretty women.

"Oh, for heaven's sake!" Anita laughed at him and let go of his arm. "Well, *I'm* going. I have twenty minutes of dinner left. It's room 512, if you're interested. Private. Of course."

"I'm not interested."

"Suit yourself." She grabbed his cracker packet and took the uneaten one, popped it in her mouth. "Eat your soup. You're too skinny."

She flounced away. At the doorway of the cafeteria, she saw more people she knew, and greeted them with a cry. "Guess what!" and they followed her out of the cafeteria.

Alan sat, unable to focus, to think. He couldn't believe it. He just couldn't believe it. Not Bell. Not this. It was a vicious rumor; he knew how fast gossip traveled in the hospital, and how much of it was a load of crap.

His stomach growled. During the long minutes he sat there, the soup developed a film over the surface. A membrane. He stared at it, thought about puncturing it. Making an incision. Making it the way it had been.

With a sigh he covered it with his napkin. Rest in peace, cream of spinach soup.

He jumped out of his chair when St. Pierre, a fellow resident, clapped him on the shoulder and said, "Jesus, Al, you hear about the old man?"

"Yeah." He wiped his face. "Yeah, I did."

Then he went into the men's room, thinking he would vomit. Instead, he cried.

At one in the morning, he went to the fifth floor. The nurses were busy at the station; he wore a doctor's coat and had a doctor's "I belong here" gait, and no one challenged or even noticed him.

The door to 512 was ajar. There was no chart.

A dim light was on, probably from the headboard.

He stood for a moment. Gawking like the other sickos, like someone slowing at an accident. Shit. He turned to go.

Couldn't.

Pushed open the door.

He walked quietly in.

She lay behind an ivory curtain; he saw the outline of her in her bed. The lights were from the headboard and they reflected oddly against the blank white wall, a movie about to begin, a snuff show. He walked past the curtain and looked sharply, quickly to the right, to see her all at once.

Oh, God. Black hair heaped in tangles on the pillow. IV's dangling on either side. An oxygen cannula in her nose. He drew closer. Her small face was mottled with bruises and cuts, but it could have been pretty, with large eyes and long lashes, and a narrow, turned-up nose. He couldn't tell what her mouth was like; it was too swollen.

She stirred. He didn't move. He was a doctor. He had a right to be here. He flushed, embarrassed with himself. All right, call it professional curiosity.

Gawking.

There were stitches along the scalp line. Jesus. He reached toward her but didn't touch her. Stared at the bruises, the long lashes, the poor lips. He saw in his mind Dr. Bell manacling her to the wall, doing . . . doing things . . .

. . . making her heart stop, my God, my God, what a fucking monster . . .

But what about her?

He wouldn't let that thought go farther, wouldn't blame the victim. He'd been commended last month for his handling of the evidence collection for a rape case. Dr. Bell had written a glowing letter: "Dr. Jones has shown a remarkable sensitivity toward his patients."

Dr. Bell. God. *Dr. Bell.*

How could she? How could she let him? Until her heart stopped. Until she was clinically *dead.*

Mrs. Magnuson had clung to life with a ferocity that had proven to be her detriment—cream of spinach—making her linger and suffer, almost literally killing the fabric of her family as they began to unravel under the strain.

He stared at her. And suddenly, he felt a rush of . . .

. . . anger . . .

so fierce he balled his fists. The blood rushed to his face; he clenched his teeth, God, he was so pissed off. He was—

"Jesus." Shocked, he took a step backward.

She stirred again. He thought she might be trying to speak, coming up from whatever she was doped up on.

In the corridor, footfalls squeaked on the waxed Linoleum. He felt an automatic flash of anxiety, a little boy sneaking around in places he shouldn't be. Mrs. Magnuson had called him "son" and "honey," and he had liked her very much for it.

The footfalls squeaked on and he shook his head at his reaction. There were few places in the hospital he was actually barred from entering. His mind flashed on Dr. Bell shuffling through the morgue like some demented ghoul; sickened, he shut his eyes and decided to leave.

Instead, he found himself standing closer to her. His hand dangled near all those black curls; and for an instant, he thought hard about picking up some of those curls and pulling—

—hard—

"Jesus." He spoke the word aloud again and wiped his face with his hand. What the hell was wrong with him?

He had a hard-on. He couldn't believe it; he stepped backward and hurried from the room.

Down the corridor, where the physicians' showers were, he washed his face with cold water and dried it with a paper towel. His hands shook. He staggered backward and fell onto a beechwood bench that lined the wall. Across from him, gray lockers with names loomed over him: Jones, Barnette, Zuckerman. Dr. Bell had no locker here; of course he had his own office, his own facilities.

Hurting her.

Jesus. He buried his face in his hands, still shaking. Mrs. Magnuson would be absolutely incapable of believing what he had been thinking while he was in 512.

And what had that been?

He stood and walked out of the room. It was time to go home; he was overtired, overstimulated. Too much coffee, too much work. Losing the old lady. Mrs. Magnuson. She had a name. They all had names. But what was *her* name?

Mrs. Bell. Ms. Bell. What was the difference?

He hurried back down the corridor and back into 512.

She lay behind the curtain; the play of shadow and white somehow frightened him, but her silhouette drew him on. He almost ran to her;

he was panting. He had another erection, or perhaps he had never lost the first one. He was propelled toward her, telling himself he didn't want to be here, didn't want, to, didn't. She was unconscious: Sleeping Beauty.

He touched her forearm. There were bruises, cigarette burns. Scars. Didn't her friends wonder? Did she have no friends? Bell was so friendly and outgoing, kind. He would have had lots of parties. He talked about barbecuing. His special sauce for ribs.

His chess proficiency, teasing Alan in a gentle way, telling him how he'd beat him if they ever played.

Beat him.

Alan found a place that had not been harmed and pressed gently. He moved his hand and pressed again.

On top of a bruise.

Pressed a little harder.

His erection throbbed against his scrubs. His balls felt rock-hard; God, he wanted—

—he wanted—

He pressed again, this time on a cigarette burn. Touched his cock. It was so hard. He was short of breath, and he wanted her so badly. He wanted—

He pinched the burn with the tips of his fingers, his short nails. He felt so dizzy he thought he might fall into her bed; he hoped he would. Swimming through something hot and active and moving; with volition and something so powerful, he stretched out his hand and cupped her breast. Squeezed her nipple. Squeezed harder.

She stirred. Her two blackened eyes fluttered open. He did not remove his hand. More blood was rushing to his cock, if that were possible. He was swaying with desire. The room spun. Those black eyes, staring at him, filled with tears as she smiled weakly.

"It's . . . okay," she whispered.

He jerked his hand away and drew it beneath his chin as if it had been severely injured.

"It's okay," she said again.

"I . . . I . . . " He averted his head as bile rose in his throat; he was sick to death; God, what had he been doing?

Her voice came again: "It's okay." Pleading. The hair rose on the back of his neck.

Oh, Christ, she wanted him to hurt her.

He wanted to do it.

As this time the vomit flooded his mouth, he ran from the room.

He didn't take a shower or change his scrubs. In the cold light of his car, he avoided the rearview mirror. He dropped the housekeys twice. His mouth tasted of sickness; he thought of Mrs. Magnuson's cream of spinach soup.

His roommate, Katrina, who was also a doctor but was not his girlfriend, had left on the TV without the sound; a strange habit of hers—she did that when she studied. There was a note that someone had called about the bicycle he wanted to sell. The bicycle. His patient had died and he had molested—

—tortured—

—crash cart—

He opened the fridge and grabbed a beer. Put it back and got Katrina's bottle of vodka out of the freezer. Swigged it. He felt so sick. He felt so disgusting.

There were sounds in her room. Deliberately he reduced his noise level; if she asked him what was wrong, he wouldn't be able to tell her.

Because he didn't know.

An hour later, puking his brains out. Katrina hovering in the background, muttering about God knew what. Praying to the ghost of Mrs. Magnuson, dreaming of Ms. Bell.

Of her versatile heart.

Of the power and the need of that heart.

that so often stopped,

that so often started.

Oh, God.

"What happened tonight?" Katrina was asking, had been asking, over and over and over. "What happened?"

"Lost a patient," he managed between bone-rattling heaves. His knees knocked the tequila bottle and it arced as if they were playing Spin-the-Bottle; they had agreed to be platonic and it had never been a problem. He liked her enormously, respected her.

"Oh, God, Alan. Oh." She stroked his hair. She had a glass of water at the ready; she was solicitous that way. If she'd known what he had done, she would probably move out. At the very least. Maybe she would have him arrested and thrown out of medicine.

"Mrs. Magnuson." He had told Katrina about her.

"Oh, I'm sorry." Soothing, sweet. He could feel himself shriveling inside. He was sick.

He was sick.

"Alan, drink this water." Rubbed his back, rubbed his shoulders. *It's okay.*

He sobbed.

A few hours passed; he dozed, then slept. Finally at about seven he woke and realized he hadn't been very drunk; except for a draining sensation of fatigue, he was all right. Katrina left him some toast and a couple of aspirin and a note that said, "I'm really sorry. Hope you feel better."

He showered and changed his clothes, forced down the toast but not the aspirin, had coffee, and drove to the hospital. He had to talk to her, to apologize, to make what couldn't be right, right.

No one paid him much notice when he went into the hospital—a few bobbed heads, a mild expression of surprise that he was back so soon. He pushed the button for the staff elevator; as he waited, a young nurse whose name he couldn't remember joined him. She said, "Did you hear about Dr. Bell?" His terse nod cut off the conversation.

The elevator came. They both went in. He pushed five and stood apart from her, his hands folded. He watched the numbers; at four she left with a little smile. She was very pretty. As pretty as Ms. Bell might be.

The doors opened. Her room was to the left.

He turned right and walked into one of the supply rooms.

Got a hypo.

He put it in his trouser pocket and headed back toward the left. Perspiration beaded his forehead and his hands were wet. He felt cold and tired.

Filled with nervous anticipation.

Sick, Sick. He was almost to her room. He felt the hypo through the paper wrapper. He was going to stick it someplace. Into her shoulder, maybe, or her wrist.

Or her eye.

His erection was enormous; it had never been this big, or hard, or wanting.

God. He sagged against her door. Tears spilled down his face. He held onto the transom and took deep breaths.

He was going to go in there and she would want it.

"No," he murmured, but he was about to explode. "No."

"Hey." He started, whirled around. Anita Guzman stood in the hall. "You okay?"

"Man." He wondered if she could see his erection; as she stood looking at him, it started to go down.

"They're going to fry him," Anita hissed, lowering her voice. "Fucking fry that *chingada* asshole."

"What . . . ?" he asked faintly.

She blinked. "You don't know." She made a helpless shrug. "I had to pull an extra shift. Alan, Bell's wife died last night."

His heart jumped. "No."

She nodded vigorously. "It was her heart. They took her to ICU but—"

"No." He ducked his head inside the room. The ivory curtain was there, the form stretched behind it. He walk-ran toward her, his chest so tight that his breath stopped.

The dark curls, the small face. He whirled around. Anita stood in the doorway. He said, "But she's still here."

"No. I had the room wrong," she whispered, wrinkling her nose in confession. "Mrs. Bell was up on the sixth."

His stomach cramped and the room began to tilt crazily; with a trembling hand, he gripped the edge of the bed. "Then . . . who is this?"

Anita came around the curtain and barely looked at her. "I don't know. But it isn't Bell's wife. This place is full of battered women, you know? Well, I gotta get back." She gave him a wave, which he didn't return.

Not Bell's wife. Not Bell's work.

But partly his.

Dr. Bell, so kind and generous. Dr. Jones, so sensitive.

This place is full . . .

The woman opened her eyes. Her gaze met his, held it, would not let him look away. His penis bobbed inside his underwear.

"It's okay," she murmured. Her broken mouth smiled weakly. "Please. It really is."

WALL OF WORDS

Lucy Taylor

I burned the Wall of Words last night, right before I headed south on Highway 87 toward Colorado.

It torched just like a big old funeral pyre, and I watched 'til the last ember sizzled and charred and the last vowel crisped and the final consonant became just so much soot.

Pa's famous Wall of Words, the talk of northwest Nebraska, that people came all the way from Denver and Sioux Falls and Kansas City to see, now it's only so much blackened kindling.

No more words.

Just silence, except for the breeze whistling through cinders and ash.

Enough silence now even for Pa, I 'spect.

We never talked much around our house in Hay Springs, Nebraska, mostly 'cause Pa forbid what he called "idle gabbing," that is, conversations that wasn't absolutely necessary.

Myself, I guess I wouldn't have minded a bit more talk, but then Pa took up his carving hobby, and I figured we had words to spare, more words than I ever knew existed: long complicated words like *fornication* and *serendipity* stacked up on the mantel, peculiar words like *quandary* and *abacus* on the coffee table, chunky words like *gash* and *brood* stoppering the doors.

I never did know what most of 'em meant and Pa, he probably didn't either. He just found 'em in the dictionary and liked their shape and sound, figured they'd look right attractive on somebody's dressertop or what-not shelf.

Pa, you see, was a wordsmith. Not some wuss with nothin' better to do than peck out words on a typewriter or a computer, but a real wordsmith. He *made* words. In the shed back of the house, what I reckon some people would call his studio, Pa carved words out of balsa and pine and cherry and other things besides.

It started soon after Pa came back from prison two years ago, when I'd just started tenth grade for the second time. Pa'd been a champion bull rider and calf roper during the years my older brother Josh and I was little, and he spent the best part of the year on the road. Then he got convicted of attempted murder after knifin' a rodeo clown that Pa claimed drove him half crazy singin' Gene Autry tunes all the time. When Pa got out of the joint after six and a half years, that was the end of his career on the rodeo circuit.

I guess maybe he developed a taste for silence in prison, though, 'cause after he come home, Pa started to complain that Ma talked too much. She was a "jabberjaw," as he put it, and Josh weren't much better; Pa called him a "yakkity-yak." Pa forbid Ma to say anything that wasn't absolutely necessary, which I always figured was why she communed with Jim Beam so often and so long. One night, though, after Ma'd threatened to leave Pa the first time some drinkin' buddy offered her a ticket out of town, she screamed, "If words was money, Ben Foley, you'd be the richest man in Nebraska, the way you miser every syllable away!"

Well, that musta' give Pa an idea. Next day he bought some wood and sharpened up the old carving knife he used for whittlin' back in his rodeo days and he started to carve out words.

At first Pa carved ordinary words—folks' names and a few inspirational words, but he tired of that real quick. He bought a dictionary and browsed in it for longer and more unusual words whose letters lent themselves to squiggles and corkscrews: long words and short ones, adverbs and nouns and adjectives, swear words and sex words (which he always carved small, but with a lot of fancy doodads), even a few foreign words—*Himmel* and *merde* and *Kindertot* are a few I recall.

Pa didn't just carve words, you see, he made works of art. He'd spend all afternoon curlicueing the ends of the "l's" in *languid* and *lewdly* and *longitude* or turning the "b" in *betrothed* into a fire-breathing serpent singeing its own tail.

The more Pa carved, the less he talked and the more he enforced the No Idle Chatter and No Speakin' Unless Spoke To rules. And Ma, she took to drinkin' in nearby towns like Rushville and Chadron, and sometimes didn't come home for days at a time. When she did straggle in, Pa wouldn't say nothin' at all, but from the door of his workshop he'd hurl a word at her—*slut* or *bovine* or *perversity*—as she teetered on up the walk with her hair teased like a bird's nest and her clothes rumpled and soiled.

And Ma'd retaliate by letting loose a stream of words fit to shame Old Nick himself.

"You daft old coot, you with your woodcarving, you got woodshavings for brains! Why can't you *talk* to me, holler or yell, like any normal man?"

But Pa'd just glare and pull his silence round him like a cloak and turn his back to her.

By this time, Pa'd bought a router and an assortment of attachable drill bits and cutters, so he could make his words bigger and more complex. Some of the letters stood two or three feet high, and the shed where Pa worked was so full up with words the walls looked like pages out of a dictionary.

Finally, I come in from school one day and saw he'd commenced to building something with the words. At first, I thought it was some kind of sign or joke or pun, but I soon realized the words stacked up in the backyard held no particular significance or sense. *Thimble* and *kissing* and *macaroon* formed part of the base with *slurp* and *bereavement* and a very highly ornamental *clannish* topping these and then some other words, short ones, on the third tier. Pa'd driven nails into the wood to hold the words together. The wall rose maybe four feet high then, at its tallest point, and stretched 'bout ten feet long.

Soon after the wall went up, my older brother Josh, who had a small farm of his own across the highway, stopped by the house one Saturday to ask me would I go with him to talk to Pa about what we referred to as "Ma's pasttime."

I agreed to go, but my heart was heavy . . . havin' a conversation with Pa was about as easy as gettin' milk out of a chicken.

But Josh was always better'n with words than I was and less afraid of Pa, too, him bein' older and livin' on his own.

"We gotta do somethin' about Ma," Josh said, standing there in the shed while Pa carved. "Put her in the hospital or something."

Pa was working on the tail of the "y" in *chastity*, and he finished it before he replied, which took a good ten minutes.

"A drunk tank?" he said finally.

"No sir, I was thinkin' more like a treatment center."

Pa carved on. Five minutes later, he said, "She's like the lot of y'all. You gab too much, fritter away your time. Jabberjaw and yakkity-yak, all day long."

He blew loose wood shavings off the letters.

"But Pa, I think . . . . "

He looked up, eyes hooded and hawkish, woodchips clinging to his beard like dark beetles. He stared at me, and I felt just like he'd turned the router on me and was drillin' out parts of my gut.

"How 'bout you, Billie-boy? You gonna have your say, too?"

I couldn't have admitted it then, not even to myself, but I was scared of Pa. He wielded silence like a club, and the few words that he ever spoke were more the kind that separate than those that might make bridges.

"No, Pa, I ain't got nothin' to say."

His eyes carved me up in sections, and I thought about that rodeo clown back in Denver and how many stitches they said it'd took to put his face back together.

"You goin' into town today?"

"Yessir."

He nodded, concentrating on the wood.

"Be long?"

"Few hours mebbe."

"Bring me back some Copenhagen . . . "

"Yessir."

" . . . and your Ma some whiskey."

"But Pa . . . I . . . "

Pa reached for his dictionary and opened it to choose another word. I peered over his shoulder and saw his long fingers pick out *scrumptious*.

" . . . about Ma, I think . . . maybe . . . . "

But he wasn't listening anymore, and I knew if Josh and I stood there all day long, we'd get no discussion from him.

❖   ❖

Not long after Josh tried to talk to Pa, Ma went out on a drunk, and didn't come back. I figured she'd turn up in a few days, like she always did, but when a week passed, I decided she musta' gone and done it, run off with some man who asked her like she'd been threaten' to do ever since Pa took up his carving. I didn't say nothin' about it, not even to Josh. I missed Ma, but I felt happy that she'd run away. For a while there, I had dreams of me and Ma together, in a fancy party at a big castle, where everyone talked and laughed about their hopes and dreams and fantasies, and the words just flowed all over each other, all rainbow-colored and glowing like fireworks in the dark.

I hoped wherever she'd run off to there'd be lots of people she could talk to.

Meantime, with Ma gone, Pa worked even harder.

The Wall of Words, as people had begun to call it, was getting higher, longer. Pa added *elephantine* and *gargoyle* and *parsimonious*, carved vertically like totem poles out of huge beams of wood with smaller words connecting them horizontally like in a crossword puzzle. People started taking notice from the road and dropping by to look around, but Pa wouldn't let them inside the shed no longer. He kept it locked, and hardly ever came out at all 'cept to take a piss and nail another word onto the Wall.

Meantime, the visitors that stopped by took pictures of each other by the Wall and let their kids crawl over it til finally Pa put up a fence around it and a sign saying *Do Not Touch* and *Quiet Please*.

Over the next few weeks, dozens of other words were added, *obsequious* and *foreboding* and *juvenile*, *malcontent* and *kindness* and *adroitly*, and the Wall just kept getting higher and longer, and some letters were as big as fireplugs and others fancied up with vines and buds and scrollwork, and Pa kept addin' to it, sometimes two or three words a day.

Josh stopped by my room one afternoon while I was laying there, having me a little sip of Scotch and daydreaming about Ma and me gossiping together at some fancy party. He was all fidgety and nervous and had that clenched jaw look he gets when he's been grindin' his teeth at night.

I stood up and offered Josh a pull from my bottle, but he just sneered and said, "Now that Ma's run off, you gonna be the family lush?"

"Helps me relax," I said, which was true. With enough booze in me, I could kinda float in and out of that grand, high society party in the castle where Ma and I drifted among high class nobility, with Ma chitchatting to her heart's content and me confiding my life story to a beautiful big-bosomed lady in a low-cut red gown like one I saw on some old pirate movie one time.

"Look, we got to *talk,*" Josh said.

That made me uncomfortable. It's one thing to fantasize about somethin', another thing to do it. Josh knew we didn't talk in our family. That wasn't our way.

I shrugged. "'bout what?"

"The goddamn Wall."

"Yeah?"

"Have you *looked* at it lately? Since Pa put up the fence and started makin' it longer?"

"I glance at it from time to time."

"Some of those words, Billie . . . "

"Yeah?"

"I think . . . "

And we stood there, staring at the floor, the windows, everywhere but at each other, 'til I took another swig and lost my balance and plopped back on the bed, and Josh said, "Ya damn drunk . . . when you can see straight, just go take a look at the Wall."

"Where you goin'?" I said as he walked out the door.

"To talk to Pa," Josh said.

And that was the last I seen of him.

After that, it was hard to gauge how many days passed, 'cause most nights I'd drink and doze off or pass out maybe, and the sun would be comin' up and I'd haul my ass off to school, but like as not I wouldn't go at all. School was a lot like Pa's Wall . . . just words on top of words that made no sense, all meaningless and stupid.

But when I went by Josh's place sometime later to see would he lend me a few dollars to go buy some hooch and I seen Josh's truck was there but he wasn't anywheres around, I got a little worried. I knocked on the door of Pa's shed to ask if he'd seen Josh anywhere.

Pa unlocked the door and stood there, his big frame blocking my view of everything but one end of his workbench, where the router lay with a particularly vicious-looking cutter slotted into it.

"Josh?" said Pa. "Ain't seen him."

"Not this week?"

"Naw."

"Last?"

"Yep. He stopped by to talk."

This surprised me. "'bout what?"

Pa actually smiled, but on him it looked unnatural, the muscles at the corners of his mouth hunched up like the hind end of a rutting dog.

"He come by 'cause he got the idea he'd like to sign up with the rodeo fer a spell. I give him the names of some buddies of mine he could call up in Laramie and Denver. Told him they could help to get him started. He was all fired up about it. We sat up 'til past midnight with me tellin' him my stories. If he ain't been around of late, I reckon he done left to join the circuit. Reckon he'll do right fine, too. Takes after me, Josh does."

And Pa shut the door in my face.

It was the most words I'd ever heard Pa speak all at one time.

It got me to wonderin'.

✦   ✦

That evening I studied the Wall, looking at the words that had been added since Ma disappeared. There was *mercenary* and *idolater* and *spinnaker,* and below that *porous* and *euphonious* and dozens of others, words of all shapes and sizes and different materials, and I noticed it then. The two long, light-colored words. Nearly white. Smaller than most and stuck into spaces between the bigger words that were carved out of pinewood and balsa.

There on the side of the Wall, I saw *jabberjaw* and a little ways from that was *yakkity-yak.* They was half hidden by some bigger words, but their paleness made them stand out real sharp.

I musta stared at them two words half an hour or more, running my fingers over each letter, learning their shape and their feel and trying to realize their meaning.

And when I thought I understood, I wrenched loose a word near the top that was carved out of teak, and I went lookin' for Pa.

✦   ✦

Words. In Mexico, where I'm headed, I'll hear them, but I won't understand. They'll fall over me like so much freezing rain.

And if I start to understand, I'll move on. To Japan or China maybe, anyplace where the words, to me, are nothin' more than decoration—singsong, meaningless sounds like birdcalls on a hot summer morning.

'Cause I can't go back to Hay Springs, Nebraska, never.

That new length of the Wall, the earth below it had been disturbed, dig up and then repacked before the words were piled on top. And them white words I found—*jabberjaw* and *yakkity-yak*—they was carved from bone.

And Pa? Well, right before I burned the Wall, I cornered him in that shed of his with all the bloodstains on the walls and I killed the silence-loving, murdering old bastard.

With *kindness,* right between the eyes.

METASTASIS

David B. Silva

"It's back," Melanie said.

The bedroom window was open, the curtains drawn back. Midnight had swept through half-an-hour or so earlier. The month was July. Nine days earlier, a high pressure system had locked in over the coast, bringing high temperatures and sopping humidity. It was rarely comfortable inside the apartment before the sun went down.

"What's back?" I whispered.

"The cancer."

"Jesus, Melanie."

The moon had risen above the apartment complex across the way. Its light poured into our bedroom, grayish-white, and fell across her body like velvet. "I can feel it inside me," she said.

I sat up, and stared numbly out the window. There was nothing I knew to say. Nothing that could express the dryness in my throat, the fear in my stomach. We had both known the cancer might return. It was just that . . . that things had been going so well. I ran my hand across her bare back in wide circles, not saying anything at all.

"I love you, Jimmy."

"Maybe it's something else," I whispered.

"Maybe," she said, not really believing.

I stared through the bedroom window at the peaceful night, wondering when it was all going to end, this cancer stuff. Night became a conscious, faraway dream for me, dark and sulking. The silence between us became a bottomless pit, its mouth open wide, waiting to taste the next spoken word.

There were no more spoken words that night.

We slept in late the next morning, till nearly ten o'clock. It was Saturday and the only item on the calendar was a mailing Melanie had promised to do for a local environmental group called Earth Care. The newsletters (which focused on a recent *Time* article about the greenhouse effect and global warming) had been delivered the day before. They were sitting in stacks on the dining room floor, a little more than a thousand copies altogether.

It was noon by the time we finished breakfast and moved into the dining room. Melanie cut a handful of newsletters off one of the stacks, and sat down at the table. "Get a chance to read the article?"

I nodded. "Last night. Before I came to bed."

"And people think nuclear war is scary."

"It *is* scary."

"I know," she said. "I didn't mean it to sound like that. It's just that no one seems worried about what's going on in our own backyards. The things we eat. The way we acquiesce to every scientist and politician and quote — professional — unquote who happens along. Doesn't it make you wonder sometimes if we aren't giving away too much of ourselves?"

I stared at her, trying to look past the words, because they didn't sound like they belonged to her. "Are we still talking about the article, or are we talking about something else?"

"The article," she said.

I didn't believe her, but I left it alone.

We worked on into the afternoon.

It was another wicked day. Mid-nineties. High humidity. The air conditioner had given out its last breath of cool air on the previous Wednesday, and the manager had promised to replace it within the week. For the time being, though, we were forced to keep the windows closed and the drapes drawn during the day. Inside, it felt dark and oppressive and peculiarly isolated.

We worked in silence for another ten or fifteen minutes. The process becoming almost mechanical, a chance to drift off into your own thoughts. Then Melanie looked up from the newsletter in her hands, and said evenly, "I've decided to make an appointment to see Dr. Perry."

"You already have a check-up scheduled, haven't you?" I looked at her, realizing unmistakably that I had secretly hoped last night had been the end of her cancer talk. It was a bitter realization, followed by an equally bitter taste of guilt.

"That's more than a month away. This won't wait that long."

"You really believe it's the cancer?"

She nodded solemnly.

"Want me to call him for you?"

"No, I'll do it."

✦   ✦

Ovarian cancer.

Melanie had been thirty-three years old when the doctors first diagnosed it, almost two years ago. She liked to swim at the Y in the afternoon, and play volleyball at the high school on Wednesday nights. She liked to read mysteries before she fell asleep in bed, and bake berry pies when the berries were in season and she could pick them fresh off the vines. Maybe that was the thing I loved most about her, that indefatigable enthusiasm, she had for life.

We had lost our only child, Ruby Ann, to a miscarriage in '86. It was a loss that nearly tore apart our marriage. A year went by when everything had seemed shrouded in a thick, dismal fog. Sometimes I would wake up, the bed next to me cold and empty, and I would find Melanie sitting at the kitchen table, drinking a warm cup of coffee, staring blankly out the kitchen window. I wondered at times like those if I would ever have her back again. In the end, though, she stubbornly pulled herself out of her depression, and for awhile we were able to piece our fragile lives back together.

Until the cancer.

The awful, consuming cancer.

"There's nothing showing up on the scan," Dr. Perry told us a week after Melanie had first brought it up. We were gathered together in a cramped examination room; Dr. Perry on a small stool in front of us; Melanie sitting on the examination table, dressed in a hospital gown, her fingers gripping the rounded edge of the stainless steel table.

"Then you've missed something," she said quietly.

For God's sake, I thought, listen to the doctor.

"We didn't miss anything, Mrs. Slayden."

"Yes, you did."

The good doctor sighed. "Your white cell count is normal."

"So was the scan, honey." I took her hand in mine, as if she were a child (later, I'd hate myself for patronizing her like that, for not listening to her). "And so was the doctor's examination."

"We're talking about my body. I know what I'm feeling. I've felt it before. The cancer's back."

I looked to the doctor, who folded his arms and leaned back on his stool. He had seen this reaction before. Maybe many times before. "I know you've been through hell and back . . ."

Melanie's chemotherapy had ravished her body nearly as much as the cancer it was supposed to fight. They had kept her overnight when her temperature hit 104 after her first session. A few days later, she received a blood transfusion for her anemia. Then her hair fell out, and it was at that point the secret was out and denial had become pointless.

She slept long hours during the six months of chemo. Sometimes I would stand in the bedroom doorway, studying her, thinking how different she looked from the woman I had married. Her face lost its color. Her eyebrows disappeared. By the end of her chemo she had vomited away nearly fifteen pounds.

When her hair finally grew back, it was dark and curly. She didn't care much for the way it looked. For months afterward, she would stare at herself in the bathroom mirror, fingering her hair or her cheeks — which had become sallow and sunken — turning from one profile to the other, wondering out loud what had happened to her.

She *had* been through hell and back.

And she had survived.

Listen to the doctor, I thought.

Three or four weeks filed by, temperatures consistently hitting the low-to-mid nineties, the humidity hovering right around eighty percent. The air conditioner still hadn't been repaired. At night, we opened the windows to the cool breeze blowing in off the ocean. Mornings, we woke up early — before the temperature had started to climb — closed the windows, drew the curtains, and hoped the night breeze would keep the house cool a few extra hours.

The summer had turned out to be one of the hottest on record.

More than the heat, though, Melanie had been bothered by our last visit with Dr. Perry. On the way out to the car, she had hardly said a word.

"What is it?" I asked during the trip home.

"I want a promise out of you," she said without looking at me.

"What kind of promise?"

"I want you to promise that whatever happens to me, you won't call a doctor."

"Don't be silly."

"I mean it, Jimmy."

"You're just upset."

"Promise me."

"How can I—"

"*Promise* me."

I shouldn't have — in fact, I remember crossing my fingers, like a child trying to make peace with a little white lie — but I did end up giving her my word. I guess I figured that would be the end of it.

After that, a slowly-widening abyss seemed to grow between us. It was more than just between the two of us, though. It was between Melanie and the rest of the world. She became withdrawn, silent. Sometimes it felt as if a dark cloud had settled over the apartment. I would look at her from across the room while she was reading or watching television and a foreboding somberness that belonged to her would stir inside me. That was as close as she let me come.

More honestly, that was as close as I wanted to come.

Between Melanie and the doctor, I wanted most to believe the doctor.

Melanie wouldn't let me do that.

In mid-August we sat down to do the next Earth Care mailing. The *Cupertino Courier*, a local newspaper, had run an article a few weeks earlier about a study in western Ontario where scientists had slowly made Lake 302 more acidic by adding sulfuric and nitric acids to the water. The purpose was to observe and chronicle the chemical and biological damage.

"Did you get a chance to read it?" Melanie asked as we were working.

"Not all of it."

"Nearly all of the species in the lake, in adapting to the higher acidic levels, went through an evolutionary change. The crayfish developed harder shells. The white suckers adopted larger eyes. That kind of thing."

"Over a period of how long?"

"The changes came relatively early, but after seven years there wasn't a species in the lake that could reproduce. Even the white suckers, which had initially thrived, had begun to disappear." She placed the last newsletter on top of a stack, then studied me for a reaction. "Every form of life in Lake 302 died out, Jimmy."

"Isn't that what they expected?"

She stared at me a moment longer, as if she couldn't believe my question, then she turned quietly back to folding newsletters.

"Well, isn't it?"

"I suppose," she said softly.

"Then what's the matter?"

"I don't know. Nothing, I guess." She shrugged. "I was just thinking . . . how sometimes it feels like we're turning the world into a giant science lab. I mean we've got test-tube babies and lakes with experiment numbers and—"

"That's how we solve problems, Melanie."

"Yeah, I know. It's just that . . ." She stopped there. Her gaze, both faraway and thoughtful, drifted toward the open window.

"Hey, are you okay?"

"I don't think so," she whispered.

"What is it?"

"I'm scared, Jimmy."

The apartment became an empty church at midnight, hushed and listening. I moved around the table, put my arm over her shoulders, and she melted warmly into me, one frightened soul into another. Entwined with her, I felt both helpful and helpless. Maybe we both felt that way. "I love you, babe."

"I know."

"What can I do?"

"Nothing."

Late afternoon faded into evening, evening into night.

Before going to bed, I pulled back the curtains and opened most of the windows in the apartment. The cool breeze off the ocean had shifted south. Here, the air was stagnant and hot, the temperature hovering near the 85 degree mark. It reminded me of the time we went down to Texas to visit Melanie's sister. That had been in the middle of a late-summer heat wave as well.

"Jimmy . . ."

"Yeah?" I climbed into bed next to her. It was the first time in weeks we didn't immediately roll away from each other, looking for sleep in the wallpaper patterns of opposite walls.

"Do you believe in God?"

"Only when I need him." I thought she would smile, but she didn't. "Why?"

"I don't know, just wondering."

A familiar silence maneuvered its way between us, and I caught myself thinking back over the past few weeks, wondering what was happening to Melanie, to our relationship, to everything I had always held close to me.

"What's happening to us, Melanie? Why won't you tell me what's bothering you? All this silence, it's driving me . . ." I stopped short of saying it, though I'm not really sure why. It was the truth. I had already inched up to the edge and looked into the abyss that was threatening to swallow us both. The blackness, the quietude, were maddening. "It's the cancer-thing, isn't it? The visit with Dr. Perry?"

She didn't answer.

"We can try another doctor, if that's what you want. Someone from a different hospital."

"No," she said firmly. "No more doctors. You promised."

"Then what do you want me to do?"

She paused, and even in the shadowlight I could see her switching emotional gears again. Softly, as if it hurt getting it out, she said, "You can hold me."

◆　　◆

We held each other for a long time.

Sometime around midnight, the heat inside the apartment finally broke. Melanie opened her eyes for the first time in nearly an hour. "I love you, Jimmy Slayden."

"You're such a fool," I said lightly. I snuggled up against her, inhaling her wonderfully sweet scent, not wanting to ever lose the memory of that smell. "Just don't lock me out, okay?"

"I won't," she whispered.

But she did.

✦   ✦

That night proved to be the last time we made love together.

Shortly after that, Melanie began to change. Perhaps that's what she had been trying to tell me, that she knew she was going to start changing and there was nothing I or anyone else could do about it.

The changes came gradually, over a period of three or four weeks. She grew increasingly fatigued during the day, awake and active during the night, after the outside temperature had cooled down. I guess I'll never know if she was bothered by daylight, but she seemed more comfortable secluded inside the apartment with the curtains closed, the lights off. Often, I would come home after work, only to find her standing in the shadows, a ghost-like form frightened of being seen.

Then one night, after nearly two days without anything to eat, she began vomiting up a brown, watery liquid. I sat next to her on the bed, holding a stainless steel kitchen bowl under her chin because she no longer had the strength to make it to the bathroom.

"I've got to call the doctor," I told her.

Out of the corner of her eyes, she peered up at me. Her face was sallow and sunken, much the same as it had looked after her chemotherapy. She shook her head.

"You're not eating . . . nothing seems to be staying down . . . Jesus, Melanie, you'll dehydrate if this keeps up."

"No doctor."

"At least take some Compozine."

Her stomach lurched again, a dry heave this time. I wiped her face with a damp washcloth. "You've got a couple bottles left over from the chemo."

"No."

"This is getting crazy, Melanie." I wrapped her hands around the now-warm sides of the bowl, and got up from the bed, wanting to distance myself from what was taking place. "I can't sit and watch you killing yourself like this."

"I don't want anything else in my body," she said. Then she coughed — or it might have been another heave, I'm not sure — and the convulsion bent her almost in two, loosening a soft weeping sound from the back of her throat.

I sat down, and rubbed the back of her neck. "I feel so helpless."

"I know."

Her skin had lost a great deal of its elasticity. As I rubbed her neck, I realized layers of skin were beginning to crumble and flake. Underneath, I touched something hard and scaled.

A chill rattled through her. "I itch all over," she said, showing me her hands. The fingers were swollen, and the backs of her hands were peeling much the same as the back of her neck. "They put that crap inside me, Jimmy."

"What?"

"I never should have let them do that." Another chill shook her. I took the bowl out of her hands, placed it on the nightstand, where it wouldn't be staring back at us. She leaned back in the bed, her eyes already closed.

"See if you can get some sleep, okay?"

"Okay."

Over the course of the next few days, she seemed to improve slightly. The nausea ended, and she began taking soup once a day. For a brief time, I actually held out the hope that the worst might be over. But there was an irritating voice at the back of my mind that said she wasn't really improving at all, she was simply adapting to her cancer.

The days continued to be unusually hot. I had grown accustomed to watching Melanie pace the apartment once the sun had gone down. She rarely slept with me now. I quit asking why, and I quit begging her to let me take her to a doctor. As cold as it might sound, it had become easier to filter out the bitter ground of what was happening to us and toss them out as if they didn't matter.

The night she died, I woke in a sweat around three-thirty in the morning. I was alone, and for a while, I stared at the grayish-yellow cast of a streetlight across the bedroom ceiling, wishing I could fall back to sleep. Then, from the living room, I heard something that sounded a bit like the rustle of dry autumn leaves.

"Melanie?"

I found her lying on the couch, under a blanket, her eyes closed. The room was dark — except for a sliver of light sneaking in from the bedroom — so I stopped and switched on the lamp.

"Oh dear God."

Her face was a thin scab of flesh pulled taut across the skeletal structure. Flaps of dry, dead skin were peeling from her forehead and her right cheek. Underneath, I could see a thin, crusty layer with a pattern of scales.

"I'm dying," she whispered hoarsely.

"Jesus, Melanie." I knelt beside her, feeling more helpless than ever. My hands were trembling, but I managed to brush the hair back from her dry forehead. "You're burning up."

She grinned from faraway, and I wondered if she was even aware of me. "Dox . . . or . . . u . . . bicin," she said deliriously.

It didn't make any sense, and I didn't have the time to worry about it. "You're too hot, babe, We've got to cool you down." I worked my arms underneath her — one at her shoulders, one at her knees — as gently as I could.

"Bleo . . . my . . . cin."

I had to kick the bathroom door open with one foot, and use my elbow to flip on the light switch. She wasn't heavy — in fact, she was frighteningly light — but it was awkward guiding her through the door and lowering her into the tub. I was haunted by the thought that one of her bones might snap.

"How's that?" I grabbed a towel off the nearby rack, placed it under her head for a pillow. "Is that comfortable?"

She settled back in the tub, her movements slow, her eyes wide and never leaving me.

I ran the tap until the water was cool enough to bring down her fever without making her uncomfortable, then turned on the shower. Melanie smiled. "Oh God, babe, I'm sorry. I should have listened when you told me the cancer was back. I should have trusted."

"It isn't the cancer," she whispered. Her eyes had darkened a bit. "It's the chem . . . i . . . cals."

I brushed the wet hair back from her face. "Shhh . . ."

"The chem . . . icals from the chemo." She reached out and touched my face with the back of her hand. There was still some softness to her touch; the shell-like underpinning was still partially buried. Then she smiled, a pure childlike grin that stretched tautly across the front of her skull. "I love you, Jimmy."

I held her hand against my face, afraid to let go.

"Dox . . . or . . . u . . . bi . . . cin," she said softly. "Doesn't that . . . sound awful?"

She closed her eyes.

"Melanie?"

Cool droplets of water were sliding off her body and lazily snaking their way down the porcelain tub to the drain. It seemed as if the world had slowed down some. Everything became crystal clear. I stared dully at the way her collar bone and ribs had stretched the skin across her chest. There were places where the scales underneath were showing through now. The water around the drain gradually turned dark from something horrible that was leaking out of her. Her hand slipped out of mine and fell against the side of the tub.

Everything crystal clear.

It's only been a few months now. Melanie never opened her eyes again. I was grateful for that. I wasn't sure I could stand to look at what was behind them. The heat wave hasn't broken. Though it doesn't feel as unbearable as it once did. I keep the window open at night, welcoming in whatever breeze happens to blow in off the ocean.

The nights seem longer without Melanie. I don't sleep much. When I close my eyes, I see her again, the way she was at the end. And I can hear her struggling with those damnable syllables, trying to recite the names of the chemicals the doctors had used to flush out her cancer. It's an ugly sound. I don't much like listening to it.

WRAPPED UP

Ramsey Campbell

As they neared the camp the archaeologist began to sing. Twill started violently and tried to hush him, but Long shook his head. The rheumatic groaning of their jeep on the cliff road must already have woken the camp. "That's your tent, isn't it?" Long demanded loudly of the archaeologist. "Over there, by the tomb?"

"There's my tent," the man said, pointing amid the camp; then, as he began to doze as if the effort of squinting had exhausted him, he added, "We're just passing the tomb."

Driving, Drabney smiled at Long's cleverness. Now they knew exactly where to go. The swaying headlights fastened on the tents and coaxed from the darkness behind them the outlines of palms like split and splintered poles. He made to switch off the lights, but restrained himself: it would look suspicious.

They were helping the archaeologist out of the jeep when a shadow rose up stiffly in one of the tents, like a joke-shop mummy. "All right," the archaeologist shouted, without slurring. "It's only me and some friends in need." They half-carried him to his tent, where he commenced singing at the darkness and offering it a drink. Then they hurried back to the jeep, whose motor was still running.

As they passed the place where he'd said the tomb was, Long and Twill jumped from the vehicle, clutching the sacks on which they'd been sitting. At once Drabney accelerated and drove loudly away, grinning. He couldn't believe it was going to be so easy.

When they'd seen the archaeologist in Cairo they had been dumbfounded by their luck. They had been sitting in a sidewalk café, so downcast they were almost prepared to drink. They'd had to flee Britain and America, where their faces were known. That had infuriated Drabney. All right, so they took wealth from people who were gullible enough to part with it. But it was because the people were susceptible to alcohol or other drugs that they left themselves so open. They were the ones to blame. The three had decided that a long time ago.

They'd heard that Cairo was full of drugs, but none of the susceptible people had seemed worth the effort. Then Twill, gazing dully on the packed dusty street, had recognized the archaeologist. The man whose last expedition had almost been ruined by his alcoholism! Who could only be here on another dig!

Twill knew something of archaeology, and it had taken only half a bottle to pry loose the location of the dig, and the other half to make the man forget he'd told Twill. Then they'd merely had to camp nearby before the archaeologist and his party arrived, to become known locally as geologists on their own expedition, and to greet the archaeologist eventually as someone he vaguely remembered. "What a coincidence!" Twill had exclaimed. But even they hadn't expected their second encounter to coincide with the day the dig reached the tomb itself.

Once he was out of earshot of the camp Drabney parked the jeep and began to walk back carrying his sack, checking his path intermittently with his torch. It had sounded as if the archaeologist was even going to leave the tomb open for them, the fool. "We aren't worried about the workers pilfering," he'd said. "I told them the mummies were those of magicians."

"That was clever," Twill had said.

"True, as well. The people who made this tomb for themselves blasphemed the whole Egyptian concept of life after death." Then he'd drifted off muttering about tomb-robbers not daring to touch this tomb.

That's natives for you, Drabney thought as he walked. Gullible. Believed us when we said we were geologists. Full of drugs, probably, all of them. The rough cliff-top bit bluntly into his soles through his shoes. He reached the place where the tomb should be, and blinked his torch down the dark cliff at a faint glow. In a moment the torch-beams turned outward from the tomb twenty feet below and winked slyly at him.

They lit the stepped path while he clambered down. Then, as he entered the mouth, the beams swung about and gouged a rough narrow passage of tawny limestone brightly from the blackness. Rubble gnashed underfoot.

"Whoever they were, they must have impressed the people of their day," Twill whispered. "Notice there are no false doors, no pitfalls. They were sure nobody would dare to venture in. Still, it must have been easy enough to frighten people then."

Thirty feet into the cliff a stone door stood ajar. "We managed to move it a little," Long said. "They must have closed it again in case air harmed anything."

Dust billowed thinly about them as they strained at the door with crowbars. Dust swarmed in the bowls of light balanced on the upturned torches planted on the rock floor. As the three heaved at the stone, chafing themselves against the rock and against each other, their tethered shadows struggled overhead, bloating as if air were being squeezed up into them. When the door gave, a sudden blacker shadow engulfed Drabney's. They inched out from behind the partly open door, then Drabney probed the gap with his torch.

He was expecting walls crowded with bright figures, the looming lustre of golden coffins. Instead, his abashed torch revealed only rough limestone coffins with cracked lids, eight in all. The walls, when he turned to them, were muddily plastered but otherwise almost bare. In the corners, or what passed for such in the crudely hollowed room, stood dark vague shapes like half-opened buds. Drabney wavered, disappointed and bewildered. It seemed less like a tomb than a cave-lair.

"He did say they didn't believe in possessions," Twill said anxiously.

"If you'd been him," Long reported, "what would you have said? He wasn't that drunk."

Drabney realized why he'd thought of a lair. The hot unpleasantly musty air which hung in the tomb reminded him of a zoo. The air, and something else. There was a faint creaking rustle in the depths of the room, beyond the dim edge of the light, as if something was crawling torpidly in its lair.

"Go on," Twill said impatiently, and pushed him into the tomb. The light of his torch staggered forward as he did. The figure standing in the darkness, against the furthest wall, seemed to step forward jerkily to meet the light. It creaked softly, like leather.

Drabney felt as if a pitfall had opened in his stomach. Only the others, pressing close behind him, prevented his instinctive flight. When his torch-hand steadied, when the figure's wrappings of shadow had ceased to flap and writhe, the three stepped forward between the two ranks of coffins to see what was standing there.

It was a mummy, featureless and brown with wrappings. Yet somehow it was unlike the mummies Drabney had seen. The wrappings looked less like bandage than thick dry skin. He was sure he'd seen something like them before. The entire tall body creaked. As Drabney bent closer and the erased face peered blindly above him, he saw that the wrappings were minutely but perceptibly shifting, as if filling out.

"That's the change in temperature," Long said. "Come on. He's no use to us."

But Twill had stooped to pick up an object near the mummy's feet. It was a gilded sceptre two feet long, surmounted by a stylized pair of spread wings. "This is a symbol of power," Twill said. "A high priest's, I'm sure it is. Why's a high priest standing here?"

"Maybe he put them all to bed and then couldn't tuck himself up."

"Come on, come on," Long said. "Time enough to joke when we're out of it."

Drabney hadn't intended his remark entirely as a joke. He watched Twill wrap the sceptre and put it in one of the sacks. How it looked as if Drabney were playing the fool instead of filling his sack. Just because he didn't twitch like Twill didn't mean he couldn't equal him.

He shone his torch on a coffin and began to prise the lid apart along the crack. The lid was lighter than he'd expected; it parted easily, and the halves smashed on the floor. Drabney froze, trying to hold the silence still, as the others glared in speechless disgust. At last, when he was sure nobody at the camp had woken, he dared to move. He sank his light into the dustily fuming coffin.

The mummy within was clasped in wings of gold. The golden case which contained the body was almost featureless. The golden head was round and entirely blank, the feet were merged into a tapering tail. The rest of the case embraced itself with two enormous ribbed wings. Otherwise the coffin was empty. Shadows stirred the ribs of the wings as Drabney's torch moved.

"This one's the same," Long said when Drabney told him what he'd found. "The bastard, he was telling the truth. They weren't interested in anything but their religion. Look there."

He jabbed his light at the walls. In the centre of each, faded and crumbling now, a stylized series was painted: a man, a mummy, a winged figure poised to fly. "And there," Long said, snatching the shapes in the corners forward with his light. They were carved stone wings, about to open and reveal their ill-defined bodies.

"Maybe this is where the idea of angels came from," Drabney said.

"No need for that kind of talk," Twill said.

"No need for you to shout just because you can't find anything. What's wrong, is your friend there upsetting you?"

The mummy behind Twill was still creaking, with a sound like the stealthy flexing of disused leathery muscles. "Yes, it is," Twill said harshly. "How long is it going to make that row?"

He strode challengingly to the figure and thrust his torch at it. "Sometimes you act as if you need a shot yourself," Drabney said.

As Twill whirled furiously, brandishing a huge vague club of light, the end of his torch caught the mummy's neck. There was a sound of tearing.

All three lights seized the figure, like nooses. A long ragged strip of wrapping hung down its chest; the head, with its rudimentary face, was tilted askew. With a rush of horror, unable to bear the grotesque parody of what might lie beneath, Twill began to rip the wrappings from the mummy. Before Long could restrain him he had uncovered the head.

Perhaps they'd tried to make it look taller than it was. Or perhaps it hadn't been wrapped properly, and had partially decayed. Whatever the cause, the bald yellowed head within was barely half the size of its wrappings. It must be decay, Drabney thought, because the face looked sucked into itself, its features half-absorbed into the skull. Their lights wavered over the face, disturbing its shadows.

The face was moving. It wasn't the shadows at all. The head was shrinking, the eyes were collapsing into the skull. The head withdrew into the shoulders of the wrapping, and as it sank it fell back for a moment, as if with a soundless jagged-tooth laugh. It was the exposure to air, Drabney thought; the mummy was hurriedly decaying. Yet he felt uneasily that it was less like decay than like something else he'd once seen.

"I don't know what that achieved," Long said, hurrying through a capering of shadows to the door. "Come on, let's get these sacks filled and go."

"How?" Twill demanded shakily.

"Like this, since we have to." Long had removed the lid from the coffin nearest the door; now he plunged in a crowbar and began to wrench free pieces of the golden mummy-case. Twill recoiled, but Long said, "We've no time to be delicate now. We want to be finished and out." Drabney hurried to help him, looking away as he shook out the contents, which the crowbar had crushed and broken.

From the back of the tomb came a large incessant rustling. Drabney imagined the figure collapsing entirely within its wrappings. Sweat crawled on him; the inert air pressed close. All three men fastened their lights determinedly on the coffin and the sacks.

They glanced toward the camp as they emerged, but it was dark and silent. They forced themselves to walk slowly, so as to hush their rattling sacks. Ahead was an inkling of dawn which had yet to touch the rock underfoot. At least, Drabney thought, they weren't so loaded that he would have to risk driving the jeep back to the others. He walked automatically, musing. Now that he was out of the tomb he wanted to remember what he'd almost recognized in there.

He was still pondering when he heard the sound on his left, away from the cliff-edge: a faint creaking rustle. He peered, but sky and rocks had seeped together. Twill had heard it too, and started jangling his sack. "Palms," Long explained. "That's all, for God's sake." But they could feel no wind. They began to hurry, heedless of the loud sacks at this distance from the camp.

Drabney struggled to unlock his mind. The dry leathery case of the mummy, the way its head had writhed and shrunk within – these were things he recognized. But from where? He strode faster, shaking his head violently to dislodge a dark blot which it carried at the edge of his eye, seeming to pace him where sky and rock were dimly separating.

When he heard the creaking again he was sure it came from beyond the cliff-edge, from the void, moving leisurely with them. It was an acoustic effect, Drabney thought, an effect of the air which was congealing hotly about him as if it had clung to him from the tomb. That was all. For God's sake, he was fighting panic as if he were drugged. And all because of something he couldn't even remember, buried deep in his mind.

A dim form stood ahead, against the hint of dawn. It was not a rock. It was the jeep. "There was something not right about the tomb," Twill chattered, relieved, panting. "Those mummy-cases. Mummy-cases were a kind of sympathetic magic, you know. They were made to represent what you hoped to be after death."

"That wasn't what struck me as wrong," Long wheezed. "I'll tell you what I want to know. If that mummy standing against the wall really did attend to all the others, then who wrapped him?"

Suddenly Drabney remembered what he'd forgotten, and his heart began to thump him, urging him faster, faster. He ran, the treasure in his sack scraping harshly together. Somewhere, beyond the vast perspectiveless grey that hung close to his eyes, he heard a slow rhythmic creak and rustling, not at all like the sound of palm trees. It was drawing swiftly nearer.

"Come on!" Drabney shouted wildly, grabbing at the jeep, bruising himself as he struggled in, cursing the ignition key as it squirmed out of reach in his pocket, cursing the others as they fumbled into the jeep. He could see nothing but the memory that had jarred loose at last, of what he'd seen that had been like the mummy: a chrysalis, writhing in the throes of its final transformation.

He was still scrabbling at the ignition when the shrunken glaring wide-mouthed head pressed itself against the windscreen, smearing the glass as it clambered over and enfolded them all beneath its wings.

DEPTH OF REFLECTION

David L. Duggins

Schulton saw thick black curtains, a canyon of bronzed light between; the dull glimmer of red-stained plastic covering the bed; a mirrored opposite wall, a dark smudge of shadowy movement behind him contained in one reflective pane.

His profession demanded that he analyze a situation, draw conclusions and act on decisions quickly. Schulton was consummately professional.

He barely had time to move before the knife went in.

He was immersed in the reports of the first three victims when Eldridge phoned him concerning a fourth. Schulton picked up the receiver on the first ring, certain of who it was, what it was about.

"Who, where, when, and what?" he said tiredly, opening his notebook, pen ready.

"Woman, late twenties, walking lakeside in Abernathy Park late last night, we figure between midnight and one. She left a friend's house alone. Probably cut across the park to save time."

"So much for the 'Break-in Killer.'" Schulton lit a cigarette, dragged deeply; the smoke grated his lungs raw. His head throbbed. He hadn't slept in twenty-eight hours.

"Pretty sure this is our boy again. Multiple stab wounds with a heavy, narrow blade, four in a row beginning at the base of the neck and terminating just above the left eyebrow."

"Body?"

"Eviscerated."

Schulton's head sagged. Eviscerated. The word was a dark canon in his mind.

"He leave a note?"

"Yep. Weirder than the last one."

Schulton sighed, rubbed his temples.

"Is Talbot with you?"

"He's here."

"Send him home. Take his notes. Get Kelly in there and brief him. Tell Talbot to stay home for the next two days. I'm changing rotation."

"Who's relieving you?"

Schulton shrugged, laughed. "I've got no weekend plans," he said.

"Bullshit," Eldridge said pleasantly.

"Any trace? Did he go in?"

"Penetration after death, as before. No pubes, no semen. Careful."

"Rhythm method."

"More than that." Eldridge paused. "They've done her smear out here with the Mobilab. Identified a neutral PH lubricant."

Schulton frowned. "What's that about?"

"Our boy's using a condom," Eldridge said.

Schulton grimaced as the blade ground against rib, sank into tough muscle tissue. Stabbing a person was not like slicing butter, he knew; skin and sinew are elastic, stringy. The steel stopped short of internal organs.

The hand powering it began to twist clockwise. Anticipating agony, Schulton brought his right arm across his body to lock the wrist. The hand froze. Sliding his own hand toward the fingers, he pressed down on the knuckles until the pinky and ring fingers loosened around the hilt. Using his thumb as a lever, Schulton clasped the fingers, drew them up toward the back of the hand, then jerked and twisted. There was a sound like icicles ripped from metal guttering. The man backed off, gasping.

Man, Schulton thought. Definitely a man.

He withdrew the knife. His teeth ground together. The edge was serrated.

The man was crouched, holding his fingers, moaning; Schulton pistoned his foot up for a roundhouse kick to the temple.

A heartbeat later Schulton was flat on his back. His ankle would bruise and swell; he would be lucky to have children. The kick had been blocked, countered offensively by an ill-placed groinchop. Half-an-inch left and Schulton would have been singing soprano.

His mind seized details: Combat training. Field techniques. Maybe 'Nam. Special Forces.

A dark hurtling shape filled his vision, and he shut his mind up.

The first three were: Jessie Allen Harms, male, age twelve, stabbed to death, face mutilated with four upward cuts, right to left, eviscerated, sodomized, July 12; Oliver Abry, male, age seventy-eight, stabbed, body mutilated with weapons identical to Harms boy, also sodomized, August 19; Marie Essex, female, age nineteen, stabbed, body mutilated, eviscerated, raped, August 30.

Common denominators: All victims attacked at night, in their own homes (Exception on file: latest case), no evidence of forced entry to premises. No witnesses. Evidence of similar or same weapon used in all cases; bodies treated similarly and penetrated in one or more orifices following death. Notes left on corpses. No trace evidence, until this morning's case turned up condom lubricant in the victim's vagina. Not exactly helpful.

Until the Essex girl turned up, they thought they might have a female killer, performing penetrations with an artificial phallus to throw suspicion. Now they weren't sure. Marie Essex had been a student at East Windsor school for the handicapped. She had been getting dressed for a movie with friends; the killer entered through either open window or unlocked door while she sat at her vanity table putting on makeup. Marie was a quietly pretty girl. She had a mental age of five.

The killer seemed to enjoy catching his victims primping.

Schulton was on his feet cat-quick, in a defensive stance. His side sang pain. The late-afternoon light was bad, getting worse. He wouldn't see blows coming until—

A hand sailed out of darkness toward his throat. Schulton blocked, dropped, punched where he thought gut might be. He connected high, just above the breastbone. The man went back, lost balance, found it and sidestepped out of the path of a leg sweep.

Schulton tightened his throat against a wave of pain and nausea. If he kicked with the left leg again, tearing the stab wound, he would pass out. He turned his body sideways, jabbed solid darkness with his right hand. He heard the man back off. Schulton slid forward, pressing the advantage.

There was movement in his peripheral vision. But the man was in front of him, Schulton was certain. Sound painted this picture clearly.

A second man!

Schulton stepped back, sought a position. He glanced over.

A flash of light caught the mirror. Sundown, outside.

"Oh fu—" Schulton began, and then he was down, under punches.

At ten-thirty Schulton drove back to the office from his combat karate class, feeling stronger, fresher, invigorated. He could tackle another eighteen hours; he had sparred against Sensei Deaton and dropped him in three quick moves.

He locked the door and unlocked the file.

Common denominators. Links to personality, psychological profiles, comparisons to existing files in Washington's big computer. That was something.

The notes were the best of them. They were run off a word processor, but they were still valuable. They were a peek into his head.

Pinned to Harm's body: You will understand/the nature of divine/when we join in reflection/your cold hand in mine.

Abry: Beowulf took Grendel on field of battle fair/Sword and shield on tooth and claw — cries echoed in the air/Beowulf, victorious, stood proud as Grendel died/Beowulf, the fool, not knowing Grendel was inside.

Essex: First springtime in Eden/saw the first Snake born/Snake he tempted Adam/but met with Adam's scorn/Snake said I can't crack him/Maybe Eve will find me true/Snake offered Eve the apple/She said 'don't mind if I do.'

Schulton stared uncomprehendingly at the blocks of computer-generated verse, thinking of facts and connections. Victims. Evidence. Commons denominators.

When we join in reflection/your cold hand in mine.

Except for the latest case, his victims had all been looking in a mirror when they were attacked.

Sweet, Schulton thought muddily. Japped by my own reflection.

He brought his right leg up to clear a path through the hammer-hail of punches, jabs and chops; rolling sideways, he crawled until his head gave him leave to use his feet. Putting the mirror behind him, he stood, waited, listening.

There. The chug-chug-chug of labored breathing.

He's tiring, Schulton thought. Figured he'd take me out with the knife; didn't count on a stand-up.

Kneeling, Schulton swept both hands over the floor. His right encountered a metal bowl; his left closed around the leg of a chair. He rose. His knees popped; his left side howled; the cold, vicious contents of the bowl spilled down his arm.

He could guess what was in the bowl. There was no time to think about it.

He threw the chair and the bowl at right angles to his body. The sudden sounds from widely separated parts of the room would startle the man, give away his position and cover Schulton's lunge toward him.

No. The chair struck the man, startling a shout from him. Schulton had completely misjudged his position. He moved very, very quietly.

Close enough, Schulton thought, and dived at the sound.

"New theories," Eldridge said. "Very little blood around the last body, the woman in the park. He killed her elsewhere, probably in her home like the others, and moved her immediately after. Realized he was getting predictable, maybe. No doubt he's got a hideout somewhere. We also think he wears rubber."

"You told me that already."

"No, I mean all over. Maybe military issue chem warfare gloves. We found prints in the mud by the lake. Strange track, shallow and wide, weird shape. Could match overboots worn during military chem warfare exercises. The rest of his stuff might be surplus as well."

"How many warehouses in the borough?"

"Five," Eldridge said. "We're checking. But they could be mail-order."

"It's something," Schulton said glumly as he hung up.

He put his shoulder forward and went airborne, connecting solidly with a shape that stumbled and lost air with a muffled "Whmph!" They went down, Schulton using the man as a sled; head connected with wall and the man lay still. A runner of blood coursed down the side of his nose.

Schulton's fingers closed around his neck.

The man's hands flew up, clawed at his upper thighs.

Still on his back, the man's hands grasped and dug. Schulton tried to break away.

The left hand — used to deliver a near-fatal groinchop — found the knife wound in Schulton's side.

Schulton struggled desperately, with frenzied strength.

The fingers pried the lips of the wound apart.

Schulton gasped.

The hand dove in.

Schulton screamed.

He stepped out for a burger at twelve-thirty, eyes bleary from reading straight off the CRT.

The phone rang as he came back in.

"Enlighten me," Schulton said, expecting Eldridge.

"Indeed I will," a stranger's voice replied. "I'm five-seven, black hair, one eighty-five. Dark, swarthy complexion. Brown eyes. Blood type O positive. You'll never get prints, you'll never get trace and you'll never, never catch me."

"We've got trace, you son-of-a-bitch," Schulton said, unsure if caller was killer but wanting to throw a scare into whoever it was. The caller had already hung up. Schulton wrote furiously with one hand, dialing Eldridge's car phone with the other.

"He called once," Eldridge said. "He'll call again."

Eldridge had nothing new on his end. Schulton hung up, frustrated, and requested line-tap gear. Then he sat staring at the phone for the next two hours.

At four-seventeen it rang again.

The killer also had a car phone. He hung up after ten seconds. He had only called to laugh.

Schulton drove his fist into the back of the man's head, grinning fiercely at the sound of teeth breaking against the hardwood. The hand dropped away from Schulton's wounded side. Schulton gained his feet and dragged the man up. Spitting teeth, he punched out; Schulton grabbed the fist and lowered it, wrenched the man around and ran the arm up his back. He dug his other hand into the hair at the back of the man's neck.

He listened to the fury at work in his mind. He dragged the man backward, then sideways. The man struggled, kicked at his ankles, struck out with his free hand.

Schulton drove the pinned arm higher and slid the unwilling man across the floor toward the mirror.

He had to sleep; thirty-two hours awake was robbing him of his concentration. They were still collating data; it might take weeks to track down the computer that generated the notes, months to trace the military gear.

The parking garage was across the street from his office. He trotted through light mid-afternoon traffic. A little girl, maybe five or six, stood by a blue hatchback across from his Pontiac. Waiting for Mom, probably. He grinned at her haggardly. She recoiled, pulling back. He wasn't surprised; he must have looked as awful as he felt.

The little girl said, "I don't want an apple."

Schulton turned, grinned again, uncertainly.

The little girl pouted. "That's what I told him and I told the man to go away. I told him I didn't want an apple and to go away."

Schulton's eyes glinted. The girl stepped back again, regarded him seriously, her own eyes dark with worry.

"Who?" Schulton approached her slowly, knelt, putting them eye-to-eye. "Did someone try to scare you, honey?"

She nodded. "Like in Billy Goat's Gruff. But I didn't want an apple and I didn't want a poem and I told him to go away."

Schulton resisted the sudden urge to reach out and grab her shoulders. "Who? Who asked if you wanted a poem?"

"The troll," the little girl said. "He was big and smelled bad. I told him to go away."

"Which way did he go, honey?"

"He was a troll but he didn't come out from under a bridge," the little girl explained. "He came out from under the car."

She pointed to his Pontiac.

Schulton turned, got down on all fours, and looked.

A small black box, barely two inches wide, was attached just beneath the driver's seat.

Schulton turned to the girl again. "Which way?" he hissed pleadingly.

The girl pointed. "That's him," she said.

Schulton looked.

Average height. Black trenchcoat. Cool, smooth walk. Three blocks away, moving west, toward downtown.

Schulton had run twenty steps when the car exploded. Bad wire, Schulton thought. Most such devices were triggered by the ignition.

He whirled.

The little girl was there. Her feet protruded from the shattered windshield of the blue hatchback. They were burning. Blood darkened the glass.

Her head had rolled under the right front wheel. Open eyes, pretty green eyes, stared out into the street.

Schulton looked back. The man kept walking, didn't look around.

Schulton called Eldridge.

Eldridge tailed him personally, Kelly behind.

Schulton waited until they called in the address, and then he came too. It was five thirty-five when he approached the front door.

"I'm going in," he told Eldridge. "Alone."

"Fuck you are," Eldridge replied amicably.

Schulton grabbed him by the collar and slammed him against his car. "Don't follow me," he breathed.

Eldridge swallowed, shook his head. "You're looking at suspension, man."

Schulton strode up the front walk. He took off his shoes, went through the front door in his sock feet.

Inside, he drew his pistol. Black curtains, plastic bedcover, mirrored wall and movement. He was struck from behind and the gun was knocked from his hand and the knife came up—

◆   ◆

He jerked the man in front of the mirror, shoved his face against the glass and for a moment the man's eyes were like mirrors, opaque, silvery, reflecting twin fisheye images of himself and Schulton.

Schulton drew his hand away from the glass. The man began to whimper.

"No," he said. "Please."

Schulton hesitated.

"No."

Schulton stared at their reflected images.

"Please."

Schulton heard the fury.

"No, God, please *don't throw me in there!*" the man suddenly screamed.

Schulton's mind filled with red-stained porcelain, hot screams and lunatic shadows; his grip tightened and he was judge jury and executioner a black grinding death-engine with blood-greased gears he was a cauldron boiling a Snake telling Eve to eat the apple he was Grendel and Beowulf all in one and his hands were cold he was—

—calm, his fingers, relaxing, eyes fluttering, breath ragged. He inhaled, gagged, spat blood. Nosebleed. He couldn't remember being punched in the face.

The man quivered. The man moaned.

Schulton grabbed him by the shoulders and threw him into the glass.

He sank up to his chest and stuck. Glass rippled like water.

And something grabbed him.

Schulton was paralyzed for an untellable span of seconds; then, forcefully animated by sudden adrenalin he leapt forward, grasped the man, pulled. He didn't budge. His legs began to kick. He was yanked sideways. His back arched. Schulton tugged, and the more he tugged, the more the man kicked and squirmed.

He grabbed the man around the waist, shuffled back a step, planted his feet, and pulled. All of his weight was behind it.

The mirror shattered, raining glittering fragments, and the man fell free. His face was bloodrag, with knowing eyes. His shredded lips moved and his throat clicked and one hand clutched at nothing, and by the time he hit the floor he was dead.

Schulton stared at four deep ragged cuts, left to right, across the man's face; at the cavern of his upper abdomen, trailing loose purple coils.

His left arm was cut deeply, his right hand severed, but these injuries had been caused by sharp edges of broken mirror glass.

The face . . . and the disembowlment . . .

Schulton looked into the mirror and wasn't sure what he saw.

There were three bodies downstairs, two women, one man. Schulton stood in the doorway while lab roaches crawled the place and sprayed, collected, collated, indexed, dusted, printed and photographed. They laughed, scuttling efficiently through the ruins of three lives. Upstairs, the man's body had already been bagged and taken away. "What a mess," one of the guys in the crew had said. "He's not even all here. Where the fuck's his—"

"Just take what you see," Schulton snapped. The guy shut up.

The three downstairs were hollowed out. There were no notes; instead, an apple had been placed in each chest cavity, where the heart had been.

At home, he undressed carefully, ran a warm menthol bath. Sparring with Deaton was civilized compared to this afternoon's romp-and-stomp. A half hour's soak left him feeling more human. He moved to his bedroom, toweling off and slipping into a robe. He sat on the edge of the bed and worked the back of his neck with the heel of his right hand.

You will understand/ the nature of divine/ When we join in reflection/your cold hand in mine . . .

Rising slowly, Schulton opened his wardrobe cabinet. Inside, his overcoat hung neatly beside suits he never wore.

The pocket bulged invitingly.

There was a full-length dressing mirror on the inside of the door.

Schulton pulled a chair up to the mirror, sat again.

He reached into his overcoat pocket.

More than anything, he wanted to see the killer's face. He wished for a camera, but knew it wouldn't matter, just as he knew his gun wouldn't matter. Staring at his own white, fatigued face in the mirror, he understood almost everything.

There had been at least an inch of separation between the cuts across the victim's faces.

Whatever the killer was, it was large.

Perhaps it would look a bit like Grendel. A bit like the Snake.

It seemed to need flesh to work through.

Schulton removed the severed hand from his coat pocket.

He just wanted to see its face.

When he threw the hand at the mirror, he was sure he would.

THE MOLE

David Niall Wilson

The slimy water rose to his waist, then to the center of his chest as he sloshed forward through the moonlight. It was soothing, easing the fiery itch of mosquito bites and the paper-thin cuts of plants, leaving fever to grow in their place. A vine slapped across his face and he grunted, gritting his teeth against the fear that threatened his thoughts, tantalizing him with visions of panicked flight and almost certain, half-desired death. The fear was not strong enough, not quite. Gus wanted very much to live, to feel Sarah's smooth skin flow beneath him, warm and soft like the river, to drink a beer. He continued to move steadily ahead, blanking his mind as thoroughly as possible and concentrating on the shadowed, muddy banks. He would be there soon, and it would be easy to miss it in the dark. Especially with every nerve, every cell of his brain screaming, "No!" in deafening, discordant protest.

A long, sinuous form slid past him, running its silken length across his thigh, and he stopped, shuddering violently. His breath leapt wildly from tortured lungs, refusing to be replaced immediately, and forcing him to stand helplessly, recovering.

"Damn," he muttered, hearing the single, muffled word as though it were a thunderclap, echoing through the jungle, drawing them near. He did not repeat his curse, but moved on instead, still working to force his heartbeat back to a reasonable rate.

Then he was there. It yawned dark and ominous, beckoning like the throat of some huge, slumbering serpent. Chilled to a depth his conscious mind could barely comprehend, he stared, hypnotized.

The wind brushed through his hair, twining the stray ends like tiny snakes. His scalp tingled with fear, on thin, spidery feet, marched in a relentless tide down the length of his spine.

For a second, one short breath, he nearly broke. This was it, the moment of success or death, the test. It was always like this before going in. Nobody could understand who had not been there. The tunnel faced him, dark emptiness and damp terror. He faced it in return, battling the acceleration of his heartbeat and praying monotonously to a god he no longer believed in, and who, in any case, had long since been bumped from his fear list. Action was the only answer, the only means of relief — either to run or to enter. There were no other choices.

Checking his belt, with its water-proof pockets and sealed pouches, he grunted satisfaction and pulled his knife. Starting forward, he gripped the double-edged blade tightly between his teeth. The smooth, hard surface was difficult to grip. Despite the apparent ease of this portrayed in Tarzan movies, the art of holding the knife tightly and securely without slicing the jaw was a tenuous security at best. It freed his hands, which was necessary, but breathing was difficult enough in the tunnels without the aching jaw and nervous sweat. If it hadn't been for the rats, he'd have been tempted to leave it sheathed. No way, though. Scars on his forearm and cheek reminded him of the rats every time he got near a mirror. He'd carry the knife. The hell with his mouth; it would heal.

Walls hugged him on both sides as he slid, belly flat in the muck, into silent, eerie darkness. There was about a foot of space above him, no more, packed mud, clay, and carefully placed stone — drainage from the camp a quarter of a mile away. He blanked his mind, concentrating on the forward motion, sliding, pulling with his hands and pushing carefully with his feet, never slowing and, God forbid he should stop. He'd tried once to rest in a tunnel. The reality of the thousands of pounds of earth spreading around him had clutched at his mind with such intensity that he'd panicked, his mind reeling in frantic, dizzying haste to claw free, to escape. His breath had seemed to evaporate from his lungs, the dark air to solidify, becoming like mud in his throat. Only a headlong forward rush had saved him, thrown him a lifeline of dimly recalled sanity to draw him onward. The last thing one wanted in the tunnels was to think. There was only movement, slow breath, and the constant watch for rats; all else ceased to exist. The two ends of the tunnel connected to reality, but the tunnel was dislocated from it, a warp in the fabric of the world. Rational thought there was as counter to the continuation of life as it was necessary outside. It seemed he crawled for years, and there was no 'light at the end of the tunnel,' as Sarah was so fond of striving toward, only more blackness.

A gently blowing breeze ushered him from the shadow and into reality, illumined him with the silver-bright face of the moon, impossibly bright after the lightless void that lay behind him. No rats, no more snakes. He would have grinned, but it would have cost him the side of his mouth. The knife had inched its way deeper between his clenched teeth, slicing his tongue. Ahead, in the moonlight, lay the mission — his mission — and then the return. It would be quicker going back. The tunnel was on an incline toward the river. This facilitated the dumping of waste water and refuse. On the way down, he would nearly slide. Momentarily he paused, wondering why there was no screen, nothing to block his exit from the tunnel. Shrugging, he moved on.

There would be time for speculation later, if he still cared; now was death. If he wasn't careful, quiet as breath and quick as a sliding cloud of shadow, it would be his own death. He shifted the knife from his mouth to his right hand, spitting softly to clear the clotting blood, and rose slowly, straightening cramped limbs and rubbing joints to limber them. He was, for the moment, concealed from view by large, drooping ferns. They shifted slightly, rustling in the grip of the night air. As his eyes and senses reoriented to the light, he moved cautiously toward the edge of the cleared camp area, darting his eyes about as though each shadow held death. It might.

Parting the heavy foliage, he could see, perhaps a hundred yards distant, the nearest of the hut-like structures that served as barracks for the enemy. It was ominously quiet, and he searched the area quickly and meticulously for the guards. Their presence was not in question, but with luck, and he had always been lucky, their attention would be focused outward — he was already inside. Surprise was his strongest ally, it had watched his back and kept him alive longer than any partner could have hoped to. "The Mole" — for that was how they called him, watching him with loathing, fear, and a morbid curiosity from behind guarded eyes — worked alone. It was his way.

There were three of them on this side of the camp. One moved slowly along the perimeter, eyes scanning the surrounding jungle. The other two were perched midway up trees to the east and south, undoubtedly mirrored by others on the north and west sides. Clasping the small crucifix he always wore about his throat, firmly attached to his dog-tags, he moved into the open, staying low and covering ground rapidly. The roving guard was nearly out of sight, not yet doubling back, and he slipped easily into the shadowed growth along the building's nearest wall. He had not been seen.

The door was unlatched. Nothing disturbed the silence but the monotonous buzzing of insects and steady breathing from the shadows within. He moved without pause for thought; that was his only option. Inside lay death, sleeping death. Only quick, certain movements and precise actions would insure that it did not waken to claim him.

Fear was the reasoning behind his existence. Slip in, destroy, slip out, sliding through tunnels, impassable pits, escaping without a trace. Terror followed in his wake. It was demoralizing, the kind of thing to take the edge off an enemy blade and tip the scales in favor of the intruders, his comrades. Enough to help even up a battle they didn't properly understand. They needed him, though he saw in their eyes a fear and loathing nearly equal of those he stalked. They could not, would not enter his world of shadow and death, could not comprehend one who could. They would have chained him, locked him away to ease their own minds, but for their fear, and for their need. Without the advantage he gave, real-estate would become available back home, widows would grieve. They left him to his solitude. He did what he could to maintain sanity within. It was a partnership of blood, deep as life, certain as death. He was their secret weapon. Even their superiors didn't really know. They would never understand.

He slipped through shadows, avoiding obstacles and treading the feather-light tread of utter concentration. All else was shut out — he existed only to kill, and the object of his existence called to him with deep, even breath. This was a different barracks from those he was used to — more room, fewer bunks. He guessed it to be some kind of officer's quarters. All the better, men without leaders would win few battles. He moved to the first door and entered without pause, moving to the side of the bunk within. Something was wrong, something he could not place. The breathing remained steady — steady but short. It was wrong.

He forced the ice from his veins, moved while he could still get his hands to cooperate. Nothing was wrong, it was his nerve that was slipping, his control. He snatched at the long black hair beneath his gaze and reached for his knife. Lightning reflexes slashed, the blade left a glittering trail of echoed light to snatch hypnotically at his eyes. Screams erupted, surrounding him with sound, shocking him to immobility.

How can he scream? His mind couldn't accept it. *How can he scream with no throat?*

Hands clutched at him from behind. Light suffused the room, incandescent brilliance that stole his sight. The screams went on, the head in his grasp — too small, he suddenly noticed — shook violently from side to side. *Not possible! No screams, no shaking without a throat . . . the knife, he . . .*

Blackness sprouted from the point of impact on the back of his head, staggering him. Rereleasing the hair, he spun, stumbled toward the door. Hands reached for him again, eyes hated him and promised death. *The clothes were wrong — the eyes were wrong.* Backing, he managed to reach the door, crashing around it into the corridor and nearly falling out the door into darkness. Curses — not Vietnamese — wrong!

The tunnel was close. He dove headlong for the weeds and tumbled down the muddy embankment. Behind him, cursing again, more light, sirens? *Wrong! Wrong!*

Darkness slid about him again as he clawed frantically forward into the tunnel. Only escape was left. Don't think, never think in the tunnels, only move. A little at a time, and Damn! He'd forgotten to put the knife in his teeth! His thoughts filled with the feral, yellow-eyed memory of rats, and his breathing became labored, gasping. Damn! It was all wrong!

" . . . the facts of this bizarre attack are not clear, as yet, though police claim to have a lead on one Gus, 'The Mole' Gronden, recently reported missing from the Windhaven Hospital for the Mentally Ill . . ."
— *New York Times*

"He sat quietly every day he was here, never spoke. Came straight to us from the war. I never thought he was dangerous . . ."
— Tom McCord, Director, Windhaven

"Started waving my Sally, my little girl, around like a rag-doll, all dressed up in a hospital gown and acting crazy. Looked like he thought he had a knife, and I'd swear he was sayin' somethin' like 'wrong.'"

— San Valencez Chronicle

"A thorough search is being conducted of the city drains, he can't stay out of sight forever. Until then, he should be considered possibly armed and definitely dangerous. I don't know where they get these damned psychos, but I know where we'll put him."

—Inspector Tommy Doyle, San Valencez P.D.

Below the city, trailing after a thin web of sanity long since beyond the limits of those above, Gus sloshed onward. Already his mind was fogging. All he knew was that he must be almost there. He had to be careful, or he would miss it. He had to clear his mind. Ahead, the tunnel loomed.

SAVIOUR

Gary A. Braunbeck

"Madness is the first step toward unselfishness."
—Kahlil Gibran

I laid out the rifles.

Loaded the shotguns.

Stacked up the cartridges along the wall.

It occurred to me that, when this was over, the authorities would expect to find some kind of note. A concrete explanation. *Why do you think he did it?*

I looked out at the yard where my family was gathered and knew what people would say: *It must have been his family's fault. You've got to pay attention to your loved ones or else—*

—or else, indeed.

Monsignor Kappes at the seminary: "If you don't stop disrupting the studies with your outlandish questions, we shall have no choice but to take severe disciplinary measures. I know an inquisitive mind is valuable but you raise arguments that border on the blasphemous. You must learn to cooperate or else—"

I opened the window, quickly checked the scopes, then grabbed a piece of paper and began writing.

Why did he do it?

✦   ✦

It began, I suppose, as all things must: with seeds. A man came into the store around three a.m. carrying a large brown paper bag. For a while he contented himself with losing money in the pinball machine and annoying what few customers there were. I stood behind the cash register and watched them all.

From eleven-thirty p.m. until eight a.m. I am their sentinel. They come in with tired and bloodshot eyes, chain-smoking filterless cigarettes. The dead of spirit wander into this store for snacks, beer, cold cuts, sometimes just to play the pinball machine. They never smile, never stand straight, and their sex is of little consequence. They shamble in from the darkness to this house of light, supply themselves, then vanish back into the night with the same familiarity as walking up the steps to home. I often wish I could do something to help them.

"Would you like to buy some flower seeds?"

I snapped out of my reverie and looked at him. I expected him to stink of liquor but he didn't; he smelled like talcum powder. His clothes were old but well-kept. His cheeks sagged and he could've used a shave, but I knew immediately that he'd been at this all day and hadn't had the time.

"What are you selling them for?"

"I'm sellin' them for my daughter," he said, pronouncing it *dodder*. "She's a Girl Scout and they, well, they got this contest, see, and whoever sells the most seeds wins a scooter."

"A scooter?"

He looked worried by the question. "Look, I know this must seem kinda weird but she's been really sick and . . . well, she was doin' so good before and I just don't want to see her lose out again, you know?"

I did see. And I believed him. Standing before me was a man who'd probably worked hard his entire life to provide for his family but never managed to give them the things they *wanted*. There is a certain sparkle that drifts into the eyes when desperation sets in, and the seedman's eyes had it.

"How much?"

"Seventy-five cents a package. I know that might seem steep but—"

"—it's for a good cause, I know." I reached into my back pocket for my wallet. "Tell me about your daughter." I genuinely wanted to hear about her.

He smiled, full of pride. "Her name's Pamela."

Pamela. What a pretty name. Gentle, lyrical, maybe a velvety laugh, perhaps she wore glasses, small, thin but not frail . . . .

"She's ten and she's been a Girl Scout since her mother died four years ago." His voice was soft and milky, not at all what you'd expect from someone of his rough appearance, and I thought that if satin could speak it would sound like a man pitching seeds for his dodder at three in the morning.

He spoke as if he were composing a poem to be written down for the ages yet to come. A turn of the page as he told me of the fishing trips his family used to take when his wife was still alive, the way his mother would put her hand against her bosom whenever she laughed, the certain look Pamela would give him whenever she told a fib, another page, a new stanza to his poem of satin and seeds, the way his wife died of lung cancer when she'd never had a cigarette in her life, another verse, a new line composed, the hidden ridicule he saw behind the eyes of people when he tried to sell them the treasures from his bag, the sounds his dodder made when she was a baby, and I listened enraptured as he carefully chose his words, finishing the verse, one last line, there; he folded the sweet, gold, sad, bitter, triumphant memories of his life into a perfect paper diamond and gave it to me for safekeeping.

He looked at the wall clock. "I'm sorry. I didn't mean to go on so long. How many would you like?"

"How many do you have?"

"Fifty-eight."

"I'll take them all."

He asked me if I was serious, I assured him that I was, I gave him the money, he gave me the seeds, smiled, thanked me for his dodder, and turned to leave.

"She'll be proud of me," he said.

She should be, I thought. Of all the sights in this world, of all the valleys and forests and temples and pyramids and rivers and mountains, there is nothing so eternally powerful as the sight of a human being doing something out of love.

I waved at him as he left—

—then his back was to me—

—so I made my hand into a fist, stuck out my index finger, lifted my thumb and snapped it down.

"Bang," I whispered. There. You'll never know hurt again, never taste humiliation, never feel like a failure. I love you. Your dodder will be proud.

Anima Christi, sanctifica me. Corpus Christi, salva me. Sanguis Christi, inebria me. Aqua lateris Christi, lava ma.

I said the prayer in thanks.

Seedman had given me my answer.

I suddenly recalled the look on Monsignor Kappes' face the day I left the seminary. He looked genuinely sad to see me go. Who would he have to argue with now? I remember as I was loading the last of my luggage into the taxi, I turned to him and asked, "Tell me one thing, Monsignor; your brother has made a nice fortune from manufacturing weapons for the government. How do you reconcile that?"

"I don't understand."

"How can you teach us of the love of God, the holiness of forgiveness, the sanctity of life, while members of your own family provide the world with tools of death and destruction?"

"Decided to leave on a cheery note, eh?"

"I'd like an answer, please."

"So would the rest of us," he said, not looking at me. "If we had an answer, we wouldn't be here."

"Oh, that's just great," I had snapped, slamming closed the trunk of the taxi and opening the rear passenger door. "I should've expected as much from you. I give you a carefully considered argument and a complicated question, and you give me a 'Damned-If-I-Know.' What's next, 'Shit Happens?'"

"Please," said Kappes, "I don't want things to end like this."

"Fine, I'll let that one drop, but—hang on." I leaned over and told the taxi driver to start the meter, I was going to be a minute or two, then I faced Kappes again and said, "What say we finally finish our little argument about what is and what isn't miraculous? As far as I'm concerned, you never did get out of that one."

Kappes almost sneered at me. "I shouldn't *have* to 'get out of it,' as you say. Your arguments about miracles are perhaps the most cynical and offensive I've ever come across."

"So as a good Christian you should ignore them?"

"No, I'm saying that—oh, all right. It's been a while since that day, you'll have to—"

"You said that miracles are the supreme proof of God's existence."

"Yes."

"But that's not fair. You can't offer up miracles as evidence of God because that makes your argument circular. 'Miracles prove the existence of a Being who produces miracles.'"

"Then what about Jesus walking on the water? What about the loaves and fishes?"

"Parlor tricks. How can you claim to be an intelligent human being and still believe a bunch of tall-tales written thousands of years ago by a group of zealots who were only interested in promoting their own brand of spirituality?"

Kappes shook his head. "Good Lord, how can you even go on *existing* on a daily basis with that kind of cynicism?"

"You're begging the question."

"Then be specific."

"Okay. If this taxi suddenly rose nine feet in the air, would you call that a miracle?"

"That's an absurd—"

"Watch it. I'm sure that many of the folks in the loaves and fishes crowd thought the same thing when Christ announced he'd feed them."

"There is a great difference between a floating taxi and Jesus Christ."

"There's something you don't hear every day. I'll bite: What's the difference?"

"Jesus was the son of God and possessed supreme power."

"And that was a miracle?"

"Yes."

"And as such proved God's existence?"

"Of course. God moves in mysterious—"

"Next question: If God is the Supreme Being, possessing Supreme Power, why does He need miracles to prove His existence?"

"Because mankind's faith is weak and—"

"You're quoting the textbooks. You're also not listening to the question, big surprise, so I'll try it again: Why does God need miracles to prove His existence if His power is absolute?"

Kappes blanched. "I'm not sure I understand."

"An omnipotent God, Who created and rules the entire universe, *all* the universes, a God Who can do anything, make anything happen, Who gave us the stars and dreams and astrophysics and Kool-Aid and compassion and Vietnam and cheeseburgers and Elvis and UFOs, Who is so majestic and wise—this God would have no need of miracles. If He doesn't want some infant dying of AIDS, He could prevent it from contracting the virus from its mother in the first place. If He doesn't want two hundred people to die in a terrorist bombing in Oklahoma, He could stop it from happening. If He doesn't want thousands to die of starvation in Third World countries, He could pick up the cue from His kids and do that loaves and fishes thing. Why shouldn't I regard miracles as evidence that God has lost control of the universe and is stumbling around in a panic trying to patch up the damage?"

"Because He's not trying to patch up anything. He is demonstrating His divine love through miracles."

"Then why be so fucking vague about it? Why not just burn a proclamation into the sky or turn the moon tartan or something irreversible like that? Why not stop the spread of all epidemics? However wonderful a few freak cures at Lourdes may be, the stockpile of human misery is still enormous! The pain is still there, we're still bleeding and starving and freezing to death and lonely and angry and heartbroken and feeling like there's nothing we can do to make it better! What you define as a miracle seems to me to be unworthy of such a majestic, loving, all-powerful God. Walking on water and a little mojo-man action with a loaf of bread and a couple of dead carp looks like a cheap conjuring act."

"Did you ever stop to think," said Kappes, "that maybe He *is* averting disasters all the time?"

"Bullshit. Anyone can claim the same thing. If I say that by standing on my head each morning while naked and chanting the words to 'M-m-my G-generation' I prevent aliens from outer space from landing in Hoboken, who's to say that I'm wrong? I could cite as my evidence that aliens, have, indeed, *not* landed in Hoboken."

Kappes glowered at me. "Why can't you be content with the bald fact that the universe and God and His miracles exist? Everything has to have a concrete explanation for you or else it's just so much smoke—and if someone doesn't agree with you, you mock them. I am sick to death of your looking down your nose at the Church and its beliefs—beliefs I happen to embrace. *I* believe that God exists and that

He reaffirms His existence through miracles. In most cases He does this in common, small, natural ways—gravity, the light from the sun, a baby's laugh, *The Firebird Suite*, a really hot Charlie Parker sax riff—but sometimes He departs from the norm and has to employ more dramatic means. It's not a question of your not being able to believe in miracles, it's a question of your being too damned arrogant to accept anything that does not fit into your cynical little universe."

I looked at him for a moment, then clapped my hands together; slowly, three times, in a lampoon of applause. "I guess all it requires is a little faith, right?"

"Yes!"

"And God will do what He will do?"

"Yes."

"In other words, 'Shit happens'. Beautiful, Monsignor, just beautiful." I climbed into the taxi. "And just so you know, my 'cynical little universe' has no room for half-assed theologians who waltz blithely through life dropping platitudes like some kind of cosmic Noel Coward. And it sure as hell has no room for their brothers who provide the world with the means of further pain and destruction—unless, of course, you want to reverse the Church's stand on, say, suicide or euthanasia. Don't forget to renew that NRA membership." As the cab pulled away I turned to look at him. I think he might have been crying but I'm not sure.

I was forced to leave school because my father had been injured in an industrial accident at the steel mill. A series of maddening complications set in and the sick pay ran out, he was denied unemployment benefits because he didn't fit the bill of being both *able* and available for work, and what my mother brought in from the laundry wasn't enough to cover all the bills. On the night Seedman gave me the answer to the question I'd asked of Kappes, my father had been out of work for nearly eleven months. It was killing him. When I collected my paycheck every week, I left the store, waited down at the bank until it opened, deposited my check into my parents' account, and took the bus home where I handed the deposit slip to my father, who always took it with a sad shame in his eyes. Once a month, at his insistence, I kept one check for myself; I'd just given Seedman one third of it but I didn't care.

At the donut shop the waitress smiled at me with tired eyes—always there are tired eyes—and served my breakfast. Her pale skin with too much makeup told me how much she wished she were lovely, just a little. She told me a joke as she refilled my coffee, and it was a good joke, and I laughed, and she laughed, and something might have passed between us then but I'll never know. Too often laughter is mistaken for the sound of happiness.

As I left she told me to have a nice day. I wished her the same. Once outside I pointed at her through the window but she didn't see.

Bang.

There.

You'll never have any more nights longing for the warm body of a lover next to you, touching you. You'll never again have to smile when you don't want to. I love you. Thanks for the joke, it was a good one.

Passio Christi, comforta me. O bone Jesu, exaudi me. Intra tua absconde me. Ne permittas me separari a te.

The bag of seeds tucked under my arm, I began the long walk home. I needed to walk today. I had to plan things.

By the time I passed the church I'd scattered twenty bags of seeds.

Outside the church, crouched like a thief, an old priest was tending a garden in front of a statue of the Virgin Mary. I stopped to admire his flowers.

"They're lovely," I said. He thanked me for my kindness in noticing. I told him there was no kindness involved, that beauty creates its own reward.

"That's very nice," he said, then returned to his work.

"Father?"

"Yes?"

"Might you be interested in some seeds for your garden?"

He waved me away. "I haven't any money to buy anything from you."

I set Seedman's bag down next to the old priest. "I don't want to sell you anything. I just want to give these to you for your garden."

"I'm grateful."

"I only ask that you listen to a story I have to tell."

He considered this for a moment, then gave a slow nod of his head.

"I'll be able to make the place quite lovely with these," he said, picking up the seeds. "Please, then, your story."

I knelt next to him and began.

"On a Florida beach one afternoon, while everyone was sunning themselves and playing volleyball, a figure in a flowing white robe descended from the sky. He said He was Jesus. The fun-in-the-sun crowd didn't believe Him and asked Him to prove it. 'Feed all of us with this bottle of mineral water and fish stick!' said one girl. So Jesus blessed these items and soon everyone was munching away. But that wasn't good enough for them. 'I can't swim because my left leg is lame,' said one little boy. 'Heal me.' So Jesus touched the boy's leg and restored it to health. Still the crowd wanted more. 'Walk on the water!' someone shouted. So Jesus got into a row boat and went out several hundred yards to where the water was deep. Everyone watched breathlessly as He stood up in the boat and touched the surface of the water with His toe. 'I do this so sorrow and hunger and pain and loneliness and despair will never again touch you,' He said. Then He stepped out of the boat, onto the water—

"—and immediately sank. He swam back to shore and crawled onto the beach where everyone was laughing at Him, calling him the 'Swimming Saviour' and other mocking names. Finally Jesus, with tears in His eyes, stood tall and proud and drenched in the center of the beach and said: 'Give me a break! The last time I did this I didn't have holes in my feet!'"

The old priest fixed me with a cold stare. "I don't think that's very funny, young man."

"Neither do I. I think it's very sad. Perhaps someday you'll see." I rose to my feet.

"See what?"

"That even failures are born out of love."

And with that I left him in the garden. I turned back once to look at him. He might have been crying but I'll never know.

I have no idea how long I walked, the places I went, the people I smiled at, waved to, spoke with. All I could see was the sparkle in their eyes, the one you recognize from working nights. All of them needed something so deeply, needed a sense of comfort, of belonging, of being loved and having that love mean something.

I pointed at them all, Bang, took it away, gave them peace. *Tell me, Monsignor, how do you reconcile?*

A small retarded girl was playing in her front yard with a doll. She seemed so contented. There was no pain in her life for me to take away and I immediately felt a special affinity for her, a special love. I wanted

to embrace her, kiss her, tell her of all I had learned. Only she would
have understood.

I waved at her and she smiled.

"Dolly," she said, holding up her treasure. "Dolly dress."

"I love you, Dollydress," I whispered. Then walked the rest of the
way home.

My father was in the back yard, hobbling around on two metal arm
crutches, trying to start the grill for a cookout. He liked cookouts,
considered himself to be something of a backyard gourmet chef. I stood
by the broken fence and watched him. The way he stacked the charcoal,
the measuring of the fluid, tossing the match in just so. Things like this
were his big projects now. Skilled hands going to waste, attached to a
broken body that would never properly heal. He saw me and smiled, so
proud.

"Hope you're hungry, workin' man," he said.

"No problems here," I replied.

My sister was placing paper plates on an old card table behind him
and trying to arrange the lawn chairs. She had recently lost out on a
cheerleading position at school. I could see she still hurt.

Do you weep? I wondered. Do you cry at night because you buy
all the latest records, read all the right magazines, dress in the latest
styles, and thumb through the paperback books that tell you how to be
more popular, but your weekends are still spent in front of the television
with the rest of the family? Do you lie in bed wishing for a boy to call,
someone who's noticed all your efforts and wants to be your friend?

She looked at me and stuck out her tongue, then giggled. I always
made her laugh, though I don't know how or why.

Inside the house, my mother was sitting in front of the television
folding clothes. All day long for twenty years she worked pressing
clothes at the town's only dry cleaning store, and here she was on her
day off doing basically the same thing. She looked so tired, so worn
and sad, but at least she had her favorite programs to look forward to.

Why, mother? I thought. Do you dream. Do you? Do you imagine
that someday you'll get lucky and hit the lottery? Is that why you buy
ten dollars' worth of tickets every week? And in this dream is your
family happy? Do we all smile and embrace you and tell you how the
money doesn't matter because you've been so good to us? Are these
the things you dream about while pressing clothes and breathing steam?
Does it help you when your back is killing you with pain? Does it

comfort you when you go to the grocery store knowing that your family will have to eat macaroni and cheese three times again this week?

I don't know what I was feeling as I watched her; I just hoped it wasn't pity. I leaned over and kissed her cheek.

She seemed so interested in the television program.

"What're you watching?"

"Huh?" She looked at me, then the television. "I don't know, just . . . some show." She looked at her hands, cracked her knuckles, and sighed. "Did you remember to get some of that new kind of aspirin for your dad? You know, them capsule ones with the flag on the label. His hip has really been bothering him and those seem to be the only thing that helps."

I produced them from my pocket and she smiled.

"You're a good boy. You always were. Your dad was just saying the other night how proud he is of you. You didn't say 'no' when we needed you."

"I love you, Mom."

"I love you, too, honey. Where have you been? It's almost noon. I was gettin' worried."

"Just out walking," I said. "Nice day for it."

"I guess. I been folding clothes all morning. Ain't that a pisser? One day off a week and I spend it . . .." She shook her head and laughed. But just a little.

How do you thank someone for caring for you? I don't mean loving you, I mean for the little things. The laundry and the food and the extra change when you're a little short. How can the words 'thank you' erase the ache of a lifetime of feeling that all you've done has come to nothing?

I started up the stairs. At the top hangs a charcoal picture of Christ. The eyes of this picture follow you everywhere and until I was fifteen I avoided going near it; now I stood in front of it, wanting to cry like I'd never cried before and hating the peaceful expression on the Saviour's face.

"Why?" I asked it.

. . . *if we had the answer none of us would be here* . . .

Tell me.

They've tried, they really have, we've all tried to get by and keep alive a faith in something bigger, the idea that it will all work out in the end.

How do you reconcile?

. . . and beneath it all is the hope that one day you'll hit the lottery, nothing spectacular, mind you, just enough to help even things out. You do the washing, you stack the charcoal, you sell seeds for your dodder, and you try to believe. But every time you're lost in a pleasant reverie something happens and snaps you back and you find yourself sitting in your living room on furniture that isn't paid for, just like the television and the house and everything else around you and you know that your accomplishments are fleeting but by God there has to be a reason—

"I'm waiting," I said.

The charcoal eyes stared at me.

—no dollydress scooter for the garden because love is a failure—

. . . to work all your life to provide for those you love, to do this thing, this seemingly inconsequential thing, and ask for nothing in return, to work like that without complaint or hope of getting ahead with the next check, to say your prayers at night and hope that someone listens as you ask for courage and strength because your children gave up something just so you could afford to *live*, and you want them to have all the things you never could but now they can't even have less because the union turns its back on you when you're hurt and people get rich from selling death and the only person who understands is cooing over her dolly . . . and you sit there in front of an 18 x 20 inch box, hoping that something good is going to come across the screen and make you laugh, make you think life isn't the dumper it seems but it is and you know this because God, the Saviour, Great Saviour, greatsaviour who loves you and gave you gardens and dollydresses and weapons and television and unions, this greatsaviour is also a sadist and doesn't even know it.

. . . *border on the blasphemous.* . .

I knew now how one reconciled.

I went into my father's room and unlocked the gun cabinet. He used to go hunting with his brother but dear brother didn't come around any more. Dad kept the guns cleaned and oiled in hopes that he'd get to go hunting again someday.

I laid out the rifles.

Ab hoste maligno defende me.

Loaded the shotguns.

In hora mortis meae voca me.

Stacked up the cartridges along the wall.

Et jube me venire ad te . . .

A note. The authorities would look for some kind of note.

I crossed to my bookshelf until I came to a collection of famous quotations. I thumbed through the pages until I found the one I was looking for, the one which had been a great source of friction between Kappes and myself. I wrote it down and taped it to the edge of the window overlooking the back yard:

> "Regarding my actions in this world, I care little in the existence of a heaven or hell; self-respect does not allow me to guide my acts with an eye toward heavenly salvation or hellish punishment. I pursue the good because it is beautiful and attracts me, and shun the bad because it is ugly and repulsive. All our acts should originate from the spring of unselfish love, whether there be continuation after death or not."

I smiled at the quote from Heinrich Hein's *Das Bader von Lucca* and picked up the rifle.

Opened the window wider.

My mother had joined my sister and father in the back yard.

I felt a tear brimming in my eye.

I wanted to take it all away and make the reconciliation flesh. To erase the sadness and loneliness. Make you forget about all the ways you've lost out in life. To give you something golden and true.

I took a deep breath as I focused Mom in the scope.

—so proud of you—

Forgive me, all of you.

Ut cum Sanctis tuis laudem te. . .

I wanted to save you.

—didn't say no when we needed—

Hold your breath, that's it, focus, steady, c'mon, c'mon . . .

I wanted so much for you.

In saecula saeculorum . . .

But I've got holes in my feet.

Amen.

The first shot was easy, just squeeze the trigger snap back and the recoil feels so good like the Confirmation slap, the smoke spit out, threw

the greatsaviour's kiss, this is how I reconcile, and I saw something
register on Mom's face and for a moment she looked just like—

—like—

—like the time she lost twenty dollars from her check after she
cashed it to go to the grocery and I remember, Mom, how you cried
because your feet had been hurting so much that week and that was
money you had to stand for four hours to earn and now there you were
having to put stuff back in the checkout line and four hours of your pain
was for nothing because your family couldn't have some extra goodies
like you'd wanted and I cried just like you did Mom and your tears were
seeds and I saved one for you, here—

She caught it just below the base of her skull, my kiss, and fell back
over the table, wine spilling from her mouth, flowing wine, come, you,
and drink from this, the cup of my blood which shall be shed for your
sins, but then my sister was screaming so—

—so—

—so what if nobody asked you to the homecoming dance? You
can go by yourself a lot of people do and *I always go by myself I want
to have a lot of friends or even just one* but you never did, my sister,
because you're plain just like me and the world doesn't embrace the
plain to its bosom, we have to make due with the powdered milk of
human kindness so I give you—

—the smoke of a dozen blackred roses. She took them to her chest
and clutched them there, calling out, her mouth opening and closing but
there was no sweet sound because suddenly my father, no fear in his
voice, brave old broken man, was running toward her as I took a deep
breath and sent—

—sent—

—sent me to the store on my birthday because you knew how much
I liked to roast marshmallows in the fireplace so I went because I knew
you were planning something special and I got the marshmallows but
you met me on the way home and we walked together and you had your
arm around me and I knew there was going to be a big roaring fire
waiting for us when we got home but when we came through the front
door there was nothing left of your fire but smoldering ashes and you
looked so ashamed because you'd tried and failed again and you looked
at me and said I wish—

—and I sent him his wish, sent it right to his face, all over his face,
through his face, and then there was the smoke and the heat from the

gun and soon nothing but peace and silence and I knew I was forgiven because even in the bitter smoke of failure there is still beautiful, fulfilling, triumphant love.

I fell back sweating. I. Had. Done. It.

I had saved them. I had made the reconciliation.

I sat up, removed my shoes, pulled off my socks.

Perfect feet.

The neighbors started screaming then, pounding on the doors. The yard was suddenly full of people so I grabbed the nearest rifle and began sending them peace as the sirens came screaming down from the distance and the pounding downstairs gave way to an explosion and the sound of many footsteps running up the stairs toward my room—

—getting closer, they were getting closer so I turned toward the scene in the back yard, blew my family a kiss, chambered a round in my father's favorite rifle—

—only one left now—

—screaming, yelling, footsteps getting closer—

—I turned toward the sound—

—took a deep breath—

—and the door flew open.

"Are you coming down to eat or not?" Mom stood there, out of breath. She shouldn't have climbed the steps. Her feet hurt so much.

"I was on my way."

"Didn't you hear us all yelling for you?" She noticed the rifles and shotguns laid out before me. "What are you doing with those old damn things?"

"Dad said maybe he'd start hunting again. I thought if I cleaned them he might, you know, feel like getting out one of these days."

She winced. "One of these days, my foot. Put them things away. You might hurt yourself."

"Yes, Mom. I just thought maybe I'd go along with him. We haven't had time to do anything together for so long."

In the yard my father and sister were yelling at us to hurry up before it got cold.

"Oh, hon," said my mother, "you don't have it in you to hurt a bug."

"I suppose." But I knew.

I had reconciled.

In saecula saeculorum. Amen.

She reached out and tousled my hair. I put down the rifle.

"I don't know about you sometimes," she said.

"I love you, Mom."

We started down toward the feast.

Mom looked back at the rifles. "Maybe one of these days."

"Yeah," I said, putting my arm around her. "One of these days."

GREAT EXPECTATIONS

Kim Antieau

I hate this apartment. It's small and has rats, and I'm always hungry here. We live on the east side now, far from our old house in the northwest, the one we had before Mother was laid off and Father wasn't given tenure at the university.

"Times are tough all over," my father said when we moved, "but we're strong. We'll survive."

They talk about survival a great deal.

Soon after we moved here, our culture hour began.

"We are poor monetarily, but we shall not be poor culturally," my father told us by way of explanation. I know the real reason for these performances. My parents haven't the money to feed us all, so they have to find out which of us is fit to survive. I've studied Darwin in school; I know what's going on here.

Now, every night we sing for our supper. Well, Maggie sings. Trina reads poetry. I don't have any particular talents, so I try everything and anything to show them that I am fit, I *am* worthy.

I haven't succeeded. Every meal, my portions get smaller: I am never the one who gives the best performance and gets the most food. I pointed out the difference in food portions once to my mother.

"What nonsense, Dollie," she said. "You all get equal portions. Really! You're too old to whine about such things."

I don't mention it anymore.

This night I am more hungry than ever, but I have to wait until the performances are over. Maggie, my older sister, sings an aria. Father and Mother smile contentedly, pleased with their sixteen-year-old daughter. She sings her last note and we clap loudly.

Next Trina, my younger sister, stands up. She holds a piece of paper which she occasionally glances at as she recites her poem. I watch my father as Trina talks; her words are rhythmic, beautiful, creating images in a kind of verbal dance. My father's eyes fill with tears.

My hands begin to perspire as Trina nears the end of the poem. It is my turn next. I am so hungry.

We clap for Trina. She bows slightly. I wonder, as I often wonder, how a ten-year-old manages to write such sophisticated poetry. All three of us are beyond our years, I have been told. But it is possible that someone helps Trina write her poetry. And that would not be fair.

Everyone turns to me now with great expectation. I have tried singing, reading, acting, writing. I excelled in none of these areas. Now I hold up a picture I've drawn of the five of us at the dinner table.

I hand the picture to Trina; she gazes at it for a moment and then passes it on to Maggie. Finally, it is in my father's hands.

"We all have talent, my dear Dollie," he says, looking at the picture, "you just haven't found yours yet. Don't worry." He stands and claps his hands together once. "Now, children, let's have supper!"

My stomach growls as I watch them file into the kitchen. I know I will not be getting the biggest portion tonight.

After everyone is asleep, I leave my sisters snoring in the beds beside mine. It's easy for them to sleep with full bellies. I tiptoe through the darkened apartment to the kitchen.

I don't need light in the kitchen. I have every part of the room memorized. I go to the bread drawer. No one will notice a few pieces of bread. I pull out the loaf and begin shoving slices into my mouth. I have to eat fast in case someone comes in and tries to take it away from me. I've been caught before. I eat two slices, three; suddenly the loaf is gone. I have eaten every piece of bread.

I drop to the floor, ashamed of myself. I roll the bread bag into a tiny ball and push it down deep into the garbage. I wish I could be good enough. I hurry back to bed.

When I get home from school the next day, something is different in the kitchen. It takes me only a moment to discover what has changed. There is a lock on the pantry door. I open the cupboards; they are empty.

Every scrap of food which doesn't require refrigeration is now locked in the pantry. I jiggle the lock. My stomach knots in panic. Now what will I do?

Maggie comes into the kitchen eating a sandwich.

"Where did you get that?" I ask.

"Mother made it for me," she said. "I couldn't get it myself because all the food is locked away. And we know why, don't we?"

"Did you tell Mother about last night?" I ask. Maggie chews on the sandwich slowly. My mouth waters.

"I didn't need to," Maggie says, leaning against the cupboard. "She knows. If you're hungry, why don't you eat like a normal person? Do you have to eat everything in sight?"

I want to hit her. It's so easy for her. She gets enough.

"Hello," my mother says as she comes up behind Maggie. She rests her hands on Maggie's shoulders. "Are you hungry, Dollie? Would you like me to fix you something?"

I stare at her. How can she be so cruel? She has the key to the pantry, the key to my survival. She knows I am starving. She doesn't care. I feel sick, like the time I found out Grandma was dying. It seemed so final. Like now. They are taking food away from me and I am the one dying now.

I run from the kitchen and into our bedroom. I slam and lock the door.

I hear Maggie call me a brat. Mother says I am going through a difficult period.

I sit on my bed. Butterflies tickle my stomach. I almost throw up. I don't. The sickness passes, and I know I must find a way to survive.

At dinner, Trina excuses herself and goes to the bedroom. She is not feeling well. Mother divides her food between Maggie and myself.

Suddenly, as Mother scrapes my share of Trina's food onto my plate, something clicks inside of me. Shifts into place. I wonder why I have not thought of this before. If Trina and Maggie eat less, I get more. I don't have to perform. I don't have to be good. They just have to eat less.

I finish my dinner slowly, savoring this knowledge. I am certain I will soon get my fair share.

In the morning, Mother unlocks the pantry for me when I offer to make breakfast for the family. I fix my parents scrambled eggs. Then

I take my sisters' cereal bowls into the pantry and sprinkle a little sugar and a little rat poison over their Rice Krispies and sliced bananas.

"I'm glad to see this change, Dollie," my father says as I place the cereal bowls in front of my sisters. "We're a family, you know, and we've got to stick together to get through the bad times."

When I get home from school, Trina and Maggie are already there in bed, complaining of stomach cramps.

Mother and Father spend the evening with my sisters, reading them stories. Mother asks me to make them dinner. As I cook, I taste-test everything. When I bring the trays in to Trina and Maggie, they don't eat much.

Later I sit in the kitchen, alone, I eat everyone's meals. I have never been happier.

"It's just the flu," Mother tells Father as they go to bed. "They'll be over it in a few days."

This night I fall asleep instantly, my belly full.

Maggie and Trina do not get better. They get slightly worse each morning after their cereal. For days I have free rein of the kitchen. The pantry is left unlocked. Mother is grateful for my help. Father goes to work each day a little sadder, a little more worried than the day before.

I am not worried. I've given Trina and Maggie enough to keep them sick for a time — long enough for me to get enough to eat. To secure my survival.

Then one morning, Father and Mother bundle up my sisters and take them from the apartment. Mother kisses me goodbye.

"We've got to take them to the hospital," she says. "We trust you to take care of yourself until we get back. Don't worry."

As soon as they are gone, I bake my TV dinner and eat it. Then I heat up a leftover chicken. Next I eat a bag of Oreo's with a gallon of milk.

Soon after, the police arrive and things become confusing. A social worker takes my hand and tells me everything is going to be all right. Someone snaps photographs. They wear white gloves and go through the apartment. One of the police officers tells me my parents won't be coming back for a while, so I have to go to some kind of home for orphaned children. For a moment I am afraid my parents have died, but then I hear they have been arrested and charged with murder. "How could someone give their own children rat poison?" someone whispers.

I lock the pantry and then I follow the social worker out of the apartment.

I am always hungry. Every night before dinner, our beds have to be made correctly, and our faces and hands must be clean. I have watched. The girls with perfect beds get more food. It isn't fair. Most of the other twenty girls have been here for years. They know how the house parents like the beds done.

Sometimes the house parents let me help in the kitchen. Food is stuffed into every nook and cranny. In that huge kitchen, I feel safe. At night, they lock the cupboards.

I am wasting away again. If things don't get better, I know what to do. They have problems with rats, too.

All I want is to survive.

Sometimes after lights out, I sneak downstairs and stand in the huge shiny kitchen. My mouth waters as I imagine the feast that is soon to come.

SHELL

Adam Corbin Fusco

The steady *whupp-whupp* of the blades made a heartbeat over his head, flying low over green, lots of green, and the crackle in his headset, that was Maddog, liking to clip the tops of the trees with the chopper blades if he could, Maddog giving his captain's account of how they're approaching the village of Phu Lai, fasten your fucking seatbelts . . . and McKraken steadied himself against the green metal of the chopper, scrunched in his flak jacket, this was the time of the silver fear, the kind you taste in your mouth because death is a roll of the dice, and Maddog didn't give a shit and McKraken didn't either, since that would mean the end of the mud and bullets and fire . . . even now as he lies flat on his back with a tube up his dick and a tube in each arm, this VA hospital dispensing the best government care a taxpayer's dime can give him, which means green industrial paint and yellowed pans, sheets white as bone and twice as hard, he can still hear the *whupp-whupp*, angry growl, touching down, get your ass down on the fucking ground, helmet bobbing on his head, and explosions from the shelling bubbling in his eardrums, you feel it before you hear it, deep in your gut, and in another place you feel the screams . . . he feels them now, as he turns his head to see the IV drip once more, smelling the saline solution, like the sea . . . Charlie had sprayed Phu Lai for weeks, so that the trees were withered husks, you could see them bent, the village lay exposed in the light of day, all you had to do was clean it up, so good old 84 company, being himself, Maddog, Dickey Spears, Randy Candy, and the others, rounded up the villagers and if any gave you lip then it was a *pop-pop-pop*, do what you had to do, you're too scared not to . . . and some are dead, or cowering, they got their little rice bowls, and the women are wailing, and how come these people can't even get *clothes* for themselves, and a stick-figure man was pleading with Dickey Spears, because he'd got himself one of the gook women . . . he tries to shift on the bed, but his back has been sweating, he's stuck to the sheet, he can move his head and see the other beds lined up and down the room, their occupants asleep or dead, and he can smell the salt of his sweat, a doughy smell coming from the bed, he wishes he could think of other things, like why he joined up in the first place, a chance to escape the brewery that imprisoned his father, escape Milwaukee, man, got to travel, make a career out of it, but it had been so long ago, when in Phu Lai he stepped into the hut to escape the sun and saw in the corner the little gook girl, shivering . . . her arm had been smashed by a bullet, she was rocking with pain, and half her face was burned, a blackened mess, and cracked, because the pus was pushing through, breaking out . . . she'd never walk again, the shelling had pinholed her legs with shrapnel . . . he stood there breathing hard, erasing salt-sweat from his face, it would be mercy if he did it, it wasn't from anger, it wasn't because he hated them, it was because he wanted to save her . . . he raised his 16, it was mercy, through and through, and it would be better if he did it in the skull, because it would be quicker, you'll only see a big white flash, little girl . . . her eye as she turned it to him was black, all pupil, wet and glistening, rolling slowly in its orbit like she was an animal gone to ground . . . and then the back of her skull blew apart, cracking like an egg . . . when Maddog caught up with him he stared a long time, but McKraken had this real sick feeling deep in his gut, God man, she was like this when I got here, look what the shelling did, happened a while ago, but there was this little creaking sound that Maddog heard which was the bowl of her skull rocking on a reed mat . . . Maddog smiled and left, and turning to follow, McKraken saw in a little reed cage one of the hermit crabs they keep around for luck, and it must have outgrown its shell, because it was slithering half out of it . . . McKraken had done it out of mercy, not because he was mad; he wasn't mad when they had captured that hill where Randy Candy took a slug in the groin and lay bleeding, grabbing himself like it was almost funny, but doing it to keep the blood in . . . and they had found the bunker thing in the hill, which was really a part of the tunnels . . . what good was spraying when they got tunnels, but try telling that to fat men in leather chairs, and McKraken waited down in the bunker, feeling guilty because he wasn't with Randy like the others, but they would take care of him, he just wanted to be deep in the ground, safe, down here where all the sounds were muted, you heard your own breathing mostly, leaning his back against the muddy wall, his boots sucking in the gooky gunk, maybe not so great here, he just wanted a bit of peace, and black tree roots had sprung up in the mud . . . when his eyes adjusted they were moving, slithering in the wet, leaving trails, or maybe they were snails, 'cause weren't slugs just the same as snails, 'cause they came out of their shells once in a while?. . . the saline drips again, he imagines every drop traveling down the tube, tries to time it, how long does it take to get into my arm, that particular drop, it's one of the few things he can look at . . . the spray had gotten to him, he's flat on his back, legs paralyzed, all the legislation in the world wasn't going to cure shit, he can look down at the floor, near the foot of the bed, and now he sees a trickle of wetness spreading from under the bed, the IV must have a leak . . . they protected him, it wasn't going to be a secret with Maddog, he told everybody, must have made it sound like soft McKraken had some balls after all, no sissy boy here, he *blammed* that gook girl but good, they wouldn't say a word, but it ate at him, the thoughts kept spinning in his mind, he did it because he wanted to kill, or he did it because he wanted to give her mercy, but maybe she could have been given some care, some healing, even a goddamn drink of water . . . they had reached a glittering sea on a pink dawn, support for 67 though they didn't need it, a cake walk, just walk along the beach, nothing here for us to do, God knows they must have sprayed here, there weren't no fucking trees, that's why you call it a *beach* . . . Dickey Spears was pissed because he'd had some buddies in 67 and they'd found bodies and thought Dickey was going to get himself some revenge . . . but walking along the sand, with the cold water shushing up around his toes, McKraken came up to Dickey where he was kneeling in the sand and holding in his hands a helmet, and Dickey was crying because he said it was the helmet of his old friend Johnny Max . . . McKraken looked at the helmet, it was black, and glistening with salt spray, bulbous towards the front, flatter towards the back with a spiky thing pointing behind it, and turning it over there was this membrane thing coating the inside, pink turning black, the army didn't issue no black helmets, and McKraken knew it was one of those horseshoe crabs, or at least what one of them had left behind . . . it is the time of day when the sun would start inching around the iron-barred windows, it is already tickling the IV bottle with a pinprick, and McKraken has to look away down at the ground, and he sees that the wetness on the floor has spread, couldn't see it actually moving, but it has gotten bigger, and fear nibbles at his throat because he cannot move . . . one of the few reprieves they got was when they actually went shopping, it was all these little stalls and huts, and behind the curtained ones you could get drugs or whores, but there were souvenirs, and one place had turtle shells all painted up in yellow designs and McKraken thought about buying one, turtles were lucky too, gooks were ape-shit over them, matter of fact they had come across a pond near the sea, must have been a nesting place, but the sun was mighty strong or something, it was hard to see in the haze, you saw these shapes crawling over the sand, making for the water like desperate, and their backs were pink, not green, little beads of pus decorating them like pearls . . . McKraken must have been really doped up, because in the pond he saw a big shape swirling around, and it started to come out of the water, a big round thing, the hooked face, but soft, its body was soft and bloated with bits of tissue hanging off of it, he hugged himself with his flak jacket and hightailed it to the chopper. . . he could have told them about the girl at the hearings, but that's not what he was there for, he hadn't *sprayed* the girl, he had shot her, wouldn't have done any good to tell, it was too late, and he'd have been exposed, it was way too long ago . . . but still nothing had taken away the racing thought of it, every day, lying immobilized flat on his back, with the sun now creeping down the IV tube, how long would it take to reach him, maybe it was heating it up more than usual today because he could smell it, a tangy smell of salt and sea . . . he can feel the kiss of the sun on his cheek, God he wishes he could roll over on his side, just on his side, he pushes out with his hands, but can't rock his hips, he is stuck to the sheets with sweat . . . the sun crawls along his skin, making it gleam, bone-white, sun-white, and shaking his head in frustration he glances down at the floor . . . the pool of wetness has made a large circle and he can feel the scream of something slipping over it, under the bed . . . the sheet has slid to his hips, and his belly, fish-white, burns where the sun hits it, he can't move, can only look at the floor where he sees a hooked face and an eye, a large rolling eye that is all black, all pupil . . . and he wonders how long it has taken to get here, how fast do they move under water? . . . the sun bakes his skin as he flounders, I did it out of mercy, I did it because I hated, and the dripping from the IV says, you are one of us.

It came slithering from under the bed.